Polly's Pride

Sunday Times bestselling author Freda Lightfoot was born in Lancashire. She always dreamed of becoming a writer but this was considered a rather exotic ambition. She has been a teacher, bookseller in the Lake District, then a smallholder and began her writing career by publishing over forty short stories and articles before finding her vocation as a novelist. She has since written over forty-eight novels, mostly sagas and historical fiction. She now spends warm winters living in Spain, and the rainy summers in Britain.

Freda LIGHTFOOT
Polly's Pride

CANELO

First published in the United Kingdom in 2015 by Harlequin MIRA, an imprint of Harlequin (UK) Limited

This edition published in the United Kingdom in 2024 by

Canelo
Unit 9, 5th Floor
Cargo Works, 1–2 Hatfields
London SE1 9PG
United Kingdom

A CIP catalogue record for this book is available from the British Library.

Print ISBN 978 1 80436 552 6
Ebook ISBN 978 1 80436 553 3

This book is a work of fiction. Names, characters, businesses, organizations, places and events are either the product of the author's imagination or are used fictitiously. Any resemblance to actual persons, living or dead, events or locales is entirely coincidental.

Cover design by Rose Cooper

Cover images © Arcangel, iStock, Shutterstock

Look for more great books at www.canelo.co

Printed and bound in Great Britain by Clays Ltd, Elcograf S.p.A.

I

Chapter One

The residents of Dove Street knew that summer must be coming because it was already seven o'clock and the lamplighter had not yet appeared. They looked forward to his coming; watched for the long pole with its blue light at the end to come dancing past their windows. When the gas lamps were lit, lads would shin up the lamp-post, open the glass and light their cigarettes, more often than not scraped together from the dimps they'd picked up in the gutters. The women, wrapped in their woollen shawls, would normally linger on their doorsteps only a little while longer, enjoying the glow of dusk and the rare blink of a star glimpsed through the thick grey smoke that blanketed the city, billowing like dragon's breath from the hundreds of mill chimneys.

If they were lucky the barrel organ man would come along and they'd find a penny or two between them so they could hitch up their skirts and kick up their legs, making their clogs spark on the cobbles. He might play them *Irish Eyes Are Smiling* or a piece from an Italian opera. There was nothing the people of Ancoats liked better than a song and dance. Then each mother would call in her own children from whatever street game they were playing and send them up the 'dancers' to bed, welcoming the opportunity to put their own feet up and perhaps enjoy a glass of stout if they'd the money to pay for it.

But tonight was different. Tonight the door of number twenty-three, like all the others in the street, was shut fast. It had been slammed so firmly closed that the piece of board, still bearing the words 'Ceylon tea', had come loose from the hole it was meant to be blocking and swung freely on one nail.

Inside the house a young woman with hair as dark as a raven's wing, but with a hint of fire in its depths and a fine Irish temper to match, railed at the injustice of life.

'I'll have you know my house is clean. Don't I scrub it with me own hands from top to bottom every week? I'll not hear anyone say otherwise!'

Polly Pride, green-grey eyes glowing with passion, spoke as if she challenged the older woman sitting opposite to dare disagree – which of course, being her mother-in-law and set in her own opinions and prejudices, she usually did. But then Florence Pride, as she was often heard to say herself, was not afraid of speaking her mind.

'Nay, don't take on so. Yon council can't pick and choose which house they gas and which they don't. D'you expect them to come knocking on t'door saying, "Good morning, Mrs Pride, have you any bugs in your house that we should shift?"'

She put back her huge head and laughed at her own wit, screwing up her small eyes and cackling with joyous mirth. Being a large woman, heavily built rather than fat, with arms on her that some might think could challenge Randy Billy in his next wrestling contest, she was generally known as Big Flo. She could have made three of her skinny daughter-in-law who was such a whirlwind of energy that no flesh would stay on her for more than five minutes, even on the days she ate well, which admittedly were few.

Big Flo watched with a mixture of suspicion and curiosity as Polly went about her work in the small kitchen, movements brisk as she brewed tea from the big black kettle puffing out steam where it sat, like a welcome friend, on the hob. She looked like a child who had outgrown her strength. Short dark hair cut into a sensible bob; eyes like bruises against the pale skin of her elfin face. It was a wonder she'd managed to produce two healthy children when to look at her it seemed a breath of wind from the Pennines would blow her clean away. What Matthew had ever seen in her, Flo couldn't rightly say. He should've married a good strong Methodist lass, like she'd told him to.

As if reading her thoughts, which had been made plain more times than she cared to contemplate, Polly wagged a condemnatory finger at her mother-in-law, her other fist planted against her narrow waist. 'It's because we're Irish Micks, as you call us.'

'If the cap fits...'

'Well, you're wrong. I'm only half-Irish.'

'How d'you work that out? Your parents both hailed from Ireland, didn't they?'

'Yes.'

'And thee were born there?'

'So? I've lived in England since I was six years old, which makes me half-Lancashire.'

Big Flo gave her loud rumbling laugh. 'Says you!'

'It's true. Yet for all the Irish have been in Manchester for nigh on three hundred years and built the railway from here to Liverpool with their own muscle, not to mention fighting in the Great War, still you call us immigrants.'

'The whole of Ancoats is full of immigrants.' Flo pronounced the word with a disapproving sniff. It was true she'd no truck with foreigners, nor anyone in fact who differed from her own fixed views – which included those who worshipped idols, built fancy altars, swung incense and needed anyone to intercede on their behalf before the Almighty, instead of talking straight with the good Lord Himself, as she was fond of doing. This ruled out pretty well every religion under the sun, barring her own nonconformist persuasion, including Baptists and Congregationalists, Church of England, Jews, and many other less established religions. Big Flo was a rebel at heart, a dissenter not a puritan, anti-establishment rather than a woman with a mission. That burden she left to her elder son Joshua, who relished following the law of Primitive Methodism to the letter. But she shared his hatred of papists, like this little madam, for they were the worst of the lot in Big Flo's unbending opinion.

'There are Italians, Polish and Russian Jews, even a few from Burnley living here. Bugs ain't fussy, they'll bite anybody. And if there's one thing we're not short of in Ancoats, it's bugs.'

Polly blinked back tears. 'Will you not try and understand for once how I feel? It's shamin', so it is.' She loved her little house for all some might call it a two-up-and-two-down slum. There were many worse. The Murphys' next door, for instance. They'd only one bedroom, and them with four boys and two girls and Davey Murphy having recently lost his job. What a terrible thing that was, to have no work. Worse than being accused of being filthy and having your house fumigated, whether you needed it or not.

She brought flour from the pantry and began shaking it into a large brown bowl. If she hurried, she might have time to make some potato cakes with the leftover mash from yesterday's dinner. 'And we have to stay in Ardwiek Barracks with the soldiers while they do it.' She could at least make sure they took their own food with them. Polly began to mix the flour and potato together.

'Aye. And take nowt with us.' Seeing what she was about Big Flo began to chop onions, which would add a delicious flavour to the cakes, once they were fried. She was rather partial to a few potato cakes for her supper. 'They'll need to chuck powder over everything; make a right mess they will. Stink to high heaven for days will that gas. But with the warm weather coming and the bugs stirring, what else can they do, eh? We'd be overrun with the blame things if they didn't.' She considered the girl with a keen glint in her eye. 'What're you fratchin' about anyroad? It happens every year at this time. I reckon you're more frightened of them soldiers than you are of the blackjacks and lice and what-have-you.'

Polly did not deny it. What loyal Irish girl would not be? Her memories of the old country were vague, having come to Manchester as a small girl when her parents were seeking work in the mills, but Irish memories were long. Her own mother, who told tales of the Fenian bombings, had been terrified of the soldiers, having lost a younger brother in a riot. She was dead now, which Polly regretted deeply, while her father was very much alive – an even deeper cause of regret. Somewhere she still had brothers and sisters but she never thought of them. When she'd announced her intention of marrying a Protestant, they'd made such a fuss she'd packed her bags and left. Even so, for all her defection from her homeland and family, she knew that nothing good had ever come out of an English barracks so far as her family was concerned, and despite her years of living on English soil unmolested, Polly felt the same.

She did recognise, however, the problem with the bugs. Despite Polly's best efforts with gallons of washing soda and disinfectant, cockroaches still crept out every night from under the fire grate, though there were none in her pantry, thank God, nor in the meat safe that sat proudly in her yard. And there wasn't a flea in the place. Didn't she take the lighted candle to the bedsprings every night of her life? And her children grew tired of her nightly ministrations with the fine tooth comb. So she hated to think of anyone considering her house as bad as those in the Dardanelles, for instance, or the notorious district of Angel Meadow.

Polly Pride put money in the poor box every week for those less fortunate than herself, for all she rarely attended mass these days, preferring to worship before a picture of the Sacred Heart and a crucifix in her own front parlour. Since the church considered her husband to be a heretic bound for hell, and this being one piece of their doctrine to which she could not subscribe, Polly had not set foot in a Catholic church since the day she wed Matthew Pride fifteen years previously. Sometimes she would have liked to find a church in the city where she wasn't known and quietly attend mass and make her confession. But this was a comfort she had so far denied herself, if not her children. They'd both been raised in the Catholic faith, to the bitter disapproval of Matthew's family and in particular his brother Joshua.

If she and Matthew were outcasts, what of it? Weren't they happy enough without the blessings of either church? Generally speaking, with the exception of Father Donevan, Big Flo, and a few like them, within Ancoats itself nobody much cared one way or the other who you were, where you came from, or whether you attended church. They had far greater problems to contend with than religion.

What mattered was whether you had enough food in your belly, a roof over your head, and were a good neighbour to those about you, ready to lend two spoons of sugar whenever necessary. As a result of this pragmatic philosophy, it was where you lived and the allegiance you had to your own street that counted most, not which banner you carried on the Whit Walks. Each was cheered as loudly as the next in any case, and Polly appreciated that fact. Although if it rained on the Friday when the Roman Catholics walked, Big Flo would say the sun only shone on the righteous.

'Live and let live' was largely the order of the day. The one thing that could set apart neighbour from neighbour in the district was trying to appear better than the rest. Getting above yourself was the real sin.

'Thinks she is someone,' they'd say with a sneer if anyone put up new curtains or dared to, set fresh flowers on their windowsill instead of paper ones bought from the tinkers. The next day there could be a half-brick thrown through it.

But still Polly had her pride, and could be fussy about her own curtains – when she had any. Her house was clean, no doubt about that, so fumigating it was entirely unnecessary and filled her with shame for all she understood it couldn't be singled out from the rest.

'What if the soldiers won't let us back into our own house?' Or what if, despite all the Derbac and lye soap she used, they found something wrong with her children and took them away, saying she wasn't a fit mother? 'What if they put Lucy and Benny in Ancoats Hospital or, worse, a children's home and I never see them again?'

'Nay, lass, you're getting all a-flunter over nowt.' Big Flo, who knew exactly where she stood in life, had never been troubled with 'nerves' while this lass seemed full of them, so far as she could see. Polly lived in constant fear of her two children getting into trouble, pinching something and ending up in the reformatory. That's if they didn't walk under a tram, get TB, diphtheria or any of the other dread diseases that stalked this street almost daily, it seemed. Moreover she didn't seem to appreciate family ties, and wanted out of Ancoats, for all it was one of the friendliest places on God's earth, if also one of the muckiest.

By the time Big Flo had gone back to her own house, which she shared with Joshua, just four doors away, for once Polly couldn't blame her mother-in-law for feeling exasperated. She had indeed worked herself up into a fine lather with largely imagined terrors. Every year it was the same. Being turned out of her own home, even for the annual fumigation, filled her with insecurity. She longed for Matthew to come home, knowing he would understand her fears and soothe them.

Her husband was good and kind and strong. She felt herself lucky to have been courted and wed by such a man. He didn't drink all his money away like some, but brought it home for the care of his children, and the wife he loved and cherished above everything. She'd looked forward to his coming home all day, as she always did, but tonight there would be no easy chat over supper, no time to cuddle up beneath the blankets and old army greatcoats in their own bed. But he'd be there all the same, her rock, so really she had nothing to fret about at all.

When Matthew did arrive home, exhausted after a day spent up and down the Rochdale canal on the narrow-boats, it was to find his wife and children standing forlornly in the street, herded together with his neighbours, ready to be carried off like refugees.

'Hello, lad,' Connie Green hailed him, 'Here we go again, on us holidays.'

'Aye, who wants to go to Blackpool when they can lie on t'floor of Ardwick Barracks?' quipped Bet Sutcliffe, who owned the old clothes shop a few doors up the street.

Matthew managed a smile but, distracted by problems of his own, didn't come back with a joke as he would normally have done. He could see Davey Murphy ordering his wife about as usual while trying to disguise the fact that she sported another bruise. Matt nodded to him, acknowledging his presence, then turned away, not wishing to appear over-curious. Instead he put his arms about his own wife and drew her to his side, knowing how she hated this annual ritual.

The smell of the gasworks, rubber works and chemical factory was strong in his nostrils, but to this would soon be added the stink of the fumigating gas. The men were already busily sealing fireplaces, windows and doors with sticky tape. Then they would set fire to tins of powder which would hiss and spit as they ran out, slamming the doors behind them, sealing each one with a sheet of rubber to keep the gas in. By the time the occupants were allowed back from their sojourn at the barracks, the houses should be blessedly free from their unwelcome visitors, for a while at least.

Matt felt Polly shudder in his arms and, experiencing a rush of love for her, gave her a little squeeze. 'Don't fret, love. It'll be over soon enough, and think what a blessed relief for us to be rid of the blackjacks for a while.' He helped her climb aboard the truck which would take them to the barracks, where he knew they'd spend an uncomfortable, cold night sleeping on bare boards. Not that he minded. The way he was feeling right now, sleeping on a clothes line wouldn't trouble him in the least, he was that tired.

'I've told them my house is clean, but they'll not listen.'

'The bugs would still come, love, clean or not.'

'I know.' She admitted with a rueful smile, feeling better already just to have him there.

He smiled back at her, a gentle giant of a man with fair hair and blue-grey eyes that did not quite meet her gaze as they usually did, so that he could hide his own insecurities and fears. He'd been doing reasonably well lately, getting three, or sometimes four days a week regular work, fewer shipments due. As a result, pay and hours would be cut and a restlessness was growing among the men, with renewed talk of unions which employers viewed as a threat to their power.

Matthew did his best to avoid such talk and patiently hoped for the best. He'd no wish to involve himself in any political protest which he knew could degenerate with frightening swiftness into something violent and unpredictable. Besides, hadn't he had a bellyful of fighting, enough to last him a lifetime? Let someone else take on this battle.

He lifted up eight-year-old Benny and told him to be a good lad and sit still for once, then helped twelve-year-old Lucy climb aboard. She went at once to take hold of Polly's hand.

'Don't worry, Mam. It'll be over soon. They'll be doing Jersey Street tomorrow, then Hood and Blossom Street. Row by row, everyone will have their turn.'

'Stay close, mind. I want naught to happen to the pair of you.' As she spoke, Polly glanced anxiously about for her young son, but he was happily nattering to his friends.

Reaching up, Matthew planted a kiss on her cheek. 'Nowt will happen to either of them. Stop your fretting. It's only the bug brigade, not the bloomin' coppers.'

'You daft bitch!' A sudden shout rang out, making everyone in the truck lean over the sides and crane their necks to see what was going on. Dove Street was never short on entertainment.

'What the...?' The body of a woman thudded against Matt, knocking the wind out of him and jarring his shoulder against the truck. Poor Mrs Murphy, suffering yet another bruising blow from her husband.

'*You bloody whore!*' As Matthew bent to help the woman to her feet, she was whipped away from his hands and flung back with a loud crack as her head met the wall.

'Hold on, what the blazes...' But Matthew got no further as a fist connected with his nose; the kind of punch that left his teeth rattling and his head spinning. He could hear Polly screaming, and fought to keep consciousness even as he lunged for Murphy yet again. But he lost his balance and punched nothing but air.

Then from the door of number five emerged one of the railway guards, who really oughtn't to have been there at all, and would almost certainly have remained hidden had the fumigation squad not unexpectedly flushed him out, and Davey Murphy had not been deprived of his usual pint or two at the pub that evening. Murphy shook off Matthew as if he were no more than an irritating gnat.

'So this is what you get up to, woman, while I'm out looking for work, day after bleedin' day. You entertain your fancy man in me own bloomin' house.'

'I weren't, he only called—' But whatever it was he'd supposedly called for, they were never to discover. A scuffle broke out as the two men flung punches at each other, Davey Murphy connecting more than the guard who was getting the worst of it, being less practised in fisticuffs than the big Irishman.

Then before anyone could guess what he was about to do, Davey swung round, letting fly at his wife with one balled fist. There was a terrible sound of crunching bones, a piercing scream, followed by a sickening thud as she fell to the ground.

'Dear God, he's done for her.'

Even as blood spurted and her arms stopped flailing to defend herself, the rain of blows and clamour of shouting and swearing did not let up until Matthew and the fumigation men finally managed, with great difficulty, to drag Davey off her. The winner and the loser of this terrible contest were by now patently obvious. Moments later it was the sound of police whistles that broke the awed silence which had descended on Dove Street.

Davey Murphy was led away, no doubt to Strangeways, with his hands in cuffs and not a trace of remorse on his face. The children would be found places in an orphanage somewhere while his poor wife's troubles were over at last, at least in this world.

'Why do we live here?' Polly said in a hoarse whisper, wanting to retch as she held her children protectively close, for all they had seen similar occurrences time and again. But for once there were no soft words of comfort from her husband, and his voice was uncharacteristically harsh as he answered her.

'Because we've no choice.'

Filled instantly with remorse and guilt over her fussing, which now seemed ridiculous in comparison to the horrific fate which had befallen poor Mrs Murphy and her children, Polly slid an arm about her husband's neck the minute he came and sat beside her in the truck, leaning against his shoulder as if she could will the strength of him to flow into her own body. With his fair hair, blunt chin and hatred of embarrassing emotional scenes he was a typical Englishman, yet she loved him for it.

'I'm sorry, Matt, for making such a blather about everything today. At least we're happy, are we not, and don't have the problems the poor Murphys had, you being in such a fine good job an' all. Is that not so?'

'Aye, 'course it is,' he agreed in his bluff way, thinking how lovely she was, and how silky her skin as he kissed her cheek; holding her protectively close as the truck jerked into motion. But his eyes were glazed over the dark sheen of her hair as she lay against his shoulder; the unseeing inward vision of a man with more troubles on his mind than he cares to admit.

Chapter Two

The night in the barracks was every bit as cold and uncomfortable as Polly had feared. Stripped of their clothes while they were deloused, the whole process seemed to her thoroughly humiliating.

The young students from the Roundhouse Mission, operating under the auspices of the University Settlement, offered fresh second-hand clothes to those who wanted them. Few took up the offer. Ancoats folk hated charity above all things. And there were some who'd rather do a bit of light-fingered fending for themselves, which at least necessitated taking a risk, than accept a hand-out; a perverse philosophy with which Polly sympathized though she did not subscribe to it herself. She frequently made a point of drumming into both her children the possible outcome of any such misguided outlook; how they might be clapped in the reformatory for seven years, just for looking as if they'd stolen something.

Polly herself gladly accepted the offer of clothes, thanking the young man in his tweed suit and striped tie as he stood guard behind his table, making him gaze with startled wonder upon this raggedly dressed woman who had such a bewitching smile and skin as fine as porcelain.

'I'll not wear it,' young Benny complained as Polly popped a 'new' cap with a smart blue peak upon his head.

'Sure an' you will if I say so.'

'They'll laugh at me.' She'd already kitted him out with an equally 'new' cotton shirt that only had one darn in it, and a pair of grey trousers which hung from his braces to well past his knees so would last him quite a time. He still wore his own clogs, for which he was thankful.

'And won't they just wish their mams had been so clever as to take up this fine young man's offer?' She smiled at the student again, causing him to gulp.

Benny sulked. He loved his mother dearly but she didn't always understand the ways of the world, not Dove Street ways anyroad. It didn't pay to be different. He had no wish to stand out in a crowd, yet his mam did it all the time. Grown-ups could be very confusing. She'd sometimes quite happily let him play out on a Sunday when all his friends had been marched off to church but then in the evenings, when he and the lads were just starting to enjoy themselves, she'd be the first to fetch him home.

'You'll not learn your lessons without a good night's sleep,' she'd say. 'Work hard and one day you'll be the best reader in the class, Benjamin Pride, so you will.'

Benny had no wish to be the best reader in the class. Reading was for cissies. Everyone knew that. But would she listen? She'd even gone so far as to have Mr Reckitt, the Dolly Varden man who lived two doors away, look out for books among the rubbish at the better-off houses. She'd been given *The Old Curiosity Shop* that way, and after weeping over it herself, gave it to Benny to read. A more boring book he had yet to find.

Worst of all, the Dolly Varden men, so called because they wore a wide-brimmed hat like the famous Dolly Varden, a music hall singer of the naughty 90s, emptied the rubbish bins, so the book stank.

And what Georgie Eastwood would say when he saw the blue peaked cap, Benny dreaded to think. Georgie wouldn't be seen dead in a cap like this. He wore a union shirt, open at the neck to reveal a blue muffler, waistcoat, jacket, and long trousers held up with a wide buckled belt. On his feet were a pair of clogs with the fiercest metal toe caps Benny had ever set eyes on.

Georgie and his gang waited for him night after night when school had finished for the day, or would prowl around the recreation ground where Benny and his mates went to play football.

Why they picked on him he couldn't quite work out, but Georgie would poke him in the ribs with a stick, or threaten to clout him with the buckle of his belt if he didn't agree to pinch a few sweets from Vera Murray's toffee shop.

So far Benny had always managed to escape, thanks to the intervention of his friends. They sometimes talked of setting up a gang of their own, here in Dove Street, but Benny worried about how they could ever hope to stand up to the Eastwood Gang. Didn't Georgie claim that his dad had once been leader of one of the legendary Napoo Gangs? And he meant to be equally famous. But even if they did get one going in Dove Street, it was perfectly clear to Benny that a leader of a gang would never wear a blue peaked cap.

Now he pulled the offending article off his head and pursed his lips till his jaws ached with the effort.

'I'll not wear it, I tell you. I won't,' he insisted one more time. But because his mam had that determined, warning light in her eyes, fists stuck into her waist in that fierce way she had, further protests quickly died and he surrendered to the inevitable. Then Benny obediently lay down on the cold floor, closed his eyes and feigned sleep. Inside his head he prayed that Georgia Eastwood's mother would also have got him some 'new' clothes, but didn't hold out much hope. The Eastwoods had their own way of getting what they needed, and didn't depend on others to provide it.

Polly settled herself beside her son, and called for Lucy to join them.

'Aw, I'm having a natter with Sal,' Lucy protested. 'I won't be more'n a minute or two.'

'See you're not then,' Polly scolded. 'It'll be black as pitch in here when all the candles are put out. You'd never find us in the crush.'

Lucy only laughed, too used to her mother's anxieties to pay them much heed. Besides, Sal had a brother Tom, who she knew had a shine for her, though he'd not admitted as much. She might not be old enough yet at twelve to go out on the monkey-walk on Eccles New Road, which was what they called the stretch of road where the girls and lads normally got together, but she could surely seize on this opportunity to bring him to the point of asking her to be his girl.

It made her go all fizzy and warm inside just to look at him, as if she'd eaten a lemon sherbet. Even if he didn't say anything, it would certainly be more fun to tease Tom Shackleton than talk to her parents. Dad was engrossed in an argument with Uncle Joshua as usual, Mam acting as referee, while Grandma Flo was enjoying herself sitting with all the other matriarchs of Dove Street, having a good old chin-wag.

Matthew was, as Lucy suspected, deeply embroiled in a discussion that encompassed hopes for the revival of the cotton industry, the iniquities of the benefit system for the unemployed, and endless grumbles about miserly bosses who objected to any hint of a union amongst their workers. His brother Joshua, long limbs coiled uncomfortably on the wooden floor, lean face looking almost cadaverous in the candlelight, seemed to pulsate with cold fury. He spoke with that measured, assured calm which drove Matthew to the limits of his patience.

'If we sit back and let them, they'll continue to abuse us. It's up to us to fight. We're all working men – in this together.'

'How can we stand up to those who hold the purse strings?' Matthew wanted to know. 'Them bosses would turn us off without a second thought if we put one foot wrong. Out on our ear, we'd be. It's all right for you, Josh, a single man. Some of us have a wife and childer to consider.' Joshua glared at his brother with the kind of intense gaze which made lesser men shiver. He'd heard this argument too many times to be persuaded by it. In his opinion Matthew made his wife and children the excuse for every decision or action he ever made, or rather those he failed to make. He put the Irish woman before everything, even his own family

– which in one instance, as they both well knew, had proved disastrous.

Polly, ever wry of these confrontations between the two brothers, attempted to mediate. 'You're both right, in a way. But standing up to the bosses would need every working man to be in agreement and on one side, and you'd never achieve that.'

'And how would you know? You're only a woman.' For all the fury in his ascetic features, Joshua's voice remained cold and expressionless, commanding respect and deference from his listeners.

Polly could only look into his nasty pale eyes and think how different he was from her gentle Matthew. There'd never been any love lost between the pair of them, for her dislike of him dated right back to the war and the way he'd blamed Matt for the death of their younger brother, Cecil. A scandalous and cruel accusation for which she'd never forgiven him. In her opinion, Joshua Pride hadn't one morsel of compassion in his entire being so if he talked of his concern for the working man, she saw only his own need for power and influence.

He was still talking, addressing the men gathered about with the kind of authority they appeared to respect. Since many of them attended Zion Methodist Chapel, where he acted as lay preacher, they were used to heeding his words. 'There are unions everywhere now, so why not here in Dove Street? The bosses will continue to put the squeeze on, keep reducing our hourly rate and putting us on shorter time, if we don't band together and stop them.'

'Happen that's what Band of Hope should be doing, instead of trying to make us all go teetotal. They've about as much chance of success,' said Percy Williams, well known for his droll sense of humour. But he soon wished he'd kept his mouth shut when it was his turn to bear the heat of Joshua's scorching glare. 'Aye, well, it were only a thought like,' he mumbled.

Matthew, who liked to approach life with more caution than his brother, gave a scornful laugh, 'How can we make the employers, union or no union, agree to any changes if the work isn't there in the first place? The major industries have been on the slide for years. Now we've sold looms to India, the competition is beating us at our own game.'

'My argument entirely,' his brother insisted. 'We should think ahead, think of our own future, stick up for the working man.' There were murmurs of assent, while others began to call out obscenities about their own particular employers. The gathering in the stinking, overcrowded room quickly grew as heated as a political rally.

'How many folk work in these bloomin' mills?' one man asked, trying to illustrate how dependent the district still was on cotton, even if not as completely as it once had been.

'About half of 'em, lazy so-and-so's,' quipped one wag, who'd grown tired of the argument. Everybody laughed and tension instantly eased, the conversation moving on to other, less contentious topics.

If it hadn't been for the good humour of her neighbours, Polly decided, the night would have been miserable indeed. Instead, almost a party atmosphere developed as one or two folk started to sing in the darkness, others joining in. The last song was arousing rendition of 'Sweet Rosie O'Grady' before silence finally settled upon the overcrowded room, or what passed for it among the snuffles, burps, grunts, snores and other less edifying sounds that went on under cover of darkness.

In the distance could be heard shunting and banging from the railway goods yard. Soon Matt was snoring gently beside her, but Polly lay listening to every sound while turning over in her mind how she could rid her house of the smell of gas, whether anything would have 'gone missing' during the fumigation process, and where she would find the money for Lucy's white frock for this year's Whit Walks. Even when sleep finally claimed her, these thoughts continued to crowd her dreams.

Benny was happily fitting the sounds of the railway to pictures in his mind. One minute he was the driver of the magnificent

Prince of Wales, stoking the engine so that steam soared from its short fat chimney; the next he was the man working the turntables, routeing each wagon on to its correct line. As he slid contentedly into sleep, he was speeding through the countryside, the wind cold upon his face and the sound of the engine whistle screeching in his ears.

None of them was aware of Lucy, stumbling back to her place beside them, nor heard her quiet sobs under cover of this multitude of nocturnal sounds.

—

Poor Mrs Murphy was buried with little fuss by the remaining members of her family. They raised a loan from the Eastwoods in order to pay for it, knowing it would cost them dear in repayment, but not wanting her to suffer the humiliation of a pauper's funeral. With her husband and children gone, the residents of Dove Street felt it incumbent upon themselves to turn out in force. An ineffectual, rather foolish woman, yet she surely deserved a last show of respect. She'd been married to a brute of a man, after all.

Polly and Big Flo made it their business to attend, removing everyday aprons and shawls and slipping on their Sunday coats, though along with the other women it meant begging a half-hour off work in order to attend. Polly from her job at the Yates's Temperance Tavern, Big Flo from the daily chores. Matthew too asked for time off, the gaffer being far from pleased by this request but willing to allow a short break on condition he made up the time during bis dinner break. Consequently Matthew told Polly he couldn't be there for the service but he'd be sure to attend the burial, as was only right and proper, them being next-door neighbours.

'Eeh, I don't think I've ever been in a Roman Catholic church before,' Big Flo said, looking about her as if she half expected the good Lord to strike her dead upon the spot for daring to do so now.

Polly laughed, though for her own part she was welcoming the peace of the church, the smell of the incense and the familiar rituals, wondering if she dare ask to take the sacrament yet knowing she'd be refused. 'It's quite a while since I was in here myself.'

'You must live in fear of the priest coming to call?'

'Why should I? We had our disagreement years ago. Father Donevan has his job to do, whether he likes it or not, and we get on fine despite our differences.'

Big Flo looked disbelieving. She knew all about these Romans. How they were half-starved because their priests took all the money; how they weren't allowed to touch a Bible, and had queer ideas about the holy bread they swallowed. It was no surprise to her that only the priest got a taste of the wine. In Zion Methodist they drank blackcurrant juice, which was quite adequate for the purpose and didn't lead you into evil ways; a measure some of these so-called holy priests would do well to follow, in Flo's humble opinion. She told her daughter-in-law as much now, not for the first time. Polly merely sighed resignedly.

'Let's not fall out over religion, Flo. I didn't ask Matthew to turn for me, and rarely attend church myself. I only insist that our children be brought up as Catholics. Surely that's not too much to ask? And we're happy. What more d'you want?'

Joshua leaned across his mother to whisper to Polly in sonorous tones, 'You could attend chapel with your husband, like a good wife should.'

'Aye,' Big Flo agreed, nodding. 'Have you done that yet? Have you hecky-thump!'

'Matthew hasn't asked me to, nor will he.'

Joshua snorted his disapproval. 'Which only shows his own lack of faith. You would not be so neglected were you my wife. He places your soul in jeopardy by pandering to your fancies.'

Polly could barely suppress a shudder as she looked into her brother-in-law's set face. Thin lips screwed into an unforgiving line, he was a living example of all she hated most: a bigot and a hypocrite. There were some who said Joshua Pride wasn't quite the good Methodist he claimed to be, that he had a few sins of his own which he kept carefully concealed, including a married woman in Chatham Street whom he visited after chapel. It almost made Polly giggle, the thought of this sour-faced man embarking upon an illicit affair. She knew it was quite impossible to win an argument with him, yet his bigotry irritated her so much she could never keep silent in the face of his jibes.

'I am what I am. Each to their own, that's what Matt and I agreed when we married. It's a pity everyone else can't take the same view.' And having made her point she lifted her hymn book and began to sing, aware of the blistering glances Joshua sent in her direction but paying them no heed.

–

Lucy had every intention of telling her mother about the occurrence at the barracks. She'd never thought of herself as either sensitive or soft; you couldn't survive in Dove Street if you were either of those things. But the words she had heard still rang in her head, even now, days later. There'd been the breath of evil in them somehow, the stench of something corrupt clinging to every syllable, as if each utterance brought the speaker intense satisfaction.

The voice had come out of the darkness, after the last candle had been quenched and she'd been making her way back to her parents. Stumbling over prone bodies as she recalled with growing trepidation her mother's warning about getting lost amongst them.

'Whore! Harlot!'

She hadn't recognised the voice, hissing so low against her ear, but as she'd tried to hurry away and escape it, a hand had gripped her arm, holding her fast while the words were repeated like a litany of vilification in her head.

She had felt violated, as if in some way they had penetrated the sweet innocence of her childish flirtation. Lucy would never have thought Tom Shackleton capable of such horrible, hurtful words, and the thought that he had directed them at her had at first made her feel used and degraded, upset her so much that she'd quietly sobbed herself to sleep that night.

Now she was filled with anger. How could he have behaved so dreadfully? She'd only been having fun, fluttering her lashes and teasing him.

Lucy had liked and admired Tom Shackleton, who was two years older than herself, for weeks, and had hoped he'd notice her. He had lovely warm brown eyes and gentle hands, and didn't have that sickening stink of poverty about him, or not as badly as some. Nor did he have anything to do with the scuttlers who enjoyed causing mayhem in the streets of Ancoats, whether it be pulling girls' hair, pinching goods off the back of carts or riding the rails at the goods yard.

Yet what Tom had done to her by using such words was, in some ways, worse. She'd never known such bitter disappointment.

Upon reflection, however, Lucy had decided against mentioning the matter to her mother. Wouldn't she only make too much of it? She'd want to know if he'd touched her where he shouldn't, maybe accuse her of encouraging his advances, of being no better than she should be, and remind her she was still a child for all she was well on the way to thirteen. Didn't mothers always take that line? Lucy knew her mam was perfectly capable of going round and tearing a strip off him, or even complaining to his own mother. She went hot with embarrassment at the very thought, and misery sank deeper into her stomach, making her feel sick. No, best to put it out of her head, dismiss it as the kind of nastiness that lads found amusing.

But she would tell Sal, her best friend, what she thought of her precious brother's behaviour! Lucy tackled her the very next day in a corner of the playground.

Being in the top class, the two girls took no part in the younger girls' games, but sat on their coats to talk or dream of the day they would be free of the tyranny of spelling tests and Miss Clarke's sharp-edged ruler, which could come down so heavily on those, like Lucy, who were prone to daydreaming. They'd talk of their hopes to get a job in Paulden's maybe, where they could serve high-class ladies with frocks and furbelows. Or, more realistically, at the railway cafe where there would at least be no shortage of food.

But there was no such girlish chatter this morning.

'I wasn't suggesting anything improper, I was just being friendly,' Lucy insisted to an open-mouthed Sally. 'So what right did he have to say such nasty things?'

'He wouldn't, not our Tom,' Sally protested, her voice weak with shock.

'Didn't I hear him with me own ears? What sort of a girl does he take me for?'

'He might be as daft as most lads his age but he isn't cruel, and he wouldn't know such words anyroad. He'd use "totty" or "pro".'

'Not if he wanted to upset and frighten me, which he did, I don't mind admitting,' Lucy insisted, finding her eyes once again filling with tears, to her great mortification.

But Sally's reaction was not what she had expected or hoped for. Instead of taking sides with Lucy, all girls together as it were and agreeing to make her brother apologise, she took offence on his behalf. Snatching up her coat she flounced off in high dudgeon. Lucy was left with the bitter taste of not only having been vilified for no apparent reason by the boy she liked most in all the world, but had now lost her best friend.

Chapter Three

It was a Saturday afternoon and although Joshua felt bone weary after a hard week in the mill and would much rather have spent the afternoon reading or resting, he kept on walking. He was working his way along Great Ancoats Street, taking detours round side streets, handing out leaflets along the way, stuffing them in letter-boxes, sticking them on shop counters or lamp-posts, wherever he could think of.

You need power. You need a union. You need Joshua Pride to run it – the poster boldly stated. Controversial, daring, radical, but necessary. Underneath were details of a meeting he'd called, which he hoped dozens if not a hundred or so working men would attend. He'd paid out a fair sum of money to have the leaflet printed, but Joshua liked to think that not a penny of it would be wasted. He was perfectly certain that the meeting would go ahead, a union of mill-workers would be formed, and he would be elected president of it.

He'd just finished Pollard Street, including Vulcan Works, Victoria Mills and others as far as the row of shops at the bottom, He'd even ventured into a few pubs, one at the corner of Norton Street, another in Long Street, where he'd been met with a mixture of jeering laughter and cautious interest.

Now he crossed the canal, meaning to visit every house around the wharf as far as Little Italy. He was concentrating his efforts on the part of Ancoats that was saturated with mills, factories and canal workings. He'd even spent an hour outside the dark red brick gothic edifice of Ancoats Hospital, handing out leaflets to folk as they queued up for their medicines.

Joshua Pride meant to leave no stone unturned in his quest to win support. He would launch a union if it was the last thing he did, and he would somehow persuade his brother to join. Matthew owed him that much at least. From the first moment he'd set eyes on that Irish woman, only seventeen at the time, he'd been besotted by her. Within weeks he'd cast aside a lifetime of worship and worthy endeavours in the chapel and married her, a Roman Catholic. He'd claimed that there was no time to waste with war having broken out, and that he couldn't live without her. He'd refused to listen to his family, caring nothing for their opinions. He thought only of love and raising a family, and other such sentimental nonsense.

Flo had been devastated by the shame of her son's behaviour, but wisely left it to Joshua, as the elder brother, to put forward arguments on the pitfalls of a mixed marriage and to attempt to pressurise him into calling off the wedding. Even at the last moment on the day itself Joshua had attempted to make him see sense by refusing even to attend the register office where the ceremony was to be held. But it had done no good, the marriage had gone ahead with no more than a couple of witnesses present. And look where Matthew's obstinacy had led.

He'd promised to watch out for Cecil, the youngest of the three brothers, but only Matthew had come back from war. If he'd not been so obsessed with saving his own skin, for the sake of the wife he'd left back home, Joshua was certain his youngest brother would still be alive today.

He pushed these memories from his mind, feeling the familiar rage and bitterness eating away at him as they had done for years.

It was as he reached Meadow Street that he remembered a certain young widow he'd met at chapel one Sunday. He called to mind her comely figure and pleasing ways; not brash or loud-mouthed like some. She'd made a point of asking for his help, since she was at her wit's end as to how to cope following the death of her young husband. He'd told her that he could do nothing for her, but perhaps he might try after all. The visit might serve to lift his spirits. Joshua liked to make himself useful, particularly to vulnerable young women.

As he neared her house, instead of stuffing the leaflet through the letter-box he glanced quickly about him, noted only a few children playing with cigarette cards against the wall, and tapped sharply on the door.

It was opened by a child. Dressed in a filthy jersey and patched trousers, the small boy considered the stranger with lacklustre interest, shuffling his bare feet and wiping a none-too-clean nose on his arm as he did so.

'Is your mother in, lad?'

The boy said nothing, not even a shake or nod of his ragamuffin head, and Joshua felt a stirring of irritation. He must be seven or eight, surely old enough to understand plain English? Then he heard a rattle of clogs on the wooden stairs and the woman herself emerged from the dimness of the house. She wore a grey skirt and a blouse that might once have been white. Joshua made a mental note to fetch her a bar of carbolic soap next time he called. He preferred his women clean but for now would overlook the ragged state of the garment in view of the way it fell open at her throat, and the thrust of her young breasts as they rose and fell with enticing breathlessness beneath the thin fabric.

'Oh, Mr Pride, I didn't hear you knock. Come in, won't you? I'll put t'kettle on. Kevin, you go out and play with your sisters, there's a good lad. I'll call you when supper's ready.'

Over a cup of weak tea, Joshua lent a sympathetic ear to the young widow's plight. Kate Hughes was clearly still in deep shock after the loss of her young husband from consumption and, as she said herself, sorely in need of advice. The last thing she wanted was to end up in the workhouse, with her three children taken into care.

'Only too happy to help, Mrs Hughes. I'm sure I can put you in the way of suitable employment. I shall make enquiries for you as I go about my work.'

She was filled with gratitude, thanking him profusely. Even so it took a minute or two before he persuaded her to remove the offending blouse.

'Perhaps you have money to pay for my assistance, instead?' he queried, when she hesitated. 'Or I could always call the Poor Law Guardians.' He got up as if to go, noting with satisfaction the way fear glinted in her eyes.

'No, no.' Kate Hughes knew when she was bested.

But then women rarely put up any sort of resistance once they saw he was not a man to be trifled with. Joshua did not believe in asking for anything to which he was not entitled, and the body of a woman was a pleasure sent by God to satisfy a man's natural needs. He did not suggest they venture upstairs, for who knew what horrors may lurk in the dark recesses of her bedroom? The rag rug in front of the mean fire served just as well and her breasts were every bit as soft and yielding as he had hoped. Nor did he trouble to remove the grey skirt, simply lifted it, checked she was wearing no drawers, was reasonably clean, and got on with it. She cried out only once when he entered her.

After that, he promised to let her know the moment he heard of anything suitable.

'I expect I shall see you at chapel on Sunday?'

Kate, seeming too stunned by his attentions to speak, managed only a nod as she stared at him, wild-eyed.

He dusted down his jacket. 'I shall call again, when I have news.' And satisfied with his afternoon's efforts, he departed, not forgetting to leave one of his leaflets on her kitchen table. As a mere woman she would have no vote or say in union matters, but he suggested she may care to pass it on to someone who had. Every little helped.

–

Polly was worn out but happy. She'd spent days cleaning what had already been cleaned by the fumigation men, as if determined to reclaim her own home.

The stink had been everywhere. Even when she laid her weary head on her pillow at night, she felt as if she too were being gassed. 'I can't breathe, Mam,' Benny had complained, and Lucy's lovely face had run with tears from the fumes.

So she'd washed their only pair of well-darned sheets, the blankets and pillowcases, plus their nightdresses, vests and pants, which were all covered with the evil-smelling powder. It had taken two full days of possing and scrubbing, mangling and drying, and another to press them all with the flat irons she'd heated on the range.

At least no damage had been done. Nothing had been pinched, and each morning when she came into the kitchen to riddle the fire and put on the kettle, it was a delight to find no sign of a blackjack.

After her assault on the beds, Polly swept the horse-hair sofa, beat the rag rugs on the line in the yard, shamed by the amount of dust and powder that came out of them, and black-leaded the fire range till she could see her face in it. Then she scrubbed the rough deal table with bleach and washing soda, a lethal mixture which would either clean it or rot it. Then she gave the same treatment to the stone-flagged floor till any remaining bugs would surely call it a day.

Finally she polished the mahogany sideboard that took pride of place in the small front parlour. This was their most treasured possession, being the first item of furniture they'd bought when they married. It had taken two years to save up for it and not a day went by without Polly giving it a rub of her duster. The only other items in the parlour, which was used for special family occasions, was a small leather buffet, a clean new rug and Matthew's armchair. They'd not done too badly, she decided, considering they'd started with nothing, and wasn't she proud enough of her little house?

This thought brought a smile to her face now as she donkey-stoned her doorstep, seeing many another woman doing the self-same thing or cleaning their mucky windows, as if they didn't know they'd be filthy again in five minutes from the foul smoke belching from the numerous chimneys near by. The women would chat together as they went to collect water from the tap in the street; 'having a natter' or 'doing a bit of camping' as they called it, over the problems of the day.

Every now and then they'd walk in pairs down to the University Settlement buildings where they'd bathe their children, five or six at a time, then climb in themselves for a quick once-over. The rest of the time they had to make do with a sponge-down from a wash basin, or a painstakingly filled zinc bath by the fire. Was it any wonder it was hard keeping the bugs at bay with no running water in the house except what ran down the walls?

Polly had once asked Big Flo if she'd ever thought of leaving. 'Nay,' the old woman had said. 'I'd be lost if I left Ancoats.' Manchester, even Ancoats, wasn't too bad a place to live in, Polly supposed. Her loyalty to her own home country had faded somewhat in recent years, and she was happy enough here with Matthew, though truth to tell she wouldn't be against something a bit better for her children. Wasn't that always the way of it? But if Dove Street was poor in material possessions, it was rich in friendships. As Big Flo was fond of saying, 'Break your ankle and the whole street limps.'

–

Within days of poor Mrs Murphy's funeral, new people moved in next door, a family with four girls this time who might at least make less noise than the Murphy lads, now probably much subdued in a children's home, bless them.

The mother introduced herself as Eileen Grimshaw. She seemed too young at twenty-two to have had so many children, though she looked older. But Polly liked her. She was small with a mane of red-orange hair and a cheerful grin, despite seeming worn out half the time, and even thinner than Polly herself.

'They eat like hawks and me like a sparrow,' she said on that first day when Polly, seeing she was worn out by the move, asked her in for a cup of tea and offered her a bit of sad cake. 'Are you sure you can spare it?' Eileen was gazing longingly at the pale crust of pastry.

'It's not got any currants in it, nor have I any butter to put on it either, but it's fresh baked. Go on, get it down you.' The crumbling pastry, still warm from the oven, was gone in seconds and Polly wished she had more to offer, the girl looked so frail. But she'd saved the rest, one piece for each of her family for supper. Even so, the girl was starving, it was plain as the nose on your face. Polly gave Eileen her own slice. 'Go on, I had a piece earlier,' she lied. That vanished too, as quickly as the first.

'By heck, I wish I could bake like that! My mam allus said I were useless. Terence tells me so all the time.'

Polly smiled. 'Is Terence your husband?'

'Says he is, so I reckon he must be. They're his childer anyroad. Mostly,' she finished with a grin.

Polly decided not to follow up that enigmatic 'mostly'. Eileen was not like the other women in the street. She refused to wear a shawl or cover her head in any way when she went out. Nor did she wear the usual drab-coloured dresses or skirts the other young women wore beneath their apron. Her dress was bright green and very short. She claimed to have been given it by a woman she'd once worked for. The hem was loose and since she wore it every day, it wasn't overly clean.

Eileen continued, 'Terence likes me to look smart. Not like these old besoms round here. Miserable old sods! And at least they'll see me coming, eh?' And she cackled with laughter, bright blue eyes flashing.

Nor did she wear clogs. 'Nasty, noisy things' she called them. 'They're good for your feet,' Polly pointed out, giggling. Eileen Grimshaw was going to bring some light and laughter into her life, she could sense it. 'Keep them dry, with plenty of room to wriggle your toes.'

Eileen's feet, Polly was to discover in the days following, were often bare, but today she wore a pair of old boots that might once have belonged to a tramp. In the evenings, if she went out for a beer with her husband, she wore the kind of shoes that round here were called 'fast'.

There was a knock on the door and Big Flo walked in. It wasn't the custom to wait to be asked. 'It's only me. By the hangment, what has the wind blown in?' Arms akimbo she considered Eileen from top to toe. 'Thee's come from t'music hall, right?'

Eileen took this as a joke and chuckled. 'I once went to the Variety with me pals. Eeh, that were a right good do? We saw Albert Modley. Oh, he was a laugh, he was. Pretended to be driving a tram.' She stood up to demonstrate, as if operating the driver's handle. '"I'm goin' to Duplicate," he says.' And she bent double with such joyous laughter that soon she had Polly giggling too, and even Big Flo couldn't hold back a smile.

'So what brought you to Dove Street? Are you married? Have you any childer? Where did you hail from? How do you earn your crust?' Flo tossed a string of questions at the visitor while Polly brewed fresh tea, mugs were refilled and the women settled themselves for a lengthy chat.

'Sparkle Street,' Eileen informed her interrogator. 'So that's what I try to do. Sparkle.'

'You come from the Dardanelles?' The scorn in the old woman's voice was clear. 'There's bloody murder done in the Dardanelles every Saturday night.'

'Aye, that's true,' Eileen blithely agreed. 'Which is why we've moved up here to this, posh neighbourhood.' This brought a stunned silence. 'Posh' not being a word usually associated with Dove Street.

Big Flo mildly remarked, 'Aye, well, happen you were right to come. They'd rob their own mothers in the Dardanelles.'

'That's because the mothers don't put their daughters on the stage – they put 'em on the game,' said Eileen, giving that by now familiar chuckle. 'Only I was lucky. I escaped that fate by marrying Terence.'

In the stunned silence that followed this amazing confession, Polly strove to restrain the laughter that threatened to erupt.

Finding her voice at last, she asked, 'Did you call for any special reason, Flo?'

'Nay, I were just passing.' The old woman set down her mug with a snap and got briskly to her feet, ready to give the lie to this with her next words. 'Whatever's ailing that child o' yours, thee'd best 'ave a word with her and sort it out. She looks like she's lost a shilling and found a tanner.' And, having shed this worry concerning Lucy, Big Flo departed, surprisingly light on her feet for a woman so big and muscular. At the door, she turned and addressed her parting remarks to Eileen.

'What does yer husband do?'

'He's unemployed at present.'

'Well then, you won't spoil a pair.' And having delivered this damning indictment of feckless folk who didn't work, she departed, arms swinging like an all-in wrestler's.

'Sorry about that,' Polly said with a wry smile after the door had slammed shut behind her mother-in-law. 'She's harmless enough really.'

Eileen gave a wry smile. 'I don't mind. Does this mean we're going to be friends?' It struck Polly as an odd thing to say, but she answered as cheerfully.

'I should hope so. Isn't that the finest thing in the world, to have lots of friends? Call in any time you've a mind, and I'll pop in to see you.'

'I'll rather come in here, if it's all right with you? Terence doesn't care for strangers in his house. He likes to keep himself to himself.'

'But we wouldn't be strangers, we'd be neighbours.'

'I know.' Looking troubled for a moment, Eileen shrugged it off with a laugh. 'It's with me being in t'family way again. He says I've no time for nattering, I work slow enough as it is. And he's right. But then, I've generally childer draped round me neck like a bloomin' necklace. Me mam's taken them today while we get moved in.'

31

Polly couldn't disguise her astonishment. The girl looked too thin to sustain her own life, let alone that of another. 'You're pregnant?'

'I am, aye.' The two young women looked at each other, one wondering how much to tell, the other whether this was a moment for congratulations or commiserations. The answer came in a bubbling flow of words. 'Not that I wanted another, you understand. But you can't stop them coming, can you?' And for all the self-deprecating smile on her new friend's rouged lips, Polly sensed desperation in the question.

'I'm a Catholic, so perhaps I'm not the best person to ask.'

'But you've only the two. How did you manage that?' Then, surprisingly, the girl blushed bright red and got hastily to her feet. 'Eeh, listen to me. What a thing to ask. Terence allus says I put me foot in it every time I open me mouth. I'd best be off.' But as she fled to the door, Polly stopped her.

'I don't mind your asking. I didn't do anything special. No more came, that's all. I did want another baby for a while, but then I counted my blessings. Two's enough to keep, eh?' Again she considered the frail figure of the girl with her determinedly cheerful countenance. Underneath that mask of bravado, Eileen was clearly suffering.

'You do get a bit of rest every afternoon, don't you?'

'Oh, aye, Terence lets me have half an hour. He's very good. He even holds the door open for me while I fetch in the coal.' And she chuckled at the joke, 'That's one of Albert Modley's. Though it's pretty accurate so far as Terence is concerned, lazy sod.'

Polly smiled too, then impulsively put her arms about the girl, apparently weighed down by children though she seemed little more than a child herself. 'Half an hour is no time at all. You need to take better care of yourself than that. You come in here every afternoon. I'm usually home by four. What men don't see they won't worry over, isn't that the way of it? And you and me can have a bit of a natter. Now wouldn't that be grand?'

'Oh, aye, it would that. I will come in, whenever I can. It'd be grand to have you for a friend, Polly.'

And they grinned at each other in perfect understanding. Then Eileen was on her way to the door, clearly itching to be off. 'Mam'll be fetching t'childer back soon, and I should be getting on with cleaning and tidying, and washing nappies.'

'Ach, a woman's work is never done,' Polly smilingly agreed as she watched her new friend hurry away. Privately she vowed somehow to find the answer to her new friend's question. There was surely a limit to how many babies a woman was supposed to have, and some way to prevent them. If ever a woman was in need of help, Eileen Grimshaw was.

Chapter Four

Polly sang as she worked, letting her voiee trill loudly on the old Irish melodies, for didn't she have a secret?

Big Flo was right, Lucy had been in one of her moods for days, but little thought was needed to give Polly the reason why. The poor lass wanted to take part in the Whit Walks as she always did, and because money was even harder to come by than usual, hadn't dared pluck up the courage to ask her mother if they could manage it this year. But she needn't have worried. Tattered and poverty-stricken though they may be, nobody in the whole of Manchester would miss taking part in the Whit Walks. Like everyone else, Polly had been saving all year for this purpose. Her 'nest egg', as she called it, was hidden away in a tin beneath a loose floorboard.

Besides working at Yates's Tavern, she'd been lucky enough to find extra work, cleaning. Perhaps she'd got the job because she'd presented herself so well, showing some pride in her appearance, shawl neatly pinned at her throat, skirt clean, clogs shining. She'd certainly not told her new employer where she lived, which had surely helped. No, there was nothing her daughter heeded that she wouldn't provide, if it were at all possible.

Not that she'd told Matthew yet about the new job. Did that mean she was turning into a cheat? Polly worried. But indeed why should it, for wasn't it only for her family's good that she worked? It was right what she'd said to Eileen. Men worried too much. She completely forgot how anxious she'd been over the fumigation.

What Matthew failed to appreciate was that the children were growing fast and so were their appetites, and however hard he worked, it wasn't enough to feed them all adequately, let alone provide all the other things growing children needed. She'd no choice but to work, and deep down he knew that.

As for the Whit Walks, well, they were special, taking place only once a year. They brightened everyone's lives, and what was wrong with offering witness to the Almighty? The problem was they all needed new clothes or boots for this grand occasion, and Lucy a beautiful white dress. Now she had achieved her purpose, Polly knew that it was time for her to tell the truth, admit to her secret and face her husband's ire. Then she could at least put her daughter's mind at rest.

–

There was a break in the canal wall at the end of Dove Street, quite close to the mill. It was here that the narrow-boats tied up. Some of them brought in coal all day long, carried along two planks that ran from the boat into the entrance of the mill fire-hole. It was one of Matthew's jobs to fill a wheelbarrow with slack, run it along the plank, tip it into the hole then go back for more. It was casual labour, paid by the hour, but glad of the work, he'd happily do this task for twelve or sometimes fourteen hours a day. If it was a tiring, back-breaking slog, he never complained or even seemed to notice. It was employment, casual or not, for which he was grateful.

On other days he might be employed at the dock in Ducie Street. Here he would help unload bales of cotton from the three narrow-boats pulled by a steamer all the way from Liverpool. Later the bales would have to be sorted and reloaded for the final stage of their journey on to smaller narrow-boats or carts for those mills without access to a canal or the River Medlock.

Though Matthew didn't work in the mill as Joshua did, he was as affected by the state of local industry as his brother. If orders for finished cotton went down, workers like him were laid off or put on short time. Then there was less demand for the coal and coke which kept the boilers going, or for the great bales of raw cotton that came down the Ship Canal from Liverpool, and Matthew spent half his life shifting one or other of these commodities.

Today, as he worked, he thought of Joshua's words that night at the barracks. Following their argument, Matthew had finally been persuaded to attend one of his brother's meetings, trying to appease Joshua's ill temper as he so often did. It had, as Matthew had anticipated, been no occasion for a celebration of brotherly love.

He knew that Joshua was hoping to lead a group from Dove Street to speak against their employers and form a union of cotton employees. This would include all who worked at the mill, and those who shipped the cotton either in its raw or finished state. Joshua was right in saying that the industry was not what it had been; the days when cotton was king long gone, with increasing fears for its future. New orders were badly needed, though where these would come from was anyone's guess.

The meeting, which had been poorly attended, passed a resolution that what they needed most was someone to lobby Parliament; make them do something about the cheap imports which were flooding the market. Trade had been poor for years, and the general strike hadn't helped. The election of a Labour government in the spring had seemed to offer new hope at first; now no one was quite sure. Nothing was really being done to improve matters. The bosses could still call the tune.

Matthew was not alone in dreaming of that seemingly impossible goal, a full week's work. Even then, the pay would be so low he knew he still couldn't hope to keep his family on it without the few extra shillings Polly brought in.

'You must join us in our fight,' his brother had insisted. 'Then you'd have a proper living wage to take home and your wife wouldn't have to work in that beer-house.'

Matthew had bridled, reacting badly as always to any hint of criticism against Polly. 'It's not a beer-house! It's one of Yates's Teetotal Taverns, as you well know. She spends most of her time serving lentil soup at a penny a time, and making sure the customers don't hack the spoons off the walls to which they're chained.' Still it shamed him to have his wife work so hard. And he hated to have his brother point out his inadequacies as a provider.

'The men've asked me to stand for election as president of our local group, but Cal Eastwood is standing too. He'll be a tough opponent to beat, since he has ways and means of making folk vote for him. Nevertheless, I believe right prevail and I'll be chosen, but I shall need all the support I can get, Matthew, including yours. You must be my right-hand man and make sure I win.'

Matthew was shocked. 'What can I do?'

'Canvass for me. Help put out leaflets, talk to people, persuade them to see me as the right candidate for the job. You surely owe me some loyalty? Or does your sense of self-preservation exclude even that fundamental requirement in a brother?'

The derision in Joshua's tone left Matthew bereft of words. They both knew to what he was referring. It went right to the core of the bitterness between them. They'd never been close, not even as young boys, but Cecil's death had soured their relationship for all time.

Even now, fifteen years later, it hurt Matthew to remember his younger brother, the eager young idealist who had volunteered along with his two elder brothers for action in a war he did not comprehend. As luck would have it, he and Matthew were posted together to France and Matthew had promised his mother faithfully that he'd look after the boy. In the event it had been a naive and foolish vow to give, empty of meaning once they'd seen what was waiting for them over there.

They'd lived day by day, sleeping in the same tent, eating the same food which was all too often caked in mud, even sharing the same stinking trench and the same devastating battlefield. But it hadn't been enough.

Matthew could still bitterly remember the day of his young brother's death. It was etched into his mind as painfully as any physical wound. Given the choice, he'd gladly have cut off a limb to have Cecil alive and well.

He recalled the preparations they'd made with painstaking care, the plans, the instructions, the mockery of rehearsing a battle charge. He remembered the September mists, the stink of gas, the poplar trees gently rustling in the breeze.

Encumbered with equipment, rations, rifle, pick or shovel, flags and Ayston fans, for clearing gas out of dugouts, they'd struggled to take up position in a long winding trench or in one of the few dugouts or gun emplacements. Matthew had tried to help the boy by offering to carry some of his load, but he would have none of it.

'Don't treat me like a child,' had been Cecil's constant cry. So Matthew had treated him like a man. And like a man he had fought and died.

They'd spent a miserable, cold night with precious little sleep and nothing but mouldy bread and cheese to eat. Then it was time to abandon the majority of their equipment so they could 'chase' the enemy. The view of Hulluch and Loos, high on the ridge above them, had seemed benign, even beautiful in the early mists of dawn. Except that the road ran right through the German trenches. No one was in any doubt about that.

They learned it was time to go into action when they received a message from the Adjutant. He ordered the attack to be carried out with bayonets fixed. The two brothers had done as they were bidden, then looked at one another, each silently acknowledging the fragility of this defence. Their battalion had three machine-guns and a bag of Mills bombs. Matthew had 150 rounds of ammunition; plenty, he believed, to see him safe. He checked on Cecil, despite his protests, and seeing he had 50 rounds fewer, split the difference with him, so each had 125.

'Keep your bloomin' head down!' was the last thing Matthew had said to him. Cecil simply grinned and winked in that cheeky way of his.

The first thing to go wrong was the wind. It blew the gas they'd thrown right back into their own faces. Matthew could remember men falling down, choking from its effects.

And it took no time at all for them to realise the inadequacy of their preparations. They'd been hopelessly outnumbered. There were German gun emplacements or bomb throwers every few yards. They'd walked openly up the hill as if on parade, the morning sun winking on their tin helmets, and marched straight into the jaws of hell.

Men fell all around, swallowed up by the banks of mist and swirling smoke from the bombs, rolling in screaming agony down the hill they had just climbed. One minute Cecil had been there beside him, solid, firm and alive, firing for all he was worth. But by the time Matthew had reached the German wire, he'd been quite alone. He'd set off running then, skirting the fringes of the defences, desperate to find his brother. A blow to his shoulder had flung him into a shell hole, already occupied by two dead men and one who quietly died with the cigarette Matthew had given him still between his lips. Matthew had lain half buried in that stinking hole for what seemed like days but must have been six or eight hours, perhaps as many as twelve, he couldn't tell.

Acutely aware that going forward he would be shot and going back would mean facing a court martial He could do nothing but remain where he was. Every time he risked lifting his head, the thud of a bullet hitting the ground inches away would send him scurrying back like a rabbit into its hole.

It was a miracle he hadn't been hit again. His own shoulder wound had been superficial, but the battalion was well near annihilated, scarcely anybody left. Matthew would never forget the sight of all those prone figures; those young-old faces frozen in death.

Those left alive crawled or staggered any way they could to get back to safety, in a silence so terrible it was almost tangible. It was as if even the Germans were sickened by what they had done.

Cecil had not been amongst the living.

Ever since that terrible day Joshua had insisted that Matthew could and should have done more for the boy. He shouldn't have lost sight of him, should have brought him out so he could receive first aid for his injuries. He refused to acknowledge the reality of the situation; how their own officers would let none of the men back on to the field to collect the wounded, not in the middle of a pitched battle.

In response to this explanation, Joshua added his accusation of cowardice, charging Matthew of saving his own skin at the expense of his brother's, of wanting only to return safely to the new wife he had left waiting for him at home. He swore Matthew had reneged on his word and blamed him entirely for not guarding Cecil more carefully. How could Matthew disagree? Didn't he blame himself even more for Cecil's death? The hatred engendered between the brothers as a result had festered and grown ever since that day.

Florence, of course, had stoically borne her grief in silence, believing her youngest son had died bravely and nobly.

Matthew grieved for the brother he'd lost as keenly as anyone, if not more so. He'd torn himself apart with guilt; suffered the agonising pain of his memories and refused to speak of the war for years afterwards. He was saved from madness only by Polly's unfaltering love and devotion.

'Are you planning on doing yerself in, lad?' hissed a voice in his ear, bringing Matthew sharply back to the present. 'You've been gawping at that mucky water so long, I thought you were about to jump in it.' The voice was that of his gaffer, Jim Taylor, a man prone to fault-finding even where none existed.

Matthew started. 'No, I'm grand, ta very much.' Hot with panic at his own carelessness, he grabbed the wheelbarrow handles and shot up the plank at a cracking pace.

The man followed him to stand on the deck of the narrow-boat, shaking a fist at him. 'If you don't shape yourself, you'll be turned off, Matthew Pride. You've gone slack lately. You were late back after that so-called funeral you went to, t'other day.'

Matthew stopped, startled by this accusation. 'It was the funeral of my neighbour, I told you. And I wasn't late at all.' He heard the intake of breath of his fellow workers, sensed a frisson of sympathy and something very like fear emanating from them, and knew he'd made a mistake in arguing. It wasn't wise to engage in a spat with the gaffer.

'Are you calling me a liar? You were late back by two minutes, I timed you.'

It was a lie, and everyone listening knew it. Matthew Pride had never been late for work in his life, funeral or no. It was all too clear management was starting a policy of discouraging some of the regulars as work grew harder to come by, and perhaps having heard about the meeting, Jim Taylor was anxious to make an example of anyone not toeing the line to prove what could happen if they didn't all watch out. Gritting his teeth, knowing why he was being baited, Matthew wisely said no more, merely continued stolidly with the task of refilling the barrow.

'We'll have no shirkers getting paid money they don't earn. We can do without lazy louts taking too much time off and idling instead of working.'

Red in the face with the effort, yet Matthew held his tongue.

'Though you manage to find time to attend meetings and visit your lady friend, eh? It's common knowledge one of you Pride brothers is servicing a young widow woman.' And Jim Taylor looked about him with a smirk on his face, as if he'd said something very clever.

It was too much for Matthew. Though conscious of the way his workmates were silently willing him not to react, he felt driven to speak up by this terrible slur on his character, and on his lovely Polly. White to the lips, he said, 'That's not true. I've always been faithful to my wife, which is more than most can say.'

'You're not trying to tell me it's that Holy Joe brother of yours who services the woman? He doesn't look capable of such a manly pursuit.' And the foreman laughed.

Matthew flushed a darker red. 'I wouldn't know. I'm not my brother's keeper. You'll have to ask him yourself. It's nowt to do with anyone, least of all me, what Joshua does. And what if I do attend the odd meeting? It's not a crime, is it? I give a good day's

41

work for my pay, and nor was I shirking just now. I was thinking, while I stopped to catch me breath for a minute.' He was keenly aware he hadn't defended Joshua quite as ably as perhaps he might, but knew it was too late to say more. And he had perhaps defended himself too well.

'Thinking, eh? My word, we've got Einstein among us and didn't know it.' The foreman looked around him again as he chortled with laughter, expressing his scorn of the very idea that Matthew might have a brain in his head to think with. Some of the other men judiciously joined in the enjoyment of his little joke. 'Well then, perhaps you should share these grand thoughts with us all. Give us the benefit of your wisdom like.'

Matthew was furious with himself. He clenched the handles of the barrow so tightly his knuckles whitened. 'It wasn't anything important,' he said, and set off down the plank, anxious to be done with this dangerous conversation and get on with his work.

'Don't you turn your back on me!'

It happened so quickly that afterwards Matthew couldn't work out what exactly had gone wrong. One minute he'd the irritated voice of Jim Taylor buzzing like a fly in his ear; the next the whole caboodle was at the bottom of the canal. Had he somehow rolled over the edge, or had he really seen a stick flicked under the wheel to catapult it into the water? One glance into the foreman's sneering face suggested the latter, and his next words confirmed it.

'That's you finished, lad. Collect what's owing to you and go. I'll not have troublemakers on my shift. This is the last time you'll get work on this wharf.'

When Matthew told Joshua what had occurred as a result of his attending the meeting, and that Jim Taylor had accused him of bothering with women, his brother gave him a cold assessing glare, the barest hint of a frozen smile on his thin lips.

'Are you trying to lay the blame on me, because you were idling and got yourself sacked?'

'I didn't say that, and I've told you, I wasn't idling.'

'What were you doing then?'

Suffering torment after years of guilt, Matthew thought, yet not for the world would he admit as much to his brother. 'Does it matter?'

'Dear me. What will the little wife say about you losing your job?'

'Damn you to hell!'

'No, Matthew, I don't think so. You're the one who'll end up in hell.' Joshua pushed his face up close, nostrils flaring with a cruel resolve which did nothing to brighten those dead eyes. 'And perhaps I'll be the one to put you there.'

Chapter Five

Polly chose that very night to reveal her secret. As soon as supper was over, she went to fetch the dress, which she'd stored in a drawer wrapped in a piece of unbleached cotton. She carefully unfolded it and held it up for them all to see.

Lucy was almost speechless with delight. 'Oh, you're the best mum in the world! Where did you get it? Did you make it yourself?'

'Wasn't I stitching away whenever the house was empty for five minutes?'

Lucy hugged and kissed her mother, and even Big Flo, sitting by the fire with her feet up on the steel fender, smiled.

'Well, go and put it on then. Let's have a look at it.'

Lucy turned and ran, bare feet skittering on the wooden stairs, giggling like the child she still was.

In the silence which followed her departure, Benny said, 'I'm not walking in no cissy procession.'

For once it was his father who answered, telling him to hold his tongue and do as he was told. If his son considered further protest, he soon thought better of it as the atmosphere in the room dropped to freezing.

Matt, seated on a wooden chair polishing his clogs, knew this was the moment he should admit to Polly that he'd lost his job, and that he might well have kept it if only he'd buttoned his lip a bit tighter. It was guilt over this which now held him silent. Instead he asked in clipped tones, 'And how did you manage to find the brass to buy such fancy stuff?'

Polly's cheeks grew red but she answered in a firm voice, bracing herself for his disapproval, 'I got another job, cleaning.'

44

'Cleaning what?'

She shrugged and moved to the table, flicking unseen crumbs away, wiping down a surface that had been wiped ten times already. 'Whatever needs cleaning. Sure, and isn't there plenty of that around here?'

'And where did you do this cleaning?'

She could hear the tightness in his voice, feel his anger. She glanced anxiously at her mother-in-law, waiting for Big Flo to wade in on the side of her favourite younger son, as she so often did. But for once the old woman held her tongue.

'Well?'

Polly sighed. 'At the Peveril of the Peak near the Hippodrome, if you must know. It's a decent enough pub. Better than most, I dare say. The actors call in during the interval, and the money is good so...' Her voice tailed away as she watched his face darken. Even so, it was her mother-in-law whose outrage was the first to surface.

'You've been working in a pub! Where hard liquor is served and lewd actresses with Red John on their cheeks parade themselves before men? Was it that slut next door what put you up to it?'

'Eileen isn't a slut. She had a bad start in life, that's all. Anyway, I wasn't serving at the bar,' Polly protested. 'Only cleaning up every afternoon while it was closed for an hour or two. What can be wrong with that, may I ask?'

She stood with arms folded as she faced her husband, but her eyes weren't so much defiant as pleading with him to understand. 'How could I buy our Lucy a frock to wear for the Whit Walks, or Benny the new coat and boots he needs, on what we have coming in? Would you have me children look like beggars?'

Matthew was on his feet, anger making his face ashen. 'So that's what you think I achieve by grafting all hours on the canal? Making my children look like beggars.'

'No, I didn't mean it how it sounds...' But it was too late. Matt thrust his feet back into his shining clogs, clipped the clasp on each, then picking up his jacket strode from the house, clog irons sparking on the stone floor. Polly knew he'd be back later, after he'd walked off the worst of his temper, but it pained her to see how she'd hurt him.

Big Flo chose this moment to put in her twopenn'orth. 'Now see what you've done! You shouldn't show your husband up, not a fine proud man like our Matthew. You should be ashamed of yourself.'

'I only wanted to help.'

'No brains, like all Irish.'

Polly was so used to this accusation, she managed a tight smile. 'But plenty of heart, Flo. You have to admit that.' The two women considered one another in silence. There'd been many times when her mother-in-law claimed to have given someone 'a good talking to' and Polly always felt great sympathy for the poor miscreant. But her silences could be worse. Matthew had once told her they could be so condemning as to bring his father, as strong a man as you could hope to meet in a long day's march, to his knees, begging forgiveness for whatever misdemeanour he'd supposedly committed. After that poor man's death, from exhaustion some said, Flo practised her well-honed skills on other unfortunates. Now Polly found herself on the receiving end of that forbidding gaze and saw exactly what Matthew meant.

Whether she would have found the courage to break the silence she was not to discover as a sound of clattering feet and excited laughter intervened. A breathless Lucy stood before them in her new frock.

'Where's Dad?'

'He had to go out. Don't worry, he'll see you on the day. Oh, and don't you look fine and dandy? A proper beauty.' As indeed she did. So lovely with her fair hair curling softly on her shoulders and her grey-blue eyes bright with a youthfulness and innocence that quite took Polly's breath away. The dress was lovely, too, a blaze of startling white in the shabby room.

'It was worth every stitch, to be sure,' said Polly, swelling with pride at the wonder of her own daughter's beauty. The hours of labour on her knees scrubbing and cleaning had also been worth it, no matter what Matthew might say.

'Aye,' Big Flo softly agreed, equally bowled over by the transformation from ragged urchin to something very like a fairy princess. 'Happen you're right there.'

–

Matthew came home late that evening, quietly undressed and slid beneath the blankets. He told his wife that her job at the' Peveril of the Peak was over. He'd called in and informed the proprietor she'd not be returning. 'You can keep the job at the temperance tavern, but nothing more. You've enough to do coping with that and looking after us.'

Polly was shocked. She had expected him to grumble, even rant and rave for a while, but never before had he attempted to override any decision she'd made, especially when they needed the money so badly. She attempted to say as much, but he wasn't listening.

'There's an end of the matter, Poll.'

She was forced to bite back any further argument, seeing that he meant it. Matthew could be very obstinate. For a long time they lay stiff and silent, side by side, shivering slightly as the nights were still cold and there was a dampness in the air. Then she reached out a tentative hand and gently touched his arm. 'It's cold I am. Will you warm me?'

He made no move so she tried again. 'I didn't mean that you kept us like beggars, Matt. We might be poor but there's plenty worse off than us. We don't go short of anything we really need. Aren't you the finest husband any woman could ask for? And the best of fathers. It's only that I want the best for our children, to have them look fine and beautiful before God, so's I can thank Him for giving them to me.'

'I know, lass. But happen you want too much sometimes,' he stubbornly insisted.

'Mebbe I do, and you're growing tetchy in your old age,' she teased, mimicking him as she curled her body against his. She kissed the cold stiffness of his cheek, moving on to tease his lips, and heard him groan her name. Then his arms came around her to pull her tight against his bare chest and, chuckling softly, she wriggled herself beneath him. It didn't take more than a few moments for all differences between them to be forgotten, and he was her loving Matthew again, and she his lovely Polly.

But still he hadn't told her the truth.

Nor did he tell her in the days following. He got up at the same time every morning and went off to work as usual, but though he turned up in good time for his usual shift he was always ignored, overlooked in favour of one of the other men. He tried the dock at Ducie Street but there were few steamers coming at present since orders were down.

He then set about combing the other wharves and docks. He picked up the odd day of casual labour here and there but nothing certain, nothing regular. It was as if word had gone out that Matthew Pride was trouble and therefore unemployable. Every foreman, gaffer and stevedore had his favourites, of course, and those vacancies which did come up were generally spoken for, often promised over a pint in the pub the night before. As the days slipped by Matthew began to despair, for he couldn't keep up this pretence for much longer.

He made Joshua swear to keep the information to himself, which caused his brother some amusement. But he appeared to keep his word for Polly was entirely unsuspecting. Though how she would take it if he was forced to own up to having lost his own steady job while making her give up hers, Matthew didn't like to think.

He pawned his suit and his only pair of boots, hoping he'd find better work soon which would bring in enough money to redeem them before he had need of them for Whit Week. He was lucky and got two days labour at Trafford Park, which meant he could once again postpone telling his wife.

Polly had done her best to like Terence Grimshaw but had failed miserably. Mostly when she went next door, which admittedly wasn't often, he would be sitting with his feet propped up on the fender, reading the *Sporting Chronicle* or the *Manchester Evening News,* while Eileen fussed over her brood like a clucking hen. There seemed to be so many children in the tiny living kitchen that every surface was crowded. Even the ceiling, Polly sometimes thought.

As well as feeling too small, the room had a sweetly sour smell about it, as if too many unwashed bodies had lived within its four walls, which was probably the case. Even now half a dozen grey nappies hung from a string looped above the fireplace, drying in the drift of smoke that emanated from the small pile of coals below.

'Our Beryl needs changing,' Terence would inform his wife as she stood at the sink peeling potatoes for tea. Or he'd complain that the child was crying. Polly didn't know how she managed to bite her lip and keep from interfering. Only once had she risked it.

'Eileen's busy,' she'd casually remarked. 'Why don't you give the child a cuddle yourself? I reckon that's all she needs.'

He'd looked at her as if she'd blown in straight from Prestwich Asylum. 'The child needs her mam. And we can do without strangers telling us what to do with us own childer.'

Polly reminded herself now of her embarrassment on that occasion, as Eileen had abandoned the washing–up to rush around, gathering up crying children, while Terence continued with his litany of demands for a fresh mug of tea and a jam butty.

'And mend this fire while yet at it! Look sharp, woman, I'm fair starved.'

It was Polly who flinched at the belligerence in his tone, and very nearly reached for the coal scuttle herself to save Eileen from lifting the weight of it, but a warning glance from her friend kept her in her seat. Instead, she strove to lighten the atmosphere by making conversation. 'Are your girls going to walk in the procession?' she asked, trying not to watch as Eileen rushed from task to task.

Finding the coal bucket empty she'd rushed off down the back yard to refill it. Rosie and Agnes drifted after her while the twins' wails increased in volume. Polly tried to signal to Eileen to stand up to her husband, to speak her mind and tell him to fetch the coal himself for once, and help with the children.

'Procession?' said a voice from behind the paper. 'We've no money to waste on daft things like fancy frocks.'

'Oh, but everyone will be wearing them. I'm sure the girls would love to walk in the procession. Except for Meryl and Beryl, of course, who can't yet.' She tickled one of the eight-month-old twins under the chin, not certain which it was, and waited for a chuckle. When none came she looked up helplessly at Eileen as she returned with the laden bucket, but she didn't seem to notice this lack of response from her child. 'I was just saying that Rosie would love dressing up in new clothes, and so would Agnes. We could nip down the market now, find a bit of fabric. I'd help you sew them up.'

'She has better things to do with her time. And we're not looking for charity.'

Polly was appalled by his attitude, but struggled not to show it. 'I wasn't offering it. I was simply being neighbourly. It's an old Manchester custom.'

'Aye, well, no doubt you're in a hurry to get off home, Mrs Pride. We won't keep you.'

Unable to avoid the hint, and feeling personally responsible for the man's ugly temper, Polly cast an apologetic glance in her friend's direction. Three-year-old Rosie, dirty knickers hanging round her knees, was at that moment reaching for a pan handle on the hob and Polly just managed to stop her before she pulled it over. Eileen simply looked anxious as she wiped her hands on a tea cloth and made for the door.

'Where are you going?' growled her husband.

'To see Polly out.'

'I reckon she can find the way herself, since she found her way in.'

Eileen stopped in her tracks and looked longingly at the door, as if it represented escape to a world of freedom only Polly was permitted to enter. 'Ta ra, chuck. Thanks for calling.'

Polly said goodbye, smiling sympathetically, and after whispering urgently under her breath for Eileen to call on her the next day, quietly let herself out of the house. She heaved a sigh of relief as she closed the door on the fetid atmosphere and breathed in the relative freshness of the air in Dove Street, then returned to her own home as gladly as if it were a palace, for by comparison it surely was. What a lot she had to be thankful for.

–

Eileen was back in number twenty-three the next day, asking if Polly had meant what she'd said about helping her sew some dresses for her girls.

'You're right. Meryl and Beryl wouldn't be able to manage taking part in the procession, but our Agnes is nearly six, and Rosie too would love to dress up and walk. Trouble is, I can't afford to buy them anything.'

'I'll see if I have something we could cut down.'

A thorough search produced a length of unbleached cotton and some scraps of satin left over from Lucy's dress. They bleached the cotton, drying it in the sun to make it all fresh and white. Then, after damping down and ironing it with a hot iron, they cut out two tiny dresses for the little girls, trimming the edges with the satin and making a matching sash of the same fabric for each dress. They looked like doll's dresses, turning out much better than either woman had expected.

Eileen was so thrilled you'd have thought she'd been given a fortune. Tears ran down her cheeks as she told Polly that never had she had such a friend before, in all her life. 'Nobody's ever given me owt, except a clout round the lughole and these blessed childer. Eeh, and won't they look a treat? I'm that pleased, Polly, I don't know how to thank you.'

'There's no need. It's God we're thanking at the Whit Walks, for His goodness in giving us such fine healthy children.' And the two women beamed with their shared joy and pride.

–

When Whit Week arrived, Polly had the pleasure of seeing Lucy preen herself in the new white frock, walking tall and gracious as a princess as she held the ribbons of the Sunday School banner.

'A real beauty she is,' Polly said, heart swelling with love and pride for her daughter.

'Just like her mother,' Matthew agreed. They smiled warmly at each other, united as always in their shared love for their family.

Benny was less happy since he'd been prevailed upon to wear a white shirt instead of his usual grey, which he thought girlish, and a blue and grey striped tie to match the hated cap. The only good thing about his outfit were the new boots and the belt he'd been allowed to wear in place of his braces. He hadn't wanted to walk in the procession at all and had repeatedly asked to be excused, but to no avail. He didn't fail to notice that Georgie Eastwood wasn't walking.

'I don't care if I'm still paying for that dress till Kingdom come, it was worth every penny,' Polly insisted.

A shadow crossed Matthew's face, but he kept it turned well away from her. 'Aye,' was all he said.

It was also worth her efforts to see the two eldest Grimshaw girls decked out in their little frocks, frees shining clean for once. 'Like little fairies they are,' Polly said. 'Did Terence object?'

Eileen shook her head, eyes twinkling, proud as punch as she stood on the kerb watching her children walk by, the twins draped about her neck as usual. 'Not a word. Mind you, I told him that my mam had made the frocks, and he daren't argue with her.'

It was indeed a glorious family week. The Protestants walked on Whit Monday, the Catholics on the Friday, and a string of other churches in between, including Zion Primitive Methodist to which Matthew's family belonged. Matthew himself did not walk but Joshua, straight-backed and solemn-faced, was one of the bearers carrying the banner.

Big Flo led the group of matriarchs who met regularly on a Thursday evening at the chapel, not simply to gossip and read the Scriptures together, but to discuss their personal responsibility for the provision of tea and buns at special chapel functions such as New Year's Day and the Sunday School Anniversary, a task which necessitated considerable organisation. The feast, if that was the right term for the one potted meat sandwich and single bun after the procession, was likewise their responsibility.

The streets were crowded as far as Albert Square with people eager to catch a glimpse of the walkers; the banners festooned with ribbons and flowers and statues bearing the words 'Ave Maria'; the dark-haired Italian girls in their long skirts, pretty blouses and waistcoats; and the men and young boys in fine white shirts carrying the Calvary. Last came the magnificent plaster Madonna decorated with dozens of flowers. Music filled the air, and everyone was happy and excited. All those long evenings of planning and preparation in the Green Dragon seemed to be paying off.

The men of Dove Street got their suits out of hock especially for the occasion, wearing boots, if they were lucky enough to possess a pair, and bowler hats instead of caps. The women set aside their shawls and clogs and wore their best Sunday frocks and hats they'd made or trimmed themselves, though the breeze was brisk and demanded they be well skewered down with hatpins. The children too looked smart and pretty in their new clothes, no sight or sound of clogs amongst them.

Even the milkman's shire horse had its mane and tail plaited, just as it did on May Day, with coloured bows and ribbons woven in. And what a glorious sight it was, with its already glossy coat groomed and brushed till it shone like new paint.

The brightly coloured banners flapped ferociously in the wind, one or two almost breaking loose so that the strong men who took turns to carry the poles were nearly lifted off their feet. But there were no real disasters and everybody had a grand time. It was like a holiday for a community who had little opportunity for such pleasures.

There was a good deal of drinking, and rowdiness, but excuses were made with even the police turning a blind eye in view of the occasion. Late each evening the Salvation Army band would beat their drums and play their bugles as they led the inebriated down Ashton New Road, along Every Street and Junction Street to the Mission Hall where they could sleep it off till morning.

The street sellers did a roaring trade, selling such delights as hot pies, black peas, or muffins. Mr Ruggiere, with his waxed moustache and fancy waistcoat, was kept busy selling the finest ice cream in the world from his beautifully decorated hand cart. There was even a man selling song sheets. The residents of Dove Street, as ever, knew how to enjoy themselves, popping in and out of each other's houses on the slightest pretext, besides the usual borrowing of a pinch of tea or drop of milk, then staying on nattering for hours, revelling in the unaccustomed freedom.

There was no smoke coming from Dove Street Mill for five whole days. What a treat! If some considered this as much a cause for concern as jubilation, no one was saying so out loud.

During the festive atmosphere of Whitsuntide, Eileen's cheeks almost bloomed, Polly noticed, as she fed her toasted currant teacakes with just a dab of margarine, not forgetting the ever-present and greedy trail of clinging children. Polly quite lost count of the number of teacakes, barm cakes and arrowroot biscuits she baked that week, every one consumed by various neighbours and family members who popped in. Benny and his cronies were constant and regular visitors to his mother's kitchen. Even Joshua unbent enough to praise her culinary skills.

'Matthew is a fortunate man to have so talented a wife,' he told her as he accepted a barm cake, well buttered for once, and stuffed thick with ham.

'My word, I'd like you to tell him that,' she said, flushing with pleasure at the unexpected compliment.

'Generous to a fault she is,' Big Flo said, but Polly only laughed.

'Sure and if you can't feed a few friends in Whit Week, when can you? And don't we have it to give?'

'It's a pity you aren't so generous over more spiritual matters,' Joshua commented.

Casting a quick glance at his face, which looked as if he'd supped a pint of sour milk, for once Polly refused to be overawed by him. 'Oh, Joshua, will you leave over blathering about religion. There's other things in life.' She caught a glimpse of fury in his face and almost apologised for her outburst, it being Whit Week, but decided against it. Instead she turned to her husband, sliding one arm possessively under his as they all stood together on the pavement, enjoying the latest procession of white-clad witnesses. The gesture was meant to remind Joshua that he had no control over her for she was not his wife but belonged to Matthew. Had she but known it, this was a fact which rankled with him, no matter how often he spoke slightingly of her.

In the days following everyone knew that 'Uncle' Joseph, the old pawnbroker who occupied the corner shop on Dove Street, would be kept extra busy as the locals handed back suits, boots and Sunday frocks, for a few essential coins to pay off some of the debts accumulated during the festivities. For a while, money would become an even rarer commodity.

'Aw, but wasn't it worth every penny?' Polly insisted.

Matthew said nothing, simply swallowed his growing fear and nodded in agreement.

Chapter Six

The next Sunday, thinking that perhaps she'd overstepped the mark in a few directions recently, yet grateful for the joy of the processions, Polly decided to pay a visit to one of the churches in the city, taking a penny tram ride in order to do so. She may be a lapsed Catholic, she told herself, but a little healthy contrition now and then was good for the soul.

It was a cool, rather damp morning for June as she caught the number 25 that ran down Bradford Road, past McConnell's Mill, on to Ancoats Lane and Millers Lane then to the terminus at Victoria Station.

'Hey up,' said the conductor. 'Warm up thy pennies. Winter's back.'

Sitting on the hard seat of the tram as it jerked and rattled along the tracks, grateful to be in the dry while the poor driver at the front was getting a terrible soaking, Polly had ample time to confront the worries gathering in the back of her mind. Matthew wasn't at all himself. He'd barely spoken a word to her since Whit Week was over, nor to the children for that matter.

The white dress now hung on a nail in Lucy's room, and Polly could tell he was still sensitive about it because when the child anxiously sought reassurance that they wouldn't need to pop it, he'd turned his face away and refused to give her the assurance she needed.

It had been Polly who'd done that. 'Of course we won't pawn it, love. You can wear it for Sunday School this summer, if you like.' Matthew didn't say a word, making the excuse of some urgent business he needed to do out of the house.

Polly got off the tram and walked for what seemed like miles, first along Cheetham Hill Road and then down a myriad streets that were largely unfamiliar to her. She took the opportunity to stop and ask about work whenever she passed a likely place but didn't strike lucky. After a while she began to feel uncomfortable, vulnerable in this strange neighbourhood. She must be somewhere near Strangeways Prison and remembered poor Mrs Murphy and her violent husband, no doubt languishing inside at this very moment. Polly half glanced over her shoulder once or twice, as if she were being followed, but then laughed at her own timidity. Could it be any worse here than Ancoats? In any case, there was no one there, the street being quite empty save for a line of people gathering outside a church, clearly Catholic. The church was quite unknown to her but as good as any, she decided. She joined the line and went inside.

'Bless me, Father, for it is... a few weeks since my last confession,' she began, and hurried on before he could ask exactly how many, to recount the sin of pride that had led her to take on work in a public beer-house of which her husband disapproved.

'And was it food for your table you were after needing?' the priest asked, judiciously not pursuing her faltering over the time since she had last felt the need to cleanse her soul.

'No, Father, but clothes for me children.' She didn't like to mention that it was in order to buy a frock for Lucy to take part in the Whit Walks in case that should sound as if she weren't really sorry at all.

Father Thomas hadn't worked in Manchester twenty years without being able to assess a situation shrewdly. He was aware of the date on the calendar, barely a week since the processions, so it didn't take a genius to work out the source of the problem. There were many times when he thought with despair of money spent on frocks and suits that would now be on their way to the pawn shop, while hungry bellies went empty.

'Pride is a terrible thing, but 'tis a human weakness we all suffer from at times. It's lucky you are that you've enough food on your table when so many haven't. Be satisfied with what you have, daughter, and don't ask for more than your man can reasonably provide.'

'I won't, Father.'

'And you'll come and see me again, not simply when you have the need for confession?'

'I will, Father.'

And she would, Polly vowed, she really would make an effort to find her way back into the Church, for didn't she miss it sorely? The three Hail Marys she was given, and the candle she lit, made her feel better for a whole half hour before Polly again boarded the tram and let her mind slip back into worrying over Matthew's behaviour. She seemed to have gravely underestimated the effect of her taking on the job at the public house. Weren't Methodists a law unto themselves, indeed?

She was surprised when at the first stop after the church, Joshua climbed on board. He came and took the seat beside her without a word of greeting.

'What are you doing in this part of town?' she asked, struck by the coincidence. And then a terrible idea formed in her head. 'You weren't following me by any chance, were you?' She didn't care for the thought of him spying on her. The man had an unsettling way of watching people, as if they had committed some great sin which he was carefully noting.

Even now, when he turned to meet her enquiring gaze, she experienced that prickling sensation at the nape of her neck she so often felt when he looked at her.

'Perhaps I think someone should keep an eye on you,' he said. He noted the swing of her dark hair, the way the light turned her eyes from green to grey and back to green again, and experienced the familiar tightening of envy bite deep into his guts. Was it any wonder that Matthew had fallen head over heels for this Irish imp, thinking her so entirely delectable that he'd even risked the life of his own brother to ensure he had a long and happy life with her? Bewitched he was, the fool!

Polly, fidgeting beneath the intensity of his gaze, was incensed by this casual remark. 'If that's true, which I deny absolutely, wouldn't the task be better carried out by me own husband?'

'My brother seems incapable of taking care of anything or anyone at the moment. Not even himself. Haven't you noticed he's troubled?' Now a shaft of sunlight had caught in her dark hair and revealed fiery threads there. Joshua watched it sparkle and glow, entranced despite himself.

Polly was forced to confess that she was indeed concerned for Matthew. 'It's true he's been either biting me head off or lapsing into silence quite a lot lately. For days, in fact,' she admitted.

'I think you'll find it's more like weeks. You should ask him what's on his mind. He may tell you.'

'Are you saying you know what's wrong?'

'I might. I might not.' Following this enigmatic remark. Joshua would say no more and they completed the journey in uncomfortable silence, each deep in their own thoughts.

–

Polly fully intended to tackle Matthew on the subject that very evening, but he seemed to be in a more cheerful frame of mind so she was afraid to spoil it. He asked if she felt better for having been to church and she agreed that she did.

'It makes me feel guilty to rob you of your religion. You shouldn't abandon it just for me.'

'I didn't, you daft galoot,' she said, softly kissing him. 'Didn't the Church abandon me? And guess who I saw on my way back?' She told him about Joshua on the tram.

Matthew laughed, a hint of scorn in his tone, proving the two men were far from close. 'Wandering the city now, is he? What Josh is in need of is a good woman. Perhaps he was looking for one?'

'The divil he was. He said he was watching out for me, which you should be doing.' Polly said it in a teasing way, smiling mischievously at him, but Matthew's face darkened and she regretted having done so.

'Aw, will I bite off me own daft tongue? What is it between you two? I know you've never got on, but I've never properly understood why.'

Matthew's frown deepened still further before he seemed to shake it off, his laughter, when it came, sounding forced and unnatural. 'Neither do I, Pol. He was always jealous of me, even as a boy. Thought I was Mam's favourite.'

'That's true. You're the apple of her eye.'

'Oh, I'm not so sure. Anyroad, now he's jealous of what I've got and he hasn't, and who can blame him for that?' And reaching for her, he pulled Polly on to his lap to start tickling and kissing her till she was giggling uncontrollably and begging for mercy.

'Sure and he wouldn't know what to do with a woman if one offered herself up as a human sacrifice,' she said, and then they were both laughing, if with some small sense of guilt that they'd made fun of an unmarried brother who chose to devote himself to chapel rather than family.

They went to bed early and made love beneath the warm blankets. Afterwards, as Polly lay contentedly in his arms, Matthew made a mental note to speak to his brother and ask what business it was of his if Polly should choose to visit a church of her own religion, but he made no mention of this decision to his wife. Nor did Polly deem it wise to investigate too closely her husband's state of depression which, for the moment at least, to have passed.

–

Matthew, worn out by his fruitless searching and low morale, for the first time in his life overslept. In his rush to leave the house, he left his snap tin sitting on the table in the kitchen. Polly noticed it just as she was about to dash off to Yates's Temperance Tavern. 'Would you believe it? He'll be half-starved without a proper dinner.' The children had already left for school and she decided

60

it wouldn't be far out of her way to slip to the north end of Dove Street before setting off in the opposite direction to her own place of work, so long as she hurried. Pulling her shawl over her head, she set off at a quick pace.

She found the men busily unloading the coal from the narrow-boats, running down the planks into the mill as usual, but Matthew wasn't among them. A few enquiries told her he hadn't been there for a while; a week or two in fact, one youngster admitted, before getting his ear clipped by an older man more used to the ways of men in keeping such details from a wife. Pale of face, Polly thanked them and walked away stiff-backed, feeling it was a miracle her legs kept her upright Not been there for weeks? Then where *had* he been working? He'd made no mention of a new job to her.

There was nothing she could do right now but go on to her own work. She didn't dare be late in case she got turned off, so half ran down Dove Street, along Ancoats Lane towards Oldham Street, trying not to think too deeply about the implications: Could this have been the trouble Joshua had hinted at?

Jesus, Mary and Joseph, she hoped not!

Her four hours serving bread and soup seemed like eight, but the moment she was released Polly paid a quick visit to the market to buy a few vegetables for supper. She'd decided that she was probably only fussing again and Matthew was most likely in Ducie Street where she knew he often worked when not on the canal. It was past two o'clock by the time she got there, but not too late for a bite. He'd be glad of these sandwiches to keep him going through the afternoon.

She searched and searched but couldn't find Matthew, a few enquiries told her he wasn't here either. Stupefied with fear, she began to visit other wharves and docks, growing increasingly desperate for a sight of her husband. Finally forced to abandon her search, since she knew the children would be home at any moment, she set off through the back streets of Ancoats, heartsick and weary. Why hadn't he told her he couldn't find work? Was she such an ogre that he couldn't bring his problems home to his own wife?

Tight-lipped, she made up the fire, set the kettle to boil and began chopping vegetables for the broth pan with a hand that wasn't quite steady. Perhaps she was wrong. In her heart she prayed she was. How many wharves and docks were there in Manchester? Dozens, at least, and she'd hardly visited half that number. There was other work too, besides the tugs and barges. He could be working in a warehouse somewhere. He'd surely be some place she'd never thought of.

Eileen came in as usual for a cup of tea but somehow Polly wasn't in the mood for her determined cheerfulness so the girl, seeming a bit low herself for once, didn't stay long. Even so, Polly noticed with a start of fresh concern that she seemed to get no bigger in her pregnancy, for all the weeks were flying past.

–

When he'd set out that morning only one thing had been on Matthew's mind: where he was to find the money to turn over to Polly this evening. It was Friday and he'd nothing left to pawn. With no work of any sort this week and not a penny coming in, he'd finally been driven to swallow his pride and queue at the Labour Exchange to sign on the dole.

He went laboriously through the soul-destroying task of answering the many questions and filling in the necessary forms to be paid the money which was rightly due to him. He learned it would amount to a little above a pound a week, and when he protested that no family could live on such a small sum, was told to take it or leave it. Since he was only too aware that many people still thought of the unemployed poor as a feckless grey mass who enjoyed a high degree of comfort living off the state, the least he could do was to keep his dignity intact, and accept whatever bit of money was due to him. This wasn't the moment for answering back, so for once Matthew managed to swallow his pride and stop his tongue running away with him. Even so, he worried over the dole lasting only a short time.

'What happens when the six months is up, if I still haven't found work?'

'The dole stops,' said the young clerk. 'Can you write?'

'Of course I can write. Give me the form, I can fill it in myself.' It took twice as long, since there were a great many questions to be answered and his skills, despite his bravado, were limited, but Matthew completed the task eventually. The young clerk picked fault with his efforts and wanted to know all the places he'd already tried, in order to prove he was genuinely seeking work. Matthew told him, and made the necessary alterations to the form, breaking the nib of the pen as he struggled to hold on to his rapidly diminishing patience.

'That's a laugh, that is.' The grimness of his expression belied his words. 'Since there aren't any jobs round here to be found.'

'That's not my fault. Sign here, please.'

Of course it wasn't the clerk's fault and, stricken with remorse for his sharpness, Matthew felt bound to apologise to the young man. He pointed out that his situation was purely temporary. 'I'll have found myself a job before the six months is up, you'll see.' The clerk merely looked at him pityingly and said nothing.

—

Lucy and Benny arrived home later that afternoon in a flurry of wet coats and squabbles, Polly gave them each a slice of bread and beef dripping and packed them off out into the street again. More than anything today, she needed to be alone.

When she heard the scrape of Matthew's clogs on the flagstones at exactly the right time, and he came swinging into the house with his usual tuneless whistle, she heaved a great sigh of relief. Here she was, fretting over nothing as usual, when all that had happened was that he'd forgotten his snap tin and failed to tell her where he was working, so was it any wonder she couldn't take it to him? What a soft-head she was, always worrying over

63

something and nothing. She smiled to herself as she ran and kissed him.

'Hey, that's a grand welcome for a chap,' he said with a smile, swinging her round while he kissed her some more. He felt big and strong and warmly loving, his arms tight about her sending shivers of excitement through her. 'Where's the childer? Would they notice if we popped upstairs?'

'Will you behave? They'll be in for their teas any minute.'

'Well, just one more kiss for a working man, eh?'

She made no mention of the forgotten snap tin until the children were in bed, then she showed it to him. 'Will you take it tomorrow instead? I've kept the lid closed so the bread won't be too dry.'

'Aye. Daft of me to forget it,' he said easily, unclasping his clogs in preparation for giving them their nightly polish.

As Polly set about the washing-up and clearing away she teased a trail of soap suds over his head and down the back of his neck till he grabbed her and pulled her onto his knee. 'Will you lay off, wife? Can't a chap find a bit of peace, after a hard day?'

'Where've you been working today then?'

'Here and there. Usual places.'

'I went looking for you,' she confessed, wriggling free as the kettle started to sing. 'Pity I didn't find you, then you wouldn't have gone hungry all day. Where should I have gone? Then I'll know next time you forget it.'

'I'll not forget it again.' He'd make damn sure of that.

She turned to look at him. 'You might if you were in a rush like this morning.'

There was the slightest pause before he answered which, on any other day, Polly might not have noticed. 'Ducie Street. So no, you wouldn't find me on the canal. Not today.'

'That's obviously why I missed you then,' she quietly agreed, and as she poured hot water into the sink, stared bleakly into space for she recalled quite clearly that they hadn't seen hide nor hair of him in Ducie Street either. Not for weeks, they'd said.

They lay in bed together, comfortable and warm in the darkness, replete after their lovemaking. The wind rattled at the curtainless windows and the tiny bedroom was filled with draughts and creaks, but neither of them noticed. The light from a fitful moon, criss-crossed with cloud, seemed to blink at them and they smiled, for they were content and happy together as always.

It was a long time before Matthew spoke. He'd had weeks to find the right words, but still he hesitated. Yet he knew the moment could be put off no longer. It was a miracle nobody had 'shopped' him by now. Only the way men stuck together through hard times had saved him from that particular humiliation. They knew it might be them next time and, like Matthew, would hope to have a new job before having to face the shame of telling the wife.

'Wasn't Whit Week lovely? I doubt Lucy slept all week, the excitement fair bubbled in her,' Polly murmured.

'Aye.' This single syllable was followed by a sigh so deep it ran the length of his body. Polly resolutely ignored it. If he'd something to say, he'd get round to it in his own time.

'I wondered if we couldn't take a picnic out to Platt Fields one day this summer, if the weather is kind. We could manage that, couldn't we? A family outing would be grand, don't you think?' She turned to kiss his cheek, wrapping her arms more firmly about his warm body.

'I've summat to tell you, lass.'

'Oh?' She wanted to jump out of the bed, run away and hide, anything to avoid hearing his next words.

'I've lost me job.' There, it was out. He'd spoken the dreaded words. Now he waited for the skies to fall in on his world. It was common enough for marriages to collapse under the pressure of unemployment. Threatened with being half-starved or even sent to the workhouse, many a wife simply packed her bags and went off to live with another man, one who could afford to keep her. Matthew couldn't imagine life without his lovely Polly. The pain in his chest expanded till he could hardly bear it, while he waited for her reply.

'I know,' she said.

'You know?'

'Well, I guessed. You're not very good at hiding things. Aw, you should've told me right away, you daft galoot! D'you think I only love you for your riches?'

'When did I ever have riches?'

'There you are then. What is it your mam says? If you have nowt and you lose it, then you've less than nowt, so it can't get any worse, can it?' And her greeny-grey eyes sparkled with mischief, as if this were all some merry joke and not a question of survival at all.

Matthew could only gaze at her in astonished wonder, entranced by her lovely elfin face, the sheen of her fine Irish skin like pale silk in the flickering moonlight. Then he was kissing her over and over, and their lovemaking this time was more intense, so wanton and abandoned it was almost as if they wanted it stated between them that their love for each other was all the riches they required.

Chapter Seven

With the dawn came a return to common sense, and an accept-
ance that it was vitally important Matthew should find regular
work as quickly as possible. What he needed was a good solid job
with a steady wage. He was skilled on the tugs and narrow-boats,
so it was to the wharves and docks that he returned that morning,
as on every other. After that, he vowed to try just about anywhere
he could think of.

'Won't they jump at the chance to take on so fine a man?'
Polly's love and belief in him sustained him throughout that long
day and the next. But as the days and weeks passed and summer
turned to autumn, then into winter, it became clear there was
little work of any kind available.

Eileen lost her baby and very nearly her life six months into her
pregnancy, but even from this she came back smiling, determined
to find a silver lining in her dull grey world. Sitting in Polly's
kitchen with Rosie and Agnes playing at her feet, Meryl sprawled
asleep on her lap and Beryl draped about her neck as usual, she
didn't offer one word of complaint except to say, 'What a place
to bring childer up, eh? If this lot survive it'll be a miracle, or the
goodness of your sad cake, Polly.'

'I've none today.' Her flour bin had been empty for over a
week.

Her own children were poor, Polly thought, but Eileen's were
pitiful, dressed in clothes with more holes than cloth. Unlike
Benny and Lucy, who were scrubbed regularly from top to toe,
none of the Grimshaw children were clean and all so painfully
thin it hurt to look at them, for all they bore the evidence of a

recent meal involving jam. When she remarked upon this, Eileen merely shrugged her shoulders and grinned philosophically.

'I do me best, and I'm just hoping and praying I don't fall again or we'll have even less to eat.' Now the smile did slip, to be replaced by something very like panic.

'Have you asked him to wear a rubber? You know, a...' Polly flushed as she ran out of courage to use the correct word.

'Dear Lord, if I told him how to stop making babies he'd be spreading his favours everywhere. He wouldn't want me then. No, I'm the one who has to stop 'em coming, if I could but work out how. I've tried laxatives and gin. All they do is make me feel sick. I've sat with me feet in a mustard bath, and even tried daft things like a wet sponge and cocoa butter.' She snorted with laughter, falling quickly silent. 'God knows what I'll do next time.'

'There are safer ways,' Polly said, knowing she shouldn't even be talking about such things as a Catholic, for all she was a lapsed one. Yet the poor girl needed help, and the fear of her doing something desperate to herself or her next unborn child was never far from Polly's mind. She told Eileen the address of a clinic she'd heard of which helped women, in strictest confidence, to control the size of their families. 'You mean, they won't tell Terence?'

Polly shook her head. 'If you ask them not to.'

'I wouldn't want him to find out, see, or he'd think I was on the game again. They won't think me – you know – loose, will they?'

'Why should they?'

'I don't know.' Eileen pulled the too-short skirt of her dress over her scrawny knees. 'Only it doesn't seem right to try and stop them, do it? I mean, if you don't want water, you don't take your bucket to the well, do you?'

Polly smiled. 'That would make you very thirsty.' And both women chuckled with embarrassment. 'You'll try the clinic? It's above a cooked pie shop in Salford.'

Eileen frowned. 'If it's free, and secret, I'll happen give it a go. Otherwise I'll have to take me chances. Women's lot, eh?' And she shrugged and grinned. The subject was closed.

–

By the spring of 1930 Matthew felt utterly desperate.

'There'll be more work now, with summer coming up,' Polly had comforted him, but the more he searched, the more of a battering he took.

He felt as if he were no longer a man, as if he'd been robbed of some essential part of his character. Every morning he went down to the Working Men's Institute where he would scour the papers, seeking anything that looked likely, but even if there were a job advertised, which was a rare enough event, he'd find a score or more men there before him, no matter how early he got up, or how quick off the mark he was.

He asked among the barges at Castlefield, the warehouses in Water Street, Irlam Park Wharf, Stanley Street, and any number of other wharves till he quite lost count. He talked to all the big firms, including the Bridgewater Department of Ship Canal Company itself, among others.

Never had he known it so bad. He stood in a crowd of men every morning, like cattle to market, all praying for work. The word would go out that a foreman was looking for a couple of gangs. Backs would straighten, eyes would brighten and in ten minutes or less it was all over with the foreman having picked his favourites, as always. If Matthew had had the money in his pocket he'd have paid for a bit of favouritism himself. As it was he would jam his cap more firmly in place to hide the fear in his eyes, thrust his hands deeper into his pockets and stride to the next dock, walking a little slower each day as hope gradually diminished.

He even swallowed his pride and called on his old boss at the narrow-boats to ask for his job back, but to no avail. All he managed to find was the odd day of casual labour here and there, for which he was grateful, but nothing regular. With nowhere near a living wage coming in, he felt close to despair.

Within months of the start of the New Year, there were rumours of a financial catastrophe that became known as the Wall Street Crash. It had taken place over in America a few months previously, and began to have an effect even in Lancashire. It ruined a good many cotton barons who lost their shares or invested capital, their savings disappearing overnight. Add to that the problem of increased competition from abroad, Ghandi conducting his boycott of British goods, cotton in particular since his own people produced it now, that it began to look as if the industry was in its death throes. Cotton districts began to resemble ghost towns.

And then, to the dismay and terror of the entire street, Dove Street Mill announced its intention of laying off more than a quarter of its workforce. The workers were instructed that in future they'd be expected to run six looms, instead of the usual four.

Even Joshua's job was at risk.

Matthew was astonished. 'But you're well thought of, a tackler no less. Why would they lay you off? They'll still need you to fettle the looms.'

'I was told that since I'm a single man, my need is not so great as a married one with a wife and family to keep. They're the ones, apparently, who need the work while I don't. In addition I live with my mother who has a pension of ten shillings a week, so you see how well off we are.'

Polly listened, appalled, for it seemed like the beginning of the end. But at least the two brothers were in entire agreement for once regarding the selfish greed of the bosses and politicians. Who else could they blame?

'If we'd had time to get a decent union going,' Joshua said, 'they'd never have dared do this to us.'

The union was new and raw, a mere fledgling power against the might of the bosses. And since not every cotton worker was a member, largely ineffective. Many folk were only too willing to operate six looms rather than face the alternative of no work at all. It caused dissention between families, open brawls in the street, even a near-riot on one occasion outside Dove Street Mill.

Joshua stood proud on his soapbox, gesticulating wildly and shouting at colleagues and neighbours, many of them women since it was they who normally did the weaving. But there were men there too, supporting them, needing the money their wives brought in; spinners with a deep knowledge of the industry; and other tacklers employed by the mill to be in charge of a number of looms. In addition there were those whose jobs were linked in some other way to cotton, perhaps in engineering, chemical dyeing or transport.

Joshua brandished a fist. 'You should have listened to me in the first place. Now we must all stand firm, as one against the bosses.'

'It's all right for you,' one woman shouted. 'My husband's unemployed and I've childer to feed, which is more than you have, Joshua Pride.'

A chorus of agreement rippled through the angry crowd, the words pricking deeply at Joshua's rawest spot. As a young man he'd enjoyed walking out with one or two attractive girls but those relationships had come to nothing. Women, he'd discovered, were fickle creatures and although he enjoyed, and took, his pleasures like any normal male, he didn't regret his single state. It gave him more time to concentrate on the business of the chapel which was far more important to him. But he hated this lack of a wife to be used as a weapon against his perfectly sound arguments. He stuck firmly to his argument.

'If nobody agrees to take on six looms, the bosses can do nothing to make us.'

'Aye, they bloody can!' a man at the back of the crowd called out. 'They could sack the lot of us and there'd be no shortage of folk ready to take our places.'

The Dove Street managers did indeed win the day as sufficient workers agreed to operate six looms. The rest were sacked, including Joshua himself, by way of retaliation for his 'incitement to riot'.

It was a glum if united family who, for once, sat together long into the night, talking over possible ways out of their troubles. No immediate solution presented itself and they all finally retired, red-eyed and weary-hearted, to their respective beds.

Only Joshua had the strength to make a resolution. He didn't want simply to survive but to progress, to achieve power and sway over the community; to make everyone listen to what he had to say and carry out his orders without question. He did not believe in meaningless dreams, only in realistic plans, which appeared to be in jeopardy.

In addition to settling his long-held grievance against his brother, he meant to find a way to succeed in his political ambitions. If this was not to be through a union then he'd find some other way, whatever the cost, and whoever he needed to step on in order to do so. He'd not shrink from doing whatever was necessary to achieve his own ends.

–

'Can I go to the Palmy Picture-drome, Mam?'

Polly stood at the sink, hands deep in sudsy water as she rubbed a pair of socks together and considered her son's bright face. 'How much would that be?'

'It's only sixpence if you sit on the benches at the front. Or ninepence for a proper seat at the back.'

'Is that all?' She wiped her hands, took a purse from out of her pocket and opened it to show him. It was empty, as she had known it would be. 'And here's me without a penny for a pinch of tea.' She gave him a rueful smile. 'Mebbe next week, love, eh?'

Benny's birthday had been two days ago, during early September, and his mother had given him a glass bobber for his marble collection. It was so big, he was sure it would win him many more. She'd also given him a lollipop to suck after his tea. Oh, it'd been a grand birthday but he knew, deep down, that marbles and lollipops were for children, and he was growing up. Benny longed to branch out and see how much more he could achieve on his own. 'Now I'm nine, couldn't I get a bit of a job? Earn a bit of pocket money?'

'Ach, Benny. I promise, I'll find sixpence for you next week.'

'I was thinking I could be an errand boy, or happen get a job at London Road Station as a nipper, carrying people's bags, unloading carts and such?' He couldn't disguise the eagerness in his voice. It was his dearest wish to work on the railway.

Polly looked at her son with a sadness in her eyes, knowing how sought after such jobs were these days, and how rare. 'I reckon they might think you a touch young, m'cushla. In a year or two mebbe, when you reach twelve or thirteen. Won't that be grand then for you to get a fine job at the station?' And patting her son's tousled head, she told him to go and play in the street and be a good boy. 'Don't be late home now, the nights are drawing in. And keep away from those big lads.'

He nodded, the lump that suddenly blocked his throat preventing any further attempt at persuasion. He walked stoically out of the house before his mother could catch sight of the tears he feared might show in his eyes. It was vital he get sixpence for the flicks. It was a Buster Keaton film and he was desperate to see it. All his mates were going, or most of them anyway. He didn't want to be left out.

More importantly, he was even more desperate to join the newly formed Dove Street Gang. He'd asked them again this morning if he could become a member and they'd laughed, telling him he was still too young, that you had to have money in your pocket to prove you were a man. He was already sick of being hine. It was scarcely any better than being eight.

And it seemed so unfair for he knew that once they let him in, he'd learn all the gang's secret passwords and the codes they used to send messages to each other, and also gain some protection from the other marauding gangs like Georgie Eastwood's lot who continued to pester him. He might even learn where the good part-time jobs were to be found, who to see to get one and what to say, which he really needed to know. They'd teach him other things too, of course, about girls and something called sex, but Benny wasn't interested in girls. Girlfriends were for cissies. He wasn't ever going to get married, not if he could help it – except perhaps to Mary Alice Ferguson who could swim and dive amongst the rubbish in Rochdale canal as well as any lad. Not that they were supposed to swim in the canal and his dad would leather him if he ever found out. They always went in behind the electricity works, because the water was warm there from the waste they pumped in; much better than Philips Park open air baths which were always freezing.

Aw, but he did want to work on the railways! He'd consulted his friends, Liam, Joe and Don. They were eleven and already in the gang. They'd told him to get hold of sixpence, or better still ninepence for the flicks, and then the rest would agree to let him in.

'Did yet get it?' Liam asked now as Benny came back out into the street. Mournfully, he shook his head.

'What're you going to do?'

'I don't know.' The four boys began to walk dejectedly up the street.

'We could sneak you in with us?' they suggested, but Benny shook his head.

'Too risky. That Mr Spaghetti, or whatever his name is, would catch me and give me a walloping. How'll I ever get in the gang if I never have any money?'

They turned a corner and walked almost smack bang into Georgie Eastwood. He seemed bigger than ever at such close quarters, and had his pack of loyal henchmen close behind.

'No money, eh? Well, well. There's ways and means round that one. You have to use your wits – if you have any. Let's see...' And snatching the blue peaked cap from Benny's head, he tossed it to one of his mates who immediately threw it to another member of the gang. They played catch with it, high above his head. Red in the face, Benny ran from one to the other in helpless rage, desperate to rescue the cap before they flung it in the canal.

'Give it 'ere! That's mine.' His mam would kill him if he lost it.

Georgie grabbed him by the lapels of his jacket and pushed him up against the brick wall of the ginnel, leaning so close Benny had to suffer his stinking breath. 'Go on then, what'll you do if I don't?' He gave Benny a push, sending him spinning, only for him to be caught by one of the other lads and tossed back again, like a top being whipped just fast enough to keep it moving. It went on for so long, back and forth, Benny began to feel dizzy and sick. The gang were all laughing at him, as if it were a great joke.

'Have you got them sweets we asked for?' Miserably, he shook his head.

He tried to run then, but Georgie grasped hold of his braces so all that happened was that he ran on the spot, like one of those daft cartoons he'd seen at the pictures.

'Then it's time you did – if you know what's good for yer.' A final push sent him into a puddle where Benny fell to his knees, right next to his cap. 'When you're man enough, you can join a proper gang. Not this miserable shower,' Georgie said, indicating the three boys huddled together some distance away. Then hitching up his trousers with the wide leather belt, he went on his way, whistling.

'Thanks a lot,' said Benny, rubbing mud off his knees and wringing water out of his cap. 'Lot of use you were.'

The three exchanged glances ripe with guilt. 'Forget him, he's not important. We were going to the flicks, remember,' said Liam.

'You mean, you were going,' Benny dolefully reminded him. The four boys stood looking at each other for a long miserable moment, each embarrassed by the incident and not quite knowing how to save face.

'I've an idea,' said Joe. 'Follow me.' He winked, then started knocking at doors. Each time a woman appeared, he'd ask, 'Any jam jars, missus? We're collecting for the poor.'

'Get off with you,' was the usual response. Or, 'Get to your own end o' t'street, you little heathens.'

'But we're not,' Benny protested.

'Not what?'

'Collecting for the poor.'

'Aye, we are. You're poor, aren't you?'

Benny nodded.

'There you are then.'

He still looked doubtful but then they reached the house. Daft Betty. Everyone knew Daft Betty wasn't all there. Harmless enough, and always good for a laugh, but soft in the head. She lived with her sister Nellie, who watched out for her like a hawk. Nobody messed with Nellie Sidebottom. The boys waited until they saw Nellie go out, basket on her arm, shawl pinned tightly about her head. She was off to market and wouldn't be back for an hour if they were lucky.

Liam nudged Benny in the ribs. 'Go on, it's you what wants to join. Get on with it. Live by your wits, like Georgie said.'

Benny swallowed, then tapped gently on the door. Betty came at once, all sunny smiles on her friendly round face. 'Hello, Betty,' he said. 'We're collecting jam jars for the poor. Do you have any?' Betty had. Giggling, she led them into the back kitchen and showed them the darkest corner of Nellie's cupboard where several jam jars were carefully stacked, waiting to be taken back to the shop.

'Eels, thanks!' The boys grabbed a couple each and fled. It took no more than five minutes to trade in the jam jars for a penny each and then they not only had sixpence for Benny to go to the Palmy Picturedrome, but twopence left over to buy Bull's Eyes for them all.

'A good day's trading,' Liam said with a grin.

'Aye, we'll happen try that one again,' Joe agreed.

Benny grinned awkwardly. He felt guilty about tricking Daft Betty in such a way, worried her sister might find out and come after him. 'Does that mean I'm in the gang now?' he asked.

'Aye, it does,' Don agreed, his cheek bulging with toffee. 'Fully paid up member.' And as the four of them went off happily, arms wrapped about each other's shoulders, Benny grinning from ear to ear, he decided that perhaps it'd been worth the risk after all. And in any case, who would ever know how he'd got the money?

Living by their wits became second nature for the entire family. Determined to keep their respectability each Friday they redeemed Matthew's suit and boots from the pawnbrokers before 'popping' them again on Monday, once the weekend was over. After the dole stopped Matthew refused to 'go on the parish' and accept Poor Relief.

'We'll manage somehow,' Polly told him, hoping she was right. 'You'll find a steady job soon. I'm sure of it.'

But the only work he could get was an odd day's labouring here and there, welcome enough but barely keeping the wolf from the door. And the few shillings Polly earned wouldn't even cover the cost of their coal.

Life at number thirty-one wasn't much better. Joshua hadn't found regular work either, though he was fortunate enough to get a three-month stint in one mill before being turned off again. Big Flo stood in her pew every Sunday and sang 'The Lord is my Shepherd, I shall not want,' as if her belly wasn't rumbling with hunger.

It was a source of great shame to Polly that often the difference between hunger and a full belly was the money they received when they pawned Benny's best boots or even, in the end, Lucy's Whit Walk frock.

Polly cried the day she had to ask her daughter if she might hock that, and was humbled by the child's reaction as she bravely handed it over.

'It was fun to wear it for that week,' she said. 'I don't need it now.'

All that effort and argument, Polly thought, to buy the dress and then they were reduced to bartering it for food.

Chapter Eight

There were days during that long cold winter when Polly was driven to asking for some item to be put 'on tick' at Connie Green's corner shop. Maybe half a loaf or a pennyworth of tea, which formed an essential part of their diet. She found she could get through most of the day on mugs of weak tea and a slice of bread and scrape.

'Just to see the week out,' she'd say, and Connie would smile and assure her that her credit was good.

'At least you pay what you can, when you can. Not like some I could mention.' Polly thanked her, even though it was shaming and she daren't tell Matthew.

Her favourite time for visiting the market was midnight on a Saturday when she could pick up a quarter stone of potatoes, a pound each of carrots and onions, and a bit of tripe if she was lucky, all for a shilling. Mebbe get a few old cabbage leaves thrown in for good measure; She'd boil the tripe gently in milk and onions, for it was Matthew's favourite meal. On one joyful occasion she bought a skinny rabbit instead which not only made them a fine stew but brought in a penny or two for the skin as well, which she sold to a woman who collected them for the glove factory.

That had been a rare treat, for the family now lived chiefly on lentil or cabbage soup, with some sort of offal or Manx kippers to break the monotony. These last she'd buy for a penny-halfpenny a pair, eight pairs for a shilling, which was the cheapest quality food she could find. And if Benny and Lucy groaned at the frequent appearance of this dish on the table, at least hunger drove them to eat every scrap.

For all she had little money to spend, and finding food for her children became an endless worry, Polly enjoyed her trips to market. She loved talking with the stall holders, enjoying the entertainment they offered.

'Any fish you like for a tanner.'

'Cheese of all varieties. Lancashire Mild, Lancashire Crumbly and Lancashire Tasty. Which will it be, folks? Make up your mind quick afore it all goes!'

'I'm not asking half a crown. I'm not even asking two bob,' another stall holder would cry, gathering a lively crowd about him. 'Give me one and sixpence. No, forget that. One shilling and threepence and it's yours.' Then some scrawny old hens or a box of haddock would change hands. Not that Polly ever had a spare shilling for such a treat, but she loved to watch.

Often she'd go with Eileen, or sometimes take Lucy to help keep an eye open for bargains. They'd walk the length of the hawkers' barrows on Oldham Street, checking every price, seeking one that was a halfpenny or even a farthing cheaper than the next. Or they'd check out Shude Hill Market and any of the other spots around Ancoats where bargains could be found.

These outings served to lighten the dull pain of their hunger. On one such occasion Polly and Lucy were standing by the black pudding stall, no more than a table with a cloth on it set by the railway arches, but giving off such appetising smells that their mouths were watering. They were counting their pennies to see if they could afford a slice each with a dab of mustard. When they found they couldn't, Lucy went boldly up to the woman and asked if she needed any regular help.

'I'm a good worker,' she said, 'I'd not complain about the long hours and I'd do as I was told.'

'Modest with it an' all,' laughed the woman, warming her hands against the heat from the glowing fire in her bucket. 'Sorry, love, wish I had a job to offer you. But keep asking around. You never know, a pretty lass like you might strike luckier than most.' And she winked.

Poverty making her unduly sensitive, Polly flushed with embarrassment at the implication and dragged Lucy quickly away. 'What were you thinking of? It's only thirteen you are, and still at school. Why would you be wanting to work for a woman like her?'

'I'm nearly fourteen. Anyroad, I could leave school now since Dad is unemployed and you've only a bit of a job. My friend Sally has. It happens all the time, Mam. They'd let me leave if I had a job to go to, which would help a bit, wouldn't it?'

Polly could not deny the fact, but the thought of her lovely daughter giving up her education for the sake of putting food in their mouths near broke her heart. 'Wasn't I wanting a fine education for you both? Who knows where it might take you? I'll not let you leave school, not on my account.'

'We have to eat, Mam. And what is it you expect me to do?' Lucy protested, knowing full well.

'Get yerself a fine job in the city, at the typewriting, or mebbe in a shop. Didn't you dream of working at Paulden's or one o' them fine shops in St Anne's Square or King Street? The kind of shop where real ladies go and don't have to ask the price. Now wouldn't that be grand?' Polly looked into her young daughter's sad eyes and saw how she bit her lip, knowing that was exactly what she wanted. She gathered Lucy into her arms and held her close for a moment. 'I don't want you to worry. We'll manage somehow. Whatever happens, you must finish your education so that you at least can get out of this rat hole.'

–

The weeks dragged by and the weather worsened, the bitter cold of winter making itself felt. Running out of coal was not to be thought of, for without a fire the family couldn't cook or even boil a kettle, let alone keep warm. To this end, Benny was put in charge of scouring for coal. He'd range far and wide with his sack, scouring the railway sidings and even the canal, picking up what bits he could find. It was a competitive occupation for everyone else was doing it too, including Georgie Eastwood.

'Hey up, look who's here. Soppy Benny Blue-Cap.' Benny started to run but too late. Georgie and his mates had no difficulty in catching him, as he couldn't run fast, being small for his age. They nicked his sackful of carefully picked coal and left him in tears. Rather than face going home with nothing, he found another old sack lying about at the back of the goods yard and started all over again.

It was dark by the time Benny arrived home but for once his mother didn't scold him. She took in the sight of his weary face, eyes like huge sad bruises in his pinched white face, and took the almost empty sack from him with gratitude. She gave him a big warm hug and planted a kiss on his cheek which, unusually, he didn't rub off. 'Aw, now won't we make a grand fire with this: What a fine young man you're growing into, son.'

Benny was granted an extra slice of bread with his dishful of hot lentil soup by way of reward that night. As he sat toasting himself in front of the fire he had provided, he did indeed feel like a man.

–

Despite vigorous effort on both their parts, neither brother managed to secure full-time employment. Joshua, having lost his job largely because of his involvement in what came to be known as the Dove Street riot, continued to be rejected in favour of a married man. Most of the mills were either on short time or demanding more of their workers and laying off the rest. Matthew considered himself lucky if he got two casual days' labour a week, unloading coal or cotton at some wharf or other, although the money he earned barely took them above starvation level.

Joshua had now switched his allegiance to the National Unemployed Workers' Movement, whose aim was to mobilise an army of unemployed to protest to the government. They held regular meetings at the Mission Hall.

'He wants me to go with him,' Matthew told Polly.

'Will you go?' Busily polishing her beloved sideboard, she felt a moment's concern, not much caring for this talk of mobilising armies of discontented men.

Matthew stood beside her in the parlour, looking fidgety and troubled. As he and his brother were now in the same boat, he felt it reasonable for Joshua to expect his support. Apathy and depression were spreading like a disease but, in common with Polly he had his reservations about militant action of any sort. 'He says it's the only way. There's talk of a Means Test where your money could be cut just because you have a pensioner living in your house, or a child that's earning, or even some decent furniture.'

He waved a hand to indicate their own few pieces in the kitchen: the deal table, horse-hair sofa and a few odd wooden chairs. Then he smoothed it over the shining mahogany of the solid sideboard with its fancy curlicues, gothic-style frame and huge oval mirror at the back. Upon it stood a glass bowl and two china dogs, all neatly set out on crocheted cream mats. He loved that sideboard, so painstakingly saved for and dearly bought, for it seemed to symbolise that they were somebody. No one else in Dove Street had such a handsome piece of furniture. It sickened him to think that if he didn't sell it, the money rightly due to him as an unemployed man with a family would be cut.

'This is our home, every last stick of it, and I mean to protect it, come what may. But it's a worry, Pol. I want to do summat to support our Joshua, but I don't want to take any undue risks. Not with you and the childer to think of. I can't make up me mind one way or t'other.'

Polly gave the sideboard a final flick of her duster and an affectionate pat with her hand, then tucking the duster into the waistband of her skirt, turned to her husband. 'Fond as I am of this sideboard, I'd let it go sooner than see my children starve, you can be sure of that.'

'They're not going to starve!' he shouted. 'I'll find some work somewhere, without help or hand-out from anyone.'

So rarely did he swear or raise his voice that Polly felt quite shocked. Then, as if all passion had been spent, Matthew dropped into the only chair in the small room and put his head in his hands. He looked what he was, a defeated man at his wit's end. Polly's heart clenched with love for him. If starving herself to death would save her children and her man, wouldn't she do it for them? But that wasn't the way. They had to keep fighting, no matter what despair they felt.

She went and knelt beside him, stroking his hands, whispering soothing words of love. 'You deserve better, all of you men do. I've read about it in the newspapers. The government is responsible for there being no work round here, through their carelessness and wrong thinking. They've overspent, so it's our throats they cut.'

'Aye, Joshua might be right. We have little control over whether we work or not, but we still have to live,' Matthew said, his voice barely above a whisper, as if dragged from the depths of his soul.

Fear was growing inside her, fear that he might never find work again. He was only in his mid-thirties, not old by any means, but there were plenty of younger and probably fitter men coming up behind him, all going after the same jobs; those who hadn't taken ship to Canada or Australia, seeking a better life. There were days when for two pins she'd sell everything, even their beloved sideboard, pack up her house and do the same. 'You're entitled to a proper living. It's not your fault there's no work. It shouldn't be looked on as charity but your right.'

'How can we live on a pittance? The government believes're all feckless. I read the newspapers, Polly, and I'll not have anyone say that about me.'

He sounded so fierce and strong again, much more like her Matthew, that she laughed, resting her cheek against his and breathing in the beloved scent of him. 'They'd have me to deal with if they dared say any such thing about my man.'

'Aye, well, the last time I went to a meeting I lost me job. I can't see how going to another will bring it back.'

So it was decided between them, Matthew would have nothing to do with the meetings, nor militant protests of any kind. He calmly informed Joshua he'd no interest in politics. 'I want no trouble. I want only to earn a bit of brass and feed my family.'

In truth Polly couldn't disagree with this. Didn't history tell them over and over how being militant led only to trouble? She'd be proud of a man who fought for his rights, but at least this way her husband would be safe. There was no shame, she told herself, in being poor.

–

Despite the everyday trials and tribulations of poverty, the Pride family were happy enough and coping. Just about. They faced each day as it came, and what they didn't have, Polly thought, they'd do without and not weep over.

If there was harshness for those still at the mill, or worse for those on the dole, it was more than made up for by the goodness found on their street. Everyone did what they could to help their neighbours. If you were desperate for a slice of bread, a dab of marg or spoonful of sugar, somebody would be sure to share with you what little they had, if only because it might be them asking next week.

Polly knew that Christmas was not going to be easy this year. Usually she started putting a bit by each week, once the clothes bought for the Whit Walks were paid for. Last year had been bad enough: this year all their savings had been used up on simply surviving.

There wouldn't be a great deal in the way of food of winter fuel, though Benny did his best to help, bless him. The children had grown used to the careful placing of pieces of coal on the small fire, and the freezing cold nights when they wore every layer of clothing they could lay their hands on. If they were lucky, and there'd been a good fire for once, they'd get a hot brick to warm their feet when they went to bed, but even that would be cold by the early hours, the worst part of a winter's night.

Polly and Lucy had spent weeks hooking a new rag rug to put before the parlour fire. It was made out of scraps of old clothes, which in themselves were becoming harder to come by these days, but Polly had been determined to have it finished in time. She always had a new rug for the parlour come Christmas, putting the one it replaced in front of the range in the kitchen, and the old one from there she'd promised to Eileen this year, since she hadn't time to make one with four children to see to.

Polly wished there was more she could do to make Christmas special for her family. It was important that it should be different from any other day of the year, or what was the point of it? How this could be brought about she hadn't the faintest idea, but she was determined to try. Even if they didn't have a single present between them, she meant it to be happy.

'We could go to the market last thing on Christmas Eve and see what we can find?' she suggested, and Eileen eagerly agreed.

'Good idea. We might be able to find a chicken, or even a goose. Then we'll buy lots of presents for the children. A spinning top for our Agnes, paints and a drawing book for Rosie, and a ball each for the twins...'

'...some blue ribbons for Lucy, and a new football for Benny...'

'...and apples and pears, enough for everyone.'

'Oh, yes, and a juicy orange each, or maybe tangerines. Ach, and I do so love nuts! It wouldn't be Christmas without a bag of nuts to chew on.' Dreaming of what they might buy at the market made it all seem possible and enlivened many a dull afternoon.

In the event, as the two women set off, arm in arm, they didn't have enough money between them to buy a rabbit each, let alone a goose and all those longed for presents. Nevertheless they did indeed have a wonderful time at the market. The air was clear and frosty, and instead of the stink of soot and smoke they smelled the tantalising aroma of the black peas stand, warmed their backsides by the hot chestnut cart and recklessly bought a tiny bag to share between them as a treat – afterwards filled with guilt at such an extravagance.

Late in the evening Polly managed to buy some bruised cooking apples with her careful hoard of money, and even some wheat flour which on Christmas Day she made into huge Yorkshire puddings, one for each of them, with onion gravy. She would dearly have loved to offer meat to follow, but it was not to be. Undeterred, she had the meal ready and waiting by the time Big Flo and Joshua came home from chapel and the children from mass.

'There, won't that fill you up grand? And there's apple pie for afters.'

'No turkey?' queried Benny, and earned himself a kick from Lucy under the table as a reward for his lack of tact.

'Praise the Lord,' said Big Flo. 'From whom all blessings flow.'

'And may He send a few more next year,' Matthew said, earning himself a reproving glare from his mother, and a stem lecture on respect and humility from Joshua.

'You are far too light-minded, brother. I seem to recall you always were, even as a boy; believing you could be as pig-headed as you pleased and still have everything fall easily into your lap. It will get you into a deal of bother one day.'

'Meaning from you, by any chance?'

'Meaning that if you want to enjoy the advances achieved by your fellow men you should help to bring them about.' Joshua was still annoyed with his brother for refusing to have anything to do with the NUWM meetings. His own ambitions as an orator were growing by the day, and he'd been asked to speak on two separate occasions which was gratifying. He'd expected his brother to be there to support him.

'Enough,' Polly said. 'No family squabbles today. A Happy Christmas to you all.'

'A Happy Christmas!'

Despite the fact there'd been little more than a tangerine and a few chestnuts in each child's stocking, it was indeed a happy day. And if there was less food on their plates than they would have liked, at least the fire roared halfway up the chimney for once, which meant they could have great fun roasting the chestnuts. Benny received much praise for his efforts in this department.

'Did you open yer own pit, lad?' Big Flo asked, punch-the child jokingly in the chest. Benny only grinned, not owning up to how he'd deprived the London and North Western Railway Company of a good hundredweight of coal, little by little, over the weeks. He basked in the role of hero, resolving to ensure that further accolades would come his way in the near future.

Living by his wits was coming naturally to Benny these days. He and his mates had never again managed to dupe Daft Betty into giving them her jam jars since her sister Nellie had locked them all away, but they picked up the odd one here and there, not least from the cemetery where they'd find them full of dead flowers. What was the point of that, they'd think, when money was so desperately needed by the living? So they'd swap the jars for pennies and go to the flicks to watch *Our Gang* or Buster Keaton. They'd take their seats on the front benches then under cover of darkness go off to the Gents and slip into the more comfortable ninepenny seats at the back on their return. If they were lucky, and the manager was otherwise occupied with his lady friend, they'd get away with it. On other occasions he'd nip them by the ear and fling them out into the street.

Sometimes they'd wander down Oldham Street, or even along Piccadilly or Deansgate, and offer to clean windows for the shop-keepers. They could earn as much as a shilling that way.

Life was far from easy for anyone, but Benny often felt that he suffered the most from their increased poverty. At school he was made to stand on his chair to show that he was entitled to free school dinners, as his father was unemployed. He then had to line up with other boys and girls, collect a ticket and be marched in twos through the streets to the Mission where kind ladies provided them each with a basin of soup and a hunk of bread. Thankful though he was for the food, he hated the humiliation he had to go through to get it. And it gave Georgie Eastwood even more ammunition to fire at him.

'Poor boy, poor boy!' the loathsome Georgie would call out whenever Benny passed by. He'd throw lumps of coal or dog muck at him, and Benny would have a devil of a job cleaning it off before he dare go home. Or Georgie would accuse Benny's father of not being a proper man. 'Can't feed his own family. *My* dad can. *My* dad don't depend upon any silly old ladies at the Mission. He's clever is *my* dad.'

'So's mine. It's not his fault he can't get a job,' Benny would cry, dreading the tears that stung his eyes because that would only make the bullying worse.

'Great soft babby! Does he want his dummy then?' And Benny wouldn't know whether to stay and fight and risk yet another bloodied nose, being so hopelessly outnumbered, or turn tail and run and suffer being dubbed a coward as well.

Deciding he'd had enough, he called a special meeting of the Dove Street Gang, now that he was a fully paid up member ever since that first jam jar collection. 'We must take action,' he announced, waving one fist in the air like a general addressing his troops, and they all vowed their support. 'Georgie bloomin' Eastwood is going to get what's coming to him! He'll wish he'd never been born by the time we've finished with him.' This was greeted with loud cheers all round.

'That's the ticket,' Liam agreed. 'We'll pulverise the lot of 'em, eh?'

More cheers. There wasn't a boy present who hadn't suffered at Eastwood's hands so they were only too willing to bring his gang down, great bullies that they were. If onlycould work out the way to do it.

—

It was the day after Boxing Day that Benny made his greatest discovery, one that was to make this Christmas special above all others, for inadvertently it changed the fortunes of the Pride family forever.

He'd been following the Eastwood Gang, spying on them as part of his campaign to find a way to pay Georgie back for his bullying. He'd still not worked out an answer to that problem but followed them everywhere, like Felix the Cat, not exactly with his hands behind his back but walking bravely through the very worst streets, then on to the better houses in and around St Andrew's Square.

Carefully tucked behind an entry wall, Benny watched as the gang rooted in the rubbish bins that stood in the yards behind each house. At first he was disgusted, then he became filled with curiosity as he saw them lift out parcel after parcel, examine the contents then run off with them, as if carrying some great prize.

When he was sure they'd gone, he slipped out to take a peep himself. Most of the bins revealed nothing more than ash and the usual collection of rubbish. He'd almost given up hope when he crept into the last house on the corner, lifted the lid and made his discovery.

Chapter Nine

'You found it *where*? Whatever made you think of doing such a thing?'

The turkey carcass sat on the deal table, almost defying Polly to object to its presence in her kitchen.

'I don't reckon you'd best ask him too closely, lass,' Big Flo warned. 'He might tell thee. Sounds like he came by it legal, anyroad, if from no very edifying place.'

Polly could scarcely believe what her eyes and ears were telling her. 'D'you mean you just took it into your head to root in someone's *bin!*' Had they sunk so low?

Benny protested, 'It's no worse than you getting them books from the Dolly Varden man.'

'This isn't books. This is food you expect us to eat.'

'It's all right. It's clean. It were all wrapped up, see, in newspaper. It's not been touched by anything, nor been there very long. And it were a posh bin, from them good houses on St Andrew's Square.'

There was a long silence while everyone considered this.

Matthew and Joshua were both out looking for work, as usual, which was a blessing in a way. It was up to the womenfolk to decide how best to deal with the matter.

Big Flo said, 'It's providence, that's what it is. No one need know. And it'd make a fine stock for a stew if nowt else.'

'And there's plenty of bits o' meat still hanging on it,' Lucy added, licking her lips.

The two women looked at each other, all too aware of the hunger gnawing at their own stomachs, let alone the naked agony in the children's eyes. The newspaper seemed clean enough, as did the turkey, Polly decided. But should she risk it? 'We might all catch some dreadful disease from it. What then?'

'Or we might die from starvation,' Lucy prompted. 'Aw, come on, Mam. I'd take the risk.'

'Me too,' Benny agreed. 'I'm that hungry.'

'By the time the carcass has been boiled, there'll surely be no danger of any disease from it,' Big Flo pointed out.

This sounded so reasonable that hunger won. The turkey carcass was indeed thoroughly boiled and scraped till every ounce of goodness had been extracted from it. Then they added chunks of potatoes, carrots and onions to the juicy portions of meat and well-seasoned stock. Big Flo took home a basinful for herself and Joshua to share, while Matthew, Polly and the children sat down to the finest feast enjoyed by man of beast. It was like Christmas all over again.

Even Georgie Eastwood won't be eating any better, Benny thought, once more relishing the sensation of being the hero of the hour.

It was only when they were all replete and sat back to rub distended stomachs, unused to so much rich food, that he thought to mention the rest of his news. He'd had to be sharp about it, for even as he'd reached for the parcel he'd heard voices coming from the kitchen door. 'Some folks must be really rich,' he observed aloud, filled with a sense of his own importance. 'It wasn't the only thing they were throwing out. I heard the woman say she wouldn't have it in the house another day. "It has to go or I will," she said.'

Polly was laughing at her son. 'What would have to go?'

'Happen her husband,' Matthew chortled, happy since his belly was full at last, despite yet another disappointing day.

'Nay, it was a carpet. These two chaps were measuring up for a new one, which they promised to fetch tomorrow. Fancy wanting to chuck out a perfectly good carpet.' Benny had never actually seen a carpet, let alone one which was about to be discarded. But he looked pleased with himself for dispensing this bit of tittle-tattle about what went on in better-off houses.

'What a waste,' Lucy said. 'Some people don't know when they're well off.'

'It's one law for the rich, another for the rest of us,' Matthew agreed, wiping up the last of his gravy with the tip of one finger. Polly tapped his hand, pursing her lips at his lack of manners. But she was unusually quiet as she cleared away the dishes that night. She didn't even speak when it was time for the children to go to bed, except to wish them goodnight. She wrapped the two hot bricks in their respective cloths, handed them over in a distracted sort of way, hugged her children but didn't offer to tell them a story, as she so often did.

'Mam...' Benny began, but Lucy frowned and shushed him into silence, dragging him away up the stairs to the room they shared. Their mother had been busy enough, what with the agonising over the turkey carcass, and the boiling and scraping of it, so no wonder she was tired out.

Her guess seemed to be correct when Polly volunteered to go to bed too, without enjoying the usual half hour of peace with her husband.

'Aye, you go on up, love, if you're tired,' he said. 'I'll bank up the fire and see to everything. I'll be up in a minute.' Polly pretended to be asleep when he slid in beside her, because for once she had no wish to talk. Crazy thoughts and ideas were whirling about her head, making her feel dizzy, and she wanted to give them time to settle before she voiced them out loud, even to herself.

By six o'clock the next morning, when she stuck the poker in the black belly of the fire to give it a good riddle and liven it to a flame for the first brew of the day, she felt a slow burn of excitement. Polly thought she could very well have the answer to all their problems.

It was a daring, reckless, some might say completely mad idea, since it involved a considerable amount of risk. If she was right, and her idea worked, Matt would forgive her, she was certain of it. If it all went wrong, then he might never speak to her again. All she had to do was find the courage to carry it out.

–

First Polly must find the right house. Over his breakfast porridge, she carefully elicited the information from Benny. Next, she sounded out her idea with Eileen.

'Don't do it,' her friend warned, sounding unusually concerned. They stood shivering on the doorstep, speaking quickly in hushed tones, fearful they might be overheard. 'No man would wear it. Your Matthew certainly won't.'

'But it'd be worth it, in the end. Can't you see that?'

'*I* can. *You* can. But will he? No, I wouldn't risk it. Polly. Think again.'

'I have thought, all bloomin' night! It's the only way. It's starvation otherwise.'

'You'll get by, as we all do. Think some more. He'll skin you alive.'

Polly did think. Her morning's work at the temperance tavern seemed to drag on endlessly. She served the soup, washed bowls out afterwards and filled them up for the next customer, then when everyone was served, ran a damp cloth round the tiled ledge that surrounded the room. But still she couldn't get the idea out of her head. She wanted more from life than simply to get by. She wanted her children to fly free of this place, not live their lives in the same cramped, overcrowded, damp conditions that had been their lot so far.

There'd been rumours of rehousing for the people of Ancoats, but so far that was all they seemed to be – rumours. And with the need for work becoming desperate, she could see no real hope of improving their condition. Now, suddenly, Polly could see a light at the end of a very dark tunnel. Wasn't it worth the risk?

By the time her shift was over, her mind was quite made up. She strode off down Ancoats Lane in the direction of the goods yard, turned right along Adair Street and finally into St Andrew's Square which was close by Helmet Street Park where there was a recreation area and bandstand.

She found the house easily enough, not half so grand as she had imagined but better than her own by far. Polly stood for a long time considering the enormity of what she was about to do. There was the roll of carpet, propped up by the back door, clearly waiting for the Dolly Varden men to take it away. The opportunity was too good to miss. She knocked gently and a maid appeared, a girl of little more than fifteen.

'Yes?'

Polly cleared her throat and asked to see the lady of the house. 'You mean Mrs Eckersley?'

'If that is her name.'

The maid sniffed, gaze moving over Polly as if she very much doubted her employer would allow such a scruff into her nice clean house. She seemed about to close the door until Polly stepped closer. 'It's very important.'

'Wait 'ere.'

After a long wait, Polly was shown into a neat parlour twice the size of her own. It was the finest room she'd ever seen in her life and Polly made a vow, there and then, that one day she'd have one exactly like it. Only not in Ancoats, near to a railway line, but somewhere really grand, where her children could have a big garden to play in, see green fields or a park out of the window. She drank in the sight of creamy lace curtains so thick that barely any daylight crept through to damage the fine mahogany furniture or the antimacassars on the winged armchairs, nor to dry out the aspidistra on its three-legged stand, or more importantly fade the colours of the splendid new carpet.

Polly looked down at her boots, which she'd elected to wear as more appropriate for visiting than her workaday clogs, and wished now that she'd taken them off at the back door. The woman was looking her over, making judgements as to Polly's fitness to stand in her front parlour. She was dressed in her cleanest, no, her only dress, which fortunately had not been returned to the pawnbrokers this week. On her head was the hat she had worn at Whitsun, skewered firmly in plane with a hatpin. She looked as clean and respectable as she could make herself, in the circumstances. Mrs Eckersley's gaze had now returned to the battered boots but she made no comment beyond a sharp, 'Well?'

Polly cleared her throat yet again and quickly gathered her thoughts. She'd worried a great deal about what she should say. It certainly wouldn't do to admit that her son had been delving in this woman's rubbish bins and that Polly's entire family had dined on the remains of her leftover turkey. Nor would it be a good idea for Mrs Eckersley to learn that her conversation had been overheard by a small boy. But seeing the carpet by the back door had solved all her problems.

Polly meant to pass herself off as a hawker, for in a way that was what she would be if she pulled off this deal. And wasn't it what her own good mother, and her less than useless father, when he was sober, had done before her? Hadn't her parents once travelled the roads of Ulster, buying and selling whatever they could lay their hands on, in order to feed their brood before giving up and coming to Lancashire? She'd been the youngest, Mary Ann Shaugnessy, fondly dubbed Polly for short. Since so many childhood memories had been blocked out as too painful, this was as far as she ever let herself think.

'I beg pardon, ma'am, for interrupting you, but I'll not take up too much of your time.' Good manners, Polly recalled her own mother telling her, would get you anything. The woman was now sitting ramrod straight with her hands as tightly clasped as her lips.

'I can give you five minutes, not a second more.'

'Indeed so, ma'am.' Polly took a breath and launched into her prepared speech. 'I was looking around, the square being a bit more top-notch than the rest of this area, hoping as how I might chance upon a bit of business. I buy and sell, d'you see, but only from well-bred people such as yourself. I never touch rubbish.'

She had no money to buy anything as yet, but that was a problem Polly would attend to if this meeting went well. Mrs

Eckersley's brow was creased by a frown, but it was more pensive than disapproving.

'And what sort of items would you be looking for? I think there's an old chest of drawers in the kitchen we no longer need.' Polly adopted a sorrowful expression.

'To be honest with you, ma'am, I don't have the space for storing furniture and suchlike in my—my premises. I deal only in carpets.' She found herself beginning to perspire beneath the woman's searching gaze, as if Mrs Eckersley could see how close to an untruth she was straying, since she didn't have premises of any kind, and had never come near a carpet in her life.

To Polly a carpet represented luxury and money, so for that reason alone she was keen to get her hands on it. Except she feared that at any moment the housemaid, or worse still, a great lumbering male servant, would be called upon to throw her out of the house. 'Begging your pardon, ma'am, but I chanced to see a roll of carpet propped up by your back door.'

'Well, indeed, that is true. What a coincidence! This new one, upon which you are standing, was delivered only this morning.' And she indicated the glorious square of patterned red carpet. Polly took a step backwards to stand on the linoleum surround instead. She felt much more comfortable there in her boots.

'It's a fine piece. Oriental, I'd say.' Hazarding a guess, since she felt she ought to sound knowledgeable. It proved, luckily, to be accurate.

'Quite.' Mrs Eckersley actually smiled. 'So I threw the old one out.' She gave a dismissive gesture, to prove it was no longer of any account and she was well enough placed to change her carpet whenever she'd a mind. Then her eyes narrowed speculatively. Doris Eckersley had married well, and her husband was justifying her faith in him by the steady acquisition of a chain of shops selling fine porcelain and tableware to the well-to-do. They still had a long way to go in their climb to the top, this house but a stepping stone along the way. Even so, Doris meant it to be so smart that well-worn carpets could not be tolerated in it. At the same time, money was not yet so easily come by that she wasn't able to see a deal when one was offered to her. This hawker woman was of the poorest class, without doubt, but appeared clean and honest.

'I'd want something for it, naturally.'

'Naturally, ma'am.' Polly's heart skipped a beat with joy. She'd done it! In no time at all a price was agreed which proved acceptable to both parties.

'And it must be collected without delay. Can you arrange that?'

Polly thought quickly. She still had to arrange the finance, and would need help in carrying the carpet. 'I'll have it collected later in the day. How would that be?'

Mrs Eckersley took a moment to consider. It wouldn't do for this street hawker to come calling during the afternoon, but then none of her friends were expected today. She'd made a point of explaining the reason why visitors would be an inconvenience on this day to as many as were prepared to listen. They'd all be here tomorrow quickly enough, to view the new carpet. 'Very well,' she agreed. 'But if you are not here by nine, I shall have it taken away by the Dolly Varden men, and that'll be your chance gone.'

'Right you are,' Polly agreed. And yours too, she thought, not entirely fooled by the gloss of respectability. Sure and wasn't her husband probably a rogue of the first water, building his fortune on the backs of his workers? The details agreed, she took her leave and hurried at once to 'Uncle' Joseph. If he didn't agree to her plan, the idea was dead in the water before she'd begun.

–

The old pawnbroker thought she had gone clean off her head. 'Is it deaf I am, or are you speaking these words into my ears and they are coming out wrong in my head? Or is it mad I've gone, at long last?'

Polly giggled. She liked Joseph Malachi. He was a gentle, kind old man who went out of his way to help people. He'd even been known to loan back an unredeemed suit for nothing for some family event such as a funeral when its owner did not have the wherewithal to pay him back. 'To be sure, you hear me right, and yes, I'm as sane as yourself. Which isn't saying much, admittedly.'

The pair grinned amicably at each other. 'Ah, well, it's a visit to Prestwich we should both be making. But then, if they'd made me right in the head, how could I go on running a shop in this Godforsaken place?'

The banter continued, taking longer than Polly had hoped. She had to convince the old man that she was indeed serious. When she had done, he sadly shook his head. 'I see what it is you are about, little one, but I am not the man to help you. Would that I were. I have not the funds for such a grand plan.'

Polly's heart sank. 'But you must help me! It would work, I'm sure of it.'

'Such faith you have. Such ambition. I remember when I was young feeling just as hungry for success, for a new world for myself and my lovely Ruth.' Joseph scratched at his beard, polished his glasses and set them carefully back in place, winding the wires around his ears. Polly could hardly breathe as she watched, sensing the hard thinking behind this little ritual. After what seemed an age he looked up at her, placed the tips of his forgers together, and smiled. 'I will do what I can. As for the rest, you could always try talking to my friend Izzy. Now *there* is a man with more money than sense. He might very well help since he was born a fool and is now a rich one.'

It took another hour to find Izzy Barnard, and more precious moments to explain her scheme all over again and capture his interest, but Polly finally felt success was within her grasp. Then it was back to her house, with many preparations and arrangements still to be made. She was in a lather of anxiety that the task be completed before Matthew's return. Finally the money was being counted into her hand, Polly found two likely lads in the street, and at long last the roll of carpet was propped up in one corner of her own front parlour. She had done it!

But that was the only item in the room.

Everything else, every other stick of furniture the family owned, had been sold in order to provide the necessary capital to pay for the carpet and set up her business. Every single chair, the deal table, the horse-hair sofa, even the beloved sideboard, had gone. The only item Polly had not sold was a small but battered tin trunk in which she kept a few family mementoes such as Benny's first pair of clogs, a lock of Lucy's hair, and a photograph of her mother. Upon this she laid out their frugal meal that night, and around it placed four orange boxes she'd got from the market. All she had to do now was wait for Matthew and the children to come home.

—

For the first time in his life, Matthew was struck speechless. He stared at his wife and then at his empty home, appalled disbelief on his face. Polly, watching her husband's reaction, experienced the first stirrings of doubt.

'Don't fret, it's me what's done this, not the bailiff.' She turned to her children, hoping to win Matthew round if she had him on her own for a minute or two. 'Would you two like to go out and play?' But for once neither had any desire for freedom. Whatever madness had beset their mother today, they wanted to hear of it.

'Well then, will you all sit down and eat yer supper while I tell you what I've done and why?' A hint of trepidation had crept into her voice, yet Polly struggled to remain resolute in spite of the dark fury that tightened Matthew's jaw as he listened to her halting explanation.

She went through the whole story twice, so great was her nervousness and so anxious was she for them not to miss the significance of it.

She explained how she'd come by the idea from Benny's tittle-tattle. She told of her visit to the house, the deal she had struck with Mrs Eckersley, and how she had managed to get a good price for their furniture from Joseph and his friend Izzy. 'And I still have a bit o' money left to buy more carpets and set us up in business.' When her voice finally faded into silence, the expression on her husband's and children's faces were indeed a sight to behold.

Benny's mouth had dropped right open and was evidently fixed there. Lucy's blue eyes seemed to have grown to twice their size, and as for Matthew – one glance at her husband told Polly that Eileen had been right. Never had she seen him in such a terrible rage. Perhaps she had put her case badly.

Haltingly, she began again but he had heard enough. With a kick from one heavy clog he sent the tin trunk toppling. Its lid broke off and clattered over the stone-flagged floor, sending baked potatoes rolling to each corner of the kitchen. But not even the ever-hungry Benny dared make a move to pick one up. His father rarely, if ever, lost his temper, but the lad was sure that if he moved a muscle it would be him that Dad would kick next, right into the middle of next week.

'I'll not eat my tea off a tin box, nor sit on a bloody orange box!' Matthew shouted, loud enough for the whole street to hear if they'd a mind to listen. Then he was striding from the house and the only sound was that of the front door slamming shut and the striking of his clogs on the setts, sending sparks flying all the way up Dove Street.

Peace descended uneasily upon the small house. Polly drew in a trembling breath, gathered up the baked potatoes and gave them a quick rub with a clean cloth. She set them back in their dish. Lucy had righted the tin trunk and Benny was struggling to fit back the lid, a terrible sinking sensation in his stomach.

'Now isn't this a grand lark?' she said to her children with a wide smile, as she took her seat on an orange box. 'It's like a picnic in our own home. Eat the spuds while're hot. We've even a dab of marg to put on 'em today. Aren't we the lucky ones?'

And Polly and her children steadfastly ate their dinner in what passed for a contented silence.

Chapter Ten

Big Flo sat in Polly's kitchen, her back as rigid as her morals. Apart from a starched white pinafore, she was clothed all in black from her shawl to the clog tips that peeped out from under her long black skirts. And the dour expression on the old woman's lined face seemed perfectly in accord. Florence Pride knew more commandments than the good Lord had ever thought to give Moses. There were the usual ones about never complaining, making do, and standing on your own feet. Being clean in thought and tongue was one of her favourites. 'Wilful waste brings woeful want' was another. 'Idleness addles the brain' was one she was particularly fond of, along with 'Hard work never killed anyone', even though it clearly did, judging by the number of miners and cotton workers dying of consumption from the muck they breathed in at their places of employment.

'Neither a borrower nor a lender be', which must include popping the furniture without your husband's permission, was the one she was airing at the moment.

'I've never seen him so cut up! The poor lad doesn't know which way to turn.'

Polly admitted that it must have come as something of a shock. It had been well past midnight when Matthew had slid between the blankets beside her, and a great relief to her that he'd come home at all. But neither of them had spoken. Even at breakfast his silence had lain heavily between them. Now she confronted her mother-in-law with face set and fists clenched. 'That being the case, it's even more important I should make it work.'

'Aye, I can see it would be. Our Josh told him he was a fool to marry you, an Irish Catholic, and that it served him right if you'd gone and lost every decent bit a' stuff you ever owned. Reverting to type, he called it.'

Polly felt her cheeks start to burn. How dare Joshua say such a thing? He'd always made it plain he disapproved of their marriage but it had never mattered before because she and Matt were happy and the two brothers not even close. But never had Joshua spoken so plainly against her and for once, it seemed, Matthew had agreed with him. It made her heart ache to think of it.

'Will you help me?'

'Me?' Big Flo's white eyebrows climbed to the heights of her wrinkled brow. She was ready to flounce out of this mad Irish woman's house for good. From the start she'd created discord between her precious sons; now she'd gone completely off her chump and thrown away everything Matthew had built up over the years. Talk about hitting a man when he was down! She'd have nowt to do with the floozy ever again, Flo decided, yet curiosity kept her on the seat, for all it was only an orange box that could break beneath her weight at any moment. 'Help you do what?'

'I mean to sell on the market. No one can afford to buy a big carpet like this, not round here, but cut into smaller pieces it'd sell, if only because it'd save the work of hooking a rug and look much better. So, will you help me clean and cut it up?'

Big Flo looked as if she'd been asked personally to pay off the National Debt. 'By heck, that's a tall order.'

'Why? It's a simple enough task.'

'You're asking me to take a stand against me own sons?'

Polly tilted her chin. 'If it works and I get a good price for the pieces, I'll be in profit. Then I can get some of our furniture back. All of it maybe, in time.'

The old woman shook her head in sadness. 'Our Matthew was right fond of that sideboard. It represented why he'd worked so hard for his family.'

Polly felt a constriction of emotion tighten her throat. 'I feel exactly the same. I did try to avoid selling it, but there wouldn't have been enough money otherwise. I doubt I could manage to get it back, not for a while anyway, but I might manage a chair or a table fairly quickly, if I can sell some pieces of the: carpet.' Then she leaned forward, eagerly grasping Big Flo's work-worn hands. 'Don't you see? I had to do it once the idea was in me head. It could be the answer. Not simply to give us something to eat tomorrow but to provide us with a future away from this Godawful place. Wouldn't that be grand?'

'Aye,' said Big Flo, consideringly. 'I can see you'd think so. I were born and brought up in Ancoats and, I'll tell you, there's worse places though I can't offhand name one. Folks are good here. But I can see you'd happen want summat better for them childer.'

'So?'

'So them's only dreams, and the likes of us can't afford to believe in dreams.'

'Why not?'

It took two pint-sized mugs of tea and a great deal more persuasion before Big Flo agreed. 'Aye, go on then,' she said at last, 'I'll help you sew this lot, but no more mind. You manage the rest by yerself.'

'Aw, bless you, Flo.' Polly would face that problem when she came to it.

'Bit you sell 'em yerself.'

'Agreed.'

–

They unrolled the carpet square and laid it out in the empty front parlour. The room was so cold there was a rime of frost on the inside of the windows. The parlour had rarely been used, save at Christmas and Whit Week. Now it looked forlorn and damp as well as empty. The two women automatically reached for their shawls, wrapping them tight around themselves and tying them in a knot at the back. Even so they were chilled to the bone, their breath cloud the freezing air.

'I'll light a fire,' Polly said. 'We can't work in this.'

'Don't waste the coal. If we work fast we won't be in here long. Once it's cut up we can take a piece at a time in the kitchen to bind the edges.'

It took longer than they expected. They rubbed the stained carpet first with the used tea leaves Polly had kept specifically for the purpose. Then they left it for an hour or two while they went to warm themselves over a mug of tea by the fire. After that, they swept it vigorously with stiff brushes to make the pile stand proud, and were delighted to see the rich browns and beiges revitalised by the treatment.

'It has a good all-over pattern, which is important since we're to turn it into small rugs.' Polly could feel a glimmer of excitement inside her. It would work, she was sure of it.

Cutting the carpet proved to be more difficult than she'd imagined. Even though she'd spent some of the precious money on a large pair of scissors for the purpose, she simply did not have sufficient strength to cut through the thick wool. After watching her for a minute or two, Big Flo took the scissors from her hand.

'Give 'em 'ere. You couldn't cut butter.' And the old woman, crawling about on all fours, revealing more of next week's washing than she realised, cut through the carpet with her ham-like hands- as if it really were butter. When they were done they had nine smaller rectangles instead of one large square.

'All we do now is bind and sew them. Still, I have the time, do I not, since there's no furniture left to dust,' Polly said, with a touch of wry humour.

'Nor a comfy spot to sit while we sew,' Big Flo pointed out, eyeing the offending orange boxes with distaste. Taking a couple of the carpet pieces with her, she marched off to her own snug kitchen.

This task was to keep them busy for days. Polly continued to work at the temperance tavern, but in the afternoons and evenings she sat on an upturned box and stitched the strips of hessian she had bought to the edges of each rectangular piece of carpet, turning it into an attractive rug.

Lucy was late home from school a few days after the cutting of the carpet, but before Polly had managed to draw breath to scold her for idling, the girl took the wind right out of her sails.

'I start work tomorrow on Dorrie Glynne's tripe and trotter stall on the market. And before you say anything, I don't care any more about Paulden's or the fancy shops on St Anne's Square or King Street, I just want us to be happy and have enough food on the table, and for Dad to come home. So I've left school and I'm not going back.'

Polly sat down hard on an orange box, every vestige of colour draining from her face. Was this what they had sunk to? In pursuing her own dream, she had robbed her daughter of hers. 'Oh, Lucy! But you should stay on, then you'd have a fine certificate to show at the end of it.'

'Things have changed. I don't care about any of that.' The tremor of her daughter's lips gave the lie to her brave words and Polly held out her arms to comfort her. Lucy came and knelt by her mother's side while the pair of them hugged and cried together, letting the tears of disappointment flow.

'Ach, this won't do,' said Polly, pulling out a hanky and starting to mop up their tears, staunchly smiling as she did so. 'You know this isn't what I wanted for you, m'cushla.'

'It'll be all right, Mam. I'm not a child. I want to pay my way, whatever you say. I can earn a bit of brass, and one day – one day I will work in a fine shop, see if I don't!'

'Of course you will,' Polly assured her, blinking back fresh tears. 'And won't that be grand? Now come and see how much I've done today.' And as mother and daughter continued the laborious hemming of the carpet rugs, they began speculating about the future.

'Happen we'll have us own shop one day,' Lucy said, her blue eyes bright.

'And why not indeed? You shall be manager.'

'No, that'll have to be Dad. I shall be the chief floor, and you'll do the buying. We'll make pots of money, eh?'

'The divil we will.' And all this happy dreaming helped their needles fly.

The next day Joshua called and ordered Polly in no uncertain terms to stop this nonsense immediately.

'And what nonsense would that be?' she blithely enquired. 'Not that it's any of your business, so for as I can see.'

'Matthew is my brother. I'll not see him made into a laughing stock.'

'The divil you won't! It's never bothered you before if he was unhappy. What's so different this time? Is it because I'm the cause of it for once and not yourself?'

'You've shamed the entire family with your worship of Mammon.'

Polly stood on her own doorstep, hands on hips, and almost laughed into his face. 'Mammon, is it? You don't think it might have something to do with needing food to put in me children's bellies?'

Joshua took a step closer, towering over her in a manner that set alarm bells ringing. In his pale, unblinking eyes there was an expression that bordered on savagery. 'Your vulgarities will not soften *my* heart, Mary Ann Shaugnessy. I have your measure.' It had been so long since she'd heard her full name used, or her maiden name for that matter, that it startled her.

'I'm thinking you're taking a bit much upon yerself,' she mildly remarked. 'This is a private matter between myself and my *husband*.' She laid particular emphasis on the last word.

'I know what it is that has set you off on this craving for money. You think Matthew has failed you.' His slack, moist mouth almost spat the words at her. 'You came out of the bogs of Ireland thinking you'd be sitting pretty married to him. Batting your eyelashes at him, coaxing him to wed you before he went off to war, selling your body in order to escape your drunken father. But it hasn't quite worked out as you expected, has it?'

She could see the hairs bristling in each flared nostril, smell the sickening odour of mothballs from the suit he always wore to his many meetings, and hated him for his worldly aspirations and his arrogance and hypocrisy in daring to criticise her own.

'May the good Lord forgive you for such terrible thoughts! I reckon you've said enough, brother-in-law.' Polly could feel herself trembling and fought to keep control, determined not to let him win. 'It may be true that my life with my parents was not what it might have been, but Matthew and I married because we loved each other and for no other reason. We still do love each other, for all we disagree on this matter. So take your dirty mind off my clean step before I knock it off with me sweeping brush!'

—

Polly tried many times to secure Matthew's support for her plan, but to no avail.

When he finally realised she did not intend to redeem their furniture at the end of the week, not even his favourite chair let alone the precious sideboard, he began quietly to collect together a few of his belongings, with a grimness that cut her to the heart of her.

Lucy's leaving school and starting work seemed to him yet another nail in the coffin of his pride. The women of the household were now gainfully employed while he saw himself as cast on the dung-heap, living in a house now bare of his worldly possessions so all the world could see his shame. It was more than any man could possibly tolerate.

He stood before them all, bag in hand, and announced that he was moving in with his mother where, he said, he could at least sleep in a bed, sit on a chair and eat off a solid table. 'I haven't fought in a war or worked all my adult life to be deprived of such basic necessities.'

'But I need you here,' Polly said, startled and afraid by this sudden decision.

'Bring back our furniture and I'll come home like a shot.'

'How can I get the furniture back, Matthew?' Though Polly had a little money left from the sale, stowed safely away in her secret hiding place, it was nowhere near enough to replace all that she had sold. Besides, she still had to buy a cart or stall from which to sell the carpet rugs. Frustration mounted in her. Why couldn't he understand and work with her on this? 'Don't be stubborn, Matthew. It's only your damned pride I've hurt. Surely you can live with that for a while?'

'You ask too much.'

'It won't be for long.'

'I'm not waiting, Poll, Not even for a day.'

'But I'm committed to this plan now. Can't you at least give me time to make it work? Or better still, help me.'

He stabbed a thumb into his chest. 'We should decide these things together, since we're man and wife.' Now the finger was stabbing the air inches from her nose, a furious energy in it. 'But you don't listen to anyone but yourself. You gave no hint, didn't even ask my advice. And why? Because you knew I'd say no.'

Polly flushed, said nothing, bleakly aware that this was true. 'We've faced enough turmoil in our married life already over you being a Catholic, without all of this.'

Polly managed a smile. 'Don't you mean because of your being a non-conformist?'

His voice sank to dangerously soft tones, as if she'd attempted to catch him out in a wrong. 'I didn't say this argument was about religion. You and me have never fallen out over that, though others have made it difficult at times for us. What I'm saying is, I've enough to contend with: a mixed marriage, my brother blaming me for summat that's not my fault, not to mention struggling to find work... without, all of this.' He waved a hand despairingly about the empty room. 'You could at least have asked me first.'

'Maybe you're right, and I was wrong not to tell you. I'm sorry about that, really I am. I thought you mightn't let me, and it's such a good idea.'

Polly dropped the piece of carpet she was stitching and went to him, sliding her arms about his waist and looking earnestly up into the face she loved so dearly. Gently she stroked his rigid cheek, tried not to notice the tightness of his jaw or the anger in his eyes. She felt he was a million miles away from her, for all he was here in her arms. 'But it's exactly because of all those things you've mentioned that I'm doing this. I want to help. Can't you see – we could have our own little business? Once these carpet pieces are all stitched and sold, we'll have made a good start. We might not be in profit right away. I'm no fool, I know we'll need to buy and sell many more. For doesn't it take time to build a business?'

He gave a snort of disgust as he pushed her away from him. 'What do you know about running a business?'

'I intend to learn.'

'You've shamed me, Polly, before everyone. The whole bloomin' street must be laughing up their sleeves to see us now, reduced to eating our dinner off the bare floors.'

'We've the tin box.' Her flippancy only served to inflame his anger still further. He flung a kick at it, the sound ringing hollowly in the empty room.

'Put my house in order and I'll be back.'

Perhaps it was the way he had attacked the box, filled as it was with her treasures, but something seemed to crack inside Polly then and all her Irish temper soared to the surface at last. '*Your* house! *Your* pride. Drat you, Matthew Pride. Can't you think of anyone but yourself? It's only a few weeks' grace I'm asking, a month mebbe.'

'No, Polly.'

'But we can do it, I'm sure of it. Till then…'

'Till then…' And he finished the sentence by picking up his bag and walking out of the house with a determination in the stiffness of his spine that told her he meant exactly what he said. Blinded by tears, and too far gone in despair and anger to control herself, she picked up his plate of broth and flung it after him. It hit the closed door, still quivering on its hinges from the slam it had received, and slid down to the bare stone where the plate split into two pieces, spilling its contents in a pool on the bare boards.

—

Polly stood as if she'd been slapped in the face. He had gone and she knew he would not be back unless she gave up her dream. Her kitchen had once been a cosy, happy place, full of life and laughter. Now it was grey and dull and desperately sad, a place with nothing in it but a pile of half-stitched carpet pieces, a few orange boxes and the battered tin trunk.

Polly could plainly see how rough and cracked were the walls, how badly in need of a coat of fresh whitewash. She could see the brown slop-stone sink with its draining board and clutter of dishes waiting to be washed, using water she would pour from the bucket that sat beneath. Even her glowing black range with its bright fire failed to warm her chilled bones as utter dejection threatened to overwhelm her.

Tears rolled unchecked down her cheeks as, unable to bear her despair any longer, she sank to her knees and let the sobs come, felt them rack her fragile, hungry body with an anguish she could no longer contain.

Oh, what had she done? If only she could go back and undo it all. Then she wouldn't lose her temper and throw his dinner at him. She wouldn't sell his lovely sideboard and his favourite chair. No, she wouldn't. She'd do it all differently.

But would she? a voice softly enquired at the back of her head. Wasn't it a fine idea that could save them all from hunger, given time? And as it came to her that she'd do exactly the same all over again, Polly cried all the more.

She knew why he had taken this line. Matthew thought she couldn't bear to live without him, would do anything to make him come back, even to the extent of giving up on her silly dream. And in a way that was true. Life without her beloved husband didn't bear thinking about. But if she gave in now, then all her efforts would have been for naught. And they'd have nothing left: no carpets, no furniture, nothing. If only he would show some patience and understand. If only he would help instead of condemn her, support her rather than leave, and have faith in her idea.

But Matthew was too stubborn, proud by name and nature, daft fool that he was. And yet so dearly loved.

The last thing she wanted was to lose him but at the same time, if she did give up, wouldn't a part of her always blame him for that? She believed in her plan. Otherwise she would never have taken such a terrible risk. The question was, could she achieve her ambitions and yet win her husband back?

A clatter of clogs and happy laughter interrupted her thoughts. Benny, coming for his supper, Lucy not far behind at a more sedate pace. Quite the young woman now that she was working, though she always seemed bone-weary at the end of a long day on the market. They'd both be hungry for it was past eight o'clock. Polly got up from her knees, wiped the tears from her eyes and quickly disposed of the smashed plate and spilt dinner. She rubbed the top of the tin trunk clean and reached for the pan of barley broth, ready to feed her family with a smile.

Chapter Eleven

Lace curtains twitched, doors stood open, and half the neighbours in Dove Street came out to view Polly's hand cart, it being early evening and most of them at home. They particularly admired the way she had painted her name and the details of her business on the side.

It said: *Polly Pride, Best Carpet Rugs in Town*. She had no way of knowing whether this was true or not, but it sounded good. Eileen stood on her doorstep in her bare feet and grubby green frock, looking vastly impressed. 'Well, I'll go to Heaton Park! Who'd've thought it. You're a businesswoman now, Poll.'

'Not quite yet, but I mean to be.'

Since she could never hope to afford a horse or motorised van, she'd bought the small cart with its long cane handles from Joseph Malachi. It had been pawned more than a year ago and never redeemed, so he let her have it at a ridiculously low price.

'It's a soft fool I am, but how else will you repay the money, so...' And he'd shrugged and spread wide his hands, beaming at her in the way that he did. Polly had kissed and thanked the old man, and now she was bursting with pride at the result of her efforts.

Finally she draped a rug from each side of the cart and one at the front, so that the beauty of the pattern was on full display. Aware they were all the same, she rolled up the rest and stacked them on top, hoping one day to buy more carpets in different patterns.

'By heck,' Eileen was saying. 'It's that smart you could take it anywhere. Albert Square or even Piccadilly.'

Polly shook her head, laughing. 'No, only the flower gazers with their big baskets are allowed on Piccadilly. It's Oldham Street for me, at first light.'

'Should be Buckingham Palace, and nothing less.' This from Bet Sutcliffe, nodding her frizzy head with a wide grin on her round shining face.

Vera Murray, leaving the blinds up on her toffee shop and the door standing open in case there should be one or two late customers, came over for a quick look. 'By heck, what are you doing, you? Are you turning into a gypsy.'

'Don't talk soft,' said Bet, 'It's our Poll, hoping to make an honest bob, aren't you, chuck?' The three women stood considering the cart, arms folded over their pinnies, their curiosity plain. Polly's heart was pumping. How she wished Matthew would come out too, to admire the cart and wish her luck. She was so keenly aware of him seated in Big Flo's kitchen, it was as if she could see him through the walls.

'What does Matt think of it then?' Vera asked astutely, rolling her eyes in the direction of the closed door. Polly twitched her eyebrows and said nothing.

'Aye, well, chaps is like that,' Bet commented, as if she'd. 'Here's to you, lass. I'd do the same, if I had your courage.' At that moment Big Flo ambled over in her carpet slippers to offer her opinion that the cart looked respectable enough. 'Though I can't imagine who would buy them rugs. Decent housewives can make their own, like I do.'

'Not everyone has time,' Polly pointed out with a wink at Eileen, who was only too eager to agree.

'I certainly don't, with the piece work I do making aprons for weavers. Not to mention four children round me feet all day, and a lazy, good-for-nothing husband to look after. I barely have time to eat and sleep.'

Big Flo said in her booming voice, 'I had three sons to fetch up, though they're grown men now and one gone to his maker. I managed to find time, then and now. For all I still have two to see to,' she added pointedly, shooting Polly a hard glare. 'I never heard of anyone buying a rug afore. But then, I'm speaking of decent folk, who aren't afraid of hard work.' And she gave that disapproving sniff of hers which was meant to speak volumes.

'Ta very much,' Eileen remarked.

'Will you not wish me luck?' Polly said. 'I'll be gone before you get up in the morning. You can't book your spot so I have to get off early, queue up and hope for the best.' And as Eileen hugged and kissed her, and Bet and Vera clapped her on the back, Big Flo merely sniffed, then turned on her slippered heel and shuffled off home without a word.

The hand cart wouldn't fit through the front door so Polly had to unload the rugs again, wheel the cart down the entry and stow it in the back yard for the night. But it would be the work of moments to set it up each morning and be on her way. Polly had been forced to hand in her notice at the temperance tavern which of all the things she had done had frightened her the most. Now she had to make this work. Otherwise she'd have no money coming in at all.

She slept little that night, half hoping Matthew would come round and wish her well. Big Flo must've told him it was her first day tomorrow but he didn't come anywhere near. If Polly wept tears into her lonely pillow, she made sure the children sleeping next door didn't hear. Matthew would come home soon, she was quite certain of it. He must be missing her as much as she was missing him. He'd soon get over his sulks, and living with his mother again would drive him mad.

'He'll be miserable as hell, the daft galoot,' Polly whispered into the darkness. And, believing this, finally fell asleep.

—

The rain was beating against the windows when she woke. The fire in the kitchen was nearly out for lack of a draught and had to be coaxed carefully back to life before it would boil a kettle.

'Drat the thing! Just when I wanted to be well organised for once.'

She finally managed to brew herself a pot of tepid tea, prepared porridge for Lucy and Benny and left it simmering, on the hob. Benny had promised faithfully to make sure he got off to school on time since Lucy would be leaving for her own work before him.

Her packet of sandwiches made, Polly rolled a few tea leaves in condensed milk then wrapped several of these small balls in pieces of paper and stowed them in her blue enamel mug. With luck she'd get some hot water from somewhere during the day, to brew herself a mug of tea now and then.

That done, and with her small stock of carpet pieces in place on her hand cart, all she had to do was walk to Oldham Street and sell them. It was as she set out up the ginnel that she heard the familiar scrape of a clog behind her. Polly whirled around, and sure enough there he was, seeming to emerge out of the mists of the morning rain.

He dipped his head, as if acknowledging her presence.

'Morning, Matthew,' she said, and her heart hammered against her ribs. She prayed for him to wish her luck, even come to kiss her. He did neither, only continued to stand in the street, spine rigid, watching her, saying nothing. He looked so tall and strong, a stranger and yet so intimately dear to her she could barely tolerate the distance that separated them. When she finally accepted that he would make no further move, Polly returned his nod, gave a hesitant wave and, picking up the handles of her cart, set out on her adventure.

No further words had been exchanged between them. Perhaps there was nothing left to be said. Matthew, face set, stalked off in the opposite direction while at the kitchen window of his mother's house, had he cared to look, he might have caught a glimpse of a grimly smiling face.

Joshua was a happy man. He believed fortune had smiled on him at last in the form of the Irish woman's stubbornness. She had achieved, at a stroke, what he had sought for years. Discord between herself and his brother. Now all he had to do was feed the resentment that had been born in Matthew, and wait upon events. Then, when the time was, he'd give fate a helping hand.

–

The hawkers' carts, many pulled by ponies, lined Oldham Street as far as Stevenson Square. Some of them had naphtha lamps swinging from the handles to light their way; others followed their instincts or the nose of their horse in the morning gloom. But despite the fact that the sun had not yet risen, the whole city seemed to be alive with bustle, hawkers and stall holders by the score, calling good mornings to each other and all apparently seeking a spot to make an honest, or not so honest, living. Polly had been quite unaware how busy the city was at this time of day.

She saw a milk cart pass by, its great churns brimful of creamy, frothing milk. Even as she watched, several of the cart holders hurried to have their jugs filled with a kit measure from the churn.

'Bit cold this morning ain't it?' the milkman remarked to one woman. 'Drink this while it's still warm, love.' Offering her a mug of warm milk, fresh from the cow.

One man hurried by carrying a hundredweight sack of potatoes on his back, which must feel twice that weight in the drizzling rain, but he called out cheerfully to everyone as he passed.

'How are ya?'

'Fairish,' someone would call back. 'And thee?'

'Right champion.'

Polly decided he might have come from the bottom of Oak Street, where she knew there were several fruit and vegetable stalls, or Shudehill or Smithfield Markets. There was an old clothes market near Swan Street. Tib Street was the place to go if you wanted to buy a goldfinch or lark, but here in Oldham Street you could find just about anything you might need, and a good deal that you didn't but were persuaded to buy by the canny hawkers. It was a prosperous shopping area, a good place to be, she decided, since it boasted many fine shops that Mancunians flocked to in droves.

They came to listen to the music emanating from Howard's, where people with money could buy a gramophone or piano-forte, sheet music for a soiree or even take piano lessons on the top floor. The well-to-do wives of businessmen might choose a fur, a pair of shoes or new costume from such fine establishments as Swears & Wells or Jones's. Polly's delight in the street had to be confined to window shopping, but the very notion of being apart of this busy scene filled her with excitement. Perhaps one day she would own a fine emporium herself, selling carpets to the cream of society.

'You're on my pitch.'

Polly, having successfully found what she thought to be a good spot, had procured a mug of tea as she eagerly awaited her first customer. Now she gazed with dismay at a man the size of a small bull scowling at her. He had a round, bullet-shaped head topped with a thatch of red hair, and powerful shoulders that loomed menacingly above her. Her feet itched to turn and run but, mindful of everyone's gaze upon her, she held her ground. If they saw her to be weak, wouldn't she be bullied by them all?

She tossed back a swathe of dark hair and managed to give her famously cheeky grin. So surprising and bewitching was it, that for a moment the man looked nonplussed.

Taking advantage of his surprise, she said, 'And here's me thinking you couldn't get a spot without queuing and taking your chance along with everyone else. So, who do I see then to reserve meself a grand pitch like this?' She could hear titters from her audience.

Recovering himself, the man almost growled with rage. 'I've stood this spot for nigh on seventeen years.'

If there'd been anywhere else to go, she would have picked up her cart and gone to it. But the street was bursting at the seams with barrows and carts of every description, and an increasing number of early shoppers. Some of the hawkers were already doing business, and this site had been the only vacant one she could find. Now she understood why. No one else dared take it.

'Leave the little lass be, Red Warren, you great bully.' The voice, sounding vaguely familiar, turned out to be that of the black pudding lady from under the arches. Polly had never been more pleased to see anyone in her life.

'Pick yer fight with her what robbed me,' muttered Red darkly. The woman stood facing Polly's aggressor with arms akimbo, head on one side and a wry challenge in her dark gypsy eyes. 'Robbed indeed! Don't you remember when you was starting out, lad?'

'This is my pitch, Dorrie.'

She folded her arms, jewellery chinking as she moved, and a musky scent emanating from the folds of her long black skirts. 'Now then, lad, you know there's no such thing. Not unless you stand the market and pay rent for a stall, like I do. This lady is jannock – honest as oats. I know that for a fact, 'cos her lass works for me on the tripe stall, so hurt her, Red Warren, and you hurts me.'

Polly was delighted to discover that her rescuer was none other than the owner of Dome's tripe and trotter stall, where Lucy was employed.

'I've never laid a finger on her,' Red hotly protested. 'I'm glad to see you've that much sense at least. You know well enough that here on the streets we takes our chances for a pitch, and pick up our barrows and take a walk every now and then so's the coppers don't nab us for stopping too long in one spot. So how can this bit of street be thine? Has it got your name on it?'

Polly was certain, from the expressions on the faces of the other hawkers' and barrow holders, that nobody else would have had the nerve to stand up to this man as Dorrie was doing. Even so, she hadn't entirely won the match, only a round in the contest.

Red Warren stuck his thumbs in his wide buckled belt and took his time answering. His leather waistcoat rode high over a belly that had seen a few pints in its day, and his legs, encased in brown serge, were thick as tree trunks, finished off with black clogs as big as shovels. Polly did not care for the look of him one bit. His silence was long and aggrieved.

Finally he announced, 'Fair enough, the lass can have it for today. But I'll be watching her in future.' And having issued his warning, satisfied he'd saved face at least, the big red-haired man climbed aboard his cart, shook the reins, and ordered his pony to walk on. Dorrie, undeterred, gold chains, bracelets and necklaces dancing, dodged a puddle and nearly collided with the hot potato man as she scuttled into the middle of the road to call after him.

'Then you'll have to start getting out the sack a bit earlier! She's a sharp one, is this lass.'

Polly was laughing fit to burst by the time Dorrie came back, a wide grin on her swarthy face. 'How do you know I'm a sharp one? You should've seen me dragging *myself* out of bed this morning, and struggling to get me bit of fire going.' But the other woman only grinned.

'Then you'll have to eat your breakfast the night before in future if you want a decent pitch. This one in particular.' It was the way the other stall holders applauded and cheered Dorrie, even slapped her on the back, as much as this grim statement which told Polly she'd been lucky to find herself a champion on her first morning. It wouldn't always be so.

–

Polly was elated. Every day that week she had risen early and gone off to Oldham Street with increasing confidence. Though she had never again managed to acquire so excellent a pitch, nevertheless she'd done well, having sold six of the carpet rugs already, mostly at a decent price despite having to barter hard. But her customers had seemed well satisfied, and she'd made a point of telling them that she'd be getting more rugs, with different patterns, in the near future. Without exception they'd shown interest.

'It's going to work,' she announced to Lucy, whirling her round the tiny kitchen.

Laughing, her daughter said, 'You've hardly anything left to sell. What happens when you run out?'

Polly sobered upon the instant. 'I'll admit it's going to take a lot of hard work to get a regular income coming in. Tomorrow I'm off to find some of those houses where folk were hit by the Crash. Even if the better off don't use pawnbrokers, they might be glad to sell off some of their treasures in private. Discreetly as you might say.'

Her mind flew, making plans, devising schemes. She'd need to arrange transport for the carpets, then start on the cutting and sewing all over again. What sort of a task had she set herself? Could she cope? Seeing the worry come into her mother's eyes, Lucy put her arms about her and hugged her. 'You can do it, Mam, I know you can.'

Benny piped up, 'I've made up the fire and put a few more spuds in the broth. Can we eat now? I'm that hungry.' And they all laughed.

'Your constant cry. Come on then, Benny me-laddo, let's eat. While we still can.'

Polly hadn't realised how hungry she was after a long day working in the open. But watching her children quickly spoon the tasty broth into their eager mouths, she slowed down, letting them take more from the pot but taking no extra herself. The only money coming into the house now was whatever she and Lucy could manage to earn.

'I wish Dad was 'ere,' Benny said, suddenly looking solemn. 'When is he coming home, Mam?' Benny did not understand this argument between the two adults in his life.

'Soon, love. Never fear,' Polly said, truly believing it.

–

Polly tried the streets around the Horsfall Museum which were a notch or two above her own Dove Street district. Here lived some of the white-collar working class with aspirations to better themselves still further. Other houses belonged to shopkeepers and small business proprietors. From these people she hoped to increase her small stock of carpets. She went the length of every Street, before finally admitting defeat.

Polly was working her way along Adair Street when a girl crossed over to say hello. 'You're the one who bought that carpet off my employer, aren't you?'

When Polly agreed that she had indeed bought Mrs Eckersley's fine carpet, the maid added a choice piece of gossip, much to Polly's delight.

'You'd never believe what happened after that! All her friends were so jealous, they started buying new carpets for their parlours. By heck, there's some folk with more brass than sense! So if you're looking for more, I'd try knocking on a few of her neighbours' doors. They're throwing out good carpets like a man with three arms.' And the girl went off, chuckling, swinging her shopping basket in time to her laughter. Polly called her thanks after the departing figure and almost ran to St Andrew's Square where at last she managed to buy not one but five large squares of faded but quality Wilton carpet.

Bless you, Mrs Eckersley. These will feed my family for months! she thought.

But however glad she was to find more stock, she needed Matthew more than ever.

Over the following weeks, Polly worked harder than ever, and soon came to the decision that she could spare a little of her takings to win her husband back. She had surely earned enough at least to redeem his armchair from Joseph. It was one of the items the kindly old Jew had agreed to take, knowing how fond Matthew was of it.

As soon as she could scrape enough together, she handed the money over, for all it hurt her to do so, since every penny she earned should really go back into the business. She and Lucy, ably assisted by Benny, half dragged and half carried the heavy chair down Dove Street and in at their front door. Few people paid any attention as this was a common enough sight, save for the odd droll example of Lancashire humour.

'Eeh, set that chair down here a minute, Poll, I could do with a rest.'

'You want to put wheels on that thing, then it'll follow you home.'

And more poignantly from Bet Sutcliffe, 'Hock it as many times as I do mine, and it'll soon know the way home by itself.'

Was this what she had sunk to, she who had taken such pride in her home, determined to keep it clean in order to prove herself better than those who had been defeated by poverty. Polly pulled herself up short. She wasn't defeated. Wasn't this what it was all about? Fighting back. And she meant to win.

Once the chair was installed, though not in the empty parlour but in the kitchen where once the horse-hair sofa had stood, and the fire stoked up to celebrate the occasion, Polly set off to her mother-in-law's house. She'd tell Matthew how well she had done, how the idea was definitely going to work, and to prove it she'd got his chair back. He was probably itching to come home by now, the daft galoot, and this would give him just the excuse he needed.

'He's not here,' Big Flo told her, keen satisfaction in her voice. 'He's gone to the NUWM meeting with our Josh, and they won't be back till late. He's standing up for his rights, as you should stand by him.'

'Or he should stand by me,' said Polly, annoyed that he'd broken his word about keeping away from militant meetings, then ashamed to find herself slamming the door of number thirty-one as she left.

Chapter Twelve

The meeting looked like going on forever. Joshua had spoken with genuine fervour, urging the men to action, to make their feelings felt to the politicians who resolutely refused to listen.

'All the government cares about is making a reduction in benefit for the poor souls out of work. So if you've relatives with a bit o' brass,' Joshua pointed out, 'a child earning a few bob or a stick of furniture you can sell, they'll cut your relief still more. The Means Test is causing outrage the length and breadth of the land, no less here in Manchester. We have to do something about it. We have to stand together.'

There were cheers in the packed hall from men who felt at the end of their tether, who would follow anything and anybody if they promised money each day and a full belly at the end of it.

They were tired of reading in the papers how they were too feckless to work, how they enjoyed living off the state and could do so comfortably on the 'dole', how most of them couldn't even read and hadn't a brain in their heads. Skilled men felt their dignity crumble daily at these outpourings in the press from the governing classes. And if they lolled about at street corners too much, hoping for someone to buy them a pint, what else did they have to do all day with no job to go to?

'We don't want benefit or charity,' shouted one man from the back of the hall. 'We want work!'

This resulted in an even louder cheer.

'Ramsay MacDonald has betrayed the working man.'

'Up the Reds!'

Joshua glanced about him with satisfaction. The mood was changing, growing more demanding, yet wasn't that what he wanted? It was true that the NUWM had communist connections, certainly several of the leaders were of that persuasion, although not exclusively so, and Joshua was not a communist himself. But its origins didn't trouble him one bit, nor did he feel that it compromised his religion in any way. He believed in equality, that the working man should claim his rights and be given gainful employment. The Union had developed from its impotent beginnings to a movement with power, and Joshua craved power. He believed the only way to stir the apathetic majority was for the vociferous few to force them into protest. Surely the end justified the means?

There were Hunger Marches being organised all over the country. One had consisted of more than two thousand people presenting a petition to the Prime Minister, demanding the abolition of the Means Test. Admittedly that had turned into a violent skirmish, with baton charges and injuries, but nothing was ever achieved without risk. There'd been fighting in Liverpool and Birkenhead, and here in Manchester too.

'The word is that more significant protests are planned for the near future, so why shouldn't we be a part of them? We might have to take up a collection to get leaflets and posters printed, but won't it be worth investing a bit o' brass in your own futures? Nothing was ever achieved without paying for it.'

And if a little money slipped in Joshua's direction for all his efforts on their behalf, how would they know? They couldn't achieve a thing without him, so why shouldn't he benefit since he was undoubtedly the right one to lead them. Wasn't that his rightful destiny?

While he cared passionately for the cause, he cared even more for his own ambitions. He was not meant to live out his life in obscurity, as an unemployed tackler in a mean street. He needed to make his mark, and this was his opportunity.

'Do you want to depend on others to put clogs on your own children's feet, and food in their bellies?'

'No!'

'Do you want to beg charity from the Board of Guardians? Have them poke their noses into every corner of your life?'

'No!'

'Or end up in the dungeon, as we call the workhouse round here, or even Tame Street Tramp Ward?'

'No!' Men were vociferous in their anger now so that Joshua had to raise his voice above the din. It was growing claustrophobic in the hall, and stuffy with the smell of poverty, making him feel almost nauseous as he battled on.

'A married man with children who receives a war pension has to take those children twice a year to the police station to prove they're still alive and dependent on him. *That's* what you get for fighting for your country. And last week Percy Williams, our good friend and a great joker, had his relief cut so low he reached the end of his tether and was driven to hang himself with his own belt, leaving a wife and four children. *Is that what you want?'*

They'd heard enough. The meeting erupted into mayhem. There wasn't a man amongst them who wouldn't agree to follow Joshua now, and pay for the privilege, once details of the demonstration were known. He had achieved his objective.

—

The next morning, when Polly finally caught up with her husband as he strode up the ginnel on his way to the wharf, she told him she'd reclaimed the chair. She was so excited she looked like a young child given a new toy. Seeing her thus, Matthew almost backed down from his intransigent stance and gathered her into his arms. But then he remembered the loss of the rest of his household goods, including their beloved sideboard.

'Does this mean that you've giving up this daft business idea of yours?'

Instantly her heart dropped. 'No, of course not. But don't you see? I've made some money. It proves that it's a good idea, that I can make it work, given time.'

'It proves nowt, except that our Josh is right. You're a stubborn Irish woman who won't listen to anyone else's point of view but your own.'

The mention of her interfering brother-in-law inflamed Polly's temper once again. 'And you're not stubborn, I suppose? I'm thinking you listen too often to that daft brother o' yours. Big Flo says you were out with him at a meeting, when you swore you'd stay away.'

'Perhaps I see now that he was right and I was wrong. I believe every man has the right to employment in order to keep his family; that he has to stand up for his principles and what he believes in.'

'And why not a woman? Why can't a woman stand up for what she believes in?'

Matthew flushed dark red, annoyed at leaving himself open to this sort of attack, yet frustrated that his own wife couldn't see the difference. 'She shouldn't do so at the expense of her husband's...'

'Pride? Is that what this is all about?' She fought to restrain her rising temper. Polly hadn't meant to quarrel with Matthew, had fully intended to use her feminine wiles and charm. Why were these always lacking when she needed them the most?

Her husband's face was ashen as he answered, jaw set rigid, and that thin white line of anger that rode his upper lip had become a sadly familiar sight. 'I've kept this family from the workhouse. I've begged the landlord to give us time to catch up on the rent, stood for hours, days, weeks, in pouring rain, in the hope of an hour's work. Yet all I've managed to hold on to is the one thing we had left: our dignity. Now you've thrown that away. Let me tell you, Polly, I'll not have it!' As he turned to walk away she grabbed his arm.

'*You'll* not have it. What about *me*! How do you think *I* feel, queuing for hours for a pig's trotter or a pair of mackerel to feed my children, then having to ask for them to be put on tick?'

Even as the words poured from her mouth, a small voice at the back of her head warned her to stop, that they shouldn't be tearing each other apart over something that was not the fault of either of them. Matthew looked older and thinner, which she didn't wonder at. He probably wasn't eating properly, wary of being a burden on his mother and brother. But then, they'd all lost weight through these trying times, including Benny and Lucy who didn't have any spare flesh to lose. Tears were raining down her cheeks now and she could do nothing to stop them.

'What about my hungry children? You made me give up a perfectly good job, yet I must do something to feed them. While all you do is go to blasted meetings!'

A long chilling moment ticked by before he answered, and when he did his voice was calm and oddly distant. 'Aye, and I'll go again to the meetings, if I've a mind to, for the sake of my children's future. Someone has to make the government sit up and listen. I don't like this situation any more than you do, Polly, but I'll not have you bring shame upon us because of some fancy notion in your head to get above yourself.'

'It's not that at all, you know it isn't.'

'I know nowt o' t'sort. You didn't even discuss it with me. But I'll tell you this,' He wagged a finger in Polly's face. 'I'd stay away forever sooner than see that happen,' And with those warning words he swung about and strode angrily up the back street, his clogs sparking on the cobbles.

Polly stood stunned for a whole thirty seconds. As if to echo the bleakness of her thoughts, the rain started to fall. It drenched her hair in seconds, ran down her neck and soaked her to the skin, yet she paid it no heed as she ran after him, slapping at his broad stiff back, snatching at his coat in her desperate efforts to stop him. Matthew tried to brush her off as if she were an annoying fly, to walk faster and ignore her, but she held on, splashing through the gathering puddles, calling his name and several other less salubrious ones.

She was out of breath when finally he stopped and turned to her, but her green eyes were blazing. 'Don't you walk away from me when I'm talking to you, Matthew Pride. At least I'm doing something positive. I can't just sit at home and watch my children starve!'

He could no longer tell which were tears and which rain, but he could see the love she held for him in every line of her beloved face, in the way she pressed her small lithe body to his, as if begging him to understand and gather her close. Yet stubbornly he stuck to his principles, hardened his heart, knowing that if he gave in now she'd go on with this dratted carpet business, destroying the last remnants of his dignity by proving him incapable of supporting his own family, and making him less of a man as a consequence.

'You think I've failed you? Is that it?' His voice was so bitter, so cold and hard, it cut to the heart of her.

Polly struggled to hold on to her patience and calm her breathing. This isn't the way, a voice at the back of her head warned. Tell him you love him. Tell him how you need him, that you'll give up the carpet stall and stand by him. Instead, she said, 'You know damn well I don't think that at all. By heck, but you can be a stubborn old coot when you've a mind.'

'And you're not, I suppose, with the fire in your hair and your dander up?' His eyes were upon her, and she saw a hint of something even at the height of his fury – admiration perhaps, desire, an echo of what they had enjoyed together through the years – and her heart instantly softened, temper diminishing as quickly as it had risen.

'Aw, Matt, 'tis awful hard living in an empty house. Will you not come home? I'd love to see you sitting in your favourite chair again. I've set it by the fire in the kitchen, exactly as you like it.'

He stood gazing down at her, considering. 'And our bed? Is that exactly where I like it?'

'After a tellingly long moment, she gave a small shake of her head.'

He pursued his point, as if needing to inflict yet more pain upon himself. 'The table and chairs? Sofa and buffet? Everything we own? Have you got those things? And our sideboard?'

Matthew looked into her silent, pale face and this time, when he walked away, she let him go.

–

There were a number of localised demonstrations and protests against the Means Test in and around Manchester in the weeks following Joshua's meeting. He and a loyal band of followers were usually present. One of the most serious was in Salford where Chapel Street was completely blocked by the marchers. Their attempt to reach the Town Hall, however, was prevented by police who charged upon the peaceful demonstrators with batons, whereupon the marchers retaliated and mayhem ensued.

'We'll not give in,' Joshua assured his listeners. 'Next month we walk to Albert Square. Thousands will take part and we'll be amongst them.' Why shouldn't his own small band of men make their voices heard and take part in this historical event? He handed over his bowler hat, which he always wore to meetings, to be passed around while grimfaced men searched near empty pockets for a coin.

'Aye, we're with you, Joshua.'

'Count us in.'

The swell of opinion and support was strong in the hall. They'd make an impression on stubborn bureaucracy this time, he was sure of it. When the hat was returned Joshua was well pleased with the collection. He and his mother would eat for another week. He would, of course, have to order leaflets and posters for this next, most important demonstration, but he'd squeeze a good price out of the printer. Couldn't have one working man making too much profit out of his fellows. Unless it was himself, for all the extra work, and effort he was putting in.

When the last of the stragglers had gone, Joshua and Matthew walked home together by way of the canal towpath.

'You'll come too, brother.' Joshua issued the words as if they were an order. Then, with a wry smile that brought a flood of angry colour to Matthew's neck, added, 'If that wife of yours will allow it.'

Matthew couldn't help but remember how he'd once agreed he would not, in any way, become involved in political conflict, and how Polly had reminded him of that fact. Then he thought of the shameful way she had showed him up in front of everyone. How she had sold all their goods and chattels on a whim and taken up life as a hawker without asking his permission, and even now refused to stop. All because he, a skilled man, was unable to find a job to support his family.

'I'll be there. I care as much as you about the plight of the unemployed. Why would I not?'

Joshua snorted with derision. 'At least I am doing something positive about it. While you are so ineffectual you cannot even control your own wife. She behaves like a loose bobbin. You should pull in the thread more tightly, brother. Keep her in check.'

Matthew almost laughed at the very idea, 'You try controlling Polly. She's a wilful woman, with a powerful Irish temper.'

'Oh, I reckon I could manage her very well,' Joshua said in his quiet way. 'Very well indeed. Given half a chance.' Matthew shot him a fierce look, not much caring for his tone but nonetheless scornful of his brother's confidence. 'The cry of all bachelors — that they understand women — when we married men know it's impossible. Fortunately your theory will never be put to the test.'

'No, indeed,' Joshua said. 'You're probably right. Women are a law unto themselves.'

Matthew's face softened. 'Polly might be stubborn, and with a mind of her own, but she came that way by watching her drunken father clout her mother once too often. Remembering what a lazy good-for-nothing lout he was makes her want to work all the harder to provide a better life for her own children. I've no quarrel with that.'

'Only the way she goes about it,' Joshua shrewdly remarked. 'I could try to speak with her, if you wish? Tell her how unhappy she is making you.'

Matthew frowned, surprised by this sudden show of concern. 'Why would you do such a thing?'

'Are we not brothers? She's your wife, my sister-in-law, and as such what she does reflects upon us all. I agree she is a hard worker, thrifty and with a good, agile brain, but a woman can be too clever for her own good. She should never set herself above her husband as Polly has done, not even consulting your wishes. Give me the chance to explain all that to her, and she'll soon see that a wife's place is at her husband's side, not selling his goods and chattels behind his back.'

'She'd run rings round you.' It might just be worth watching such a contest, for the fun of it, he thought, although he'd back Polly any day in a set-to with his brother.

'We'll see. Shall I try?'

'I don't want her upset, Josh. I just want our furniture back. My home the way it was, and a bit of peace in my life.'

'Of course you do, and you shall have it. What do you take me for? I'll simply remind her of where her duty lies.'

'Right,' Matthew agreed. 'I suppose no harm can come of you having a quiet word. I'm sure *I've* got nowhere. You see if you can do any better.'

–

Polly was too busy sewing and cutting her new acquisitions and dealing with her own problems to give much thought to political demonstrations or care a jot for her brother-in-law's opinion on her duties as a wife. She had it clear in her own mind what must be done. It was vitally important that she make her business successful, to prove to Matthew that her actions had been justified. To give up now, before she had properly begun, would mean that all their sacrifices would have been for nothing. She was too far committed to turn back, and equally convinced that once Matthew saw how successful she could be, he would forgive her stubbornness and return to his home once more, the loving husband and father he had always been.

But it was not going to be easy.

Red Warren, whose pitch she'd allegedly stolen, was doing his utmost to make life as difficult as possible for her. Twice more she managed to reach the pitch before him but after that he was always there first and no matter where else she chose to settle, there too often seemed to be some sour-faced hawker objecting. On numerous occasions she was warned by a particularly nasty young policeman to be on her way, though she'd been there only a few hours and it was nowhere near eight o'clock when everyone was supposed to stop serving. Not that many obeyed this rule, most stalls still operating at midnight.

Polly had begun to suspect that Red was conducting a campaign against her. She wouldn't have put it past him to slip the copper a bob or two to move her on. But she would dutifully pick up her barrow and walk it along to Stevenson Square, then up Lever Street, down to New Cross and back down Oldham Street. By then her pitch would have been taken, once by a small fat man selling mufflers and handkerchiefs, another time by the organ grinder, and on several occasions by a grinning Red Warren himself.

Another day she left her hand cart unattended for less than three minutes while she went to get some hot water for a brew from a friendly shopkeeper close by. The street was thronged with people all milling in and out of the many shops that lined Oldham Street. The sound of a pianola playing 'Believe Me If All Those Endearing Young Charms' added liveliness to the busy scene; queues formed outside Jones for a sale they'd started that day; the butcher's shop was packed and the scent of freshly baked bread filled the air, making Polly feel hungry.

Her nearest neighbour on this occasion was a young girl selling imperfect lengths of cotton that had flaws in the weave, or dye that had gone wrong. The girl declared herself happy to keep an eye on things for Polly while she went in search of tea and a sandwich. On Polly's return she found the girl in tears, rugs scattered all over the street, soaking wet as they lay in muddy puddles, and the handles of the cart had been snapped clean in half.

'I tried to stop him but he threatened me too,' the poor girl whimpered. Several of the other barrow holders offered sympathy and assistance, including Dorrie Hughes, who left a queue at her black pudding stall while she helped pick up carpet pieces.

'I did warn you he'd choose his moment to retaliate.'

'If he thinks he can bully me he's picked the wrong woman,' Polly said to Dorrie, gritting her teeth with fresh determination as she stacked her dripping stock back on the barrow. 'I'm not one to give up easy, even when pushed.'

'Particularly when pushed, I'd say,' Dorrie agreed with a grin. She admired this plucky girl enormously. 'You stick to your guns, lass, but watch your back. Red Warren ain't one to give up either.'

Polly had no choice but to go home early that day, dry off the carpet pieces, nail new handles on to her cart and hope to do better next time. She certainly wasn't admitting defeat.

–

Over the following days, she searched out one or two more small carpets but was finding it impossible to be in two places, let alone three, at once. She couldn't be buying carpets, sewing and selling them, all at the same time. To her great disappointment, Big Flo obstinately kept to her word in refusing to help any further with the cutting and sewing.

'Nay,' she said. 'I must stand by that lad o' mine, and so should you.' No amount of argument would make her change her mind so Polly was forced to accept her decision with as much good grace as she could muster. Eileen, however, proved to be her salvation.

'I may not have much in the way of brains, but there's nowt wrong with me sewing hand. I've made more aprons than most weavers have had hot dinners,' she cheerfully informed Polly. 'If you can pay, I can sew.'

'Oh, I'll pay you right enough,' Polly agreed. 'If you can sew, I'll find and sell the rugs. We'll make a great team, so we will.' And beaming with delight, the two women hugged each other.

Chapter Thirteen

Polly felt she had exhausted the spoils of St Andrew's Square and the area around the Horsfall Museum, so Benny was given a new role to add to that of chief coal merchant. It became his task to keep his eyes open and his ears to the ground – or to people's back doors – and to search out any other likely source of new stock. This was heady stuff for Benny. It certainly made a change from delving in the mud of the Rochdale canal whenever the locksmen lowered the level of the water, to sift out coal that had been spilled by passing barges.

Now he would swagger about the posher streets of the city, sometimes as far as Piccadilly Gardens or the streets around Philips Park, pretending to be Sexton Blake as a change from Felix the Cat, hiding round corners, eavesdropping on conversations at bus stops. What he would really have liked was a disguise, but failing that all he could do was pull the blue peaked cap down over his ears and hope for the best. Whenever he heard a couple of gossiping old matrons, he'd shadow them like the great detective himself, hoping they would let drop some titillating piece of information, or lead him to yet more parlour cast-offs. So far he hadn't struck lucky, but he lived in hope, and certainly the search was proving to be fascinating. Who knew what other delights he might discover?

He chanced to catch sight of his Uncle Joshua on his way down Wesley Street one day. Benny called out to him but he didn't hear, and before the boy could reach him he'd vanished, perhaps into one of the houses, though whose it was Benny hadn't noticed.

In fact Joshua had not gone into a house. He'd knocked on the familiar door as usual, which had been opened by an Irish navvy, of all people. The man told him that the previous occupant, Joshua's latest conquest, had done a moonlight flit, taking her snotty-nosed children with her.

Joshua was annoyed. He wouldn't particularly miss her for she'd never been an exciting companion, putting no effort into pleasing him. Nor had she shown any sign of that element of subservience which so elated him. Nevertheless it was inconvenient, a blow to his pride, and extremely frustrating even though there were any number of other possibilities he might try. He really shouldn't trouble himself over one none-too-clean widow when he had other fish to fry. And wouldn't he enjoy the eating?

He'd spoken to his sister-in-law, just as he'd promised Matt he would, and her response had been entirely as expected. She'd absolutely refused to listen, revealing her character as nothing less than a headstrong termagant, a shrew of the first order.

'Keep your prying nose out of my personal affairs,' she'd shouted at him. Words she would live to regret.

–

In addition to Benny's efforts, Polly continued to ask around on her own behalf and thus came to hear of a once well-to-do family now suffering financial hardship due to the Wall Street Crash. Bob Reckitt, the Dolly Varden man, had put her in the way of it. She took a tram to the house, according to his directions, and was shown the brown and gold carpet, drawing-room size, in need of a thorough cleaning but otherwise in good condition. She made an offer but the owner forced the price up higher than she could afford to pay and she reluctantly conceded defeat. Instead she bought an even dirtier grey one from a dreadful old woman who lived in a huge Victorian house in Collyhurst.

'I reckon that was the last time it was cleaned,' Polly said, scattering tea leaves with abandon over its dingy surface. 'When Victoria was a girl.'

'It stinks of mothballs and cat pee,' Eileen said, holding her nose, and Polly laughingly agreed, privately thinking it must indeed be bad if her friend complained.

She and Eileen spent hours crawling over the carpet in Polly's front parlour as they scrubbed and brushed and finally cut it into several rectangular pieces. Their fingers were red raw with blisters by the time they'd finished. They were not assisted in their efforts by Eileen's children who seemed to think that crawling about on a dirty carpet was some new sort of game.

'I'd leave the daft buggers at home only Terence doesn't like having them under his feet,' she mourned.

The two women were cutting lengths of edging braid when Benny bounced in through the front door, bursting with excitement as his diligence had finally paid off.

'I've heard of a good one. I followed two old crones from Union Street nearly as far as Openshaw. They were talking the whole time about an old picture house that was to change into a dance-hall, and wouldn't that be a grand thing? They liked a bit of a dance, they said, but what a shame to rip up that lovely red carpet.'

Polly listened to the tale entranced, then wrapped her arms about her son and gave him a suffocating hug. 'What a treasure you are, Benny,' she said, making him beam with delight.

She didn't even stop to think that this would undoubtedly mean Matthew's chair would have to be put in hock again. But since he'd refused to return home and sit in it, she'd rather it went than stand in her kitchen, a silent reminder of the troubles between them. Polly had only recently redeemed the deal table and four wooden chairs as well, but they too would have to go again, along with anything else she could lay her hands on. A cinema carpet? Too good an opportunity to miss.

Eileen agreed to give Benny his tea, since Lucy didn't get home till after eight. She was only too glad of any opportunity to escape the dingy confines of her own home, and in particular the constant demands of her lazy husband. When he wasn't lounging on the corner of the street, drinking or gambling money he didn't have with his cronies, he was flopped in his armchair reading the *Manchester Evening News* or *Sporting Chronicle,* in between issuing orders to his wife. His other favourite occupation took place beneath the bed covers, every night if he got the chance. Eileen had to make sure that he didn't.

The last thing she wanted was to start another baby and to that end had used every excuse under the sun, from a simple headache, to overtiredness, a bad cold, even having the curse last far longer than human nature would normally allow. He'd be bound to lose patience eventually, and then she'd be off again, she knew it. If only she could pluck up the courage to go to that clinic Polly had mentioned, but it didn't seem quite safe. If she took the risk, Terence would be sure to find out and then there'd be hell to pay. He'd report her to Father Donevan at the very least.

'I'll get started on sewing this lot. By heck, Polly, at this rate you'll make a fortune afore you're done,'

She grinned. 'And you with me, Eileen.' Then, having received directions from her son, and urging him sternly to be ready for bed by the time his sister got home from the market, she grabbed her shawl and hurried away through the darkening streets just as the lamplighter set out.

–

No sooner had Polly finished congratulating herself on success-fully agreeing a knock-down price for the cinema carpet, than it occurred to her it would be far too large to fit into her parlour. Even rolled up at its tightest she'd be lucky to get it through the door.

'What d'you reckon I should do?' she asked a frowning Eileen. 'Nay, don't ask me.'

If only she could talk through her problems with Matthew. Perhaps if he saw real signs of her being a success, he'd come back home, even though they were again sitting on orange boxes. But somehow Polly couldn't quite pluck up the courage. Not until she'd solved the problem of where to put this new acquisition which represented a considerable investment. She couldn't even have it collected until she'd sorted that out.

'What'll I do?' she mourned to Lucy, when her daughter came wearily home from the market stall the night following its purchase.

Lucy, who was already beginning to regret taking on the job with Dorrie Hughes, was keen for her mother to get the carpet business going, then she might escape the tripe stall. She didn't mind cutting up the stuff, or dealing with the trotters, but she was also expected to help prepare and cook the black puddings, which she didn't enjoy one bit. Mixing the groats, fat, herbs and onions into all that blood simply made her feel sick. She used to love black pudding with a dab of mustard; now she couldn't stand the sight or smell of one.

Sometimes it was difficult treading a diplomatic line between her parents but since the damage was done and the furniture gone, they might as well have a go at making things work. She sympathised with her father but at the same time understood what Polly was trying to do. Lucy understood about dreams. Her own job on the market stall was a far cry from her ambition to sell frocks in Paulden's or one of the fancy shops in King Street. Oh, she'd be glad enough to do something different. It was thinking of Paulden's which gave her the answer.

'Why don't you take on a shop, Mam? It's all right is the barrow, but you'll never make much out of that on its own. True, Dorrie Hughes has barrows and market stalls all over the place. But she doesn't make a fortune, and it's hard work being put in all weathers, and not so good for carpets when it rains as it is for black puddings.'

Polly looked at her daughter with new eyes, her mouth falling open in delighted surprise. 'Wasn't I blessed with wonderfully clever children? Ye never cease to amaze me, either of you. First Benny finds me this wonderful cinema carpet, and then you come up with a way to deal with it. Sure and I think you're all marvellous.' And to Lucy's great embarrassment, Polly showered her face with kisses. She was soft that way, was her mam. Even so Lucy was laughing by the time Polly had found her shawl, babbling on about what they could find for their dinner while already halfway to the door. 'Ye don't mind, do you, if I go and make a few enquiries?'

'Get away with you,' Lucy laughed, waving her on her way, used to her mother always acting impulsively, with not a scrap of patience to wait for anything. 'We'll manage. Have you told Dad about the cinema carpet?' But her words were lost in the slamming of the front door. Shaking her head with fond disbelief at the stubbornness of adults.

Lucy went to examine the stock pot.

–

Polly had indeed heard her daughter's advice, and decided that perhaps she should heed it and call in at number thirty-one this minute to tell Matthew all about the carpet and her plans for a shop. Wouldn't that be grand? Perhaps he would come and help her run it.

Big Flo informed her that both men were out and about on business, and what was Polly doing wandering about the streets after dusk? She made some excuse and hurried away, not wanting to become embroiled in an argument with her mother-in-law.

Her next stop was at 'Uncle' Joseph's, where they sat for some time discussing the progress and difficulties of Polly's business, the old man watching her pensively over the tips of his fingers, listening to the excitement in her voice as she outlined her latest plans.

When she had done, he told her of a vacant shop on Ancoats Lane which he thought might serve her purpose very well. Polly became so excited she would have gone to see it there and then had he not insisted on a more sensible time the following day, even though she hadn't entirely solved the problem of how to finance the carpet.

'And you can manage all of this?' he politely enquired.

'If you'd buy my things off me again,' she pleaded.

Joseph sighed. 'It would be difficult to refuse my favourite customer. But I ask myself where this is all leading, Polly? Matthew didn't seem a happy man when I saw him last.'

She wanted to ask where and when Joseph had seen him, if Matthew had looked well and whether he was finding any work, but dare not put her longing into words in case her emotions should get the better of her. Best to remain practical and businesslike with the little pawnbroker. 'That will all change when he sees I'm making a success of the business.'

'You take too many risks, Polly.'

She shrugged her shoulders. 'Seems to me that's the only way to survive.'

Joseph ran his tongue over his teeth while he considered her answer. 'How can you keep on selling your furniture?'

'I must use what I have.'

'But will it be enough?'

She knew that whatever sum he agreed to loan her, it would be woefully short. 'Give me a few days and I'll find the rest. Enough for the carpet and for a deposit on the shop. We still have some carpet pieces to sell.'

'What if I agree to this plan and you manage to acquire this shop, what then?'

'I will use it to expand my business. First to cut up the cinema carpet into good-sized pieces to sell.' Polly was leaning forward, keen to convince him. She had not missed the caution in the old man's voice. He had said it would be difficult to refuse her, his favourite customer, but he still might, so she was anxious to win him over. 'With more space I can make real progress. A barrow is nowhere near big enough for what I have in mind.'

'To make the money to buy back your furniture, you mean?'

'Of course, and more besides.'

'For how long, I'm thinking? Till you sell it again for more carpet?'

Polly laughed out loud this time. 'Who can say?'

'It is madness, l am telling myself. So why do I say yes, yes, yes, every time you ask me?' He lifted his hands in a gesture of despair while Polly only grinned.

'Because you, above everyone else, believe in me.'

'Which means, I am thinking, that the pair of us need our heads examining.'

Polly chuckled delightedly and kissed him fondly on both cheeks, knowing by the light in his faded old eyes that she had won. 'But you'll do it?'

'Won't your Irish charm win me over if nothing else does?' Joseph agreed, sighing deeply and shaking his head in fond disapproval.

–

As Polly headed home along Henry Street she wished Matthew could be as understanding and supportive. She reached the corner and saw a group of men gathering, and rightly guessed that yet another demonstration was being planned.

The men were lounging against the wall of the Green Dragon, though it was doubtful whether any of them could afford to go inside. To Matthew, as a teetotaller, it had never been something he missed, but to some of the other men the lack of a few coppers for a pint seemed to strike at the heart of their manhood, as if they were being deprived of their rights. She sensed their air of excitement; all conversation ceased as she approached, and she wondered why.

It was then that she saw him.

He looked so dearly familiar, so wonderfully solid and real, he seemed to fill her entire vision. It was as if he were larger than life, bigger, stronger, more handsome than she had ever properly appreciated, and her heart seemed to stop for a second before racing on at breakneck speed. She stood in front of him, feeling as fragile as a heart-struck young girl.

'Hello, Matthew. You look well.' Polly recalled how he had promised her that he'd take no part in any political meetings, and had felt certain he'd keep his word on that at least.

'And yourself?' His eyes seemed to bore into her innermost being. Polly guessed that her own must be doing much the same to him for the other men turned away, embarrassed at witnessing this awkward reunion.

'Would you walk me home? I don't much care for the streets after dark.'

He mumbled something about its never having bothered her before but nonetheless adjusted his cap, pushed himself away from the pub wall and nodded his farewells to his companions, seemingly content to walk along beside her. He said nothing as they made their way along Henry Street, overshadowed by the dark red brick walls of warehouses and McConnell's Mill. She read the words over the arched entrance as they passed: James McConnell, 1788. Sandford, McConnell and Kennedy, 1791. 'All those years,' she said, 'and now the mills are struggling for their very existence, some even closing.'

'Not if we can prevent it.'

She stopped by the canal towpath and gently touched his arm so that he would turn and she could look fearfully into his face. 'Matthew, this demonstration or whatever it is... You'll not be on it, will you?' Even in the poor light from the gas lamp she could see the tight set of his jaw. It was becoming a painfully familiar sight, yet still she persisted. 'Didn't we agree that violence was not the way?'

'We agreed a good many things in our life together, like always talking matters through afore making a decision.' He began to walk again and she hurried to keep pace. They crossed the bridge and threaded their way through the congested network of streets, mills and warehouses.

'I miss you, Matthew.'

He didn't answer. Polly swallowed the painful lump which had come into her throat and tried again. 'I can't seem to come to terms with life on me own. Will you not...'

He interrupted her, his voice harsh and accusing. 'Where is it you've been at this hour? Why aren't you at home with the childer?'

Excitement put an edge to her voice. 'I've been to see Joseph. He's told me of a shop that's going, and I might just take it. I've no space in the house and the barrow's too small. Sure and wouldn't that be fine, to have a shop of me own?' It was the wrong thing to say. She should have said *our* own. She saw at once her mistake by the way his brows met and his eyes glinted with anger.

'You'll have that much work soon you won't even notice your husband's no longer around.' But as he turned away she grasped his arm and put her hand to his face, fingers cupping his cheek.

'Don't be angry, Matthew. Be pleased for me. For *us*. I love you. I need you home. I want you to share this new business with me. Why won't you?'

'You want me to work for my own wife? That would be the last straw. I'd sooner shoot meself.' He took her wrists and put her brusquely from him. 'You're only fooling yourself, Polly. The sooner you get these daft notions out of your head, the better. You've no money to stock a shop, and you can't keep on selling every stick o' furniture we've ever owned. Once it's gone, it's gone.'

'But it isn't, and I can. I've sold some of it twice already, and how else could I fund the business? It costs me a bit in interest each time, but it's working. I am starting to get somewhere.' Matthew turned and walked away. Polly hurried after him, struggling to find the right words, but there seemed nothing left to be said and she felt strangely exhausted by the effort of trying. She managed to keep pace by half running alongside him, but they remained silent and distant, a good yard of pavement between them.

They reached the door of number twenty-three far too soon to Polly's way of thinking. 'Will you come inside for a cuppa?'

As expected, he shook his head. 'Can you not try to believe in me, Matthew? Can't you see this business will be good for both of us in the end?'

'I can see you like to get your own way, Polly, always have. And you don't seem to mind who you hurt in the process. You need me only when things are going badly for you.'

'Aw, that's not fair.'

They stood together beneath the light of the lamp like strangers, or worse than strangers, for once they had been lovers and now neither could reach across the great gulf that separated them even to manage a goodnight kiss.

Chapter Fourteen

In September 1931 Ramsey MacDonald had faced near revolt by his colleagues as Britain came off the Gold Standard, and rumours of financial collapse had been rife. The resulting coalition government had achieved little and by October arrangements were put into place for a hasty election. The result brought a landslide victory for the Conservatives, but peace in Manchester was to be less easily won.

The group of men Polly had spotted lounging with every sign of careless indolence against the Green Dragon wall became, the very next day, a key part of that city's demonstration against the Means Test.

Optimism was high and Joshua, accompanied by Matthew, led them into the fray. With them were Stanley Green, Vera Murray's husband Barry, Bob Reckitt, Norman Sutcliffe, young Tom Shackleton for whom Lucy had once had a fancy, and Cal Eastwood and his cronies, along with a score or so spinners and cotton workers from in and around Dove Street.

Manchester had seen many such demonstrations before, dating back to the dark days of Peterloo, and there wasn't a man amongst them unaware of the outcome of that protest.

Faced with the prospect of the coming clash, some of Joshua's followers began to experience grave reservations about the wisdom of their actions, suffering severe pangs of nervousness and beginning to question why they'd chosen to come at all. One or two did leave, shame-facedly shuffling back to the safety of their firesides. Sensing their uncertainty, Joshua got up on his soapbox at the corner of the street, using the full powers of his oratory to keep the rest with him. The last thing he wanted was to lose the army he had so painstakingly assembled.

'There have been many organisations who have set out to change the social fabric of their day,' he told them, lifting his voice above the hum of their disquiet, filling it with the depth of his fervour and passion for this movement in which he truly believed. 'From straightforward Socialists to the Social Democratic Federation which was more Marxist than democratic; from an Independent Labour Party under Keir Hardie to the Clarion movement of Robert Blatchford. Great names that we in Manchester have been honoured to know.'

Little by little their anxious murmuring faded away and he sensed in the hush of the crowd a growing interest and agreement with every word he spoke. He smiled to himself, intoxicated by his own powers.

'Each one has promised to raise the awareness of the governing bodies, to bring action on our behalf – we the downtrodden workers and unemployed of Manchester. Each set out to gain concessions in housing and employment, and each played his part in bringing about changes in the economic conditions of his time. Now it is our turn!'

'Aye, that's the ticket.'

'We'll show'em, Josh.'

His passion mounted as he reminded them that as recently as 1911 there had been industrial action at the docks and in the transport industries. 'So aren't we following in a fine tradition?' He chose not to remind them that none of these movements had achieved as much as it would have liked, or how many men had been injured in the course of their efforts.

Nor did he mention how there had been a backlash against such social agitation on the grounds that Socialism should be about education and building a worthwhile social culture, not an incitement to riot. So far as Joshua was concerned, none of these issues mattered. The NUWM, he resolved, would be different and achieve what its forerunners had not. This was the movement that would make a real mark on the state of the country and the history of Manchester. And on his own political career, of course.

'Freedom and dignity for the working man!' he yelled, and the crowd roared their approval back at him, as one surging forward, ready to do battle with all-comers if that was what it would take to win the day.

—

The police were ready for them, denying the marchers access to Albert Square, halting their progress at the junction of London Road and Whitworth Street. With batons raised, they set out to force the men to retreat.

'Don't budge! Stand your ground!' Joshua cried, and the marchers sat down in the road, refusing to move even when ordered to do so with the threat of arrest. It was then that the baton charges began. Fire hoses from Whitworth Street Station were brought into play and in the ensuing uproar tempers were lost and clogs thrown like bricks, causing several constables to nurse sore heads.

When one bore down on young Tom Shackleton, baton raised, Matthew flung himself across the boy to protect him from the worst of the blows which rained down relentlessly upon them both. He could hear the boy's screams, echoing endlessly in his head, followed by a terrible silence which, to Matthew, was infinitely worse. His brother Cecil had once gone silent and simply vanished from his side. And Cecil had died. His vision blurred. Matthew rubbed the blood-red mist from his eyes and reached again for the boy, struggling against a sickening weakness to lift him in his arms.

'It's all right, I've got you.' He thrashed out at the copper with his foot as once again he came swinging towards them, kicking him where it hurt most. But the policeman was only winded and within seconds was back upon them with his baton. Matthew heard, rather than felt, the sickening crunch of splitting bone as his ankle took the full force of this latest blow, sending him sprawling to the ground. He struggled resolutely back to his feet, biting his lip against the agony that shot up his leg as he tried to put weight on it. His arms were still about young Tom, half dragging, half carrying him out of the carnage. He didn't rest or pause for breath until he'd sheltered the boy safely in a shop doorway.

'Stay there while I get help.'

'You're hurt too, Matt. Stop here. We'll be safe for a bit.' The boy had a point for it seemed there was no help to be had, not a sign of a friendly face anywhere, and it was now, his mission completed, that the full force of his own injury struck Matthew. He slumped to the ground feeling nauseous and disorientated. Yet nowhere could be safe, not in this mayhem. He must do something. Find help for the boy.

'Don't move,' he cried above the din. 'I'll be back.'

Joshua, too concerned with saving his own skin to be aware of any of this, was beginning to realise that his men had little hope of winning; that the forces ranged against them were too strong and too determined. Yet stubbornly they hung on, thousands of men filling the streets with pandemonium, more newcomers arriving at every minute. He'd not give up. He wouldn't. Not while he had breath left in his body.

—

Across the city, dressed in her Sunday coat and boots, Polly stepped out along Ancoats Lane with her head held high, the practised speech which had kept her awake half the night still going round in her head. She saw the milling groups of men marching towards the city and felt glad Matthew was not amongst them, although she recognised and admired the genuine conviction with which they were taking part in the cause. They believed they could make a difference to government thinking, and for all she knew they could be right. She could sense their excitement and resolution.

'Good luck, boys,' she called, and as one they turned and acknowledged her good wishes with a cheery wave, watching with appreciative eyes as she swung along the road. It was unusual to see a woman walking abroad in her figure, without a shawl swathed modestly around her and they enjoyed the spectacle for a moment before returning to the more serious task ahead.

Polly lapsed back into thoughts of her own problems, feeling certain that if she could secure the lease of this shop, which was in a good central position in this part of Manchester, then she could really begin to make progress in her business and Matthew would see that she had been right. Perhaps then he would stop feeling threatened and they could learn to work together, sharing the struggles and hardships, and enjoying the success she was sure would follow.

She found the shop and stood back to admire its wide window. In her mind's eye she saw it filled with carpet rugs. Optimism mounted. The depression couldn't last forever, and this was surely the time, while rents were low, to look to the future.

Exploring the dusty, dilapidated premises, she did not hear the hue and cry of men's voices as they echoed far away in the city. The room behind the main shop could be their workshop, she decided, where the cutting and binding would take place. She discovered there was even space to store her hand cart in a shed in the yard. She'd need to keep that, in order to transport the stock. Polly was certain it would all be perfect. Everything now depended on whether she could afford to take it. She straightened her spine, smoothed back a stray curl, and prepared to talk terms with the landlord.

–

Over in London Road, clashes between police and demonstrators had quickly degenerated into outright warfare. Clogs and bricks were flying, whistles blowing, blood flowed, gallons of water sprayed everywhere. Many arrests were made and men were being thrown into the Black Maria with ruthless regularity.

Joshua was not amongst them. He'd backed away at the optimum moment, managing to escape the worst of the crush for he'd not liked this new turn of events. Besides, he reasoned, what good would it do the cause for one of its leaders to be arrested? In his heart, he knew it would do him no good at chapel either to be thrown in jail, but convinced himself this had little to do with his decision to make a tactical withdrawal. His men needed him, that was the truth of it. He was certainly no coward, unlike his brother who had been notable by his absence almost from the start.

Joshua could see no sign of Matthew anywhere. Where was the man? Had he run away yet again?

He was determined that his brother would not evade his responsibility to others this time. Hadn't he been seeking just such an opportunity as this for years, in order to prove Matthew's cowardice? Joshua considered the possibility that he was lying injured somewhere, but dismissed it. More likely he had found himself somewhere to lie up, as he had done while Cecil lay dying in that other battle long ago. In which case it was surely his responsibility to bring Matthew back to his colleagues, dragging him by the scruff of the neck if necessary.

Then he saw his brother, sitting on the edge of the pavement, a dozen or so yards away.

Matthew lifted his head and looked at him out of eyes that had seen too much. 'Joshua, thank God! Did you see the way they fought?'

With a jolt of irrational disappointment, he realised his brother must have been in the midst of the melee after all. Joshua said nothing. Nor did he take a step towards him.

'Did you see how they hit out and struck even young boys, without a thought for the injuries they might sustain? I tried to stop them but...' Matthew's voice thickened, faded to nothing. He was sickened by it, and by the painful memories the demonstration had resurrected. 'Young Tom Shackleton is back there, holed up in a doorway. I only just got him out in time but he's bleeding badly. He needs help. Fetch someone quickly, Josh. A doctor or ambulance. Hurry.'

Perhaps it was the manner in which Matthew told him what he must do, or the sight of all the blood lost that day, that inflamed Joshua. Or perhaps the irritating but irrefutable fact that his brother had shown himself to be a hero, saving young Tom from almost certain death rather than retreating like a coward as Joshua had imagined. Whatever the reason, rage flooded through him and he refused to accept the evidence of his own eyes.

He told himself there probably hadn't been any real danger at all, that Matthew had sustained nothing more than a minor injury. How dare he sit nursing his head as if he were the only one suffering when others were being half killed in a pitched battle?

In his mind's eye it was Cecil and not Tom Shackleton who'd been left for dead in some unknown spot. Idealistic, young and eager, vowing to do his bit and come back a hero. Reliving all the pain of that time, Joshua once again suffered the agony of knowing his youngest brother would not return from war. It was as if, yet again, he lay dying, inch by inch, in some stinking field while this man here, this man who called himself a brother, left him there to rot.

Matthew was indicating some supposed injury to his foot. 'I'd carry the boy the rest of way meself, but I reckon me ankle's broken. Some copper tripped me with his truncheon. You'll have to help me up, Joshua, I can't walk.'

The modest use of the word 'tripped' brought a sneer to Joshua's lips as his patience finally snapped and his mind lost its grip upon reality. I'd *carry the boy myself*, he'd admitted, only he'd been *tripped*. Something as simple as a cricked ankle and he'd leave his own brother to die. There, wasn't that the truth he'd always suspected, the admission he'd sought?

Afterwards, Joshua knew he could have done something to prevent what happened next. He saw the crowd lurch and shift, begin to swell and surge towards them. The movement brought him sharply, back to the present, to the fact that it was Tom Shackleton lying injured, not Cecil at all. But still he did nothing.

On Sundays, when as a lay preacher he recited his sermons in chapel, he often spoke against the creed of 'an eye for an eye', quoting liberally from the Sermon on the Mount: Matthew, Chapter Five, as a baby might recite a nursery rhyme. To Joshua it made about as much sense. He believed there were times when turning the other cheek was not appropriate. He did not love each of his neighbours, nor was he willing to give anyone the coat from his back should they ask for it. Joshua was an Old Testament man rather than a New. And he believed there were times when a man must take his punishment, times when revenge was justified.

The last he saw of his brother was the top of his bright head as the crowd swamped him, and the last he heard a piercing cry as he called out the Irish woman's name. Even then Joshua made no move to save him. But then who had helped Cecil when he had called out thus? This was a battle, and in a battle, wasn't it every man for himself?

Less than an hour later when Polly was walking home, bubbling with excitement at having agreed terms to takethe shop on Ancoats Lane, she met several straggling groups of men coming back from their march. She could not help but notice that the excitement had gone from them, to be replaced by dejection and despondency. Several were nursing cuts and bruises, one was being half supported by his comrades, his arm clearly broken.

Amongst them she spied Joshua and waved to him. Though she felt a strong sympathy for the demonstrators, yet she was eager to tell someone about the shop, the wonderful deal she had struck with the landlord and how their future was growing rosier by the day.

Surely her lovely husband would be proud of her now?

She quickened her step. 'Joshua, have you seen Matthew?' But he did not reply to her question. Nor did he hurry to meet her. Instead he stopped dead in the middle of the street and as the other men melted swiftly away, she frowned with puzzlement.

Why did he always have to make even the smallest request for help or information into a major event? Sighing with irritation, she skipped off the pavement and ran across the street towards him. It was only when she was a step or two away that she faltered, for it was then that she saw the blood. With a start, she looked up into his eyes and what she saw there drenched her in a new fear, so chilling she swayed on her feet, as if her own life blood were draining away.

–

Matthew lay in the hospital bed, his face bleached almost as white as the pillows. It was small comfort to Polly to have heard the full story of her husband's heroism from Tom Shackleton's lips. The boy thought him a hero. Safely sheltered by the doorway, he had been in no danger when the crowd had surged by. Without doubt, Matthew had saved his life.

Joshua had said only that it had been a terrible accident. Unforeseen. Tragic. Matthew got caught up in the crowd and had been dragged underfoot.

Now Polly clung to his hand and prayed to every saint she could think of with a desperate fervour she had not felt in years. He did not move. He did not even open his eyes to acknowledge her presence. Yet he must know she was here, she was certain of it. He could surely feel her presence and her pain, as deeply as she felt his. She willed him to do so.

How long she sat thus, Polly couldn't have said. In her mind she was reliving every year, every month, every day of their life together. She remembered the loving days of their courtship, their simple wedding, the belief that nothing, not even the differences of religion, could divide them. She recalled the birth of each beloved child and the happy years that had followed of joyful family life.

She was also regretting every wrong word, every foolish quarrel, every show of Irish temperament; wishing desperately she'd never thought to sell all their furniture in order to buy a stupid carpet; never sold that dratted sideboard; never hurt him in any way.

If only she could turn back the clock.

Polly knew why he had gone to the demonstration despite his promises not to do so. It had been in retaliation for their quarrel, to prove he was still a man, even though he had no job and no means of supporting his family. He needed to prove to himself, as well as to her, that he had some control over his own destiny. It was his way of retaining his dignity. Polly rested her forehead against his limp arm and wept silent, bitter tears.

At last she lifted her head, struggling to pull herself together for this wouldn't do; It wouldn't do at all. She mustn't weep. Didn't he need her to be strong? She'd take him home and nurse him, make him well again. Wouldn't she devote her life to his care?

She smiled brightly at the still figure, wrapping her arms lovingly about him. 'Come on, you daft galoot. Stop frightening the life out of me like this. Will you not open your eyes and give me one of your daft winks?'

She became aware of hands on her shoulders, hands that dragged at her, attempting to draw her away. She tried to shake them off.

'Mrs Pride. Come with me, Mrs Pride.'

'No. I must be here when he wakes. I must be.'

Again the grip tightened and Polly resisted it, 'Mrs Pride. Come and have a cup of tea. It'll do you good.'

'No, no. Matthew might wake while I'm gone.'

'My dear, your husband is not going to wake. I'm sorry to say that he has passed away. He is in a better place now, safe from all pain and trouble.'

Polly stared at the woman, slowly registering her nurse's cap perched on top of a tightly scraped-back bun. She was old and wrinkled with whiskers sprouting on her upper lip. What did this woman know about love, about Matthew? 'No, you don't understand,' Polly carefully explained. 'He always looks like this when he's asleep. He'll start to snore in a minute.'

'I'm sorry, love, but he won't. Come with me, Mrs Pride. Wouldn't you like a nice cup of tea?'

'No! Leave me alone!' Polly fought with all her might. She shouted and screamed to make the silly woman understand, but another nurse came and the pair of them dragged her away from her beloved Matthew. Polly knew then, deep in her heart, that it was over. She knew she had lost him.

Chapter Fifteen

Eileen was frying chips for the children when Polly walked into her arms, laid her head against that grubby breast and wept as if the tears might never stop. The smell of the hot fat made her want to gag but, her mouth wide open like a child, heart-wrenching sobs came from some private place deep inside where the pain lived. Yet even these could nowhere near assuage the depths of her emotion. She was overwhelmed by grief.

Nor did it get any better in the days following. How could Matthew be dead? At any moment she expected the door to swing open and to hear him walk in, the chink of his clogirons on the stone floor, the sound of his tuneless whistling filling their small home with his vital presence. But he did not come. The house remained silent, save for the intermittent sobbing of her children and the shifting of coals turning to ash in the grate; rather as her life had burnt away to nothing along with it.

Afterwards she had no recollection of the funeral. There were crowds of people standing forlornly in the vast bleakness of the cemetery, but she could not have put a name to any of them. No doubt neighbours and colleagues had supported her, but Polly could only recall holding her children close to her side and managing, throughout that endless day, not to cry in front of them. Inside she felt dry and withered. Utterly spent.

Now she lay on the bare mattress in the dark privacy of her lonely bedroom and stared into the emptiness of a grim future. Life without Matthew was impossible to envisage. It really didn't seem to matter whether she had a future or not. Her ambitions for a business and the quarrels they'd had over it now seemed petty and cruelly unimportant, serving only to mar the last weeks of his life.

Why hadn't she listened to him? Why couldn't she have told him she was content and satisfied with her lot, happy to wait until the economic tide turned and her husband was in work again? Why did she always have to imagine that she could fix things herself?

Now everything was gone and her life was over.

The tears came again when she realised how she had deprived herself even of the bed they had shared throughout the long years of their marriage. Selling all their precious belongings hadn't mattered when she still had Matthew, or even the hope of his eventual return. Now she felt as if she had given a part of him away. She wept for the solid comfort of his favourite chair which reminded her so much of him; for the chairs and kitchen table around which they had shared so many joyful family meals; for the buffet and aspidistra and other bits and bobs which had made up their home. Most of all for the glossy mahogany sideboard that had represented the culmination of their efforts together as a couple. This above all else had mattered to Matthew, and she had deprived him of that comfort.

Now she was deprived of his warm body beside her, not simply for the duration of a silly quarrel, but forever.

'Nay, don't take on so.' Eileen had crept into the darkened bedroom. Wrapping her skinny arms about her friend, she cradled her like a child. 'You have to stop tearing yourself apart, Polly. You'll make yourself ill. Matthew wouldn't want that, and Benny and Lucy need you.' The two women looked into each other's sad faces and wept together.

'Oh, Eileen, what am I to do? it's more than I can bear.'

'We bear things because we must.'

'But how will I manage without him?'

'Same answer. Here, I've fetched you some soup. Get yourself outside of that.' Eileen set a tray over Polly's knees and sat by her while she sipped it, making sure she drank every drop. 'That'll set you up champion,' she said, but a warning note crept into her voice as she squeezed Polly's hands. 'I'm off home now. Lucy is seeing to Benny, but I'll be back tomorrow. I shall expect you up and about when I come. No languishing in bed. Life goes on.'

Polly nodded, knowing her friend was right, but inside an inner voice cried out in protest. Her life, in every respect that mattered, was changed forever and the strength needed to endure it was more than she could manage to find, now or ever again.

—

Joshua felt no such despair, nor any sense of remorse at his lack of action on that fateful day. Both his brothers were dead, and that was a cross he must bear with fortitude.

Witnesses had fortunately confirmed his report that it had been a wretched accident. Matthew had been in the wrong place at the wrong time, poor man, though Tom Shackleton continued to sing his praises all over town. To have this brother, whom he had deemed a coward, the a hero was almost more than Joshua could stomach. Yet he must, for he wanted no further investigation of the matter, no questions asked about where exactly he had been at the time of Matthew's 'accident'.

He watched his mother grieve in stoic silence and felt a stirring of reluctant admiration for the old woman. Big Flo had never been one to wear her heart on her sleeve, and she did not do so now.

Any indications of her distress in the long bitter days following her son's death, she shared only with her Saviour, her great friend. Joshua could hear the subdued mumble of her voice in the bedroom above as he sat by the fire each evening.

She would be on her knees on the cold linoleum by the high brass bed, praying for strength and thanking Him for the blessing of so many joyous years with her son. In chapel she sang as heartily as ever, 'What a Friend We Have in Jesus', giving no indication to onlookers of her inner pain. There were times when even he envied his mother her simple, unshakeable faith.

For his sister-in-law he had less patience. He would give her a week, two at most, and then he would insist that she pull herself out of her self-imposed depression. There were decisions to be made, changes to be put into effect. This was no time for self-pity. He would see to it that she did not shirk her duty as a mother, nor as a member of this family.

He told himself that women were no mystery to him, they were merely selfish, physically demanding creatures, with sin on their soul that needed to be rooted out by the superior male.

He waited five days then wait to Polly and told her that it was not fitting for her to live alone.

'Not fitting?'

'As a widow with two children to care for and nourish, it's not possible for you to manage on your own. Besides, it would seem as if we, your family, were neglecting you.'

Polly struggled to take in exactly what he was saying to her, but as so often these days her brain refused to function properly. She could barely remember to get out of bed each morning, or eat breakfast when she did. Once, during the first endless weeks following Matthew's death, she'd followed Eileen's instructions and tried standing with her barrow as usual on Oldham Street. The other hawkers and stall holders, having learned of her loss, were sympathetic and supportive, but they could not run her business for her. She had lost all hope or interest in taking on a shop. Now she couldn't even manage her market barrow.

Customers came, made their purchases as usual, but at the end of the day Polly had little money to show for her efforts. She'd not had the energy to barter or haggle, accepting the first price they offered. Even in her bemused state she was aware she'd lost money. She did not go again.

Just stepping out of the door to visit the corner shop filled her with panic and confusion. She'd stand at the counter wondering why she had come. Connie Green, ever sympathetic, would put some item of food in her hands – 'There y'are, chuck. That'll keep the wolf from the door' – and send her on her way, assuring her she could pay when she'd got herself sorted. And Polly would do as she was told because thinking was too great an effort. Now she gazed into her brother-in-law's stern face and nodded.

'Whatever you say, Joshua.'

He was surprised, having expected a protest, but then he smirked, reminding himself of what he'd always believed. He'd often remarked that Matthew was too soft with the woman, perfectly certain he could manage her much better, and here was the evidence in the way she calmly acceded to every decision he made. She had only wanted a man to take a firm hand.

The next day Joshua had all the furniture moved from number thirty-one into number twenty-three because Polly's house was the larger of the two. Big Flo was packed up and carried along with it, protesting vociferously all the while for, rather like an aspidistra without its pot, she swore she'd wither and die away from her own fireside. Joshua didn't even trouble to respond to his mother's complaints. He was the head of this family now, and the women would do as he said.

-

The bright autumn days of October changed into a wet November and Polly seemed suspended in a state of shock. Lucy too was having a hard time. Tom Shackleton's life had been saved by her father. She realised now that she still loved Tom, was relieved and happy that he'd survived the dreadful baton charges that day, but in order for him to do so, her own father had died. How could she show her happiness over this without seeming to disregard the loss of Matthew? Tom once asked her out, to take a walk over to Platt Fields or in Philips Park, but she'd told him she couldn't go. It was too soon.

'In a month or two maybe,' she'd said. 'When things have settled down.' And he'd nodded sagely, understanding that the family needed time to grieve.

But it was much more than that. Though not quite to the same degree as her mother, Lucy felt her freedom slipping away.

Whenever she stepped out of the door, Uncle Joshua demanded to know where she was going. She always told him but gradually, little by little, began to resent having to do so. She'd never needed to before, for Polly had always trusted her to be sensible.

Lucy wouldn't be fifteen till next March, which seemed half a lifetime away, but once that day arrived, she vowed to go out with Tom. And nobody, certainly not Uncle Joshua, would stop her.

Benny was struggling to be a man. He knew he wasn't supposed to cry because his dad had once told him only babies and girls cried. But sometimes as he lay in bed at night, the pain in his chest hurt so much tears did come in spite of his opening his eyes as wide as he could to try and stop them. They trickled down into his ears and soaked his pillow but he didn't dare make a sound in case Lucy should hear. He felt shame at this display of weakness. He only hoped that his dad wasn't watching from heaven.

Once, when he was at the flicks with Liam, Joe and Don, they'd seen a film called *Outward Bound* which was about a liner full of people who acted as if they were alive but were really dead. A man came on board, he was the pilot, and it was his job to decide who could live and who would be left dead. Benny had wished real life was like that film and he could pilot his dad back to life again. It had been a boring film but to his horror, under cover of darkness, several tears had rolled down his cheeks and plopped on to his jersey. He'd been so scared of anyone noticing, he hadn't even dared put up a hand to wipe them away.

Worst of all was that his mam didn't seem to notice his unhappiness. He understood why that was, but he longed for her to smile again, to chuck him cheekily under the chin, even to nag him about not wearing his cap. He'd happily wear the awful thing forever, even wash twice a day and never get into a scrap ever again, if only his dad could come back, and his mam could be happy again. But since that wasn't possible, he needed her to do something, anything other than this pained silence. He hated to see her with purple bruises under her eyes, cheeks all sunken and her lips pinched.

Benny and Lucy would talk about the problem in hushed whispers before they went to sleep.

'She misses Dad so much.'

'Yeah.'

'I miss him too.'

Benny had no wish to express the depth of his emotion, not to his sister.

Lucy said, 'We have to help Mam get through this.'

'How?'

Neither of them could find an answer to that, and then Uncle Joshua and Grandma Flo moved in and everything got worse instead of better. Benny didn't mind Grandma Flo, She was old and grumbled a lot, but she'd slip him an extra biscuit at tea time when no one was looking. She took up residence in the back bedroom, complaining it was little bigger than a cupboard; Lucy moved into Mam's room, while Uncle Joshua took over theirs. Benny was given one blanket and a pillow and told to sleep under the stairs. He was appalled. Only really poor people did that, and they weren't that poor, were they?

'Mam?' he appealed, begging her with wide shocked eyes to prevent this outrage. But she only smiled distractedly and handed over his father's greatcoat for extra warmth.

Benny knew it must be a sin, but he didn't like Uncle Joshua one bit. He saw him as a stern, sour-faced man, with never a good word for anyone, least of all Benny himself. He was quite sure that, given time, he could have been the man of the house and looked after his mam and sister without any help whatsoever. The new regime also meant that he and Lucy had to hold their private conversations in whispers while they washed and prepared for bed. There was no other time when they were alone.

'You don't think he'll start telling us what to do all the time, do you?' Lucy hissed through the soap suds as she delicately lathered her face. Benny watched with interest, noting how she smoothed it over her skin with great care, as if afraid of doing damage to it.

163

'How should I know?'

'You know, bossing and ordering us about, and making us read the Bible and learn scriptures and stuff?'

This was exactly what Benny feared too and they looked into each other's faces, horrified at the thought, for they were well aware what a tyrant Uncle Joshua could be, particularly when it came to imposing his own brand of religion. And it was perfectly clear to them both that their mother was in no fit state to protect them.

'We won't let him bully us,' Lucy declared, before dipping her head and splashing her face briskly with cold water.

'No.'

She came up for air and Benny handed her the towel. 'We'll stick together.'

'Aye.'

It sounded so grand, like an army with its back to the wall or the Three Musketeers perhaps, that Benny cheerfully agreed, even felt a surge of optimism. What could his uncle do against such a united front?

-

The first challenge came sooner than they expected. The very next Sunday Joshua took it into his head to insist they all attend Zion Methodist, instead of their own Catholic Church.

While Benny chewed on his lip, wondering how he could wriggle out of this unpleasant duty, he watched his sister's face flush to a dark and dangerous crimson. Didn't he know that colour well? 'You can't mean it?' she stormed. 'We're not Methodists, we're Catholics!'

'You *were* Catholics. Now it's time for you to change. Your family are all Primitive Methodists. Your father was a Methodist. It's your duty to honour his memory by following in his footsteps.'

'Dad hadn't been to chapel in years, except at Christmas,' Benny put in and then wished he'd kept his mouth shut when he felt the full force of his uncle's glare.

Big Flo judged it wise to intervene at this point. 'That does not mean he didn't believe, or wouldn't want you to,' she said, sniffing her disapproval. Flo had no wish to think ill of the dead, but she'd often had 'words' with her son over his refusal to attend chapel, yet not once had she won the argument. Perhaps with his children she'd be more successful. The Catholic Church had too much power over its people, in Flo's opinion. She didn't hold with too much power, anybody holding sway over others, let alone a church, not recognising the very same thirst for power in her own son. She played what she considered to be her trump card. 'Our Matt never turned to become a Catholic, now did he?'

Lucy shot a glance of appeal at her mother but as usual Polly was staring mindlessly into the fire. Nevertheless, in desperation she decided to make a stand. 'Maybe not, but Dad always said everyone should worship as they please. He was entirely tolerant in that respect and wouldn't have tried to make us do something we didn't want to do. So thank you for the offer but we'll stick with our own way of worship, if you don't mind.'

'But I *do* mind. Your well-being is my responsibility and you'll do as I say.' Joshua was telling them that he was master now, and while both children itched to argue further, something in his manner advised caution.

Lucy again looked frantically to her mother, but Polly laid back her head with her eyes closed, hands lying loose in her lap. There were times when Lucy had an urge to shout at her, shake her out of what seemed like a long confused sleep. But perhaps it was too soon. She'd no wish to hurt her. Perhaps Polly needed this time in which to grieve. If it meant they had to put up with a few difficulties meanwhile, so be it. Although it went against the grain, Lucy swallowed her protests. Rolling her eyes briefly heavenwards, she sent Benny a warning glance to keep quiet too.

Polly, unaware that her daughter had just fought a losing battle for control over the free expression of her soul, was engaged in fighting her own devils, with a deep burning anger that seemed to consume her.

When ordered to do so she, like the rest of her family, dressed in her best and meekly followed them to chapel. Joshua ushered them all into the pew for which he paid a weekly rent. By paying the small sum he ensured it belonged exclusively to himself. As did the pew's occupants, in his opinion.

Lucy and Benny stood close to their mother. Grandma Flo was beside them in her best black hat with the long hatpin, singing loudly about God being our help in ages past and sheltering us from the stormy blast. Benny could only hope it was true, for he could sense many storms ahead and felt in need of a bit of shelter right now.

Eileen was outraged. Never had she heard of such Draconian treatment in all her life. Not that she would have used the word 'Draconian', being more familiar with earthier words, which she struggled to avoid using when talking to Polly.

She'd made no comment when Joshua and his mother had moved in, largely because she considered it none of her business, but she didn't much care for it all the same. Joshua continued to attend his meetings, and perform his powerful oratory on Sunday afternoons in Stevenson Square.

So far as Eileen was concerned the change had brought no good in its wake. His very presence seemed to put a damper upon the quiet intimacy that had grown between the two neighbours. Big Flo had taken over the cooking and housekeeping, and both Benny and Lucy seemed fidgety and unhappy. Polly had simply given up, sinking ever deeper into depression. Life went on around her but she took no part in it.

Joshua made no effort to stir her from her lethargy, yet. Eileen had seen how his nasty little eyes followed his sister-in-law's every move; she noted how he watched her, like a cat waiting for the right moment to pounce. She'd even seen him mix her sleeping potions when Polly complained she couldn't sleep. Yet how could she hope to sleep at night when she sat dozing in the chair for most of the day? It was infuriating.

Eileen tried to make Polly see that she was falling into a downward spiral. 'You shouldn't let Big Flo take over your house, nor give in to Joshua so much. I didn't come down with the last snow fall. He's up to summat. I don't know all the ins and outs to it, but he's after making your life a misery.'

Polly shook her head. 'Joshua knows I can't manage on my own. He's family, so naturally he wishes to help.'

Help himself more like, was the uncharitable thought which flashed into Eileen's mind, though she managed to keep it to herself.

'He too is grieving for the loss of his brother,' Polly reminded her, and Eileen felt bound to concede this was very likely true, as it was also true that he was family, kith and kin, the old adage being that blood was thicker than water. She had to admit it was only right in a way that he should play his part in looking after Polly. He'd also done a great deal for the community. A solid, worthy citizen. A stalwart of the chapel and upholder of justice, leading men into that demonstration so they could stand up for their rights.

Even so, there was something about the man Eileen did not like. She couldn't quite put her finger on what it was that so disturbed her. She only had to be in the same room with him, to watch the way his eyes lingered on Polly or how his hand pressed upon her arm as he handed her a powder, and a shiver would run down her spine. There was no doubt about it, he gave her the creeps. His behavior wasn't normal. She only wished she could work out why, which made her even more desperate to rouse Polly's once abundant energy.

'You were managing before – before Matthew had his accident. You must get going again, Poll. What about them carpet pieces that need binding and stitching?'

She simply looked blank and then put a hand to her head, as if it was all too much to think about. 'I've finished with all of that.

Look where it led. If I hadn't been so stubborn, then Matthew wouldn't have had anything to prove by attending that meeting.'

'Nay, that's daft. Thousands of men attended the demonstration, love. He were only doing what was right, and look what a hero he was, saving young Tom like that. He should get a medal from the King. But life has to go on. I'd help – with the carpets like.'

When she got no reply to this, and saw how Polly seemed to shrink further into herself, drawing up her knees and wrapping her arms tightly about her own emaciated frame, Eileen came to a decision. It felt so momentous, so startling and dangerous if Joshua should find out, that she resolved to make no mention of it to Polly. No mention at all.

She gave her friend a hug, removed her untouched mug of tea to wash it out and replace it with a fresh one, said her goodbyes and made her way towards the door.

'I'll go out the front way, if that's all right,' she said, quite unnecessarily since she usually went that way. Polly merely nodded. On her way through the front parlour Eileen collected up the half-sewn pieces of carpet rugs, together with a roll of recently delivered carpet still waiting to be cut, and transported them, an armful at a time, to her own house next door. No doubt Terence would have something to say on the matter but he could take a long jump off a short pier. Eileen meant to help Polly, come what may. What were friends for? One day, she might even thank her for it.

Chapter Sixteen

The moment Lucy discovered that the carpets had gone she was incensed, certain that Joshua was to blame. Young as she was, she bravely tackled him on the subject, tilting her chin in a way that was alarmingly reminiscent of Polly herself. She could feel herself shaking with barely controlled anger as she accused him of removing property which rightly belonged to her mother.

Joshua's brows met over his long lean nose so ferociously that she almost wished the words unsaid. 'Do you imagine that I would soil my hands by touching what contributed to my own brother's misery?'

'That's exactly why you would take them,' Lucy retaliated, clenching her fists into fierce balls of fury.

'I doubt there is any requirement for me to explain to you, a mere child, but I care little where they've gone. I am only glad that they have, since I need a place in which to do my work for the NUWM. The parlour will do very well.' Joshua spent much of his time collecting funds for the cause, though it was proving amazingly difficult to squeeze even a penny or two out of the men. Of course he knew that money was tight, many of them already suffering from the restrictions of the Means Test, but he was frequently driven to point out that the situation would only get worse if they didn't give what they could towards fighting this pernicious affliction. As a result of these efforts, his own percentage of the fund was growing nicely, but then he deserved it, since he was doing most of the work.

Lucy was saying, 'It's my mam's parlour. She might have summat to say about that.'

There was a long silence during which Joshua studied the girl in silence. Then, smiling, he stepped closer to pinch Lucy's chin beneath his finger and thumb. 'A mettlesome little thing, aren't you? I like a bit of spirit in a woman, though in a child it can prove bothersome. But then, you always were old for your age.'

Something in the way he said this, in the hiss of his breath against her cheek, caused a cold shiver to run down Lucy's spine, as if it stirred a memory she couldn't quite capture. And then the sensation evaporated as the child in her became transfixed by the way in which his pale eyes seemed to move about in his eye sockets, rather like those of a watchful lizard. In that moment she hated him simply for being alive when her father was dead. For being in her house, let alone for his determined efforts to take over their lives.

But this wasn't the moment for argument, she wisely decided, not while her mam was still poorly. Someone else would have to tackle him on the subject. It certainly wouldn't be her mother, not in her current state. Nor Grandma Flo, who never had disagreed with any of her sons, in particular this one with his slow-burning temper that could suddenly erupt when you were least expecting it.

Lucy suddenly lost all appetite for battle. Hadn't she lost two already in her efforts to resist attendance at chapel instead of her own church, and in losing the freedom to see her friends as regularly as she once did. But she continued to fret about the carpets. They represented the sum total of Polly's sacrifice. Her mother must come out of her depression eventually, and how would she feel then to discover all her stock had been stolen?

Over the next few days Lucy was busy working at the market, but then she bumped into Eileen in the street and all was explained. Their neighbour had taken the carpets into her own protection.

'I thought it'd be for the best.'

Lucy was eager to offer her help. 'I could come and help, whenever I'm not at the market. It's only a part-time job, so I could do a couple of days each week. How would that be?'

Eileen's eyes lit up and, grabbing Lucy's arm, she marched her off down a ginnel where they could talk more privately. 'Could you manage to mind the childer at the same time? If you did, then I could take the barrow and stand in Oldham Street for Polly. That would at least keep things ticking over.'

Lucy was less enamoured of the thought of Eileen's ruffian children than of carpet stitching, difficult though that job undoubtedly was, but she agreed to the plan, for Polly's sake. To see her own mother kept in day after day, like a recalcitrant child, filled her with grave unease. She may be grieving, but she couldn't go on like this indefinitely. Lucy supposed her uncle meant well, but it didn't seem right. As she strove to explain all of this to Eileen, the older woman seemed to understand perfectly.

'Aye, he'd turn t'milk sour that one, just by looking at it. I'd watch me step if I were you.'

They neither of them commented on what Polly should do:

–

Over the following weeks they put their plan into operation and it worked beautifully. Two days a week Eileen would go off at dawn with the hand cart laden with carpet rugs, and Lucy and the children would have the house to themselves. The minute Terence rose from his bed, which usually wasn't until around noon, he made himself scarce, keeping well away from any threat of activity. So long as there was food on his table, the children were kept out of his hair and Eileen gave him a bob or two to enjoy his smokes and racing, he didn't much care what his wife did with her day, so long as she didn't go back to her old ways.

Eileen developed a good line in repartee with the customers. She'd take some of the carpet pieces to stitch between sales, and the rest she would work on in the evenings. Lucy did what she could on the days when she wasn't employed by Dorrie Hughes on one of her black pudding or tripe and trotter stalls.

Both knew the plan had a limited duration. Once all the carpet pieces were sold, they weren't sure whether they would have the courage to seek more out, as Polly had done so ably. But that was a worry for the future. For now they would mind the business and bring in what money they could, just in case she had need of it one day.

Big Flo continued to do most of the cooking and cleaning for them all, while Polly meekly carried out any tasks she was given, saying little and never protesting when Joshua told her it was time to eat, or to go to bed, sweep the hearth or make the beds, ordering her to do this, that or the other. It chilled Lucy to see that her mother wasn't even allowed a trip to the corner shop by herself any more.

'A breath of fresh air might do her good,' she would constantly protest. But when he finally relented and allowed Polly to go to Connie Green's corner shop for a pinch of tea, she wandered off and was found hours later in Whitworth Street, close to the spot where Matthew had been killed.

'I remembered – that's where I've been wanting to go for so long. I had to see where it was he died, to say goodbye,' she explained, as if it had been some sort of pilgrimage, which in a way it had. Joshua made it clear that he was not pleased at this blatant flouting of his orders, and made her sit in silence for two solid hours to reflect on this act of disobedience. Wasn't the man dead and buried, with every respect already paid to him? Treated like a hero no less. Much to Joshua's private chagrin.

'See where that silly idea led,' he accused Lucy. 'Would *you* accept responsibility if anything should befall your mother next time?'

Put so bluntly, Lucy felt forced to back down from an argument, but it brought fresh worries. Was her mother truly ill? Would she end up in Prestwich? Or was Uncle Joshua only making out she was ill in order to keep her at home? But why would he do that? Why wouldn't he want Mam to be happy and busy with her work again? She couldn't grieve forever. He was like that new man who had taken over Germany, somebody Hitler, who was being nasty to the Jews. Lucy felt decidedly uneasy, but there seemed to be little she could do about anything.

Christmas came and went without any attempt at celebration. A New Year dawned and the months of 1932 dragged endlessly by, each one as long as a lifetime. Driven near mad by grief Polly felt quite unable to cope, and saw no point in trying. She came to from her lethargy sufficiently to manage everyday tasks about the house but showed no interest in resuming her work with the carpets. Her one concern was to care for her children and give them what comfort she could to ease their own grief, but she had so little energy.

Polly appreciated the care which Joshua took of her, even to getting sleeping powders from the doctor for her since she was exhausted from the nightmare of sleepless nights spent going over and over how the accident must have happened. It was months now since Matthew had died yet she felt the pain as keenly as if it were only yesterday. At least the powders brought blessed relief from her torment, and she did not object when he insisted she take one each dinner time as well, so she could seek oblivion for much of the afternoon.

Sometimes, though, the urge to take action was almost overwhelming. She would put on her shawl or coat and go out of the door almost with a spring in her step as if there was something particular she must do, some place she must go. But then she'd forget what or where that was. In any case, Joshua would always waylay her before she got very far and bring her home again, cautioning her to stay safely by her own fireside.

'You don't want for anything, now do you?' he would ask, and Polly would agree that she needed naught but her children and wasn't she fortunate to be so well cared for?

There were many who couldn't say as much.

–

The dole was reduced, for those who could get any, and the number out of work soared to unprecedented levels. For all the excitement of Amelia Earhart's solo flight in May, spirits were generally low for there was increasingly alarming news from Germany regarding the formation of a new National Socialist Party. The autumn of that year brought yet more riots and hunger marches, followed by the first Christmas wireless broadcast by King George V, an attempt to bring a little cheer, which indeed it did if no long-term optimism.

Certainly Benny didn't feel like cheering. Life for him had a remarkable sameness to it. So when the New Year of 1933 came in on a flurry of snow which he knew would turn to slush by the next day, if previous experience was anything to go by, he determined to enjoy it while it lasted. Crisp white snow was a rare commodity in this city.

Together with his friends, he fashioned a sledge from a bit of old corrugated iron, punched in a couple of holes to tie a loop of string through and dragged it to the top of Stony Brow. Here they could all pile on and whizz down the steep hill, right into the timber yard at the bottom. It was great fun, whooping and shouting as they went.

They tried every position they could think of: backwards, forwards, lying down head first or feet first, sitting with their knees bent or legs spread, one boy seated on top of another, or several locked within each other's knees. Speed and comfort varied, but the accuracy of their trajectory was constantly in doubt since the sledge could hit a stone, or the string break, and then career out of control in seconds.

Nevertheless the Dove Street Gang was having great fun and wasn't unduly worried about such details.

Until Georgie Eastwood turned up.

He seemed to have grown out of all proportion to the other Ancoats lads, apparently proving he had easier access to regular sustenance than most. His hands were big as bricks, brown hair sticking up around his bullet-shaped head, face set in a permanent glower beneath knitted brows. At fourteen, older than them by a couple of years as well as a known bully, Georgie no longer had to suffer the humiliation of wearing short trousers. So far as Benny and his gang were concerned, despite their earlier bravado, he was still not a person to argue with.

Now, as Benny climbed aboard the sledge for his next run down, he found Georgie had placed one heavily clogged foot against its front edge. 'Gerroff he said, as succinct as ever.

Benny turned to stone. If he got up and let Georgie take the sledge, his friends would think him a coward and a cissy. Yet if he stubbornly hung on, he'd be belted into the middle of next week. Georgie was bad enough on his own, but from the corner of his eye Benny could see that he was not alone. All his henchmen were close by.

'And if I don't?' He felt a singe of pride to hear he sounded much braver than he felt.

Georgie snorted derisively. 'Then you'd be sorry.'

As if to emphasise the fact, he kicked at the sledge with one iron-tipped clog and the ringing sound it made brought to a halt all activity on the hill as children turned around to see what was going on. Within seconds they had melted away, just as surely as the snow would soon melt under the press of their feet. Benny found that he was facing the enemy alone, even his three friends had decided to strategically vanish. The Eastwood Gang closed in. It comprised Georgie's two younger brothers, Bert and Mick, and a motley crew of hangers on.

With no effort at all, they picked Benny off the sledge as if he were no more than a flea and tied him with his own ball of string to the nearest lamp-post. Then they stamped and danced around him as if they were red Indians and he was the cowboy waiting to be scalped.

Benny felt quite certain that something equally dreadful was indeed about to take place, and wondered what Tom Mix would do in this situation. Shoot from the hip? Flick a lasso over Georgie's head? Without the aid of either six-shooter or rope, he could only shiver in helpless misery. In the end they satisfied their malice by kicking snow at him, and stuffing snowballs down the neck of his jersey till he was soaked through. Then they went off, towing the stolen sledge behind them and laughing at their own cleverness.

Some time later Benny's mates returned to rescue him, but he could barely look them in the face. He felt as if he had failed in some way by losing the sledge, and they too were embarrassed at having left him to his fate. Yet each was too proud to apologise or even express sympathy, and far too fearful to suggest retaliation. They'd long since given up on that score.

The situation was made worse by the thorough scolding Benny received when he got home. Not so much from Polly, who gave a vague sort of smile and cuddled him close, but from Grandma Flo because his clothes were soaking wet and he'd be sure to take a chill. She dosed him with Fenning's Fever Cure just in case, which he loathed, and made him wear a layer of brown paper and goose grease plastered to his chest under his clothing for days afterwards.

Even Lucy was scathing when he protested, refusing even to listen to the full tale. 'You great soft lump! You should stand up for yourself and not give in to bullies.'

'It's all right for you to talk,' he protested. 'You haven't had Georgie Eastwood breathing down your neck.'

'Huh, I'm scared of no one,' she protested. 'I wouldn't let anyone tell me what to do.' But later, as she lay in bed, a memory stirred of a voice whispering close to her ear, hot breath against her shrinking flesh. It spoke the kind of dirty words which had come to her out of the darkness that long ago night in the barracks. That couldn't have been Georgie Eastwood too, could it? Surely not. He was sitting nowhere near her at the time. But if not Georgie, then who? She'd never discovered.

Her eyes opened again as panic assailed her. Somewhere in the darkness she heard a faint hiccuping sob and her heart filled with pity. She got quietly out of bed and crept downstairs. From the cubby-hole beneath she could hear her brother's sniffles quite clearly. She wriggled in beside him and stretched out her hand to pat him gently on the shoulder. 'You're right, Benny love, I've never had to face up to real bullying like that. I reckon anybody would've been scared.'

'Dad wouldn't,' Benny whimpered, wishing his father were here now so that he could sort out Georgie Eastwood.

'No,' she agreed in a sorrowful voice, snuggling down under the greatcoat which still smelled faintly of her father. She thought of Tom Shackleton and again experienced that familiar ache in her chest. 'Mam never used to let anyone bully her either, once. But she does now.' On this grim thought they both fell silent and finally fast asleep, but with tears on their cheeks.

—

Unaware of the bullying her son was suffering, or of her daughter's misery at not being permitted to attend her own church, Polly began to feel an urgent need for the ritual and calming influence of her own religion. She wanted to see again the flickering candles that seemed to herald the presence of the Holy Ghost; smell the incense and hear the rhythmic chanting in Latin, most of which she had never understood but had always loved. She did once consider going to see Father Donevan yet couldn't quite pluck up the courage to do so. He'd never supported her when Matthew had been alive, so why should he now?

One morning she stood at the kitchen window and listened to a blackbird trill its merry song in the back yard. Yet another spring without Matthew. How could she endure it? She couldn't go on like this. Polly knew she must do something to snap herself out of this endless melancholy. But what?

Joshua came up behind her with one of the powders, mixed in a mug of warm milk, which he assured her would calm her fragile nerves and prevent the panic attacks which so frightened her.

'Drink up, Polly. You know it will make you well.' He sounded impatient, as if he were in a hurry.

She nodded obediently, taking the cup from him. Through the grime of the window, which she really ought to clean, she watched the sparrows peck at invisible crumbs, remembering how she and Matthew had always gone to Platt Fields at Easter to roll eggs for the children. After that would come the Whit Walks. But no, not any more. Wasn't it the Whit Walks that had started the trouble between them in the first place? she thought in confusion. Her stubborn determination had driven her to take on extra work in a public house so she could buy Lucy a new frock. Matthew had been so angry, yet she hadn't taken him seriously, even then.

If only she could turn back the clock. This single thought was repeated again and again in her head like a cracked record, and nothing would shift it.

Eileen had once told her she should get out more. Polly looked again at the sparrows and thought how lovely it would be to walk in the park. Perhaps that was what she needed to do. Perhaps she should give it a try. She set down the cup and turned to her brother-in-law.

'I think I'd like to go out for a walk.'

'No, Polly, not yet.'

Protests formed in her head but none reached her lips. Joshua continued, 'I'm off out collecting. Big Flo is sitting with Betty Sidebottom while her sister Nellie goes shopping. The woman isn't fit to be left apparently.' He'd once hated to leave Polly on her own; now he felt quite certain she would obediently drink her milk and stay by the fire. She wasn't going anywhere ever again, not until he was ready to let her, or had thought of another way to punish her.

Poor daft Betty, Polly thought, and subsiding into the chair by the fire, sipped at her milk, just as Joshua had told her to.

As he opened the door a waft of spring air blew into the little house, and a shaft of disappointment at not being able to walk in the park struck unexpectedly sharp and keen in Polly's breast. It came to her then that she didn't have to obey Joshua. She could go if she wanted to.

He was saying something about a meeting of the church elders which he must attend later and as the door clicked shut a memory stirred of another church she'd visited once, near Cheetham Hill. Polly recalled a more sympathetic priest who'd told her to call any time she was passing. Father Thomas, that was his name. He'd seemed kind and understanding, not the sort of priest to condemn a woman for loving a man with a different religion. But could she find it again?

Without stopping to think or even to put on her coat, in a mood of sudden resolve Polly poured away the sleeping draught, walked out of the front door and set out to take the tram.

As she walked along Dove Street, it crossed her mind that she hadn't seen Eileen for a long while. The last time her friend had called, Joshua had insisted Polly wasn't well enough for visitors. With the sun on her face she felt an unexpected surge of energy, like new blood pouring into her heart and lungs. Sure and she'd call on Eileen on her way home, prove to her that she was doing as her friend had suggested and getting out and about again.

She came to the tram stop and, jostled by the crowd, became suddenly confused, overwhelmed by indecision and panic as she struggled to remember what she was doing here and where she had meant to go. It seemed so strange to be out amongst people again that she could barely think. What was it she'd meant to do? Polly shivered, feeling a great desire to turn and run, to escape something or other, though from what she was escaping or where she should run, she couldn't imagine.

'Are you all right, love?' The voice sounded concerned, the eyes that looked down into hers were gentle, brown as melted chocolate and fringed with long curling lashes.

She said, 'Yes, I think so.'

'You're shaking.'

'I just feel a bit cold.'

'I'm not surprised. It's cold enough to crack a nut today for all it's supposed to be spring. And you've no coat on, lass. Here, take this.' He was whipping off his own thick reefer jacket and draping it around her shoulders. The warmth of it seemed to seep into her frozen soul. 'Charlie Stockton, at your service, as they say.' And he grinned at her. His round face, weathered by sun not normally found in Manchester, seemed to Polly in that moment the most welcome sight she had ever seen. Yet still she shivered and Charlie became even more concerned.

'What tram were you wanting? I mean, are you in hurry? We could go into that caff over the road and get a drink of something hot. Tea and a toasted teacake. How do you fancy that?'

There was something solid and comforting about the man, never mind the prospect of hot tea and toasted teacake. He was tall and broad-shouldered, with short brown hair cropped close to his head, belying the hint of natural curl to it. His clothes were rough and ready but clean, a hole in the sleeve of his pullover had been carefully darned, she noticed. It crossed her mind that he might have a wife who did such tasks for him. If so, what would she have to say about him taking a strange woman into a cafe?

'That would be grand,' she said, amazed at herself for agreeing but it suddenly seemed wonderful to be free and out of the house, talking to this friendly young man. A situation, she thought with a small spurt of rebellion, which Joshua would not approve of. But how would he know if she didn't tell him? Besides, if anyone was in need of a friend right now, surely to goodness it was herself.

Chapter Seventeen

They ate and drank in companionable silence, at first not quite looking at each other, perhaps shy of saying the wrong thing and spoiling this unexpected meeting. And then both of them started to talk at once.

'I was looking for a church,' Polly began.

'I was looking for work,' he said at the same time, and they both burst out laughing.

'You first,' Polly said, beginning to relax for the first time in months.

Charlie grinned, lighting up his whole face and making his brown eyes sparkle. 'It wasn't important. You said you were looking for a church. Any one in particular? There's a cathedral back there.'

Polly smiled. 'I need a Catholic one. Are you Catholic?' She didn't know why she asked and instantly apologised. 'Listen to me, nosy old goat, 'tis no business of mine what you are.'

'I'm nowt,' Charlie told her, cheerfully enough. 'I've attended churches of just about every religion under the sun, in just about every country, while I was in the Navy. And I've discovered there's not a lot to choose between any of them. It's the same God after all.'

Polly smiled. 'Exactly my own way of thinking. But what about when you were a child?'

'Aye, well, that depended where I was living.' Then between sips of tea he proceeded to relate his life story; how his parents had both died of TB when he was quite small, and he'd been taken into Blackburn Orphanage. 'Great big place it is. Victorian. Rows of beds, big long tables, high ceilings. Grim but well intentioned, if you know what I mean. There were worse places I could've been sent. Sometimes we were all taken out for Sunday teas, picnics, or on day trips; loaned out like a library book to worthy, do-gooding "aunties".' He said this with such a twinkle in his eye that Polly almost laughed, but managed to stop herself in time. After all, it wasn't the least bit funny for a small boy to be handed about from pillar to post.

'Were they kind to you, these aunties?' she asked instead, feeling quite comfortable asking this perfect stranger personal questions.

'Oh, yes, only I was such a rebel at the time I'd be sure to blot me copybook in some way. Like once I put salt instead of sugar in the bowl of one lady's tea set. She wasn't best pleased.'

'I shouldn't think she was,' Polly was almost bursting with her efforts not to laugh.

'Another time I picked all the roses from the garden to give to one auntie but she was furious. How was I to know they wouldn't grow back again by the next day? I was only a lad. You'd think she'd have appreciated the thought at least, wouldn't you?'

Polly was hiccuping with laughter by this time, and Charlie grinned impishly at her. 'So there you are, they always got fed up and I'd be confined to barracks for a few weeks. Anyroad the orphanage did well by me. They made sure I had an education, then I went into the Merchant Navy and saw the world, as they say. Now I'm land-locked and looking for something different.' He set down his cup and cocked his head to one side, looking very like a quizzical sparrow. 'Now it's your turn.'

'Oh, you don't want to know about me,' she said.

'I wouldn't have asked if I didn't.' Charlie liked the look of this frail young woman, was itching to know everything about her, but something about her behaviour troubled him and he'd hoped his own openness would inspire her to be equally frank. He considered her more carefully. She'd had a hard time, he could tell by the pinched look about her face, the eyes red from recent weeping. And she was dressed all in black. Common though this was among the poor, he believed it to have a particular significance in her case. He leaned back in the wooden chair and set both his hands flat on the table with a deep sigh. 'It's hard when you lose someone. I remember when both me mam and dad died. I thought I'd never get over it, even though I was but a child. You never do, of course, in a way. Just get used to living with it. Who was it you lost, lass? Your husband?'

Polly nodded, and after taking a moment to compose herself, briefly told her tale, relieved that her eyes didn't instantly fill with tears as she spoke of Matthew's terrible accident. She had no wish to cry in front of this man. She didn't want to cry ever again. For the first time she felt a surge of pride in the way he had saved that boy. 'He died a hero, and for what he believed in.'

'There are worse ways to go.'

'Yes, I suppose there are.' She looked at him with gratitude, grateful for this new viewpoint. And in the moment when their eyes met, Polly experienced a great desire to start living again. It felt good to see someone smile at her, and to feel she'd made a new friend.

He walked her to the tram stop where she hastily handed him back his jacket as a tram drew in. Jostled by the crowd as the waiting queue piled aboard, they had a small argument over it, since he was still concerned about her catching cold, but Polly won. It was just as well, for it was then that Joshua found her.

'Are you lost, Polly?' he enquired in his soft, rasping voice, and her heart sank. She shook her head and struggled to explain her purpose, her tongue somehow seeming to stick to the roof of her mouth.

Joshua cast barely a glance in Charlie's direction, dismissing him as a nonentity. 'Just as well I was passing this way, as it's time you were home,' he said, grasping her arm. 'You know you shouldn't be out on your own. Not yet.'

'I'm all right. Let me be,' Polly protested, but his claw-like fingers dug deep and she could not free herself.

'Here, mister, what's your game?' Charlie stepped forward, taking a challenging stance as if ready to knock to the ground this man who dared take such liberties with his new friend.

'It's all right,' Polly hastily intervened. 'I'm coming, Joshua. It was only that Matthew would want me to...' She struggled to recall what it was her husband would want her to do, and where exactly she'd meant to go. Why had she been waiting for the tram? Who was this young man and why had she talked so freely to him? Had she thought he was Matthew? No, her lovely Matt was dead. But he would want her to go on living. She must explain. 'Joshua, I need...'

'Looking after, I know that. You *and* the children. You've no need to fret. I will decide what's best for you all. You're certainly not fit to take care of yourself at present. Now stop being foolish and come along home at once.' Tightening his grip on her arm, Joshua marched her along Ancoats Lane. Polly dared glance back only once, to see Charlie standing watching, his mouth agape. He's missed his train, she thought. Moments later they turned a corner and it was as if he'd never existed.

Joshua jerked her to a halt and glared furiously into her face. 'What were you thinking of, wandering off like that? Who was he, that man?'

'Nobody. I don't know. He was waiting for the tram too and we got talking.' Not for the world would she tell him about the tea and toasted teacake.

'You'll not do that ever again, do you hear? I won't have you talking to strange men. He'll think you're a whore!'

Polly actually laughed out loud at that, struggling to free her arm, though without success. 'Isn't that the daftest thing I ever heard? Why would he think such a thing when I was only being polite?'

'You're not even wearing your shawl or coat. You aren't at all yourself. If you were, you'd know well enough that it isn't proper for a woman to walk abroad half dressed.'

Polly subsided, ashamed. What he said was all too true and she was instantly filled with doubt and fresh confusion. Even the stranger had been concerned about her. Why hadn't she thought to take better care of herself? Once she'd been happily in control of her own life and family, now she couldn't even judge what was right and proper. She must be sick indeed.

Joshua led her firmly back to her own fireside, only to vent the rest of his wrath on his mother, for not keeping a proper eye on her.

'Nay, this isn't Strangeways,' Big Flo protested. 'And I'm not her jailer.'

But somehow the message registered deep inside Polly that it wasn't wise for her to wander about the city alone. Who knew what might become of her, without Matthew there to guide her? She'd been ill, hadn't she? Joshua was right, she really shouldn't go out on her own, not until she was fully well again. But for a moment, with that cheerful young man in the cafe – what was his name, Charlie Stockton – she'd felt almost like her old self. Just for a few moments she'd felt life stir in her again. Was that so wrong?

Surprisingly, for once, her mother-in-law was sympathetic as Polly sat shivering by the fire trying to make sense of it all. 'Our Matt hasn't gone forever, lass. He's only crossed over to the other side a bit soon. You'll see him again, mark my words. The good Lord will see to that.'

Polly looked at Flo with bleak agony in her eyes. 'I wish that could be tomorrow.'

'Nay, lass, don't even think such things. There's warm blood in thy veins. Give thanks for that.' And the old matriarch wrapped her chunky arms about the thin frame to hold Polly close while the tears flowed, and somehow Polly found comfort against the pillowing warmth of her mother-in-law's bosom.

–

Attending chapel three times every Sunday was a ritual about which Joshua was adamant, as cast in stone as if it were the eleventh commandment. Polly, like the rest of the family, had so far offered no significant protest, but the following Sunday morning, when he announced it was time to depart as usual, she astonished them all by refusing.

'No, I don't think so.' The set of her jaw revealed the old Polly, the one willing to stand her ground against him. But then she'd been managing to avoid taking quite so many sleeping powders for a few days now, pouring them away when Joshua wasn't looking.

He glowered down at her, eyes narrowed. 'I beg your pardon?'

'My children are Catholics, like me,' she said, the tone of her voice seeming to indicate that she was reminding herself of that fact, as well her brother-in-law. 'Not Methodist at all.'

He turned away as if she hadn't spoken. 'Put on your coat, Benny, and don't stand there dithering. It is ill mannered to be late for chapel.'

Polly stood in the middle of the kitchen floor, a pensive frown creasing her brow. She stared at her brother-in-law as if seeing him clearly for the first time. 'You know very well that I was brought up a Catholic, and for all my failings I've brought my children up to be the same.'

His mouth twisted in contempt. 'And why was that, I wonder? Because of the fine example your parents set, a worn-out ineffectual mother and a drunken father? I hardly think they were the best people to decide upon the well-being of your soul.' His sardonic tones made Polly want to curl up and die.

Joshua continued, relentless in his scorn. 'No wonder you were anxious to marry into our family. Even your mother failed you by taking the easy way out into death. At least at Zion Methodist you will not be allowed to follow in their footsteps. Hard liquor is not permitted, nor is morbid self-pity. It will improve the state of your health, as well as the good of your soul if you put on your coat and accompany us. And get a move on, we haven't all day!'

If there was one thing Polly hated above everything, it was to recall that part of her life, a time when she'd felt powerless against the incomprehensible brutality of the adult world. Even now the memory of her childhood served only to resurrect an appalling sense of inadequacy, and she shrank a little inside. Yet she continued to outface him for another half minute. But as he thrust Benny and Lucy ahead of him out into the street and she heard her daughter's protesting cry, saw Benny's frightened glance back at her, Polly's spine grew rigid as steel.

'You can take a horse to water...' she said, walking past him, head in the air, striving not to hear his stifled laughter.

As she sat on the hard polished seat of the pew, the memory of her drunken father and dead mother a terrible vision clogging her mind, Polly remained steadfastly silent throughout every hymn and prayer. A small show of rebellion, perhaps, but the best she could manage right then.

Seeing how Polly suffered, Lucy did her best to be equally obedient and not cause trouble, as her mother seemed to wish, but it was all most worrying. Lucy couldn't remember the last time she had been to mass. Then one day she saw Father Donevan in the street and he tackled her on that very point.

'And why have we not seen you in church recently, Lucille Pride?' he demanded. He always called her Lucille, which Lucy hated. It wasn't even her real name.

She stared unblinkingly up at him, wondering how to explain. *Honour thy father and thy mother*, the Bible stated, but it said nothing about uncles, so far as she was aware. Yet like Benny and his wariness of Georgie Eastwood, Lucy had learned to be equally circumspect and cautious in the way she dealt with Uncle Joshua. Her earlier show of defiance had become somewhat muted, largely because her mother had become completely cowed by the new regime. And for all Lucy's own hatred of him, which she didn't fully understand or feel comfortable with since he was family, after all, something inside her shrank from standing alone against Joshua. Perhaps the priest could be an ally and supply the support she needed.

'It's an answer I'm waiting for, Lucille. Will you be telling me or must I go and have words with your mother?'

Panic-stricken, the words tumbled over themselves in her urgency to prevent such an unspeakably awful development. 'No, no, you mustn't! Don't go on at Mam. She's enough on her plate right now. You'd have to ask Uncle Joshua, he's the one in charge.'

The priest nodded understandingly. 'Indeed to be sure, but 'tis you who are responsible for your own beliefs, Lucille.' Why wouldn't he understand? How could she explain the insidious power of her uncle and his dictates, seemingly so well meant and issued in such soft whispers, not least his endless little sermons, yet in reality taking no account of anyone else's feelings or opinions. 'He wouldn't even let my mother get on a tram,' she tried, thinking she could at least get some help for Polly, but Father Donevan only clicked his tongue in sympathy.

'Joshua is indeed most protective of her. I understand and applaud such care and consideration.'

Lucy wanted to protest that her mother didn't need protecting, not in that way. Her father's accident had happened over a year ago and she could sense her mother was striving to pull herself out of this terrible depression. But how to explain all of that to a stranger? How to secure the help her mother needed?

She became aware that the priest was still speaking. 'She has always been stubborn, has Polly, although indeed she suffered a terrible blow losing your father in that shocking way. But you could all gain great comfort from the church, if you would but try. Perhaps your uncle has not quite understood how necessary it is for you to attend mass regularly. You must explain.'

And as Lucy opened her mouth to ask if he wouldn't come and do that task for her, she felt a hand grip her arm. 'Ah, there you are, Lucy. Your mother and I were wondering what had happened to you.'

Something in the way he said 'your mother and I' chilled her, as if he was not only caring for Polly in her grief, but that in some way they formed an alliance against her, Polly's own daughter.

'I was only talking to Father Donevan,' she protested.

Joshua offered the priest what might pass for a smile. 'Not saying anything untoward, I hope? I trust you explained what good care I'm taking of you all.'

The old priest found himself nodding. 'She was indeed. I was wondering if perhaps we might see a bit more of her at St.——'

'Dear me, is that the time? You must forgive us but Polly is not herself at the moment, as you will appreciate, and gets into quite a panic when Lucy is late. We must talk some other time. Good day to you.' And Joshua strode briskly away, his hand still firmly clasped about Lucy's wrist.

The old priest watched them go with troubled eyes. He recalled many fierce arguments in the past with Polly Pride during her rebellious years when she'd married outside the Faith, but she'd never refused its blessings for her children. It surprised him that she did so now.

Father Donevan had not been blind to the veiled implication that he was interfering in matters which did not concern him. Nothing in Joshua Pride's words had been in any way rude or disrespectful, yet he'd felt a disdain there, a sardonic disregard for the true Church, and for the child in his care. But then, Joshua was a Methodist and outside Father Donevan's jurisdiction, so perhaps the man had a right to object. It would be a pity to lose two fine young people like Lucy and Benny, but perhaps this wasn't the moment to interfere in family matters. The children were clearly being well fed and taken care of, which was achievement enough in these difficult times.

Having salved his conscience and convinced himself he should do nothing to interfere at present, the old priest turned his attention to what his housekeeper might be producing for his supper and went on his way.

Back in number twenty-three Joshua gave Lucy a stern lecture about not gossiping to strangers about family business.

'But Father Donevan isn't a stranger. He's my priest!'

'He *was* your priest. But since you have developed such a taste for religion, we can put it to good effect.'

Lucy faced him with an expression of outraged defiance on a young face so like Polly's in that moment, that Joshua's temper increased tenfold. He slammed the Bible down on the table before her. 'You can learn the entire Book of Samuel. That should teach you not to tittle-tattle.'

Lucy bridled, blue eyes flashing with matching anger. 'If it's a penance you want from me, then I'll do my own, thanks very much. "Hail Mary, Mother of God, pray for us sinners, now and at the hour of our death." There,' she said, on a high note of defiance, 'that's a penance!' Whereupon she stuck out her tongue in a childish show of temper and stormed from the room.

–

That night, as Lucy lay beside her mother in the big brass bed, she told her what had occurred, unable to disguise a very real sense of exhilaration. Polly listened carefully then cradled her daughter close, worrying over how this had all come about, even as she worried over how she could put things right. Although she might chide Lucy for lack of respect to her elders, for disobedience and not showing suitable gratitude to the uncle who had fed and clothed them, inside she was tormented by a growing anger. How dare he treat her precious child in such a way, simply for wanting to worship in the way she believed? Who in God's name did he think he was, lording it over the lot of them?

Lucy echoed her own thoughts, whispering fiercely into her ear, 'Mam, can't you see what he's doing to us, to you in partic- ular? He's punishing you, determined to control every step we take, and make our lives a complete misery. You've got to stop taking any more of those powders. You have to get better.'

Polly knew that she was right. 'Sleep, m'cushla. It'll be fine, I promise you. He'll not hurt you while I have breath in me body. And won't I tell him so first thing?'

The following morning Polly left Lucy getting dressed while she went downstairs to confront him, fists clenched into her narrow waist, mouth pursed upon the tightness of her anger.

Inside she could feel her heart beating twenty to the dozen, yet this time she'd not stand down. Wouldn't she fight for her children to the death?

'It's to the Catholic Church we go next Sunday, like it or not, Joshua Pride. D'you hear me now?'

He cast her a glance of scathing contempt. 'I hear you, Polly Pride.'

'You can tell us what to eat, when to get up, go out, come in, even when to wash our daft faces, but you'll not tell us how to pray to our God. D'you mind what I'm saying to you?'

Without a word, he simply smiled. Then, walking past her up the few wooden stairs, turned the big rusty key in the bedroom door, leaving Lucy firmly locked inside.

Shaking with shock and fury in her own kitchen, Polly railed at her brother-in-law while upstairs she heard her daughter's scream. 'Mam, Mam! The door's stuck. I'm locked in. Someone help me. Please, Mum!' But even as she called, her throat drying with fear, Lucy knew that despite the brave show of defiance, her mother could do nothing. Uncle Joshua was still very much in control, and there was no one in this house strong enough to stand against him.

Chapter Eighteen

It was one day at the end of May that Charlie came to the house. Disturbed by Joshua's handling of Polly at the tram stop, he'd quietly followed them home, watching from street corners as she was marched along, itching to intervene but instinct telling him it would only make matters worse for her. He hated the way the man had forced her almost to run to keep up with him. Charlie didn't like that. In his world men showed respect and consideration to women, not treated them like chattels.

Besides this very real concern, she'd looked so lovely, so fragile with her heart-shaped face and big greeny-grey eyes, that he hadn't been able to get her out of his mind ever since. It was daft of him, he knew, they'd only just met and spent no more than a few minutes together, but in truth he'd fallen for her badly. He was glad of any excuse to look her up again.

Charlie had never been short of women in his life, but nor had he ever wanted any of them to stick around. This one, he felt, would be different. What he couldn't quite decide was how to go about it. He'd stood on street corners and watched the front door of the small terraced house for weeks on end when really he should've been looking for work. All in the hope he might spot her when she came out to do a bit of shopping. But not once, in all this time, had she ever emerged, and his worry increased by the day.

Was she ill? Had she left the area? Neither thought brought him comfort so, in the end, without a plan of any kind in his head, he strode across the road with his sailor's rolling gait, and knocked on the door.

He prayed she would answer. Or perhaps a child. He assumed she would have children. A child answering the door would be perfect. He was good with children. It was opened by a large woman, with fists the size of hams.

'Well?' she demanded, in a voice which said she was ready to deal with all time-wasters in a flash, or with one flick of her brawny arms. Charlie swallowed, wishing desperately he'd learned the young woman's surname, then he could ask more politely. But he hadn't.

'Is Polly in?' he ventured, feeling very much like a school boy asking a favour of a sweetheart's mother. But then she wasn't his sweetheart, was she? Not yet, anyway.

'And who might you be?'

'A friend.'

Big Flo considered this. She'd heard of no friend, certainly not a young Jack-me-laddo like this one. 'I suppose you have a name?'

'Charlie Stockton, ma'am.' He stood to attention, very nearly saluted. If he'd been in uniform he probably would have done. The old woman's tone reminded him very much of his commanding officer. 'I'd just like a quick word.' To ask her to spend the rest of her life with me, a voice in his head murmured. Charlie struggled to ignore it 'If she has a minute to spare.'

'I'll ask,' the old woman said. 'But keep them mucky boots off my clean doorstep.' And Charlie found the door slammed shut in his face.

Big Flo marched back through the parlour, where Joshua was painstakingly making notes for his next speech, and into the kitchen. Polly was standing at the sink, peeling potatoes. 'There's a young chap at the door, wants a word. Says he's a friend o' yours.'

Polly turned, a frown knitting her brow. 'What's his name?'

'Charlie Stockton, he says.'

Joshua, who had come to stand in the doorway to listen to this conversation asked, 'And who might he be, Polly?' The expression on his face was glacial, making her shiver.

Polly realised instantly who it was, though it must be several weeks since their meeting at the tram stop. How had he known where she lived? If Joshua had forgotten meeting the young seaman, she certainly had no intention of reminding him. Seeing her own daughter locked in her room for the better part of a long day had distressed her greatly, even though Polly herself had castigated Lucy for disrespect to her elders. Joshua's behaviour was deeply troubling, as if there were more to it than simple bad temper on his part, like some sort of vengeance he was inflicting upon them both.

'I think he's one of the hawkers from Oldham Street,' she said, pulling the idea out of the air, quite certain Joshua would recognise it for the lie it was. But he only stared at her through narrowed eyes as her heart started to race at her own recklessness. 'I expect he's come to ask how I am.' She started to wipe her hands on a cloth but Joshua held up one hand to stop her.

'I'll see to him. I won't have you troubled by riff-raff.'

'Oh, but he's not. It's no trouble, I...'

'I said I'll see to him, Polly.' His tone was so authoritative, so tinged with suppressed hostility, that she could do nothing but bite her lip and keep silent, praying Charlie wouldn't start any trouble.

In the event, Joshua opened the door on to an empty street, returning to announce with some satisfaction that her so-called friend had not even troubled to wait. Dipping her head so he did not see the disappointment in her face, Polly went back to peeling vegetables.

Charlie, alarmed by the length of time it was taking the old woman to relay his message, had withdrawn to the corner of the next ginnel. From here he could see the front door of number twenty-three without being seen himself. When he saw the man step out, he recognised him instantly as the one who had marched Polly off that day. He sighed with relief at his own foresight. But there was something about this set-up that he didn't like one bit, and Charlie made a decision, there and then, to keep a close watch on the comings and goings at number twenty-three.

Later that same evening Joshua addressed Polly in the tone of voice he might use on a half-wit child. 'Isn't it time you went to bed?'

She lifted her head and met his gaze with calm defiance. For all his efforts to make the Irish woman's life not worth living, he saw in that look that she was in no way defeated. But she said not one word. It was in fact Big Flo who answered.

'Aye, it will be soon enough, but I've to fill this bath first. It's Friday remember, bath night. You'll be off out as usual, I suppose?'

Joshua felt a niggling irritation that he'd somehow been put in the wrong as he sat and watched the two women struggling to carry the large zinc bath tub from the back yard and start to fill it with hot water from the two kettles on the hob.

He hadn't believed her lie about Charlie Stockton being a hawker. Did she take him for a fool? What he needed was to find some way to cure that wandering spirit of hers. Maybe he knew the very thing.

A further pan of hot water stood waiting. Towels had been warmed, and a drop of Dettol was ready to put in the bath water, together with a bar of soap and a pumice stone. Cleanliness being next to Godliness, in his mother's view, this was the normal ritual of a Friday evening. 'I'm off out,' he said, reaching for his bowler hat.

Thinking he had gone Polly began to unbutton her blouse but, pausing in his stride, Joshua took a step back into the kitchen to cast one last lingering glance over her; smiling sardonically as her fingers froze and he caught sight of a glistening strip of bare flesh between her breasts. His eyes said clearly that she was a fine figure of a woman, no doubt about it, and that he could curb her defiance whenever he chose.

In that moment Polly felt no hint of the laughter she had once shared with Matthew at the thought of his brother with a woman. Instead, a shiver rippled down the length of her spine, leaving her chilled and more disturbed than she cared to acknowledge.

When he had finally gone, she took the quickest bath ever, acutely aware of her nakedness in the cold draughts of her own kitchen. As she hurried through the weekly ritual, she kept half an ear tuned to the sound of the front door. As if sensing her unease but misjudging the reason, Big Flo touched her gently on the shoulder and offered to wash her hair.

'You need to come to, lass. This jumping at shadows can't go on. Our Matt's gone, bless him, and all you can do is look forward to the day you meet him again. Till then, you have the childer to think of. And yourself.'

As Big Flo washed and dried her hair, Polly knew that the old woman was right. Day after day Joshua had continued to devise ways of humiliating her. He'd kept her half senseless with the sleeping powders, constantly criticised her and undermined her confidence. Whether she was scrubbing a step or peeling vegetables, he loved to find fault and point out how useless and inadequate she was. If all else failed, he would taunt her over her parents and the bleakness of her childhood. He even used his power over her daughter to hold her in check.

Polly felt as if she was pitched in a daily battle against him, yet couldn't for the life of her work out why, or what the reason for the war could possibly be.

She wished that Charlie had waited, or at least that she could find some way to see him. Remembering how lively and kind he had been, she ached for his friendship, for the chance to talk to him again. Secretly, deep inside, it had felt good to be reminded that she was a woman, young and perhaps even still attractive. Of course she wasn't for a moment contemplating anything improper between them, but for those few moments in his company she'd felt alive again.

She suddenly longed to tell all of this to Eileen, who she hadn't seen in ages despite her friend living next door. Polly couldn't remember the last time she'd talked to a woman of her own age, one who could understand how she felt. Polly knew she was done with grieving, must resolutely set aside that sense of emptiness left after Matthew's death. She longed to be in charge of her own life again, as she'd once been. But somehow this final step still eluded her.

Finding a job so that she could be independent of Joshua was becoming her chief concern. At first she hadn't cared about the loss of her business. Now Polly began to wonder if she'd thrown away her only life-line. She had no money, except for a few coins she'd kept tucked under the floorboards. The rest had been used to help feed them over the last year. She didn't even have any furniture of her own to sell to raise fresh capital. It all belonged to Big Flo and Joshua. She was trapped in a state of dependence and destitution.

As these thoughts raced through her head, Polly only half listened to Big Flo's homely wisdom. And the memory of Joshua's burning eyes haunted her all through that endless night.

-

The next afternoon, it being a Saturday, Terence was off down to the dogs. Eileen had finished her chores early for once and was feeling in need of a bit of company. She'd tried on numerous occasions to see Polly, but to no avail for some weeks now. Today she meant to succeed.

Gathering up her squabbling children and dragging Beryl away from nibbling coal from the scuttle, she set out with brood in tow, one of the twins draped about her neck as usual – and bumped slap-bang into a man in a blue reefer jacket. He was half bent down and she ran into him full tilt, knocking her nose against his shoulder in the process.

'Dear Lord, where did you come from?' she yelled, putting a hand to her nose to see if it was bleeding. Her eyes filled with tears of pain and she could see nothing but a blur. Meryl, still clinging fast round her neck, had acted like a cushion and simply bounced off him. Even so she began to yell and the man was all concern, insisting he check that the children were unharmed.

'It was my fault,' he admitted. 'I was bending to tie up me laces. I never saw you coming.' Charlie had in fact been trying to peep around the half-open door of number twenty-three, to see if the man was working in the front parlour, as he so often was. But he could see only the green curtain that shielded the vestibule from the rest of the house, no sign of anyone. Despite hours of careful watching he still hadn't clapped eyes on Polly. He was becoming seriously worried.

'D'you know next door?' he asked, as he helped Eileen back on her feet and dusted down a green frock that had seen better days. She knocked away his hand as if they scalded her.

'Now why would I?' she commented with biting irony.

'I mean, the girl – the woman – what lives there. Polly? I forget her last name.'

Eileen gave him a suspicious look through narrowed eyes. 'What would you be wanting with Polly? How come you know her, anyroad? She's never mentioned you.'

'We met on a tram. Well, not quite *on* a tram, *waiting* for a tram. She'd no coat and I lent her mine. I didn't want her to catch cold, see. But she didn't even catch the tram.'

Eileen, struggling to make sense of this garbled tale, decided he was three-ha'pence short of a shilling, abandoned the effort and turned to go.

He followed her. 'Tell her I'm here, will you? Tell her I'm still waiting.' And there was in his open friendly face such sincerity, such intensity in his soft brown gaze that Eileen found herself nodding. She was filled suddenly with curiosity about this pleasant young chap, who seemed harmless enough for all he was clearly daft as a brush.

'Happen I will. If I get chance. Why don't you come to mine for a cup of tea and tell me what it is you want me to say to her?'

—

Joshua had chosen this as the day to make his move because Big Flo was once again minding Betty Sidebottom while her sister Nellie was out at work. Putting on his jacket and hat, he informed Polly that he had business to attend to. 'You'll be perfectly safe here alone, although it's a pity you don't get out more,' he told her, in his most amiable voice. 'Why not refrain from taking a powder today? You might feel well enough to visit the market or take a walk to Oldham Street and meet up with your old cronies. Like that hawker friend of yours. What was his name? Charlie something or other?'

Joshua waited for her to supply the name. When she remained silent, he doffed his hat and left, smiling to himself for he knew she would be unable to resist the temptation.

Polly couldn't remember the last time she had been to the market, nor Oldham Street. How she missed all the lively rivalry and camaraderie of the other hawkers. But why would Joshua suddenly be happy for her to go out when he'd always been entirely against it? She was still staring at the closed front door, puzzling over this as Eileen came in by the back.

Disentangling herself from her children, she hugged Polly as if they'd been parted for a lifetime, which was exactly how it felt. 'I saw the bugger leave. Thank God they're all out for once, and I've got you to myself at last.'

The shadows in Polly's eyes seemed to clear as she smiled at her old friend. 'Oh, Eileen, I'm so glad you're here. I don't see enough of you these days. Of anyone in fact. You wouldn't believe how I've missed you.'

The younger woman flushed with pleasure. 'Same here. And I'm dying to hear all your news.'

Eileen plonked herself down on the horse-hair sofa. Provided by Big Flo, it was almost a replica of the one Polly had sold to finance her carpet business. Sitting on its prickly surface brought to mind the long hours the pair of them had spent sewing, and the desperate efforts she was still making to hold on to Polly's business while knowing it could easily slip through her fingers. It was hard, what with the children always under her feet, and Terence as much use as a wet lettuce. But she was making a profit, just about, if not as much as Polly would have done, simply because she didn't have her knack for spotting a bargain. It was such a shame!

Even so, Eileen didn't want to bother her with these problems, not just yet. She could manage for a while longer. First, Polly must be encouraged to get properly back on her feet, and to cheer up. How to do that? Then she remembered the eager young suitor she'd just met. Happen he was exactly what the doctor ordered.

'Who's this chap who keeps hanging about? I've just cannoned into him and gave him a cuppa. He told me how you two met. Not exactly the stuff of Elinor Glyn, but it had my insides turning to mush.'

Polly felt her cheeks start to burn, not knowing whether to be thrilled or fearful that Charlie had been round again. 'Ach, I've only met him the once, but when we talked it was as if we were old friends. I liked him.'

But for all Joshua's remarks before he'd left, Polly guessed he'd have a fit if she started seeing a man. 'Not that Joshua must find out, you understand? He'd think the worst, wouldn't he just?'

'My lips are sealed,' Eileen said, making some ribald remark about what she could do with such a grand-looking chap so that both women were soon giggling just like they used to. When they'd both calmed down, Polly tried to explain.

'It's just that every time I go out, doesn't himself bring me home again? He means well but he's too – protective – I suppose.'

'Possessive, more like. Nay, love, you can't go on like this. You have to break free.'

'Aw, indeed, I'm doing me best to get going again, really I am, Eileen. The trouble is, I owe Joshua so much. The care he took of the children and...'

'You owe him nowt. Get out there, girl, and live.' The sound of Eileen's cheerfully irreverent tones brought Polly to fits of laughter again. She hadn't felt so cheerful since that day at the tram stop and her meeting with Charlie Stockton.

'He doesn't think I'm well enough.'

'Bugger that for a lark! Here, I've an idea. Give us that shawl.' And grabbing Polly's brown shawl from the back of the chair, Eileen pulled it over her own head, 'Now, have you a spare skirt?

He'd know me a mile off in this green frock, but in one of your skirts, he'd think I was you. Then he could follow me to Kingdom come, and you could go off and enjoy yourself for a change. You could find this chap o' yours and fix yourself up, why don't you?' Soon they were laughing and giggling again, like young girls planning a secret assignation.

Eileen's change of clothes took no more than a moment, then while Polly slipped quietly out of the back door, smartly dressed in her best coat and hat, her friend walked out of the front, bold as brass, but with the shawl closely tucked close about her head. After a moment, a figure slipped out of the shadows and followed her.

–

It was chilling to think that Joshua had shown such an interest in Charlie. There was something in his manner these days which set all Polly's nerves jangling. He'd only tried to help her through the worst of her grieving, but still his attitude bothered her. It was as if he resented any sign of her recovery. Yet life must go on. There were still times when Matthew's death seemed like only yesterday, at others, like today, it felt more like half a lifetime.

As she searched for Charlie, a strange bud of excitement began to unfurl deep inside, and Polly wondered at herself. What was she doing seeking out a man she'd met only once? Even if she found him, she must make it clear they were but friends, and he must never come to the house again. She wasn't sure quite why, but it felt vitally important that Joshua must never discover him.

Ancoats Lane was thronged with people and heavy with traffic as she walked along feeling oddly shaky and uncertain, legs trembling slightly. But Polly was determined not to give in to a panic attack today, not after Eileen's generous offer to change places. And didn't she feel more herself again? At last she turned the corner at New Cross and reached Oldham Street. She meant to walk the length of that too, chatting with old friends. Perhaps this would help build her confidence and make her want to be back amongst them. After that she'd go on down to Piccadilly and perhaps London Road Station. She'd no idea where Charlie might be. All she could do was look and ask around. Even if she didn't find him, the walk would do her good.

She loved the breeze in her hair, the beguiling scents of the fruit and vegetable market, the appetising aroma of a hot chestnut stall which recalled that long ago Christmas. They'd managed to make happiness out of nothing in those days. She must learn to do so again. Wasn't she too young to give upon life? Even the hum of traffic thrilled her, and people going about their daily affairs in the city centre. It felt good to be out and about again, Polly decided. Time indeed to start living again.

Chapter Nineteen

She found Charlie, surprisingly enough, manning a hand cart not far from where her own used to be. Only his was much bigger, pulled by a pony, and he was doing a roaring trade in fruit and vegetables. She stood and watched him for a while, since he was too occupied with customers to talk, looking every bit as cheerful as she remembered. He was weighing rosy apples and teasing a customer.

'Now then, no complaints. Only four apples make a pound. We don't use wooden weights here.'

'Nay, the only wood is in thy head,' said the greedy customer, 'His hair had grown and was curling wildly but he was still wearing his reefer jacket, navy blue serge trousers tied just below the knee, and boots, not clogs, on his feet. They were highly polished, Polly noticed, for all the soles were caked with straw. She watched his rolling gait as he moved about the stall serving people, remembering his talk of years in the Merchant Navy. It came to her then that for all he'd told her quite a lot about himself in their first brief meeting, Polly wanted, *needed,* to know so much more.'

'Hello!' she said at last, when finally he stopped to draw breath. His delight at seeing her seemed so entirely genuine she was sure it couldn't be just her imagination.

'Polly!' He took a step towards her then paused, uncertain, wiping his hands on the backs of his trousers. 'Are you all right? I mean, are you feeling better?'

She nodded, finding herself smiling at his eagerness. 'A little. And you?'

'I've been sick too.'

She was at once all concern. 'Why, what's been the matter?'

'Heartsick,' he said, throwing caution to the winds. 'I thought you didn't ever want to set eyes on me again. I've stood outside your house waiting for a glimpse of you for weeks.'

Polly gazed at him, wide-eyed with astonishment and concern as she watched a tide of crimson flow up his neck and into his cheeks. She sensed her own face was as red. 'You never did?'

'I did too. I just needed to see you were all right. I couldn't stop worrying about you.'

'I heard you came once, but not that you'd haunted the place.' She gazed at him in disbelief, lips pursed, and finally burst into laughter. 'You're telling me porkies! I don't believe a word of it.' Her own happiness startled her, making her feel suddenly guilty for standing here laughing with this man who was little more than a stranger.

'It's true.' He looked hurt by her doubts, and she longed to reassure him but the words simply wouldn't come. His hand upon her arm was making her feel quite odd and panicky again, a sensation like cramp gripping her stomach. What was the matter with her?

Even as Charlie frantically sought a way to press his case and keep her with him, a woman approached the barrow, bristling as she poked him in the ribs with her basket.

'Are you serving or what, you? I can allus take me custom elsewhere, young man.'

'Aye, I'm serving. Hold your horses, love, till I settle me future with this lovely lady, then I'm all yours,' Charlie said. The moment he'd released Polly to speak to the customer, she'd begun to edge away.

'Get away with you.' The woman was laughing despite herself.

'Don't go yet. Please, Polly. It's not my stall. I'm only minding it for a mate for an hour or two. And we need to talk.'

The woman, who had been taking great interest in their conversation, said, 'For pity's sake, lass, say you'll wait, then I can get some taties and a large cabbage for us tea.'

A man carrying a heavy sack jostled Polly, leaving in his wake an overpowering aroma of oranges. For a moment it felt good to be in the market again, as if she were back amongst her own people. Then she caught a glimpse of a shadowy figure hovering in a doorway and felt certain it must be Joshua. Sweat sprang to the palms of her hands, and her vision blurred as if seeing the scene through tinted glasses. Was he following her? If so, why? Charlie was still desperately trying to rid himself of the talkative customer while Polly felt hemmed in, trapped, almost claustrophobic, and filled with an unreasoning fear.

Why had she come? What was the urgent message she'd needed to give him? Oh, yes, of course. 'If it's true, about you hanging around Dove Street,' she said, backing away, 'you've got to stop it, d'you hear? That's what I came to tell you. Don't come again. Joshua doesn't like it. Now I have to go.'

Polly turned, pushing her way through the crowds with a desperation that swiftly robbed her of breath and brought a pain to her breast, clogs slipping on soggy cabbage leaves and debris scattered underfoot. She could hear Charlie's voice calling to her, making her run all the faster. Then he had hold of her arms and was asking – no, insisting – that she meet him the next day, in the little market cafe.

A voice in her head told her she could not go, but somehow she had to make him release her since Joshua might walk by at any minute, as he had done once before at the tram stop. He would be even angrier at seeing her with Charlie this time than he had been back then. With Lucy and Benny, as well as herself. She couldn't risk him venting his anger upon her children, or Lucy again being locked in her room for hours on end for no real reason.

She found herself agreeing to Charlie's demands, saying anything to make him release her, so that he'd go back to serving his neglected customers and she could escape. He squeezed her hands one last time before letting her slip away into the crowds.

Polly did not stop running until she'd reached her own front door, flung herself inside and slammed it safely shut behind her. Gasping for breath and clutching a painful stitch in her side, she recalled the desperate agony in Charlie's face as she had run from him. Whatever had possessed her to seek him out? What would Matthew think of her, almost throwing herself at another man when she was still grieving for him? But she couldn't grieve forever, and'd only been offered a chance of friendship, what was so wrong with that? Now she had lost that chance. Upon these confused thoughts, she burst into tears.

–

Dusk was starting to fall by the time Eileen turned back into the entry to head for home. She'd walked about longer than she'd meant to, and Terence would moan at having been left with the children. But she'd a nice bit of pork together with some crackling for his dinner, so that should sweeten his temper.

She heard the scrape of a clog iron on stone, but took no notice. And then the unmistakable sound of a man's breath close to her ear. Eileen jumped as if stung, but even as she half turned to see who it was, she found her face enveloped in an all-pervading darkness. She opened her mouth to scream but it was filled instantly with the soft wool of a shawl, a stifling hand pressed tight against it, making it almost impossible for her to breathe, let alone cry out.

Fear was shooting through her as strong arms dragged her to the ground and she felt the hard ridges of stone cobbles beneath her back. Even when the hand lifted from her mouth it was only to tie the shawl in harsh efficient knots about her neck so that she could do no more than sob, too afraid to call out for fear he might throttle her. Hadn't she read enough gruesome tales on the billboards advertising the Illustrated Police Gazette? She could guess only too well what was about to happen, knew she had to stay calm if she was not to inflame the man's anger still further.

Shrouded by the cloying closeness of the shawl, the claustro-phobic darkness stifling her, Eileen felt herself gagging for breath, certain she must die of suffocation any minute. She struggled to form sounds in her throat but it had gone too dry. Even so, screams sounded inside her own head when the weight of him came down hard upon her, robbing her of the last of her breath.

He pinned her to the ground with one hand pressed against her throat while with the other he pushed up her skirt to explore the nakedness of her stomach and buttocks, and private parts. She could do nothing save pray for someone to walk into the entry and rescue her.

No such salvation came.

He took her with a terrifying swiftness, scarcely uttering a sound beyond carefully suppressed grunts in the rigours of his climax. It was shocking, excruciatingly painful, but blessedly quick. For an instant her body had been filled with a tearing pain, her nostrils with a cloying, unpleasant odour she couldn't quite identify. And then he was done with her. She heard him get up, heard a sharp intake of breath and a stifled oath, as if at last he realised what he had done and was expressing regret. But Eileen could only lie where he had thrust her, broken and degraded.

–

She lay shivering on the freezing stone setts for what seemed like hours but was probably no more than ten minutes before finally convinced that he had gone, and it was safe to move.

Eileen got stiffly to her feet and clung to a back yard wall, shaking uncontrollably in every limb. It took several long minutes to untie the knots about her neck with numbed fingers, and to drag the shawl from her head, by which time her sobs were almost hysterical.

She could feel a wetness trickle down her bare leg, and the smell of him clung to her, a violation in itself. She felt the bile rise in her throat and vomited into the gutter, emptying her stomach, leaving her cold and clammy with sweat.

She knew what must be done. She dare not go home. Terence would smell him upon her and think she was back on the game. Turning on her heel, she headed back the way she had come.

At the University Settlement she paid for a bath all to herself. Stripping off the borrowed clothes, Eileen took the carbolic soap and scrubbed herself, inside and out, in a desperate attempt to eradicate all traces of him. It was only when she had carefully dried herself, disposed of the dirty water and stumbled home like an old woman that she felt the tremors slowly subside.

She washed herself again that evening, then sat by the dead remains of her fire, sipping a mug of scalding sweet tea. With the children in bed and Terence seated opposite, she struggled to keep a smile on her face as she listened to him chattering on about his win on the dogs that afternoon. But her mind wasn't on a word he said.

Little by little the shock began to subside, and she began to count her blessings. He could have done much worse to her, she supposed. Whoever it was hadn't hit or injured her, nor strangled her with the shawl, though for one frightening moment she had thought that was to be her fate. At least she'd survived.

But who could it have been? And why had he covered her head? Because of his deep anger? She'd felt it simmering in him, in his terrible silence and the harsh way he'd thrust himself into her, like raining blows upon her body.

Or had he been afraid she might recognise him? The most likely candidate was one of her old clients. Did any of them hate her that much, or miss her enough to take it without paying? Eileen let the long-forgotten faces slip through her memory.

The trembling started again at this thought, and beneath her skirt she felt sore and wounded, a warm trickle of blood starting. She wanted only to go somewhere private to nurse her pain in peace.

And then she remembered that she hadn't looked like herself at all today. She'd deliberately set out to disguise herself as Polly. In which case, that was who he'd thought he was attacking – Polly. She remembered then the sharply indrawn breath, not from guilt at all but from realisation that he'd attacked the wrong woman.

Dear God, if that were the case, and she could find no other convincing reason, then Polly must be the one in danger. And from who else but that young Jack-me-laddo in the reefer jacket? She must be warned, and at the first opportunity, for he could strike again.

–

Joshua was irritated rather than angry at the mistake he'd made. The fact that he had inflicted punishment upon an innocent victim didn't trouble him in the slightest. The woman next door was of no account, so what did it signify? She'd no doubt suffered far worse in her former line of business. As for Polly, he was annoyed that she'd given him the slip. Where had she gone? And with whom? And why had that worthless chit been wearing her shawl?

Thought she was a clever minx, did she? He smiled to himself. The Irish woman would have to get up early to beat him. There would be other times, other opportunities. He was willing to wait on events. For the moment, her stubborn defiance was proving to be most entertaining, a real battle of wits. But he'd break her yet, see if he didn't. He would win this little contest and nothing she could do would stop him.

–

Eileen became almost addicted to washing. Never had she used so much soap and water in all her life, yet failed utterly to feel clean. It took a great deal of resolve, but the moment she felt the soreness begin to subside, she took the precaution of allowing Terence a taste of long-deprived favours, by way of insurance. They'd always joked that he only had to throw his cap on the bed and she was off. This man, whoever he was, had done much more than toss his cap at her.

She lived in fear through the hot sticky days of an Indian summer that he'd laid more trouble at her door than she could deal with, and when her monthly curse, as she called it, did not arrive on time, the fear intensified with each passing day. By the time the second period had failed to materialise, Eileen admitted the worst.

It was this which finally made up her mind. She'd tried and failed to see Polly on numerous occasions, and dreaded what she had to tell her, for she knew her friend harboured a soft spot for the young merchant seaman. Gathering up her children, Eileen went next door.

Fortunately, for once, Polly was alone. She sat, as so often these days, staring blankly into the empty grate. Eileen would have liked to pick her up and shake her. Instead, the minute she'd prised herself free of clinging children and sent them off in search of adventure under the stairs, she took hold of Polly's hand and stroked it.

'I have to talk to you, lass.'

She got no further as the front door banged open where both women saw Benny, face ashen, wriggling like a trapped eel as his earlobe was held in a pincer grip by Joshua. The man looked so huge and powerful in that moment, his presence seeming to fill the suffocatingly small room, just as it dominated Polly's life.

'Do you know where I found this rascal? Trying to sneak under the fence into the ground at Manchester North End on Charles Street and watch the match without paying. Which, in my book, is thieving.'

Polly offered an apologetic smile on her son's behalf. She knew that what Joshua said must be right, yet he really didn't need to hold Benny's ear quite so fiercely, or be quite so harsh in his treatment of him. Wasn't he just a lad? What boy hadn't tried to sneak into a football match without paying? She reached out her hand, 'I'll talk to him, Joshua, get him to understand about right and wrong.'

'He should understand already, a lad of his age.'

Benny gave a great hiccup. 'They were playing Glossop. Everyone else were doing it.'

'And if everyone else walked under a train, would you do that as well?' Joshua asked, and shook him even more fiercely, making Benny's teeth rattle.

Polly looked into her son's pleading gaze and felt the familiar stirring of anger. 'It's not uncommon, Joshua,' she pointed out, battening it down as she fought for calm. 'It is Saturday, the new season must have started and he does love football.'

'If you'd waited till three-quarter time, Benny, you could have gone in for nothing, when they opened the big gates.' Eileen put in.

Toes barely reaching the ground, he was whimpering with pain while manfully refusing to cry. 'But then we'd 'ave missed all the goals.' A reasonable argument which caused a chuckle to escape from Polly's lips at last. Joshua forestalled any further excuses she might have been about to make for her son by switching his attack to Eileen.

'When we want your opinion, Mrs Grimshaw, we'll ask for it.' His voice was so loud in the small room that Agnes and Rosie ran to their mother in alarm, Meryl stamped her bare fret on the rug and started to scream, and Beryl, who'd been happily tearing up newspapers in the glory hole under the stairs, chose this moment to emerge and investigate the noise. Her mouth, still stuffed with newsprint, opened in a loud wail of sympathy with her twin.

In two swift strides Joshua had reached the child, picked her up and deposited her in her mother's lap. 'Take your caterwauling brats home before I...' His face was so close to hers she could actually smell him; an indefinable masculine odour, overlaid with a lingering scent of mothballs.

'Before you what?'

It was as he dumped Meryl equally unceremoniously into her arms, one hand became inadvertently trapped between the screaming child's clinging arms and her mother's neck, that the realisation came to her.

That touch, coupled with the smell, lifted the fine hairs at the back of her neck. And from instinct born of long experience, in that moment Eileen's heart seemed to stop, for she realised that she'd been wrong in her previous assumption. She'd done young Charlie Stockton a grave injustice. It hadn't been him at all who'd done for her on that terrible night, but Polly's canting, hypocritical brother-in-law. The very same man who was still holding her friend in thrall.

'I'm going nowhere,' Eileen said, holding her twins like a shield to her breast.

Joshua didn't even deign to reply. He grasped a bunch of her orange hair and dragged her, squealing, to the door. Seconds later she was on the other side of it, and all Eileen could hear then was the sound of Polly's sobbing.

Afterwards, she told herself she'd gladly have broken the door down and gone back inside had she not been encumbered with screaming children. Yet it was with a certain guilty relief that Eileen scurried back to the safety of her own house, slammed shut the door, and for once even welcomed Terence home with more enthusiasm than usual.

–

Benny stood, stiff-backed, in the front parlour, or what Joshua preferred to call his study, by seven sharp the next morning. He'd wisely judged that the sooner he presented himself the better. And there was always the chance he'd be given breakfast after he'd taken the beating he fully expected to get. That's if he could manage to eat anything, with his stomach so knotted with fear. The last thing he'd eaten was a potted meat sandwich at dinner time yesterday. No supper had been forthcoming, and not even Grandma Flo had managed to smuggle him a biscuit.

He'd already seen his sister suffer the penance of learning endless scriptures, and being locked in her room for a day. Now, feeling he was about to go to the scaffold at the very least, Benny prepared for his own execution.

He looked into his Uncle Joshua's cold eyes and thought Lucy's description of him as a lizard even more accurate than usual. He looked as if he might flick out a long tongue and gobble Benny up at any minute. His uncle made him think of the terrible things that happened in the Saturday morning serial at the pictures, when crocodiles would come out of the swamp to eat Tarzan. Or spikes would appear through the floor of a cage in which he was trapped. Except that Tarzan usually escaped with ease, as all heroes did. Benny wished he could do the same, but didn't feel in the least bit heroic.

The lecture came, as expected, and Benny patiently endured it. All about honour and duty and obedience, about knowing right from wrong, about smoting motes out of eyes and cutting off limbs that had offended. All of which sounded pretty gruesome to Benny's way of thinking. But what was to follow proved much worse. Offending his uncle's high moral code had not been a good idea at all.

'If you're so keen on football, let's see you do some training,' Joshua told him, and Benny was marched out into the back yard and instructed to run round and round it, back and forth with his arms above his head.

'But footballers don't train like this,' he tried to explain, except that Uncle Joshua wasn't interested in hearing how real footballers trained.

It took no more than half a dozen laps to make him feel slightly queasy, but whenever he put his arms down, or slowed his pace, his uncle would emerge at the back door to glower and shout at him to put them up again and run faster.

In no time at all Benny was feeling sick and dizzy, losing his balance and staggering about the yard like a drunkard. Most of all, he was heartily wishing he'd never set foot anywhere near Manchester North End, and swore he never would again. They were a lousy team anyway, not even in the proper FA League. He could feel the dreaded threat of tears thicken his throat and was terrified that at any moment he'd be blubbering for his mam, just like a baby.

The worst of it was, he could see her standing at the window watching him. She had her two hands pressed flat against the glass as if imploring him to be brave. For that reason alone, he mustn't cry.

The wind had changed direction and a drop of rain fell on to his head, then another. Benny shivered. Within minutes he was drenched, his whole body soaked through, and shaking with fatigue and cold.

If Uncle Joshua killed him by making him run up and down with his arms over his head in the rain, then he'd be a murderer and they'd hang him and it would serve him right. At the thought of his own death which would have to take place to bring about this terrible fate, and of how upset his mam would be if that happened, Benny finally succumbed to tears. But it didn't seem to matter now that he cried, for who could tell the difference between the rain and his tears?

Chapter Twenty

Polly turned from the window to face her brother-in-law, crimson with rage at this harsh treatment of her son.

'*How dare you* do this to Benny! You've no right!'

'I have *every* right, as his uncle. The boy has no father and is clearly in need of a man's hand.'

'But this—' Polly jerked a thumb at the scene outside, the boy still running back and forth in the yard with his arms above his head in the pouring rain. 'This is inhuman. I'm fetching him in this minute.' She made for the back door but Joshua blocked her way before she had taken two steps.

Then he bent his head down to hers and hissed, 'You will not interfere. Do you understand?'

'No,' she shouted. 'I do not understand. You have no rights over him at all. He's *my* son, and I'll not have him treated so cruelly.'

Joshua smirked. 'And how do you propose to stop me?' For a moment she did not understand his meaning. To Polly the case seemed clear-cut; she was surely the one responsible for the welfare of her own family and Joshua must be made to see that. She struggled to shake off the effects of the last sleeping powder she'd taken, not even certain how she'd been drawn back into the habit. 'May the good Lord forgive you for I never shall, Joshua Pride. Benny!' she called, and flung herself at the door. Unfortunately, she was nowhere near quick enough.

Joshua easily grabbed her, vigorously shaking her as if she too were a wayward child. 'Let the boy take his punishment. He needs discipline, as does his mother. No wonder Matthew couldn't control you. You're a wicked, wilful woman who panders to her children. It does no good to spoil them. See what it's done to them. No wonder they run wild about the streets. Matters are going to change in this house, and for the better.'

He stopped speaking only because he had run out of breath, but his fury drove him to push Polly backwards and press her against the wall. 'Remember this, woman. I am not my brother. You'll find me less easy meat to push about your plate.'

Polly was shaking with emotion, desperately striving to take in the full impact of this threat. Instinct told her there must be something more to it than the misdemeanour of a child trying to see a football match he hadn't bought a ticket for, but she couldn't for the life of her think what it might be.

With an enormous effort she shook her arm free. 'Did I not thank the good Lord every day of our lives together for the fact that Matthew was not like you, his own brother? No, indeed, you'll never match him, if you live to be a hundred. A kinder, sweeter soul never walked God's earth. As for you, you conniving, scheming, nasty b—'

'Hold your tongue! I'll have no blaspheming in my house.'

Polly gasped. 'I think you have that wrong somewhere. This is *my* bloomin' house.'

'Not any longer, Polly. It is *our* house, or perhaps even *mine,* since I now pay the rent.' And he put back his head and laughed, an unpleasant sound that chilled her to the bone.

Yet still she paid no heed to the danger signals. This man didn't care a jot for her or for her children. He hadn't moved into her house out of sympathy or family duty. It hadn't been kindness he'd practised towards her but his own special brand of despotic authority, even resorting to drugs to keep her dazed and distracted. Why had she not realised this before? He worshipped *power,* not God, and had some twisted motive of his own for hurting her child, one she couldn't fathom.

Her instincts had been right to make her concerned about his discovering her friendship with Charlie. But by sweet Jesus and the Blessed Virgin, she'd stand up to him or die in the attempt, sooner than see her son suffer in this way.

'*Benny!*'

Tears were raining down her cheeks but some of the old Polly reasserted itself, and she slapped Joshua full across his sanctimonious face. The marks of her fingers were livid against the white of his skin. But even as she again made for the door, he'd grasped her wrist and with one casual flick twisted it behind her back, to push her face forward against the damp wall of her own kitchen.

'That was a big mistake, woman. You will pay dear for that little act of defiance. What did Lucy call it, a penance? That's it. You will pay a penance, as your son is doing right now. I shall enjoy devising one especially to suit your volatile temperament.'

She had never known such pain. At any moment Polly expected to hear a crack as the bone in her shoulder parted company with her arm. Amazingly, his grip tightened further, jerking the arm still higher up her back till she felt nauseous with the agony of it. Inside her head she was screaming, yet forced herself to stay silent, determined not to let him see how he hurt her.

He put his mouth against her ear and chuckled with a cruel venom. 'I like a woman with a bit of temper. Not like that madam who lives next door. She has no fight in her at all.' Polly shuddered as the hiss of hot breath caressed her ear. 'You bewitched him, my poor stupid brother. Because you're a Jezebel, a whore!'

A redness was creeping into her eyes and Polly felt so light-headed she was certain that at any moment she would pass out.

Whether she would have done so, or what his reaction might have been if she had, Polly was not to discover for at that moment the front door banged open and Big Flo's voice called out.

'It's only me. By heck, it's raining stair-rods out there.' Hearing his mother's voice, Joshua instantly released Polly from the punishing grip. She fell back against the wall, white-faced, eyes bright with unshed tears as she eased her arm tenderly into its normal position.

Her strange appearance earned her a keen-eyed stare from her mother-in-law as she entered the kitchen. Joshua was already heading for the back door, but not before Big Flo had spotted Benny in the yard.

'What the hangment is that lad doing now? He'll catch his death. Tell him to stop marleking about and get in here this minute, Joshua, or I'll have his guts for garters. And you put the kettle on, lass, the daft boy will need warming up.'

As Polly gladly hastened to carry out Big Flo's bidding, rubbing at her wrist and blessing all the saints for this unexpected rescue, she caught the old woman's eye. It came to her in that startling moment of unexpected contact that Big Flo wasn't half so ignorant, nor so accepting of her remaining son's behaviour as Polly had supposed.

-

Inside her a child was growing, more than likely a cousin for young Lucy and Benny, thanks to their uncle, did they but know it. Eileen was secretly terrified. What would Terence say if he ever found out? Dear God, she daren't think. What would it look like, this baby? They said that at the moment of birth a child looked more like its father than ever it would thereafter. She could only hope this one would be an exception.

Men took advantage of you, she knew that well enough. They used you and then threw you away like an old dish mop. Even the idle Terence was staying out later than usual these days, and it couldn't be work that was keeping him. She was beginning to worry that he might have another woman on the side somewhere. He hadn't been interested in her for weeks, and that filled her with fear too.

After supper, the minute her husband had gone out, Eileen again washed herself from head to toe, and inside and out, just as she had done night after night since the attack. She'd hoped and prayed that the non-arrival of her monthly curse had simply been due to shock, rather than the thing she most dreaded. But she recognised all the signs of pregnancy and desperation set in. Bearing a child that had been forcibly inflicted upon her was bad enough; bearing one of Joshua Pride's was more than she could stomach.

–

It was Sunday morning and Lucy had risen early so she could hurry next door to make arrangements with Eileen. There would be rugs to finish off, the hand cart to clean and get ready for the week ahead. Following his usual lively Saturday night, Terence always had a longer lie-in on a Sunday so they were rarely inter-rupted. Lucy slipped in through the unlocked back door and crept across the kitchen flags on tip-toe, anxious not to risk waking him. Hangovers did not improve his temper.

In the event he wasn't there at all. Lucy found the children sitting on the stairs, their nightdresses soaked with urine and tears rolling down their puffy cheeks. She wasted precious moments tending to them before finding that it was Eileen, for once, who was still in bed. Her eyes were closed and sunken with dark rings beneath, her face pale and pinched. Lucy was appalled and instantly alarmed.

'Eileen? What is it? Are you ill? I'll fetch Mam.'

'No, no,' she weakly protested. 'There's nowt she can do. She's enough on her plate, without me an' all.' The words were hardly out of the poor woman's mouth before she began to retch and vomit. Lucy waited no longer but turned on her heel and ran.

Within minutes she'd fetched Polly, who needed only one glance to guess what had happened.

'Sweet Jesus, what have you done to yourself this time, Eileen? What've you taken?'

She couldn't exactly remember, hadn't she tried just about everything these last weeks? By the time she'd mentioned a few, including Penny Royal and Slippery Elm, and putting laxatives where they were never meant to go, Polly was frantic with fear.

'Aw, the Lord bless us, it's a doctor you're needing, and quick. Lucy, run and fetch Doc Mitchell. Go now – fast as you can!'

Lucy ran with the wind on her tail. But by the time she'd argued the toss with the doctor's wife, who claimed that since it was Sunday and the doctor's day off he would only come out for emergencies, and could they afford to pay him if he treated this as such, it was far too late. He set down his bag, gave a perfunctory examination to the sick woman as he listened to the sad tale, then declared there was nothing to be done, Eileen's system had been poisoned by all the potions and preventatives she'd used in her efforts to rid herself of the unwanted child.

Polly stared at him, incredulous. 'What d'you mean, *nothing to be done*! We can't just let her die. *Do something, drat you!*'

Eileen was taken to Ancoats Hospital where her stomach was pumped out, but if this was unpleasant the miscarried remains of a dead foetus was even more so. Polly made Lucy wait outside, thinking it no place for a young girl.

The volunteer nurse on duty shook her head, indicating there was little hope. 'She's lost too much blood, I'm afraid. And now septicaemia has set in. We've done what we can.'

Eileen lay close to death, eyes riveted upon Polly's lovely face. 'You were me best friend. Only one I've ever had.'

'I still am your best friend.' Tears streamed down Polly's face as she grasped the frail hand, stroking it as if she could instil her own strength into Eileen through the blue veins that threaded it. 'Aw, don't give up, lass. You can fight this. Why did you do it? Why didn't you go to that flipping clinic?'

'It wasn't my fault, it were 'im.' The voice was rasping and faint, but the eyes were filled with a bitter hatred.

'Who, Terence? We've sent for him. He's on his way.'

'No, not Terence. *Him!*' The effort to speak was almost too much for Eileen and she broke into a fit of coughing. Polly hushed her, urging her to rest.

'I must talk… while I still c-can. I must s-save you.'

A cold thread of fear uncurled in Polly's stomach. She felt as if she were trembling on the brink of a precipice, from which at any moment she might tell. 'What are you trying to say, Eileen?'

'The bugger r–raped me. He give me this child.'

'Who?' Polly hardly dared ask, for some part of her was already supplying the answer.

On the faintest breath of remaining life, it came. 'Your b– bloody brother-in-law. He f–forced himself upon me. The day we swapped clothes. H–he thought I were you.'

The enormous effort this took Eileen resulted in a bout of coughing and retching that seemed unlikely ever to stop. Polly could hardly bear to watch but sat holding Eileen's hand all night, offering what comfort she could and praying with all her strength.

But despite everything possible being done, by dawn Eileen was dead. Like many another desperate woman before her, in attempting to rid herself of an unwanted child, she had succeeded only in ending her own life.

Polly put her head in her hands and sobbed out all the misery that welled in her heart. A still, frail figure, like a small wax doll, Eileen was borne away and given a pauper's funeral, since her husband didn't even have the money to bury her. Polly at least made sure it would be a decent Christian one by persuading the nurse to record the death as caused by blood poisoning, with no other explanation.

Eileen was gone, and Polly seemed to be the only one to weep for her.

On learning of his wife's death, Terence dabbed away a tear which he managed to squeeze out, blew his nose, then moved in with his 'fancy piece', who fortunately was landlady of the Bull and Bear so he'd be sure of regular food and beer. Unfortunately she wasn't too keen on children, so the four girls were taken into a home, probably the same one that already housed Polly's previous neighbours, the Murphy children.

It was not until the house next door again stood empty that Polly saw the carpets, neatly stacked in the back bedroom.

'She tried to keep things going for you,' Lucy explained, sniffing back tears. 'We both did, as a matter of fact. Eileen took out the barrow while I looked after her children and helped a bit with the sewing, though Eileen did most of that too.'

Polly was dumbfounded. All those endless months of grieving and she'd been completely unaware of the machinations going on right under her nose. Polly had found the carpet trade hard enough work, even with Big Flo helping. For Eileen to attempt it as well as see to her family and do much of the sewing in the evenings, must have been crippling. The thought of such selfless friendship brought fresh tears spilling down her cheeks.

She was even more astounded when Lucy handed her a small draw-string purse which jingled with coins.

'What's this?'

'The takings. She bought the odd bit of carpet, if someone offered it to her, but didn't have the nerve to go round houses as you did. Instead she saved every penny she could. Eileen always said it was your business, so the profit was rightly yours too, which you might need one day when you were better.'

Polly opened the purse and looked inside. She could hardly believe the evidence of her own eyes. This money could surely save them, herself and the children. 'So while I sat in a stupor, you two were working the market for me?'

Lucy nodded.

For a moment she could barely speak. Typically, when she did, it was Eileen's welfare which most concerned her. 'I hope she took proper pay for her work?' Lucy assured her that each week Eileen had taken out the sum Polly had always paid her.

'But that was nowhere near enough, not for all the extra work she was doing. She should have taken more.'

'Eileen was happy with what she earned.' Lucy smiled. 'She said it was the most pay she'd ever earned in her life for keeping her legs crossed, and you were her best friend so she owed you everything. No one else had ever cared twopence for her.' Lucy was crying now, searching up her sleeve for a damp hanky, and Polly gathered her close.

'Oh, Lucy love, what a mess.' She felt humbled, stunned by her friend's foresight and generosity. It brought back memories of the painful, lingering death she had suffered, and through no fault of her own. Polly sat down quickly on a stool and put her face in her hands. What was it Eileen had said with her last breath? That Joshua had raped her. *Your bloody brother-in-law forced himself upon me.* Could that be true? If it were, no wonder she'd wanted rid of the child.

But was Joshua capable of such a despicable act?

Without further consideration, some instinct told Polly that he most certainly was. He was a man riddled with contradictions. He may claim to be devout but Joshua Pride was nothing short of a nasty-minded, power-hungry bigot. Not only did he tolerate no other form of worship than his own, but he bullied the entire family into sharing his beliefs whether they wanted to or not. Hardly a Christian way of going about things. He allowed them no freedom, either of opinion or movement; insisting they obey his every command. Worst of all, he over-reacted when the children were naughty, not simply because he made no effort to understand them, but because, being young and naturally rebellious, they were harder to keep under control and he resented that fact.

What he had done to Benny had been unspeakably cruel, for which Polly would never forgive him. From that moment on she had seen him with new eyes.

As for herself, he'd actively encouraged her to continue to grieve and remain a prisoner by her own fireside. The blinkers off now, she recalled her futile efforts to shake herself free from her depression; the times she had put on her coat or shawl and he had taken it from her. The few occasions she'd got as far as the corner shop and he had scolded her afterwards, as if she'd committed some crime.

She remembered her trip to the tram stop in an effort to find and seek comfort from Father Thomas, and met Charlie. Then how Joshua had brought her back home like a wandering puppy. He'd kept her virtually a prisoner, both in mind and body, ever since Matthew's death, constantly telling her that she was incapable of coping or of living her own life, or even looking after her own children.

Polly recalled the day of the attack on Eileen with particular clarity. He had *wanted* her to go out, positively urged her to do so, against all his previous warnings. She'd taken Eileen's advice and gone to find Charlie, then foolishly panicked and run home again like a lost child.

In the meantime Eileen had suffered an attack meant for her, simply because she had dressed in Polly's shawl and skirt in order to act as decoy.

'Oh, dear God, what have I done?' Polly moaned.

The truth was that Joshua, her own brother-in-law, had raped her best friend. And that act of violence had led, indirectly perhaps but all too certainly, to Eileen's untimely death. Not for one moment did Polly doubt her story. How could she, since he had used violence on her too? In any case, why would Eileen lie, knowing she was dying?

Lucy, unaware of all this, thought Polly wept only over the carpets. She put her arms came about her. 'Don't cry, Mam. Eileen wanted you to make something of yourself, and now you can, thanks to her.'

As the tears flowed, Polly could only nod her head in agreement. Eileen had constantly urged her to pull herself together, if not quite so brutally. Now, thanks to her friend, whom she would miss to her dying day, she did indeed have the means to start up her business again. She even had a few stitched rugs ready for her first day's trading. Polly hugged her weeping daughter close.

'You're right. It's time to stop crying, m'cushla. We have work to do. Time to make a fresh start. If Eileen isn't to have died in vain, then from now on, you and me are going to be very busy.'

Chapter Twenty-One

Polly might very well have moved into Eileen's house there and then, was tempted to do so, but still stunned by her friend's death, couldn't get her thoughts together quickly enough. And then Benny arrived home in obvious distress with his jacket torn. While she scolded him for it, annoyed that he wouldn't explain how it had happened, another family had moved in, beating her to the house.

The woman stood on Eileen's doorstep that very same evening, arms folded, cock-a-hoop with her success in finding somewhere to house her large brood. She looked as worn out and encumbered with children as Eileen had been when she'd first arrived, or poor Mrs Murphy before her.

But this time, although Polly made herself known and was as friendly as politeness dictated, she vowed not to become too involved with her new neighbour. She offered no treats of sad cake in her kitchen, no gossipy chats over countless cups of tea. It seemed Eileen had barely been laid to rest before strangers were occupying her kitchen and sleeping in her bed, and Polly wanted none of it.

Sighing with regret, she turned her attention to her son's woes. 'I'll not have you fighting. Whatever possessed you?' And she became embroiled in a fierce discussion over whether she should go and complain to his teacher about the damage. In the end Benny was so clearly upset by this threat, that Polly felt forced to back down.

'Well, take it off then and let me stitch it. I'll not have a child of mine going about with his elbow out.' Benny obediently peeled off the jacket, hoping his mam wouldn't demand further layers to be removed, or she might discover that there was more to worry over than a torn sleeve.

Polly had indeed missed all the obvious signs of a genuine problem for her son. Absorbed in her own distress, the tears fell unchecked as she stitched, dampening the worn cloth of the jacket, while her mind inevitably replayed the events of her friend's death and the implications surrounding it.

Could Joshua's bitter grievance over religion truly have driven him to such lengths? All because she, a Catholic, had married into a non-conformist family? The man was sick. Polly paused in her stitching of the patch, staring through the window at the rain-sodden back yard, remembering Benny's agonies as he'd been marched up and down, the pain in her own arm as Joshua had twisted it. A wave of sickness filled her at the memory and she had to wait till it eased before continuing, tight-lipped, with her sewing.

If he really did mistake Eileen for her, why had he done nothing to rectify his mistake since? Was he biding his time? Watching and waiting for the right moment, so that he would in no way be implicated should some terrible accident befall her.

For the first time it occurred to Polly that Matthew's death might not have been an accident after all. Her blood seemed to freeze in her veins at the very idea. Could Joshua possibly have engineered that too? No, surely she was letting her imagination run away with her? How could he know that Matthew would be there, in the wrong place at the wrong time, trapped like an injured animal under the stampeding crowd? And Joshua was nowhere near Matthew at the time of his death. Wasn't that what he'd told her?

But what if that weren't true?

'Oh, sweet Jesus!' she cried, hearing the tremor in her own voice. If that were the case then he was not only a bigot and a heartless rapist but a murderer too.

It all seemed much too far-fetched to take in and she fought against the idea as fanciful, born of her natural distress and alarm.

In that moment she ached for Charlie, for a friend to rely on and provide the support she needed. Yet she knew, deep down, that he could very easily be much more than a friend. He wanted her, she could see it in his eyes, and had discovered she was not indifferent to such emotions herself. One day soon she would go to him, as she so longed to do. But first she had some issues to resolve.

Polly heard the sounds of her brother-in-law's boots on the linoleum as he returned home, and bent her head to her sewing with a fervent vow to keep a sharper, eye on him in future. Despite the very real grief she felt for her lost friend, Polly knew she must not allow grief to overwhelm her. This was no time for falling back into that trap.

–

The first thing she did was carefully to count out the money that Eileen had left her. There was more than she had expected: sixteen pounds, ten shilling and ninepence in fact, which would set her up grand. The very next time Joshua went to one of his meetings, she put on her shawl and announced that she was off out too.

Big Flo looked anxious. 'Where to this time? He'll ask, soon as he gets in.'

'Tell him you don't know because I didn't tell you. Get your coat on, Lucy. You're coming with me. It's not too soon for you to learn a bit of business.'

'What sort of business? Nay, Polly, thee's not off with that carpet nonsense again? He'll flay me alive for letting you wander,' Big Flo wailed, following her to the door.

'Like you once said yourself, this isn't Strangeways and you're not my jailer. Neither is Joshua.' Then Polly was striding along Dove Street with such a determined spring in her step that Lucy had to run to catch up with her. Big Flo stood on the doorstep waving a ham-like fist and shouting for her to come back this minute, if she knew what was good for her.

The empty shop on Ancoats Lane had been taken long since, of course, but the landlord, delighted to see her again, knew of something which might be equally suitable. 'Not a shop,' he told her. 'But costing less in consequence. It will happen be just the ticket for you.'

He rifled in a chest of drawers, found a rusty old key and led Polly and Lucy along Ancoats Lane, down Store Street and through a maze of interconnecting streets quite near the railway arches. Finally he stopped by a tall, soot-darkened red brick warehouse. Some of the casement windows were broken. There were many such buildings now in Manchester, following the slump.

'Chap who owned it went bump, as many others have done. There's been too much lost during the Crash.'

He unlocked the big double doors and led them into a low-ceilinged room, the length of it broken at intervals by iron pillars. It had clearly served its time as a weaving shed as well as a warehouse, but Polly felt a stir of excitement.

'We're dividing the warehouse up into sections,' the man explained. 'This bit will happen do for your carpets. There's this room, an office and a small kitchen. What d'you reckon?'

It was ideal for her purposes. There was more than enough space here to store, cut and sew any number of carpets. Polly and Lucy exchanged a quick excited glance, hastily disguised as they had no wish to be taken advantage of.

'How much? I'm not made of brass,' Polly asked, borrowing some of Big Flo's Lancashire bluntness. A fair rent was agreed, a deposit paid which was quickly pocketed, and the key handed over.

'I like a body who pays in advance. If you're looking for some place to lay your head as well as carpets, give us a shout. There's the old caretaker's flat next door.'

Polly looked surprised. It was a tempting thought, but right now it was more important that she spend her money on the business. There would be time enough, once she'd got it going again, to find somewhere other than the house in Dove Street for herself and the children to live. She smiled her thanks. 'I'd need to think about that. But I'll remember the offer.'

When the man had gone, well pleased with the deal, Polly and Lucy hugged each other in delight.

—

Joshua suffered no remorse at his behaviour. Far from it. He was well pleased with the way things were turning out. In one respect, allowing Polly to go out that day had probably been a mistake. Ever since then she seemed to be gaining strength, growing more obstinate, even rebellious, no longer willing to take the powders which had kept her in his clutches for so long.

However, he knew that although it may be diminished, he still held considerable power over her.

That young son of hers would think twice in future before he risked bringing shame and humiliation upon his family again. As for the girl... His victim on that occasion may only have been the Irish woman's son, but he'd keep an eye on Madam Lucy too, who was almost as full of sin as the mother.

Joshua smiled as he turned up his coat collar against the rain, and set off to his meeting, with a light heart.

One day soon, the Irish woman's turn would come. So far he had only chastised her, a little, teaching her the lesson she deserved for daring to display such a show of temper. But he'd enjoyed the scuffle. He'd tried once to do more, of course, and failed, mistaking that slut next door for Polly, simply because she'd been wrapped in her shawl. Not that he felt any regret over Eileen Grimshaw. She was no loss to anyone, a woman like that. But next time he would be more certain of his quarry.

He reached the Mission Hall and paused, brow furrowed in thought, barely aware of the greetings of the men as they passed by to enter the building.

He would like to have had the satisfaction of accusing her of being responsible, as Matthew had been, for Cecil's death. Joshua was convinced that if she hadn't captivated his brother so completely with her feminine wiles, Cecil might be alive today But it was too soon, he told himself. It might make her start asking questions about Matthew's 'accident'.

As it was now, even if she did connect him with her husband's death, which as an ignorant woman she surely wouldn't have the wit to do, she was powerless to prove a thing against him. He had only to bide his time, choose his moment with care, and he'd enjoy inflicting just punishment upon her all the more. In the meantime, he'd at least ensured she would never slap him again.

Now he stood before his fellow unemployed on the stage of the Mission Hall, a man well pleased with himself and life in general. He lectured them sternly on the subject of politics, the evils of the Means Test and the success of their protests to date. The men drank in every word, believing implicitly that he was their only hope.

'This is but the beginning,' Joshua proclaimed. 'Follow me, comrades, and every man amongst you will be given work, and the means to provide for your family.'

He felt like a missionary, leading an entire people to salvation, almost as if he possessed the power of the Almighty Himself. On Judgement Day he would most certainly sit at the right hand of Our Lord, as one of the most blessed among men. A leader, very nearly a prophet. Joshua swelled with pride as the shouts and cheers rang in the hall.

'We'll follow you, Josh.'

'Aye. Find us work and we'll follow you to hell and back.'

'Or Heaton Park,' shouted one wag. 'Which is the same thing.'

Joshua smiled. Only one person that he knew of was destined for hell. And he meant to put her there himself.

Afterwards he walked amongst them, taking, a collection for the cause. Cal Eastwood approached.

'You're pushing 'em too hard, Joshua.'

'Let me be the judge of that.'

'They've hardly enough money to feed themselves and their families, without lining your pockets.'

'I resent that remark. This money is for the NUWM.'

'After you've taken out your own expenses first, I reckon.'

'I am not running a charity here. There's the hire of the hall to pay for, stationery, postage, leaflets and posters advertising the next demonstration.' Use of his home as an office had also to be taken into account, as did wear and tear on his shoe leather. If he put his mind to it, it came to quite a sum. Joshua exacted a similar recompense for his chapel duties but had no wish for the men, Cal Eastwood in particular, to know the full details.

He shook the bowler hat under the nose of one man, who sheepishly dropped in a penny. His mate scurried away before he could be trapped too. Cal smirked, knowing his point had been proved.

'Much good it's doing us, giving our last pennies to these pie-in-the-sky dreams of yours. Don't look worth it from where I'm standing. Happen I'll give you a run for your money at the next elections.'

Joshua was angry but unrepentant. Not for a moment did he believe that the likes of Cal Eastwood could oust him from his position of power: He'd tried once before, when they were both in the newly formed union. He'd failed then and would fail now. Joshua would make certain of it. Call would learn that he was not a man to be trifled with, as had Matthew, to his cost.

His brother had received his just desserts, suffering the same crime against him that he himself had perpetrated against Cecil. Just as it was written: 'An eye for an eye, and a tooth for a tooth.' It didn't trouble Joshua in the slightest if some might judge him as a murderer. He didn't see himself as such. It was true he could easily have pulled his brother from the path of the advancing mob, but no one else knew that.

Dealing with his brother's wife, who was equally culpable, would bring him the greatest satisfaction of all. Admittedly it would require special care and planning, if he were to succeed in his mission without drawing suspicion upon himself.

With a sneering laugh he pocketed the money and, placing the bowler hat neatly back upon his head, turned to go. 'You're welcome to try,' he called to Cal over his shoulder, knowing himself to be inviolable.

Polly felt invigorated, almost reborn. Her head was buzzing with plans for what she would do with the warehouse. The small stock of carpets left in Eileen's parlour had already been moved there, safely out of the way of the new neighbour. The next major task, once the warehouse had been thoroughly cleaned from top to bottom, would be to add more, which wouldn't be easy in these difficult times. But Polly was in no way daunted by the task ahead of her.

'Rome wasn't built in a day,' she'd say to her children as she simmered porridge for their breakfast, watching with satisfaction as they gulped it down. The statement was to become a litany as they swept and scrubbed, mended floorboards or blocked up broken windows in the days following. Lucy was eager to help whenever it wasn't one of her days at the market. Benny too worked like a Trojan. The minute school was over, he'd be there beside his mother ready to do his bit, jacket off, sleeves rolled up.

Polly knew that however hard she must work, in the end it would all be worth it. And at least the children seemed happy. She vowed never again to allow Joshua to hurt them. She even began issuing a string of dire warnings, just as in the old days.

'Don't think you can run wild, the pair of you, just because you're getting older. Won't I leather you myself if you go wandering off down the canal for no reason, or come home again with a tear in your coat? Ye never tell me where you are, neither of you, and don't I need to know?'

Benny might once have protested against this injustice, now he would grin from ear to ear, willingly pick up the hated cap and go off to school with a jaunty bounce to his step. His mam was herself again, and it felt good.

Lucy dreamed of catching sight of Tom Shackleton. Maybe she could risk suggesting that she was open to invitations, now that her mam was well again. She made up her mind to hang around the street corner when they were done at the warehouse one day, in the hope of meeting him on his way home from work.

Because of all the work needing to be done, Polly would always eat her own breakfast at breakneck speed, anxious to be on her way, absently making the usual consoling responses to Big Flo's daily complaints of rheumatic aches and pains.

She fully intended to justify Eileen's unswerving belief in her. Nothing on God's earth would persuade her to hand over any of her friend's hard-earned money to her brother-in-law. She'd pay her way, but no longer was she willing to be ruled by him, no matter how many tantrums he might throw in his attempts to frighten her. When breakfast was over, she would quickly wash up the few dishes and reach at once for her shawl.

The question always came, as expected. 'Where you off to now?'

'Out.'

One morning Big Flo dropped her spoon and reached out a restraining hand. 'Take care, lass. He were on about that friend o' yours again yesterday, can't remember his surname. You know, that chap who come asking after, thee once. Charlie summat.' The two women exchanged a long speaking glance.

Polly, surprised by this unexpected show of concern from her mother-in-law, made no comment at all, merely tightening her lips to an obstinate line, gave a brief nod, then strode off in the direction of the city centre, taking Lucy with her.

-

As well as sweeping out the room and disposing of thousands of cobwebs, hammering down floorboards and temporarily fixing boards over the broken window panes until they had the money to replace them with glass, they'd also fashioned a long wooden slide made out of old doors. It ran the length of the room so that the carpets could be slid from one end to the other, which would make the task of moving them much easier.

Their final task had been to scrub out the tiny kitchen. It was little bigger than a cupboard with a sink and a gas jet, but it would serve. Mother and daughter sat in it now, eating a hot pie by way of reward for their labours, savouring the delicious flavour, licking the juices that ran between their fingers.

'How will we manage, Mam, on our own? You're good at bargaining and selling, but we can't carry big carpets through the streets.'

It had crossed Polly's mind to ask Charlie to help but she'd dismissed the idea almost at once. Maybe she was still a bit nervous of Joshua, but she shied away from any contact which might embroil him too closely in her life. Not till she was ready, anyway. Yet somehow this decision, sensible as it seemed, had the effect of depressing her. 'We can use the hand cart. I'm strong, and I'll get stronger,' she declared.

Lucy at once offered to help. 'I'm used to working with the carpets now, and I enjoy it. I could give up the tripe and trotter stall.'

'Not yet,' her mother cautioned. 'We need your income for a while longer. But our future is bright, love. Believe me. We'll get this business going, and later I do have a friend who may help. He was very kind to me when I got lost looking for a tram that day. He was in the Merchant Navy once but is looking for work at the moment, like many another.'

Polly was horrified to find herself blushing like a schoolgirl. 'He might be interested, he might not,' she finished, all in a rush.

Lucy, listening with close attention, thought her mother had never looked better, younger and prettier than she had seen her in years. The pinched look had gone from about her mouth, her eyes were bright and her skin glowed. She wondered, with a start, if her mam could possibly be in love, realising she'd never considered such a possibility before. Yet the prospect pleased her. 'I'm glad for you, Mam, really I am. He sounds a nice chap.'

'He's simply a friend,' Polly hastened to assure her. 'We met a few times, but only to talk.'

Oh, and how they had talked, as if they'd known each other for years! Then he'd come to the house looking for her. If she now went looking for him, something deep inside Polly told her that Charlie would be glad to see her. But it was far too soon. She wasn't ready for any more emotional turmoil just yet.

By way of response, Lucy started to tell her mother all about Tom, about how he'd once asked her out but she had refused because the family had still been in mourning. Polly listened with sympathy and interest, then patted her daughter's cheek.

'There's plenty of time. Mourning shouldn't last forever.'

'I know, Mam, and he promised to wait.' Lucy flushed. 'But I wondered if it might be all right now if I – well – if I went out with him like?'

Polly smiled and hugged her daughter. 'Of course it would. You are only young once and isn't he a fine young man? But take care. Remember all that your mam has told you.' And Lucy gigglingly agreed that she would.

'You're a good girl,' Polly said. But how much time did she have? She wasn't young like Lucy. It could take years to build her business and break free from Joshua's tyranny. Would it be too late then for her to find happiness?

As Polly pondered on these personal problems, Lucy chattered on excitedly. It was the best heart-to-heart mother and daughter had enjoyed in a long time and seemed to bring them closer together.

All too soon reality intervened.

'What about Uncle Joshua?' Lucy asked. 'What will he say when he realises you've started working again? He's not been blind to all the activity these last few days. He's started giving me funny looks, asking questions about where I'm going, and why.'

Smiles quickly faded as the two considered this in grim silence. At length Polly said, 'We could always agree not to tell him. No, that wouldn't be right, and I couldn't hope to keep it a secret forever. Well, he'll just have to lump it. He's not in charge of my life any more. I am!'

They ate in silence for a while, then Lucy continued with her questions. 'Did he – did he touch you that day he had a go at our Benny? I mean, did he hit you?'

'He certainly didn't cover himself in glory, the dirty beggar. But he'll not try it again. Nor lay another finger on either of my children,' Polly declared, with such fierceness that Lucy had to smile. Then something began to stir deep in her memory and she struggled to get to grips with it. 'Why do you call him dirty. Mam? What did he do?'

'It wasn't so much what he did, though he hurt me right enough. It was what he said. Called me by a rude word, so he did.' Polly refused to repeat it before her lovely daughter. She could see already how distressed the child was, for she'd gone death pale. 'Aw, don't fret, m'cushla, we'll get by, so we will. All we have to do is stick together.'

'No, it isn't that. Only… you remember that night in the barracks, when they were fumigating our house?'

Polly frowned, not wishing to think so far back to a time when she'd had nothing at all to worry about, since her man was still alive and well. 'I remember I made a great fuss over nothing in particular,' she confessed.

'Someone used dirty words to me that night,' Lucy said in a quiet voice, feeling hugely relieved to have got this offchest at last, after all this time. 'Whoever it was called me a *whore!*'

Polly stared at her daughter, appalled, as Lucy related her distress that night, how at first she'd blamed Tom, who had since convinced her of his innocence. They both realised in that same instant that not only were the words used the same but the voice too. Low and rasping, hissing in their ear.

Polly gathered her child close in her arms. 'May the Saints preserve us, for I'll kill him with me own bare hands if he ever touches or says such things to you ever again.' And in that moment Polly knew she would need all her wits about her, and every one of her survival skills, if she was to protect not only herself but her children too.

Chapter Twenty-Two

'Where have you been?' Joshua was standing at the door waiting when they arrived home. Polly squeezed her daughter's hand with loving reassurance.

'Say nothing and get off upstairs. I'll give you a shout when I've brewed a cuppa.'

'Watch him, Mam. If he tries anything...' Fiercely protective of her mother since their talk, Lucy could hardly bring herself to walk through the door, let alone leave Polly alone with this monster.

Yet there were some things Lucy had not been told. She was still unaware of how Eileen had come to be pregnant. If Polly had her way, her daughter would remain in ignorance. There were some things a young girl shouldn't hear, one being that her uncle was a rapist. She realised there were risks in not telling her. It would mean that Polly must protect Lucy even more closely, since being in a state of ignorance she might not think to protect herself. Some decisions, made with the best of intentions, often come to be regretted later. She could only hope this wouldn't prove to be one of them.

Without a glance at Joshua, Polly moved over to the range and slid the kettle on to the centre of the hob over the fire. Then she turned to Big Flo who sat darning a sock, fat fingers flying.

'How about a nice bowl of cheese and onion for your tea? I could boil it in a bit of milk.' Her mother-in-law had few of her own teeth left and point blank refused to consider false ones.

'Aye, that'd be grand,' Flo agreed, casting a nervous glance in her son's direction. Her expression implied that she knew there was something wrong. He wasn't himself these days, all fidgety and watchful, but she couldn't quite get to the bottom of it. Not yet. But she would, given time.

'I've bought a bit of haddock for you, Joshua. Lucy and me have already eaten. We had ourselves a treat. Stopped off at Florrie's pie shop. Sure and there's none better in the whole of Ancoats.'

'You should've fetched us all one,' Big Flo protested, feeling deprived.

'Indeed I should. Why didn't I think of that? I will next time, will I not?'

'Where did you find the money for pies and haddock?' Joshua's voice was tight and rasping. Polly had already come to dread the sound of it, but now, following her daughter's revelation, it filled her with loathing. Some of this revealed itself in the tone of her reply.

'We might be poor but I'm no pauper, Joshua. There's plenty worse off than us. Haven't I always said so? My clean floor should prove that if nothing else.' And more than that she had no intention of saying. Joshua, however, was far from satisfied, and stubbornly persisted.

'You must have a store of money somewhere, for I've given you none, and this is the third time this week you've fetched food home from wherever it is you've been spending your time recently.' He was seriously peeved that due to the pressure of work for the cause, he'd not been able to pay proper attention to her movements lately. Now he meant to rectify that, come what may. 'Was it left over from that stupid carpet business? Where d'you keep it?'

Polly began to chop onions, bringing down the knife with slashing strokes. 'Sure and I don't know what you're talking about. How would I have any money, after all this time?'

'I wouldn't know, but if you have some hidden, I want to know where it is. We all need food in this house, so you can share what money you have with us all.' She was becoming increasingly obdurate, and it worried him.

238

'Aw, you're wanting me to pay me way now, is that it? Well, I'll be glad to, if you stop complaining every time I set foot out of the house. I should've told you weeks ago, but Eileen kept some of the carpet rugs for me.' Polly slid the onions into a small pan of milk and set it on the hob, deciding that perhaps it was time to make her position clear. 'As a matter of fact, I've made up me mind to go back into business, since it's time I pulled meself together and...' She got no further as Joshua slammed his fist down hard upon the table.

'You'll do *nothing* without my permission.'

At one time she would have flinched, even cowered, and no doubt panicked and run for another powder. Now Polly turned from the fire where she'd been stirring the onions, to look at him in feigned surprise. 'I'm thinking that would be an odd thing for a grown woman to do. I'm perfectly well now, thanks very much, and quite able to earn me own living, even if you aren't.' It was a cruel taunt, but she wasn't feeling in the least bit kindly disposed towards her brother-in-law today, perhaps never would again.

The money Eileen had earned for her was now safely hidden where Joshua would never find it. Some of it in a special place at the warehouse, the rest secreted on her person, in her underclothes. He'd interfered with a woman's underclothes before, she reminded herself, but he wouldn't get within arm's length of hers or he'd live to regret it.

Feeling himself losing control, Joshua returned to the original point of dispute, his voice taking on a savage note. 'Where is this money? *Get it now!*'

Polly crossed her fingers and lied. 'I've told you, I don't have any. That's why I need to work.' It was a thin excuse, one he would surely see through since she'd plainly need capital to start up again, and she began to regret the overoptimism which had led her to buy the cheese and haddock, and tell him about the pies.

'You're lying.' Then before she could guess his purpose, he swung on his heel, pulled open the stair door, and within seconds was upstairs, clomping across the wooden floor of the bedroom she shared with Lucy.

'Dear God, the rat is going through my things!'

'Nay, don't interfere,' Big Flo cried, holding fast to her arm and giving Polly a little shake. 'He weren't allus like this, you know. I don't understand what's got into him these days. But if thee has any brass, then I'd recommend you hand it over.' She nodded her head so vigorously to emphasise her point that one of her curling pins came loose and bounced into the sugar basin, then simply stared at it, looking troubled.

'Joshua has enough money of his own sticking to his pocket linings,' Polly retaliated, and throwing off the restraining hands, flew up the stairs after him. She found he'd opened every drawer and was flinging her clothes, including her underclothing, all over the floor while he searched. Lucy was standing watching him, white-faced and trembling.

A heat rose in Polly as fierce as the boiling water that even now rattled the lid of the kettle downstairs. 'Get your filthy hands off my things!' In a way she was almost relieved she didn't still have the chopping knife in her hand, or she might have done something she'd might regret. But even as the temper soared in her Polly knew she was no match physically for her brother-in-law.

His face contorted with mocking laughter. 'And how will you stop me?' He ripped back the bedclothes, fingering first Polly's nightdress and then Lucy's lingeringly, a smile on his face, before casually tossing each aside. Then he upturned the mattress to examine the bare springs.

'Satisfied?' Polly felt impotent with rage, bleakly aware that he was right, there was nothing at all she could do to stop him rifling through her personal belongings.

He came to stand beside her, his powerful presence only inches away, making him seem even more intimidating. 'Wherever you've hidden it, be sure that I will find it, so it would be better if you were to volunteer the information. I think your temper has got the better of you today. You would do well to ask forgiveness in your prayers tonight.'

'*My* temper?'

'Perhaps you should recommence taking those powders? To cool your fever and restore rational behaviour.'

'I am perfectly rational, and I don't need any more powders. Let me alone, Joshua.'

He almost spat the words into her face. 'No one makes a fool of me, woman. I always get my way, in the end.' Then, to her enormous relief he strode from the room. Polly put her hands to her burning cheeks and counted slowly to ten to regain her calm, but the shaking in her limbs was so bad her legs gave way and she was obliged to sit down with a bump on the bare springs of the bed.

'Are you all right, Mam?' Lucy came to put her arms about her.

'I am, m'cushla. Though I'd be a whole lot better if I could rid us of that fiend.' She felt hot and cold all over, her palms sticky with sweat. 'I'll swing for him, so I will. Just give me the chance.'

'Can't we leave, Mam? Now, this minute. Can't we go and live some place else? With your friend Charlie perhaps.'

Polly gathered her daughter close, tears she refused to shed thickening the back of her throat. 'I don't even know where he lives. In lodgings somewhere. Besides, this is *our* problem and we must solve it ourselves, not go running to some man we hardly know.' No matter how much I might long to do just that, she thought. More than she cared to admit.

And then she remembered the warehouse's landlord, and his mention of the caretaker's flat. Perhaps it was still available or he had other property somewhere. But could she afford to pay rent on a house as well as the warehouse?

'Come on, chin up. Soon as we've earned a bit of money, we'll find a place so we can be together, just the three of us like we used to be. And haven't we made a good start already, with money saved, so long as he doesn't get his thieving hands on it.' And mother and daughter comforted each other as best they could before restoring the room to order.

Despite her brave words, Polly had to stifle a shudder later that evening as she handed Joshua his supper. Every time she thought of what he had done to Eileen, his cruel punishment of her own son and the dirty words he'd used on her precious innocent daughter, she wanted to scratch out his eyes. But she knew that wasn't the way. She must tread with care, for she had her children's welfare to think of. Look what had happened to Eileen's four, all taken into a home. Lucy was nearly a grown woman now, but Benny wasn't quite thirteen and mischievous enough to be forever getting into bother. The last thing she wanted was for a similar fate to befall him or, worse, for him to be taken to the Reformatory. And she didn't put anything past Joshua to bring that about.

In any case, hadn't she made great strides already, getting the warehouse and at least some carpets to sell? Accommodation wasn't easy to come by in this neighbourhood, and Polly refused to take her children anywhere that wasn't clean and decent. She had standards to maintain for her family, poor or no.

As she had feared, the caretaker's flat had already been taken. 'Eeh, you should've snapped it up while you had chance, lass.' She was more disappointed than she could say, and bitterly regretted her own caution in the matter.

Polly realised she would have to learn to be more decisive, to take control of herself and her life, or she would never get anywhere. But then she probably couldn't have it anyway. For the moment at least, she must be patient.

She did what she could by asking around locally, in case there was anything suitable. She even visited the Corporation offices to enquire about the new slum clearance scheme she'd heard of, where they were sending families to live out at Wythenshaw, a garden suburb which was the pride and joy of the city. The clerk laboriously took down her particulars and helped her fill out all the necessary forms, but gave no indication of when a house may come available, if at all.

Polly turned with renewed attention to her work, for that was her best route to escape. Finding new stock must be her priority. They were running desperately low, and without carpets she had no income, and without income, her freedom would evaporate almost as quickly as she had won it.

As for Charlie, he must remain a dream. He'd only come looking for her because he was a kind man concerned for her well-being. It didn't mean anything more than that and she'd been foolish to think any different, or to go looking for him. At least he'd kept away since, as per her instructions. She'd probably never set eyes on him again.

–

The next few months were difficult. Polly spent hours trekking round with her hand cart, knocking on doors and asking if anyone had any old carpets to sell. Unfortunately nobody had and, once she had sold all her remaining pieces, the warehouse would be empty. This was a severe disappointment, for if she couldn't make a go of her business, then her money would soon disappear and she'd have no means of earning any more, which meant no hope of escape from her brother-in-law.

There must be a solution somewhere, she thought, very near to panic. Perhaps she was looking in the wrong places. Perhaps she should try Victoria Park, Ellesmere Park or over towards Wilmslow. But if she travelled too far, how could she possibly transport the rolls of carpet on the hand cart all the way back to Ancoats?

Christmas came and went and Polly felt trapped and frustrated, close to despair, and all the time a small voice was telling her to find Charlie again and ask for his help, yet stubbornly she resisted. She wanted to prove herself first.

And then she remembered she had one asset she hadn't yet considered. Her son.

Benny was bearing his own problems in stoical silence. He was delighted to see that his mam was more herself, but his situation hadn't improved one bit. He hated sleeping under the stairs, with only an old greatcoat and thin blanket to keep him warm. It wasn't that he'd enjoyed sharing a room with his sister, or needed her comfort, for he was almost thirteen now and very nearly a man, but his candle cast funny shadows on the walls of his cubby-hole. He told himself they were only homely things, like the flat iron, the bread bin or the clothes-horse, but sometimes the black shapes on the wall looked more like a man's dismembered head, the sort of thing shown each week in the *Illustrated Police Gazette,* or even the bars of a cage. He hated it. But he hated his uncle more.

If Uncle Josh and Gran hadn't moved in, he'd have a room of his own now and be the man of the house, which was what his dad would have wanted.

In addition, Georgie Eastwood was continuing to make his life a misery. The episode of the torn jacket had been the last in a long line of taunts and tricks that Georgie played on him at every opportunity. He waited for Benny to come out of the school playground, then he and his gang would follow him home, or they would jump out at him from some ginnel or back entry. No longer at school, nor with any sort of a job, Georgie had to amuse himself somehow. Benny was the butt of his humour.

But the last thing Benny wanted was for his mother to start fighting his corner for him, as if he were an infant who couldn't stand up for himself. Nor did he want her to see the bruises on his body, left there by the many punches Georgie and his gang flung at him.

Now, when Polly came to him, he was anxious to help. Anything to help them break free from his uncle's authority. Yes, he agreed, of course he remembered the old cinema that he'd overheard the women talking about. Whether it would still have its carpet was another matter, but he'd certainly go with her to look.

They went together. With great trepidation and very little hope in her heart, Polly knocked on the manager's door. When a voice boomed out, telling her to enter, she very nearly ran away.

Twenty minutes later she was glad that she hadn't. The manager did still possess the carpet, his plans for turning the cinema into a dance-hall having suffered a set-back while he sought extra finance through the dark days of the depression. Now that he had succeeded in his quest, he was more than ready to agree a price and be rid of it. He even offered to have his own men deliver it to Polly's warehouse. She couldn't believe her luck.

'We're in business,' she whooped, whirling Benny round in a dance of delight right there on the pavement. 'Aren't I blessed with a fine son? Ye've come up trumps again, so you have.' And he puffed out his chest with pride.

Perhaps it was time to tackle Georgie Eastwood head on.

Then again, perhaps not yet.

－

When the carpet was delivered, Polly felt almost overwhelmed by the task which confronted her. It would take days, if not weeks, to clean, cut and bind a carpet this size into saleable pieces. She had no money left to pay for labour to help her, not a penny, but still it had been worth it. Lucy had promised to give what assistance she could. Benny couldn't sew, of course, but had offered to help with the lifting and carrying, eager to prove his worth and help his mam earn enough money to get them out of Joshua's clutches.

'It will be a real family business, will it not?' she'd told them.

For the rest, she'd just have to grit her teeth and set to work herself. Despite the prospect of weeks of back-breaking labour, Polly felt alive with new hope. She meant to put a sign on the windows of their part of the warehouse, just as soon as they had some pieces to sell. She didn't hold out any great hope of selling many carpets that way, but the odd sale would help to keep the wolf from the door, until she had enough stock to go out on the road.

'You look mighty perky. Have you lost twopence and found a tanner?' It was a day or two later and Big Flo was watching with interest as Polly pulled her shawl over her head, ready to set off especially early. 'You look like you've come into a fortune.'

'Maybe I have in a way. If you must know, I've bought a carpet, a great big one, which is going to set me up grand.'

Big Flo shook her head in disbelief when she'd been toldfull tale. 'A cinema carpet? Nay, you can't cope with one that size all on your own.'

Polly smiled at her mother-in-law's lugubrious expression. 'I did tell you I'd find more stock.'

'Aye, but I never thought you'd actually do it. He'll not like it, tha knows.'

Polly didn't ask who she meant. 'Well, he'll have to lump it.' She closed the door on her mother-in-law's dire warning and walked briskly away. She'd only got halfway down Dove Street when she found that she was no longer alone: Big Flo was beside her, old black shawl enveloping her massive shoulders, huge clogs clicking on the stone setts. Polly stopped dead. 'What's this?'

'I thought as how you'd happen need a bit of a hand like. If it's as big as you say.'

'Oh, it's big all right.'

'Right then, let's get cracking.'

Polly was delighted by this turn of events. Big Flo would be invaluable, with her great strong hands and arms. And she had a good eye, able to cut straight as a die.

'What about Joshua? You'd be going against his wishes.' After a long moment in which the two women looked at each other without a word being exchanged, Big Flo wrapped the shawl tighter about her massive shoulders. 'Happen so. And happen he isn't always right, eh?'

It was a major concession, one she had never made before. When Polly said nothing, she snapped, 'Come on then, lass. Weil not earn any brass standing about here gawping!'

—

The dusty days of summer soon gave way to the shorter days of autumn, with the lamplighter coming round earlier and earlier. The Italian ice cream sellers put away their highly decorated carts and made a start on the hot chestnut season.

'Annyragnbones?' shouted the rag and bone man, in the hope of picking up a few decent bits of clothing, paying his customers with slabs of donkey stone or used clog irons. He did a thriving trade.

If Polly's own business wasn't exactly booming, at least she was breaking even. She was covering her costs and able to offer a sum of money each week to pay for the food she and the children consumed. This at least gave them a sense of independence, even if they were still living under what was effectively Joshua's roof.

She stuck a small notice in the warehouse window, announcing the date they would be open for custom. In addition, following Joshua's own example, she risked some of her precious money on having a hundred or so leaflets printed and got Benny and Lucy to go round likely streets in and around Ancoats, putting them through letter-boxes.

When the big day arrived, each and every one of them was anxious to do well. Even Big Flo, who normally claimed to be untroubled by such things, was a bundle of nerves.

'Eeh, heck, what if nobody comes?'

But they did come. A full hour before the appointed time, a queue began to form outside. Lucy, peeping through the dusty window, could hardly believe her eyes. There were men, women and even children patiently waiting to view the novelty of carpet pieces which might brighten their homes and bring warmth to their cold feet. And everybody loved a bargain. Lucy was so astounded by the numbers gathering that she had to bring Benny, and her mother to confirm that she was right; they were indeed queuing up to come into the warehouse, and not simply waiting for a tram.

When the moment came to unlock the double doors, Big Flo appointed herself doorkeeper.

Polly looked a bit worried by this. 'Remember, we have to be polite, Flo. They are our customers. We want them to enjoy the experience and stay around long enough to buy.'

'Aye, I know that, but if there's any trouble, they'll be out on their ear faster than they can turn round!' She rolled up her sleeves in readiness, bringing them all to a fit of giggles at the picture this painted of people spinning through the door and landing on their ears.

The day was a great success. The crowd surged in and each one of the Pride family, Polly, Lucy and Big Flo, was kept fully occupied showing rugs and taking money. Benny helped too, earning himself the odd copper by rolling up the carpets and sending them sliding down the home-made chute, or offering to deliver the larger pieces to folk's front doors. At this rate he'd a good chance of earning more in tips on the delivery rounds which he could fit in each day after school. Life was picking up.

There was one awkward moment when Polly rolled out a largish square of carpet and a beetle scurried across it. Quick as a flash Big Flo caught the interloper in her great fist before anyone noticed and held it there, its legs scrabbling to be let out. The customer, none the wiser, paid over her money and went off happily with the rug tucked under her arm. Only then did Big Flo open up her hand to reveal the creature which was unharmed.

After releasing it out the back door, she said, 'I'd've thrown this little chap in for nowt, only I know Ida Murgatroyd already has plenty of her own.' And she cackled with laughter, for this was the best fun she'd had since last wakes week on Collin's Fairground.

Chapter Twenty-Three

During the long cold days of winter, Polly worked harder than she ever had in her life before, though never had she felt more fulfilled. After that first day, the sales became a feature, every Thursday and Saturday, regular as clockwork. Some days were quiet with no more than a few curious wanderers; on others there would be a steady flow of customers, even if they didn't all buy, which gave Polly hope. The Depression surely couldn't last forever.

The rest of the time the Pride family was busy cutting and sewing, or Polly was out and about with her hand cart, seeking more carpets. Sometimes she was lucky, more often than not she came home empty-handed. Finding stock continued to be a problem, which proved there was no room for complacency. As soon as the weather improved she'd have to try further afield, though she still hadn't solved the problem of transport. Even so, life was good.

'Sure and everything's going right for us at last.'

'Aye, you could say so,' Big Flo agreed, but there was still the slightest hint of doubt in her tone.

Lucy, having decided that her mother was back on track now, resolved to give more attention to her own affairs. Each morning she would set out early, hoping to catch sight of Tom on his way to the rail yard where he worked. Tom was a Catholic. Therefore not at all suitable so far as Uncle Joshua was concerned. Not that Lucy cared what her uncle thought. After a dozen disappointments, she finally spotted Tom, managing to come around a corner at the optimum moment to collide with him head on.

'Oh, hello, Tom, I thought you'd disappeared off the face of the earth,' she chided, picking up his snap tin which had gone spinning to the ground.

'I thought you were too busy looking after your mam.' The reddening of his cheeks told Lucy she was still in with a chance.

'I was, but she's better now, so I might be able to find time to go out now, were someone to ask me.'

She tossed the words at him with a slight lift of her chin, trying to show that she really didn't care one way or the other whether he asked her out or not; but was secretly thrilled and delighted when he grabbed at the chance.

'I've been wanting to take you out for ages, Lucy, you know I have,' the young man informed her earnestly. 'We'll go to the Palais, eh?'

The Palais was the most expensive place he could have suggested, costing ninepence to get in. She told him she'd consider it and let him know, feeling a leap of excitement in her heart, though what on earth she would wear for such an outing, she hadn't the first idea.

Bet Sutcliffe's old clothes shop solved the problem.

Though she gave Lucy a few funny looks at her enquiry, she produced a red polka dot frock rather like a magician brings a rabbit out of a hat. Lucy was enchanted.

'How much?'

Bet named a sum but on seeing the girl's face fall, dropped it a few more pence. 'Go on, I'm a fool to meself. You can have it for one and sixpence. Pay up quick afore I change me mind.' Lucy paid, the coins carefully saved from her meagre earnings. Bet threw in a pair of equally daring scarlet shoes to match out of sheer pity. The lass had obviously got herself a lad, and Bet remembered being young herself once. She was willing to keep their little transaction a secret, for the very same reason.

The *Palais de Danse* was on Rochdale Road and Lucy was well aware that even at sixteen she was still young to go. Even her mother, were she aware of the plan, would be against it. Grandma

Flo would call it 'a den of iniquity' and the women and young girls who went dancing there either 'fast pieces' or, even worse, 'scarlet women', for all it was Temperance and nothing stronger than coffee was ever served there.

But Lucy had no intention of telling anyone, most especially not Uncle Joshua. What the eye didn't see, the heart didn't grieve over, wasn't that one of Grandma Flo's favourite sayings?

She took especial care with her bath on the following Friday evening, even offering to carry extra buckets of water from the street tap so she could have clean water of her own instead of sharing everyone else's.

Polly was surprised but Big Flo reminded her of her own fetish for cleanliness, so where was the harm?

'I'd rather be on me own too, while I have it,' Lucy insisted, and after exchanging amused glances her mother and grandmother discreetly obliged by going upstairs to sit in a bedroom while the hour-long bath took place. Uncle Joshua was out distributing leaflets for the coming NUWM elections and not expected back for ages, and Benny was off with his pals as usual, so there was no one else to disturb her. Lucy lay back in the steaming water and thought of Tom. She'd fancied him for years; had dreamed of him asking her to be his girl. Perhaps tomorrow he would. Oh, she did hope so!

She heard the click of a latch which she assumed to be her toother. Her eyes were closed and the heat of the water was causing her to drift into a delicious dream of anticipation.

What would it be like? Would Tom admire her? Would he even try and kiss her? Oh, she couldn't make up her mind whether she wanted him to or not, or how she should respond if he did.

She certainly didn't intend to ask her mother for advice. The less people knew of her plans, the better. She could hardly wait.

Upstairs Big Flo settled down to her knitting to the only chair in the small bedroom while Polly sat staring out of the window, watching people pass in the street, although not seeing the one person she longed to see most of all. She hadn't set eyes on Charlie

Stockton for months but he was still there in her mind, an elusive and cherished memory. He'd probably forgotten all about her, perhaps gone off to find work to some other part of the city. Manchester was big enough for anyone to get lost in.

Big Flo said, 'Do you reckon our Lucy has found herself a lad?'

Remembering a previous conversation with her daughter, Polly smiled. 'I think that might well be the case.'

'Then you'd best have a word then, about… you know.'

'Don't be daft, Flo! I had a "word" with Lucy ages ago. She's a good girl and I'm sure we've nothing to fear in that direction.'

'I never had any trouble with my lads, but girls are different. Here, you might as well do summat as sit on that windowsill in a daydream.' Flo handed Polly a skein of wool to hold between her hands, and once she'd adjusted the position to her satisfaction began to wind up a ball of it at lightning speed. 'Grand lads they were too, all three of them. Never gave their mother a moment's concern.' Polly said nothing but moved her hands automatically to accommodate the winding process while continuing to stare out of the window.

'I know our Matthew was keen to marry young, and Cecil never got chance. But our Josh never had no time for women. More interested in his work at the chapel, and politics, and whether his shirt collars were clean enough. Always very particular in that respect.' Flo smiled fondly.

Polly thought it a great pity he wasn't quite so fussy about the purity of his mind. 'Lucy will be fine,' she said again, discouraging further conversation on the subject.

Lucy would have heartily agreed were she privy to the conversation. She felt blissfully happy, but the water was growing cold so she stood up in the bath, enjoying the sensation of the water sliding off her body.

The man standing by the crack of the door noted her pleasure, watching as she ran her hands over the firm contours of her young breasts with a movement that was almost sensual. He saw her shiver, though whether from excitement or the draughts in the old kitchen he couldn't have said. It was the body of an alluring young woman, not a child, the breasts taut, the hips softly rounded. It was almost a pity, he thought, that she was blood-related. Although the Bible permitted him to chastise her, it would be wrong for him to lust after her. But there were other pleasures which would serve to curb his own weaknesses of the flesh as well as his young niece's. She was a wanton child, growing up too fast and in dire need of discipline. But not now, not today. He'd slipped back only to collect his members' address list, which he'd forgotten to take with him. As Lucy reached for the towel, Joshua slipped quietly away.

Benny was, at that precise moment, seated deep inside a railway wagon, waiting with heart in mouth for the chap with the long hooked pole to knock it free and send it rattling away down the track. He'd worked out a new way to deal with the bullying. He'd decided that as he couldn't possibly win against Georgie Eastwood, not even with the backing of the Dove Street Gang, then he must tackle the problem head on and make friends with the enemy.

The very next time Georgie pounced, Benny had been ready. 'Wait, wait!' he'd yelled as the older boys tugged and pulled at his clothing, pushing him this way and that as if he were a yo-yo on a string. 'I want to join your gang.'

Georgie held up one grubby hand and his 'men' instantly stopped their taunting while he considered the matter. 'You want what?'

Benny had swallowed hard, wondering if this was such a good idea after all. 'I want to join your gang,' he'd repeated, deciding there was no other way.

Georgie's mouth twisted into a nasty smile, as if this were the funniest thing he'd ever heard. 'You'd have to take a test. An initiative test. We don't want no weaklings in our gang.'

'I don't mind. I'm your man. I'll take any test you like. Only I'm fed up with the Dove Street lot. They're no good. I want to join yours.'

Georgie had grinned from ear to ear as he'd clenched hold of Benny's coat collar and dragged him close. 'Now that's something I'd really enjoy – seeing you take one of our tests. That'd be a rare treat, that would. Come on then, we'll show you what you have to do to join our gang, won't we, lads?'

And so here he was.

Riding the rails had been the last thing on Benny's mind when he'd once expressed a wish to work on the railways. But he'd made the mistake of letting Georgie Eastwood know of this ambition, and so the test had been devised.

Somewhere over the wall he could hear a group of girls chanting a skipping rhyme: *'I'll tell me ma when I get home, The boys won't leave the girls alone.'* For the first time in his life, he envied them their uncomplicated lives.

But Benny wasn't interested in girls. He wasn't as interested in trains as he used to be either, he discovered. But then he'd never before been at such close quarters with one. He just had to make sure that he survived the experience. He was going through all of this, he told himself, to stop the bloomin' Eastwoods from bullying him. If he could just convince them he wasn't a coward, they'd leave him alone, he was sure of it.

He stood up to peep over the sides of the wagon. It was too high. He had to scramble up the side and cling on like a monkey with all his toes and fingers. Over by the arches he could just catch a glimpse of the Eastwoods. They were huddled together, watching the man who operated the turntables to route each wagon on to its proper line. Benny fell back into the wagon with a clatter, cricking his ankle and wincing with the pain. What had he let himself in for?

He could hear the gush and hiss of steam as trains approached the nearby London Road Station. In his mind's eye he could see its great glass dome with the clock, and the dark red brick patterned with cream tiles. How many times had he hung about that great central area hoping for a bit of a job carrying some lady's luggage, or a free sandwich from the cab men? Now, here in the goods yard, he heard the piercing sound of a whistle, the clank of rods and swish of pistons, wheels screaming on the tracks and then the terrifying boom-boom, like the explosion of a giant banger on Bonfire Night as wagons banged into each other.

He listened with keen attention because each time the man blew his horn it was the signal for the next wagon to be pushed off. It would roll fast along the track till it clanged and banged into the next and the next, running them all together faster and faster along the rails till they reached the buffers at the end. Benny had watched the process a thousand times, and admired the skill involved. This time he was inside one of those very wagons and had never been more scared in all his life.

He told himself that all he had to do was sit tight and wait his turn. Then it would be over in minutes, and he'd be a hero. His turn came sooner than he'd expected and before he was quite prepared.

There was a jerk and the wagon lurched suddenly forward so that he knocked his head on the floor as he fell. He made a grab for one of the iron grips that were stuck into the wooden sides but managed only to grasp hold of a gap where the planking had split. He could feel the pull of gravity as the wagon started to roll faster and faster and then found himself slipping, legs splaying uncontrollably beneath him, the wind whistling through his ears as though it came in one side of his head and out the other. Terror rushed through his body in much the same way.

He told himself he'd be all right. He'd be a hero like Tom Mix or Hopalong Cassidy. Then the Eastwoods would let him join their gang, and leave him alone for good. All he had to do was sit tight and hope for the best. He lost his grip just as his wagon cannoned into the next.

–

Perhaps it was watching her daughter's excitement which brought Charlie Stockton back to mind. But it seemed no sooner did Polly allow herself to think of him than he was there, standing on her doorstep with a woebegone Benny at his side. Her first emotion was a sunburst of joy that he hadn't left the city as she'd imagined, swiftly followed by relief that Joshua was out on one of his collecting rounds. For a moment she could do nothing but gaze into Charlie's eyes. And then she looked at her son.

'Sweet Jesus, what have you been up to?' Polly couldn't believe the state of him. He was covered in coal dust from the tips of his hair to the caps on his clogs, and what she could see of his clothing in between appeared to be hanging in ribbons from him. His socks were round his ankles and blood-red scratch marks, gravely pock-marked with black, ran down his legs like tram-lines. 'Oh, Benny, what have you done to yourself now?'

A pair of glistening eyes blinked at her, begging mutely for sympathy.

'He's been in a bit of bother,' Charlie quietly explained, but it was his glances over her shoulder into the house beyond which alerted Polly to the real danger. She had Benny over the threshold in seconds.

'Thank you, you can leave him with me. I'll see to him now, and get to the bottom of whatever the daft galoot has been up to.'

'Polly!' He had his toe in the door, preventing her from closing it. Panic washed over her like a hot tide.

'Don't, Charlie. Please leave before...' She didn't finish the sentence. Her son's face was screwed up tight with pain and the effort not to cry. He was clearly hurt and Polly really didn't know who to deal with first: Benny, who deserved no sympathy at all for whatever mischief he'd got himself into, or Charlie, who should be thanked for fetching him home, but risked life and limb should Joshua clap eyes on him.

She came to a sudden decision. 'Go now, please. I'll see you tomorrow, at the cafe.'

'You didn't hold to your promise last time,' he said, keeping the toe of his boot in place. 'How can I be sure you will now? And this lad needs attention.' Then, before she could do anything to stop him, he was over the threshold, half carrying the boy through into the kitchen. Dear God, Polly thought, now what should I do?

Big Flo, having forty winks in her chair by the fire, woke with a start, surprised to find a stranger commandeering her dish cloth and asking if she had any hot water to spare. And then she saw her grandson.

'By heck, he's as sooty as the fire bade! Have you been up a chimney, lad?' Benny shook his head, still not trusting himself to speak. The shame was too great. He simply hoped for lightning to strike, or the stone flags to open and swallow him up, so that Uncle Joshua might never catch him looking like this.

Lucy, swathed in dressing gown and towels, was giggling uncontrollably. 'He's welcome to my hot water.' She indicated the bath tub which she'd been about to empty.

'Ideal. I reckon you ladies had best depart. This is man's work,' Charlie said, rolling up his sleeves, and it seemed they had no choice but to obey.

Big Flo, Lucy and Polly went upstairs and sat on the big double bed, clinging to each other in apoplectic laughter.

'Did you ever see such a mess in all your life?' Polly gasped.

'Oh, hecky-thump, that lad'll be the death of us, he will really,' chortled Big Flo.

Lucy was the first to mop up the tears of mirth and put forward an alternative viewpoint. 'I bet it's that Georgie Eastwood. He's been bullying our Benny for years.'

Polly stopped laughing upon the instant. 'This is the first I've heard of any bullying. Why has he never told me?'

'He didn't want to trouble you. Thought you had enough on your plate.'

Big Flo sniffed her disapproval. 'He has too much pride, that lad. Just like his father.'

'Whatever I have on me plate, I won't have my son bullied by a worm like Georgie Eastwood. I'll knock him into the middle of next week, so I will.'

'Nay, the Eastwoods aren't a family to tackle on your own. You'd need the entire regiment of Lancashire Fusiliers to back thee up.'

Lucy agreed. 'Gran's right, you mustn't do anything. Benny would skin me alive if he thought I'd even told you. He must be allowed to sort things out for himself.'

'But how can he? He's only a boy, and that Georgie...'

'Will get what's coming to him one day, see if he doesn't. Leave our Benny to sort it out for himself, Mam. It'll be for the best, believe me.'

'Happen she's right,' Big Flo put in. 'Bullies are all cowards at heart, and unless you stand up to them yourself, they'll go on at you forever. There's nowt worse than a bully, I've allus thought.'

Polly stared at her mother-in-law, struck dumb by this little homily. It seemed strange that Flo could see in others what she never recognised in her own son. Even so Polly conceded they both had a point, for hadn't she countered Joshua's hectoring and bullying by insisting she come and go as she pleased? Yet Georgie Eastwood was big and strong and Benny was – well, he was her little Benny.

'Mebbe I could give him a bit of help from behind the scenes, without telling him. How would that be?' she suggested, and they both agreed with enthusiasm that might be the best way. But before they could discuss details, they heard the scrape of a clog on the flags outside and Big Flo beat Polly to the window by a matter of seconds.

'By heck, he's home early for once. What the hangment will our Josh say, when he finds that Charlie Stockton in his house?'

At one time Polly might have protested that it wasn't Joshua's house. But this wasn't the moment. She flew down the stairs, grabbed Charlie, still with his sleeves rolled and hands dripping from helping poor Benny bathe the cuts and lacerations to his legs, and tried to pull him away. Her son was now shining clean, swathed in the towels she'd set to. The hath water, however, looked like tar. Polly knew she was babbling something unintelligible as she struggled to drag Charlie out the back door, but couldn't seem able to get a proper grip on her words.

'What in damnation…?' He fiercely resisted her efforts.

'For God's sake, go. Quickly, Charlie. Go now! Joshua is coming.'

'I must see you, Polly.'

'Yes, yes!'

'When?'

'Anytime.'

'Tomorrow?'

'Yes, if you like. Now go. *Please!*'

Only when he saw the depth of her distress did he cooperate. 'My jacket?'

She flung it at him and closed the back door just as Joshua walked into the kitchen.

Chapter Twenty-Four

Benny's suffering was far from over. Big Flo lifted a square of red-hot pink lint from out of a pan of boiling water and slapped it, without any apology or warning, upon the victim's knee. The yell that went up would have wakened the dead.

'Is that absolutely necessary?' Polly cried, running to comfort her distressed child.

'It'll go septic,' Flo announced grimly, shaking her head, 'if we don't get all yon muck out.'

No speck of dirt would have dared resist such a thorough scalding. Pink lint was Big Flo's favourite method of first aid, that and iodine which she now plastered over all Benny's cuts and scratches, making him yell even louder. By the time she was done, his injuries were certainly clean, if a strange combination of beetroot red and orange. Poor Benny's head was also well larded with goose fat to bring down the swelling. Big Flo completed her first aid by fashioning a sling from an old belt and hooking it about his neck.

'That should keep you out of mischief for a bit, you daft barm-pot. Next time, you hit him first.'

'You'll not tell Uncle Joshua?' Benny begged. It was his greatest fear.

Both women looked at each other in silence. Having post-poned his tea for half an hour, Joshua was now in his 'study', otherwise known as the front parlour, preparing his speech for what would probably be a difficult meeting ahead. So far he had shown little interest in events taking place in the kitchen, except to be irritated by the inconvenience of bath night in such a small house. The women hoped to keep it that way.

'Get yourself up them stairs into your mam's bed for once, afore he starts getting curious.' And half lifting her grandson from the chair with her powerful arms, Big Flo gave him a little shove in the right direction. It took no further bidding to send him scampering up the stairs, injured or no.

Joshua chose that precise moment to leave his papers and emerge from the front parlour. Suspicion crept into his pale eyes as he took in the enamel basin of water, the bottle of iodine, and Polly's white face.

'What's going on here? Not more baths?'

'Nowt,' said Flo, gathering up the evidence. 'I cut my hand on the mangle, that's all. But I've sorted it now. Come and eat your tea before it goes cold.'

She placed a dish of rabbit stew in front of her son.

Still casting glances in Polly's direction, but realising he'd get no more information out of his mother, Joshua began to eat. The two women said nothing, didn't even dare glance at each other until Joshua, having finished his meal, had downed a mug of tea, read the evening newspaper from end to end, then painstakingly shaved with the hot water Big Flo brought him, in readiness for going out again.

Then he put on his best black jacket, greening somewhat with age but still giving the air of authority he craved, and collected his bowler hat. They all sat watching these preparations in silence, like children waiting for their teacher to release them from the bondage of lessons.

'I believe they may well appoint me branch chairman tonight,' he told them, 'since I've made my mark as treasurer. The unit's funds are in a healthy state, which is all down to me.'

His fingers struggled with the studs that held the starched collar to the equally stiff shirt, and his neck in a stranglehold. Joshua insisted on wearing a white collar, since it put him a cut above the rest of the men in their union shirts and mufflers, but his mother was too fond of starch. Big Flo felt it gave a shirt the necessary degree of smartness and cleanliness in direct relation to the pain it inflicted upon the wearer.

'That'll be grand, son,' she agreed, nodding wisely as she forced the reluctant stud through the slit, not in the least interested.

Polly said nothing, simply thankful that he hadn't clapped eyes on Charlie's retreating figure, and wishing Joshua would be on his way so she could go up and see Benny. The moment he had finally gone, that was exactly what she did and to her great relief found the boy fast asleep, right in the middle of the big bed.

Back downstairs again she confronted Big Flo. 'What made you do that? First you help me with the carpets, now you save our Benny. What's going on? Have you changed sides or something?'

Flo considered the question as she cleared the table and poured boiling water into the sink. 'Boys will be boys, and our Benny isn't a bad 'un. And you ain't such a bad mother either,' she added in a gruff voice: 'Anyroad, happen I think Joshua shouldn't have things all his own way. I reckon he's mebbe had a bit too much of that already.' Following which enigmatic remark, she buttoned her lip tight and would say no more on the subject.

In that moment Polly felt a huge outpouring of gratitude and without stopping to think, wrapped her arms about the great bulk of her mother-in-law, and hugged her tight. 'Thanks, I really do appreciate it.'

'Nay, don't talk soft. You're the one who's pulled herself up by her boot straps, not me.' Big Flo did not find it easy to display emotion, and Polly knew these were giant strides she had taken, both in defying her son's iron rule and in offering a compliment, however grudgingly, to her Catholic daughter-in-law.

She felt a great desire to open up the whole subject of Matthew's death, to ask the old woman if she thought it had been entirely accidental. But how could you ask a mother if she thought one son capable of murdering the other? Of at least standing by and doing nothing while he was mown down by a raging mob. It was certainly not a question Polly felt able to ask, perhaps because she feared the answer.

On the day of Lucy's first date, unaware that even at this moment her daughter was curling her hair and trying on the scarlet frock in the secrecy of their bedroom, Polly was seated in the market cafe, holding hands over the table top with Charlie. They were talking with such intensity it was as if they'd a lifetime of news to impart which, in a way, was the case.

Charlie was telling her how worried he'd been after that first meeting at the tram stop, how he'd followed her home and finally plucked up courage to call. And how thrilled he'd been when she'd come to find him on the fruit and vegetable barrow.

'You shouldn't have come to the house. Joshua doesn't like strangers calling.'

'Is that why you told me to stay away? Who is he this chap, your keeper?'

Polly stirred her tea, though it didn't need it for she didn't take sugar, staring pensively into the swirling dark brown liquid. To explain the nature of her brother-in-law's control over her seemed impossible, and made her feel uncomfortable and disloyal. Not only that, but her own emotions confused her. Should she even be here, with this lovely man? Wasn't it a betrayal to Matthew? 'I owe Joshua a lot in a way. If he hadn't been there to watch over me after Matthew's death, my children might've been taken away from me and then I'd've run mad.'

'Or you might have got on with your life a lot quicker.'

Polly met his gentle gaze and saw that could well be true. Everything was different now. At the time she'd been in need of someone to take care of her and the children. Big Flo, even Joshua in his way, had done that. The sleeping powders had helped her through the achingly long, sleepless nights, and to live through the empty days.

Now, following what she had learned of his attack on Eileen, an attack meant for herself, Polly felt nothing but loathing for him. He might just as well have put a knife to the poor girl's throat, the effect had been the same.

Yes, there was a dark side to his nature. His treatment of Benny had been inhuman, and the nasty words he had used upon Lucy obscene. She dreaded to think what he might do next. The man was sick; his obsession to control and bring them all into the Methodist fold had twisted his mind. Polly shuddered even now at the memory of his violent treatment of them all.

'I don't like looking back,' she said, the words blurted out as she continued to stir her tea furiously. Charlie took the spoon from her fingers, as if afraid she might break the cup with it.

'I'm all for looking forward myself.' His blue eyes twinkled merrily. 'Mind you, I've had a few adventures in me time that I could tell you about.'

'Go on then, tell me,' she said with relief, wanting to think of other matters. 'I love stories.' And they smiled into each other's eyes then looked quickly away, embarrassed by the intimacy of the moment.

'Mebbe you'd just best drink your tea before it goes cold.'

Polly obediently did as instructed, battening down feelings of guilt, telling herself Matthew wouldn't want her to take the veil. He'd always been warm hearted and practical, and he'd want her to be happy. This man, this kindly ex-sailor, once a rebellious young orphan, was making her feel happy again. Polly rested her chin in her hand and thought that she could listen to him all day. He was telling her now about one of his many voyages.

'And where is it, this wondrous land where there are miles of golden sand and gorgeously coloured birds that can talk?'

'Australia. I'll take you there one day, Polly. Just you and me. It's a long way, the other side of the world, so it'll take us a year or two to save up.'

'A year or two? I should think it will. Half a lifetime more like.'

'So what's the rush?' he said with a quiet smile.

He spoke as if they might well spend half a lifetime together. A faint sensation, like a butterfly's wing, fluttered inside her and Polly felt herself blushing. 'Don't you play fast and loose with me, Charlie Stockton. What makes you think I'd want to travel to the other side of the world with you, or that I'd even give you the time of day tomorrow, for that matter?' She lifted her chin in pert fashion, challenging him with her green-grey gaze.

Charlie shook his head in admiration. 'Don't I just love it when you look so sparky? You know very well, Polly Pride, that you and me were meant for each other, It was fate that took you to the tram stop that day, fate that told you not to take your shawl so that I'd take pity on you and lend you my jacket. And I don't lend it to just anyone, you can be sure of that.'

'Then it's honoured I am.'

'So you should be, to be sure,' he teased, imitating her Irish accent now.

Then they were both laughing, and he was reaching for her hands, caressing her fingers as if he never meant to let them go. Polly felt the funny fluttering sensation change to one of a burning need, so fierce that it stunned her. But surely it wasn't a sin to want to be loved?

Somewhere a clock began to strike and she jumped to her, feet in alarm. 'Lord, what time is it? I must be off.' She turned and pushed her way through the other diners to reach the door, then remembered her vow not to be bullied by Joshua ever again. She stopped dead and, turning, saw that Charlie hadn't even moved. He was still seated at the table, one hand outstretched, palm upwards, fingers curled open as if imploring her to fill them once more with her own. Very slowly she retraced her steps, weaving her way back through the crowded cafe, sat down again and did just that.

For a long time they sat unmoving, eyes locked in a compelling gaze, as if they could will time to stand still. At last Polly licked dry lips, struggling to find her voice. 'I really should go. Benny will be home from school soon.'

'I know.'

'I can't risk leaving him alone in the house with... I'm sorry, Charlie. I have to go. Don't I have work to do?' Still she made no move.

He gripped her fingers harder. 'And I meant every word I said. I'm not just throwing you a line, Polly. You're very special to me, you know that. You'll come again, won't you?'

And she felt her cheeks start to burn, just to feel his loving eyes upon her.

She wanted to lean over the table and kiss him, never to stop kissing him. She wanted to feel his body pressed against hers, to experience delights she'd thought would never be hers again. Holding hands just wasn't enough. 'If you promise to stay away from the house, I'll come. Because if Joshua were ever to find out about you, well, he'd...'

'What would he do?'

Polly shuddered. 'I'm not sure. I just know that he must never find out. He isn't to be trusted.'

Charlie's face tightened. 'He's not laid a finger on you, has he? Because if he has...'

Common sense warned Polly against revealing the beating her brother-in-law had given her. She didn't want Charlie to feel responsible for her safety. 'He can make life difficult for me, and for the children. I could meet you here tomorrow. There are things I would like your advice on.'

'What kind of advice,' He'd gathered up both her hands again and Polly leaned closer, quickly outlining her plans for starting up her carpet business again, but how difficult it was to find more stock, and transport it.

'So it's only my muscle you're after and nowt else, is that it?' he teased.

'That's right. I'm looking for a bit of labour I don't have to pay for,' she joked right back, and they smiled into each other's eyes.

'But you won't let this tyrant brother-in-law of yours keep us apart?'

She shook her head, too full of emotion to speak.

A long time later Charlie reluctantly let her go, but only after insisting she meet him again, same time, same place, the very next day.

'I can't tomorrow, it's Sunday.'

'Monday then?'

'Monday it is.' How could she refuse when she wanted him so? Finally, and reluctantly, Polly made her way home.

That same evening, Lucy found that the dance was indeed wonderful. Everything she had dreamed of, in fact. Right from the moment of meeting Tom in the foyer, where there was a horde of other young people like themselves, and older ones too out for a good time, everything was perfect. They put their coats in the cloakroom then drifted in and out of the glittering array of shops which sold sweets and ice cream and all manner of good things. Not that Lucy had any money to spend, but just to look in the windows made her mouth water and filled her with delight.

'When I've made my fortune,' Tom informed her, 'I'll buy you the biggest box of chocolates in the place.'

She smiled up at him. 'I'll look forward to that.' And they both chuckled.

Strains of swing music lured them up the thickly carpeted stairs which, being something of an expert on these matters by now, Lucy knew to be the finest wool, and of the very best quality. At the top was a splendid restaurant which Tom steered her quickly past, and a small snack bar into which he proudly led her. 'I thought we'd have a coffee before we go in,' he airily informed her, and she squeezed his arm with delight.

'Ooh, Tom. This is the most wonderful night of my life!' She could hardly breathe for the excitement of it all, nor wait to see the glories of the ballroom if the grandeur of the foyer was anything to go by.

Lucy looked at him, eyes shining, wondering how she could have imagined he could ever have used those dirty words, let alone about her. He was lovely was Tom, and she was quite certain she was falling in love with him, praying he might soon feel the same way about her. Right now, she longed for the dance to answer all her dreams.

The evening did indeed live up to expectations. Tom danced every dance with her, not letting her out of his sight for a moment or allowing any of the other blokes to get a look in. They danced the foxtrot and the Veleta, a dreamy waltz in which he held her especially close, and even the Gay Gordons which left her head spinning and quite robbed her of breath. Since Lucy had never been to a dance before, he had to teach her all the steps but she was a fast learner, and if she was at all uncertain she would simply cling tighter to him as he spun her round, which he didn't seem to mind one bit.

During the interval, when the band went off for a rest, he bought them each a glass dish of ice cream and they sat eating it on the carpeted stairs, licking up every scrap with delight. When they had finished and Tom had returned the dishes to the counter, they both sat shyly holding hands. Lucy struggled to think of something witty or funny to say to make him laugh. He wasn't even looking at her, or smiling, but seemed to be frowning very seriously. She began to worry that something had gone wrong, Perhaps he was bored with her already, or had seen another girl he liked better. Her stomach tightened painfully at the thought.

At length Tom spoke, addressing the toes of his polished boots. 'There's something I've been wanting to ask you for a while now, Lucy.' He took a breath. 'Will you be my girl? You're the best-looking lass in the whole dance hall, and I'd really like it if you would. Will you?' The words tumbled from out of his mouth as if he couldn't get them out fast enough.

Lucy was so thrilled she could hardly speak. With her own eyes fixed on her scarlet shoes, and feeling her cheeks must surely match them in colour, she nodded. 'Of course I will, I've been wanting you to ask me that for ages.'

'Oh, Lucy, that's grand.'

They cast a sideways glance at each other then, all pinkcheeked and smiling. The broad sweep of carpeted staircase, even the ballroom, seemed tinged with rose pink to their eyes. Wasn't this what she had dreamed of, night after lonely night?

Grinning from ear to ear, Tom took her hand firmly in his own. 'The band's back. Let's dance.'

Oh, how she loved him! How she loved life. It was all so wonderful. Lucy also loved the feel of the scarlet dress swirling about her bare legs, and hearing the red shoes pattering on the wooden dance floor, such a welcome relief from her clomping clogs. Tom looking equally grand in a grey suit and his best boots. What a fine couple they made.

'We'll come here again,' he announced, as if he wasn't in the least concerned about how such treats might be afforded. 'We'll come regular now.'

And as they walked home he told her all about the good job he had on the railways, how he meant to do even better in future, just in case he should happen to wed within the next year or two. Then he drew her into the shadows of the ginnel and kissed her, and Lucy discovered what it felt like to be weak with love.

Polly kept her promise and over the following weeks met Charlie just as often as she could, for all it was never easy to escape. Big Flo grew suspicious that not all her outings were concerned with carpets. Joshua spent a great deal of his time out and about on NUWM business, even so Polly continued to take great care since he was unemployed and his movements unpredictable.

Determined as she was to live her own life, Polly worried that if she saw Charlie at the cafe for lunch, or walked with him in the afternoon, they might accidentally run into Joshua. She was constantly glancing over her shoulder for fear he would appear, like a bad genie. It was all dreadfully nerve-racking.

But although she remained jumpy as a kitten, she continued to take the risk. Joshua had no rights over her. He wasn't her husband, for God's sake. Just to see how eagerly Charlie came to her filled her with joy.

They snatched moments together whenever they could, always in different places so as not to run the risk of being spotted by any of Joshua's old work colleagues either. They walked by the canal, or mingled with the crowds in the city centre, looking in shop windows on St Anne's Square or marvelling at the glitter of jewellery in Hancock's windows in King Street, as if they had money in their pockets to spend.

They might catch a tram, buying a twopenny ticket from the clippie's rack, and sit for as long as they could on the hard wooden seats, just so they could hold hands and be together. Their favourite trip was sitting on the open top deck of the Number Two to Heaton Park on a lovely sunny day, though they would scarcely have noticed had it rained.

And all the time they talked. Charlie would describe what work he had managed to get that week: perhaps a bit of casual labour chopping and selling wood, or a few days' work in a warehouse, or if all else failed minding his friend's fruit and vegetable barrow. Polly would explain how she must make a success of her business in order to ensure a good future for her children. But also they talked of themselves, their feelings for each other, and of nothing in particular, as lovers do.

The first time he kissed her, Polly thought she might die of pleasure. It was gentle and exciting all at the same time. His lips against hers were sweet and yet demanding. She knew, deep down, that she was falling in love, and why shouldn't she? He'd made it plain he felt the same way about her.

'I want us to walk out proper,' he said. 'Not creep about, in this hole-in-a-comer fashion, like a young lad and lass on the monkey-walk.'

She urged him to be patient, explaining how difficult her life still was, how she was constantly asked to account for her every movement. The children, of course, had to be considered too. They'd already guessed she was up to something, and Polly was anxious to put their fears at rest, carefully explaining to them that her friendship with Charlie did not mean she had forgotten Matthew.

'He'll always have a special place in my heart, as will you two. But one day won't you both grow up and love someone else besides me? And won't I be on me own then? So I hope you don't mind if I look for a bit of happiness myself. We can love more than one person at a time, after all.'

Lucy smiled and hugged her, happy for her mother. Benny looked rather worried. 'I'd never leave you, Mam.'

''Course you will, one day, when you're a grown man and take a wife and have children of your own. It's only right and proper.'

He considered this for a moment, rather liking the sound of it. 'But you'll not leave us now, Mam, will you?' he asked, just to be sure, and Polly wrapped him close in her arms.

'Not even a bolt of lightning let alone Joshua's evil temper, could drive me away from my precious children.'

Her brother-in-law did appear far more agreeable nowadays. Following the showdown over money, he seemed to have accepted that Polly was starting up her business again.

She did once hear him having something of a disagreement with Big Flo, apparently over the old woman's helping her at the warehouse, since Polly heard her mother-in-law remark that she was too old to be dictated to, and big enough to do as she pleased. Rarely did Flo stand up to her son so Polly had felt flattered and a little puzzled by this increasing show of solidarity. But that seemed to represent a turning point. He'd made no further comments after that, except to express satisfaction she was contributing at last, as if he hadn't been the one stopping her from getting out and about, or back to work, through all those long dreary months.

Joshua agreed that she might visit neighbours, the local shops and market, or simply go out for a walk with her children if she'd a mind. Nevertheless he instructed Big Flo to watch her like a hawk. He wasn't to know that his mother at once informed her daughter-in-law of this fact. For all she strove to keep a foot in each camp, she was leaning, more and more in Polly's favour.

'Where you off to now?' she would ask, adopting an aggrieved expression whenever Polly pulled on her shawl, and then she'd fasten a large pin at the neck for her, concerned she should keep warm end take good care of herself.

'Just down the market, Flo. We have to eat.'

'Don't be late back, mind, or you'll catch it,' she'd whisper. 'We don't want no awkward questions, do we? Our Josh don't have the patience Matthew had, so take care who you talk to down there, lass, or who's watching you. There are eyes everywhere, don't forget.' And she'd tap the side of her large nose with one finger, giving a knowing wink as if they were conspirators with a shared secret.

Surely, Polly thought, Big Flo didn't know about her and Charlie, did she? Could she have guessed?

Sometimes all this subterfuge made her feel as if she were a young girl like Lucy, who Polly guessed was secretly courting young Tom Shackleton, and not a grown woman at all. Joshua had, at first, tried to insist that she give a detailed outline of her destination and anticipated time of return.

'Sweet Jesus, I'm not a child, nor one of your weavers needing to clock in and out!' she'd said, outfacing him. 'The hell with that.'

'If you blaspheme, I'll wash your mouth out with carbolic soap, whether you're an adult or not,' he'd calmly informed her.

And looking into his cold eyes, Polly experienced a prickle of unease between her shoulder blades, fearing for so, she refused to be confined. 'I apologise for the language,' she conceded. 'Sure and you'd try the patience of a saint. Even so, I'll come and go as I please without asking your permission, Joshua Pride.'

Once outside the front door of number twenty-three, she'd turn in quite the opposite direction from the alleged objective of her errand and hurry straight into Charlie's arms, wherever it was he waited. Desperate to see him, she became more reckless and daring than she knew to be quite wise, but didn't seem able to help herself. Besides, Joshua maybe peeved by her increasing rebellion but they'd been so careful she was quite certain he didn't suspect the truth.

Chapter Twenty-Five

Joshua guessed that something was afoot, though what exactly he couldn't quite decide. This sudden and frequent desire to visit the market, or call on neighbours Polly had never previously bothered about, filled him with deep suspicion. It was bad enough that she had defied him over the matter of the carpets, but, whenever he challenged her on the subject, she'd say she was out buying stock, or living her life, as if she surely had a right to do. In his opinion, she had no such right. She was becoming far too independent.

Nothing, in fact, was going his way at the moment.

The latest NUWM meeting had been a disaster as Joshua had failed to secure the post of chairman. Cal Eastwood, of all people, had been granted that honour. He'd sent his henchmen round, urging everyone to vote for him, claiming Joshua was too radical.

This was a severe blow to Joshua's political ambitions. He hadn't devised all those clever money-making schemes to have some other man spend the funds and take all the glory. And having Cal Eastwood as chairman would badly affect his ability to take what Joshua considered proper recompense for the services he rendered as treasurer. Pilfered money had become a vital part of Joshua's income. But Cal wasn't one to miss a trick.

'Don't feel badly. You'll happen be lucky next year,' the victor had magnanimously consoled him, before going with his mates to celebrate over a pint or two in the Gaping Goose. Joshua declined an invitation to join them. Next year seemed a long way off. Who knew what state the organisation, or the country, would be in by then?

So far as Joshua was concerned, the NUWM seemed to be losing its edge. It had not allowed him to make any significant mark on the public consciousness. Most of the newspapers, local and national alike, had refused to write about it in any positive way. The greatest public sympathy had been won by the hunger marchers of Jarrow, who had no connection with the NUWM at all, were non-political, and as a result had received the best publicity.

Back in 1931 it had seemed the NUWM could do no wrong. The national membership had been strong and growing, and Joshua had believed he would go all the way to the top with it and find himself in Parliament, rubbing shoulders with the likes of Neville Chamberlain and Ramsay MacDonald, with him having a real say in the way the country was governed.

Now he was facing the unpalatable truth that, for all it was one of the few organisations to stand up for the ordinary man in the street, it had failed to mobilise more than a fraction of the unemployed. Joshua made his feelings on the subject known to his colleagues in no uncertain terms.

'Wal Hannington, our leader, blames the Labour Party and the TUC, but I blame you lot! It's apathy,' he accused them. He was doubly concerned because, little by little, the membership was dwindling, and with it his last hopes of glory.

'We're still here, aren't we?' one man shouted back to him.

Joshua slammed his fist down on the lectern. 'But there's not enough of you. No one else must leave. It's a disgrace. We must all stand together. We seem to spend far too much of our time campaigning for winter relief – of benefit to some perhaps but hardly worthy of our full attention.'

If he wasn't sticking a knife in some employer's back, Joshua felt unfulfilled.

Still without any prospect of employment, largely because of the prejudice of prospective employers who now viewed him as a troublemaker, he could see no future for himself but a slow decline. The prospect served only to increase the bitterness he harboured against life in general and those going up in the world, such as his sister-in-law.

It gave him enormous pleasure to have made her life such a complete misery since Matthew's death. Now, his present circumstances hardened his resolve to make the Irish woman suffer even further. He resolved to find out exactly what she was up to and, if she was making money, to discover where it was she kept it hidden.

He began to follow her. Day after day, with increasing persistence and dogged patience, he traced her steps as she went seeking carpets to buy till he could have recited almost every street she had tried from St Andrew's Square to Cheetham Hill Road, from Piccadilly to Miles Platting, neglecting his chapel and NUWM duties in order to do so. He would hide in a shop doorway or ginnel and watch as she knocked on door after door, feeling intense gratification at her continued lack of success.

Yet instead of looking cast down and weary, Polly remained buoyant and elated. There was a glow about her that deeply troubled him. It would certainly pay him to keep a close eye on her, he decided. All he needed was to think of some way to upset her apple cart, for things were going a little too well for Madam. Even now, the fire in her dark hair seemed alive in the sunshine, bouncing on her shoulders with a vibrant life of its own, for she was almost running down the street with the kind of excitement usually reserved for meeting a lover. But how could she have a lover? She surely had no opportunity.

Joshua turned the corner to discover that finally his patience had been rewarded as he saw her run into the arms of a man, and turn up her laughing face for his kiss. He watched with cold speculation as the man lifted her slender figure in his arms to swing her round, the naked joy on his face almost painful to see. Now he understood where she had been going, and the lies she had been telling. Not so innocent after all, but sneaking off to see this man, her lover, and take part, no doubt, in fornication.

But who was this man? And then Joshua remembered the unknown visitor to his door more than a year ago. Of course. Charlie Stockton was the fellow's name. How foolish of him to forget.

Polly decided that her own immediate area was too poor for many folk to own big carpets. It was therefore time to search further afield. 'We'll try over towards Cheshire way. There's more money round there.' Benny was in school, and had been warned she'd be late home. Lucy was working on the tripe and trotter stall, and Charlie had promised transport.

'You find 'em, I'll carry 'em,' he'd said with his cheeky grin. 'And I'll keep an eye out for something interesting too. No reason why I shouldn't do a bit of buying and selling on my own account, is there?'

It was wonderful sitting up on the high cart with Charlie, even if the horse was old and they could probably have walked faster. But the animal was strong and sure, and would come into his own when the cart was piled high with the carpets Polly hoped to buy. Inside her waistband was tucked the money that Eileen had saved for her; several golden guineas which Polly had guarded with great care.

She felt as light-hearted and happy as a young girl on a first date with her young man. She half glanced up at Charlie, loving the way his hair grew tousled in the wind, the curve of his lashes upon his cheeks, the gentleness of his fingers curled about the reins. Everything was perfect, even the weather. The sun was shining, birds were singing. It was a soft spring day with the promise of summer ahead and, as they left the city behind them, it was even possible to see the sky turn blue, with streaks of pink and white cloud.

'Did you ever see such a lovely sight?' said Polly, sighing with pleasure.

'I see a lovelier one every day.' And as he pulled her close to his side, she blushed, for there was no doubting the compliment was directed at herself.

They rode along quiet country lanes before coming to a small village, but Polly insisted they keep going. This wasn't the place to find second-hand carpets. In truth, she would have been content to drive all day with Charlie and not even think about business. At this time of year she would once have been thinking of the Whit Walks, but there were more important things to occupy her how. She had Charlie to think about, and her living to earn. She was also desperate to find a home for her family. Somehow she had to save her children from Joshua's tyranny.

'Where does he think you are today?' Charlie asked, intuitively reading her mind. Polly shrugged.

'Who knows what he thinks? Isn't he a law unto himself.'

'You don't reckon he'd follow you, do you?'

She looked at him, wide-eyed with shock. 'He wouldn't dare.' It was something she'd never considered, yet as she did so now, she felt a chill creep over her as if his eyes were indeed upon her. 'The man is capable of anything if it serves his purpose. But I hope not,' she added more thoughtfully, then snuggled closer to Charlie's side. 'Let's not talk about Joshua, or even think about him today. Let's pretend there's just you and me in the whole wide world. Wouldn't that be grand?'

'It's what I want more than anything,' Charlie said, and trusted the horse to lead them while he kissed Polly so thoroughly she was in no doubt of his sincerity. 'It's time you got out from under his jurisdiction altogether.' Charlie wished he could ask her to marry him there and then and have done with it, but what could he offer her? Nothing, He was earning little, and she less. Besides, her heart was set on this business and he knew her for an independent woman, not one to be rushed.

'Oh, I mean to leave all right, just soon as I get my business going. That's the most important thing right now,' Polly agreed, and he subsided into silence.

By ten o'clock she was knocking on a door. It was to be the first of many that morning but with no success. Most of the householders were dismissive, some downright rude. Nobody had a carpet to sell, though one or two seemed almost regretful, perhaps more ready for quick cash than they liked to admit. 'We're wasting our time,' Polly mourned.

'Not necessarily. We'll mebbe strike lucky in the next street.'
Unfortunately the next proved as bad as the first and yet foolishly,
unreasonably, they were happy.

They stopped and ate their sandwiches amongst a carpet of
bluebells beneath a spreading horse chestnut tree, pink with buds.
The smell of the flowers was heady and magical, such a romantic
setting that Polly almost didn't care if she found no carpets at all.
Wasn't she having a lovely day out with her man?

For a while they lay quietly on the sun-warmed grass together,
feeding each other crusts of bread and cheese, biting into crunchy
apples. Then they lay in the sun and slept for a while, Charlie
with his arms about her, stroking her hair with the tips of his
fingers. Polly's eyelids grew heavy and languorous even as a new
excitement burned within. She wanted him. More than she could
ever have thought possible. She lifted her face and touched his lips
with her own. 'Would you take me, Charlie Stockton, if I asked
you to?'

She felt his arms tighten convulsively about her. 'That's not
fair, Polly. You know I want you. But we aren't wed, have no
hope of getting married until we've a decent income coming in
and a home of us own.'

She sighed. 'The trouble with Lancashire folk is they're far too
practical for their own good. A little Irish romance wouldn't go
amiss, don't you reckon?'

'I agree, but romance doesn't pay the bills.' He laughed softly
in her ear. 'Don't I love every little bit of you, Polly Pride? We'll
make it come right, I'm sure of it. While you're building yourself
a fine carpet business I'll find myself a job, or do a bit of trading
on me own account, Then I'll find us a house and marry you like
a shot. Won't I then take you to my bed with joy?'

'Goodness, if we've all of that to go through then we've really
no time to waste, kissing and canoodling,' said Polly, kissing the
lobe of his ear and sliding her mouth along the line of his jaw, in
spite of her words.

As he reached for her, she pushed him playfully away to run
from him, squealing with delight, leaping over tree roots, skipping

through the bluebells deep into the woods so that he had to chase and catch her. Only then did she let him kiss her and roll her amongst the flowers, becoming intoxicated by their scent and his closeness so that it was hard for her to think, let alone resist him. And because he couldn't help himself, he wasted a good half hour returning her kisses with a new fierceness whilst struggling to keep a tight hold on his emotions. It wouldn't do to let them run away with his common sense, not just yet. What would happen to Polly if she took trouble home? He didn't care to think.

Some time later she sat up, tidied her hair, dusted off the grass and petals, and smiled into his eyes. 'Come on, laddy. We've work to do.'

Charlie set out on his own quest for household items to sell. He hoped one day to buy a horse and cart. Might even buy this one off his pal. It would come in handy if Polly were to make a success of the carpets, as well as be useful for selling his bits and pieces. He'd done well lately, chopping and selling firewood. He'd even managed to buy some boxes of early strawberries which he'd sold at a good price to the ice cream makers. But it wasn't a regular income, which was what he desperately needed, for all of this brought in barely enough to cover the cost of his lodgings.

Perhaps it was his cheeky charm which appealed to the house-wives but today he struck lucky. He bought several items which he felt sure he could sell on at a profit. An old iron mangle with wooden rollers, a pram, even a fancy bird cage amongst other practical items. He stowed them aboard the cart and went on his way, whistling.

Polly too had finally been successful.

'Yes, dear, I've an old bedroom carpet I'd be glad enough to see the back of,' came the much hoped for reply at last. 'Perhaps I can persuade my husband to buy me a new one then.'

For a moment Polly was so surprised at this positive response that she found herself suggesting the woman's husband may not care to be deprived of it, but the woman only laughed, declaring he'd been promising her a new carpet for years. 'All he needed was a kick up the backside, as you might say. What would you give me for it? I'd want at least five pounds.'

'It's not worth thirty bob,' said Polly, shaking her head, and looking suitably glum as she viewed the carpet. Inwardly she was delighted by its size. The house was a large Victorian villa, the bedroom large enough to take the whole of her own modest dwelling, and the carpet, though at least as old as the house, was thick and substantial. 'The colours have faded. Can't sell it as it is, of course. It needs cutting and stitching.' And a good clean, though she didn't like to say so.

She drove the woman down to one pound fifteen shillings and counted the coins into her hand before she could change her mind.

Later, when Charlie had rolled it up and stacked it on the cart, he expressed his admiration. 'Thirty-five bob for a carpet that size? You're a hard bargainer, Polly Pride.'

'No, just meaner than her poor husband, who'll find himself with a large bill for a new replacement.'

This success filled her with new hope, and perhaps the fact that they now carried a carpet gave them credibility, for their luck improved. They found two more willing sellers and later, as they unloaded their booty in the warehouse, discovered they'd accidentally rolled up a chamber pot with the bedroom carpet, by mistake.

'Not to worry,' said Charlie. 'We'll start a new line. It can go with the bits and bobs I've found. It'll all help to make our fortune, Polly lass.' Then he pulled her into his arms to kiss her again by way of celebration at their success, right in the middle of all the rolls of carpet and general clutter.

Finally breaking away, all pink-cheeked and flustered, Polly said, 'You've a wicked way with you, Charlie Stockton. I worry over me own daughter getting into trouble, and here I am behaving like a loose woman. Our Lucy has more sense than I have.'

Polly might well have thought differently in the weeks following, had she witnessed her daughter tossing the red shoes over the back yard wall each Saturday evening. She did guess that Lucy was not going to chat with her friend Sal quite so often as she claimed, but was in fact walking out with Tom Shackleton. Polly could only hope that Joshua was not quite so wise to the antics of young girls as a mother was. So long as he didn't suspect, there was really nothing to worry about. But then, she didn't see Lucy walking off to the Palais dressed in a polka dot dress that would have given her grandmother a heart attack.

–

Lucy always came back down to earth from the excitement of these expeditions with a rude bump as she shinned over the back yard wall, thereby avoiding the risk of clicking the latch on the gate. It also allowed her time to strip off the party frock in the lavatory and pull on the skirt and blouse she'd hidden there earlier. Shivering with cold and the residue of delight from Tom's kisses, she would wrap the dress and shoes in a brown paper parcel, carefully stowing it away in her secret hiding place behind the ash pit. Finally dusting herself down, and checking that she'd wiped off every trace of lipstick, she would saunter casually into the kitchen, usually empty at that time of night, and scurry upstairs to bed.

On one particular night she found Uncle Joshua sitting at the kitchen table reading a paper. He looked up when she entered, then pointedly took out his watch from his waistcoat pocket to consult it. 'And what time do you call this? I told you to be home by ten. It's ten minutes past.'

'I'm sorry. We got talking and forgot the time, Sal and me,' Lucy said, sticking to her story.

'Talking girlish nonsense, no doubt.'

She couldn't resist trying to score a point over him. 'As a matter of fact we were talking about Father Donevan, and how upset he is that I no longer go to church, as I have done for years?'

'Indeed?'

'He'd like me to go and have a chat with him, at the presbytery, to explain. I said I would.' The whole story was largely a fabrication, though she justified it by thinking that Father Donevan would indeed love to have her back in the fold, as she would love to get one over on her uncle. Lucy was enjoying the way he was scowling, for she knew how he hated to be bested by anyone, most of all a Catholic priest.

'Go to your room. You'll come to my study before breakfast and I'll set you some scriptures to learn on the subject of obedience. That'll teach you for staying out late, and satisfy this sudden craving you have found for religion.'

Lucy experienced such a surge of loathing towards her uncle that she pummelled her pillow till she was utterly exhausted, only wishing it were his sanctimonious face. She had expected her mother to be there in the big bed, ready to offer comfort, but Polly still wasn't back from her trip to Cheshire. Moments later she did arrive home but was so obviously tired Lucy said nothing as she slid between the sheets, and within seconds was deeply asleep.

Sleep refused to come for herself, although she was by now outwardly calm. Lucy marvelled that Uncle Joshua couldn't feel the heat of her anger through the bedroom wall. She felt as if she were walking a tightrope, and he was just waiting for her to fall off it. She vowed she would take whatever he threw at her without complaint, so long as he didn't find out about Tom. She was hoping to win her mother round to her side before her uncle discovered the truth. Polly liked Tom Shackleton, and since Dad had died saving his life, surely she would approve.

Downstairs, in his draughty cubby-hole under the stairs, Benny shivered and worried in private, subdued by deep pity for his sister and only too thankful it wasn't he who had to face Uncle Joshua in the 'study' tomorrow. He wondered if bravery was something you acquired more of as you grew older. He'd be thirteen this September. Would that help?

But by morning all Lucy's good intentions had evaporated and she didn't even hang around for breakfast, let alone meekly present herself at her uncle's study. She quitted the house shortly after five-thirty and consequently arrived at the tripe stall an hour early, much to Dome's surprise.

'By heck, you're an early bird.'

'I swear I mean to spend as little time as possible within the four walls of that house, even if it is me own home. How dare he treat me like a child? He's not even me father, only an uncle. He's no right to tell me what time to come in or go out.'

'Ah, like that is it? The baby bird growing up, eh?' And seeing how the land lay, Dorrie left Lucy to work off her temper by chopping tripe.

Chapter Twenty-Six

In no time at all, it seemed, Polly was asking Lucy to give up her job on the tripe and trotter stall and take over the hand cart on Oldham Street so she could sell the carpet rugs full-time. Lucy was delighted, feeling life had taken a turn for the better. Benny too was feeling much happier. Although his ploy to be accepted by the Eastwood Gang had failed miserably and Georgie continued to harass him, Benny was determined to ignore it because he was so happy to be working for his mam. He still had to attend school, of course, which was boring but wouldn't last forever. For now, on evenings and weekends he heaved carpets, earning himself enough coppers in tips to go to the flicks twice a week if he wanted. Life was sweet.

Polly herself spent much of her time at the warehouse these days.

She and Big Flo could be found crawling about the floor on their hands and knees, cutting carpet into strips for stairs, rectangles for fireside rugs and bedrooms, and even the odd square for those with the money to buy a decent-sized piece for their parlour. All this work demanded a great deal of stitching and binding, and their fingers became covered in calluses and painful nicks from the scissors. Bob Reckitt's wife Marge gladly agreed to work with them. Nellie Sidebottom too, once she'd found a neighbour to sit with her sister Betty, since they were in dire need of the money and Polly could pay well.

Everyone complained of aching backs and wrists, eyes blurred from tiredness, but not for a minute would Polly rest or permit anyone else to slacken either. There was no time to lose. Hadn't she wasted enough already?

Charlie too was making good progress. He'd long since grown tired of asking for work at the various factories. McConnell's were having a difficult time, Hetherington's weren't taking on anyone new at the moment. He'd tried Mackay's, Allsopp's, Cooper's, and many more besides. Now he concentrated on hawking, an unpredictable life style with an unreliable income, but at least he was in charge of his own destiny, just like Polly.

He went down to the Pension Office in Dickinson Street and applied for money out of the King's Fund. This provided him with a horse and cart, though it meant a slight reduction in his naval pension and from then on he set about the task in earnest. He would often pick items up while he was out and about on Polly's behalf. Once they shared the cost of an advertisement in the *Manchester Evening News*. As a result, notes were delivered to the warehouse by post and by hand, some with details of old carpets people had to sell, others enquiries from people who wished to buy. Polly picked up two more cinema carpets that way, and one from a hotel that had gone bump.

She would take a tram, look the carpet over, make a bid and arrange for Charlie to come along later to collect it. Sometimes it had to be cut before it could be moved, with several trips required to transport it all, but no matter how much of a struggle the work was at times, business was brisk and no one was complaining.

Sales at the warehouse became a regular feature, advertised in the local papers. Potential buyers came from far and wide to view the pieces on offer. Her next major task, Polly decided, would be to find more retail outlets, in order to spread her net ever wider. But her first priority was her family.

As a result of her increased income she was now able to consider moving house. She'd been paying her share for some time at number twenty-three. Joshua collected five shillings a week in rent from her, and seven shillings and sixpence for food, though some weeks he demanded more if he thought the children had eaten too well. Polly paid up gladly, even though she hated the way he continued to control their lives. What she wanted most was freedom, for herself and her children.

One day she took her courage in hand and suggested that Joshua be the one to leave. 'You only moved in because I was unwell after Matthew's death. I'm fine now, so if you and Flo want to go elsewhere...'

He looked at her, plainly horrified, as if the thought had never occurred to him, which troubled her greatly. 'We are family,' he insisted. 'This is *our* home now and we have no intention of leaving. Not ever.'

That was the day Polly set about seriously looking for a house of her own. She'd certainly no wish to make Big Flo homeless, in any case. But it proved to be far more difficult than she'd hoped. Then quite out of the blue Bet Sutcliffe, her neighbour who owned the old clothes shop just up the street, announced she was moving, and Polly seized her chance. True, it was still uncomfortably close to Joshua, but she'd have her own front door to close against him, and the children their own rooms.

'Can I take on your shop, Bet? Not the old clothes, you can sell those off, but the premises?'

'Gladly! I'm going to help our Dot run a grocer's shop in Wilmslow. Be a nice change for me, and in a better area. You're welcome to this one, so long as the landlord's happy.' Bet wasn't the only one to be leaving Dove Street, or Ancoats for that matter. The City Corporation had finally got around to providing better housing in an attempt at slum clearance. However, there were grumbles that the new tenants, moving into Wythenshaw for instance, were more likely to be white-collar workers with steady employment and a good wage coming in than the poorer working class in need of a leg up.

Like many another, Polly was one of those offered no such escape.

'It's small,' she warned her children, 'with only two bedrooms, but one is large enough to split into two with a curtain for you to have half each.'

'Does that mean we won't be living with Uncle Joshua any more?' Benny wanted to know, pausing from loading the hand cart, eyes suddenly alert and interested.

Polly ruffled her son's hair. 'It means exactly that, with your own bed and private space.'

'Oh, *spiffing*!' And Polly laughed at the word, so out of place coming from the mouth of her grinning urchin of a son. He'd probably picked it up from Billy Bunter in the *Magnet*.

'We won't stay there forever but it's a start, a foot on the ladder towards something better.' She also welcomed the opportunity to expand her business through the shop, small though it was. Dove Street could hardly be compared with King Street but every little helped, and who in King Street would want to buy second-hand carpet rugs in any case?

When informed of this plan, Joshua was beside himself with rage. Painfully aware by this time that without Polly's income he could barely afford the rent on number twenty-three, let alone a decent standard of living, he put forward every argument against the plan he could muster, fighting desperation with anger.

'The house is far too small for a family.'

But this time, Polly stood her ground. 'We'll manage fine, thanks.'

'And no doubt rife with bugs from all those old clothes.' Polly almost laughed. 'I reckon we've coped with that problem before. I'll call in the council before we move.'

'In any case, it's a complete waste of money to pay two rents when we can all live together on one.'

'It's my money, Joshua, so I'll spend it as I choose, thanks all the same.'

And then in near desperation he said, 'The truth is, woman, that it isn't fitting for a respectable woman to be living on her own at all.'

'Why ever not? I'm perfectly capable of looking after meself. I've had enough, Josh. I'm leaving.'

'You are not! You're going nowhere unless I say so.'

She pushed her fists into her waist and confronted him with defiance flashing in her green-grey eyes. 'Indeed I am. And no one, certainly not you, can stop me. Ye've been nasty to me and my children from the start, Joshua. It can't go on. Sure and it's time for us to go our own way, so nothing you can say will make me change my mind.' Perhaps it was joy at finally scenting freedom that made her reckless. 'I might even be getting married soon, then you won't be troubled by me ever again.'

Joshua stared at her as if she had run mad and his voice, when it came, was low and hissing. 'Don't talk ridiculous! You'll marry no one. Not while I have any say in the matter.' Polly lifted her chin, and met the severity of his gaze with fortitude. 'That's just it, you don't have any say. I'm a grown woman and free to do exactly as I please.'

There followed a long, chilling silence. 'We'll see about that.'

Before Polly had time to move one item of her belongings, Joshua spoke to the landlord and somehow convinced him she would be an unreliable tenant. The man let the property to another family without even informing her. It was only when Polly saw curtains go up in the dusty shop window that she learned what Joshua had done. Yet again he had bested her. She stood helplessly in the street, staring at the curtains in utter disbelief. 'I'll swing for him, so I will!'

All the neighbours came out to offer their sympathy as well as to fill her in on the missing details of the saga. Connie Green patted her shoulder, urging her to stay calm, while Vera Murray told her to do just the opposite and pop one on him.

But they were deprived of the joy of witnessing the confrontation as Polly stormed into the house and slammed shut the door, leaving their curiosity unquenched. The red in her dark hair glinted with the fury that raged through her as she stood before him, small fists clenched, as if they might just do as Vera had suggested. Joshua simply flipped open his evening paper and told her to get the supper on. He was hungry.

'I'm sorry, Flo, but I can't – won't – go on like this.'

It was wash day and the kitchen was filled with steam from the dolly tub, the crumbling walls running with the resulting damp. Behind the wainscot they could hear the scratching of tiny feet, for all their efforts with mouse traps and poison. Polly felt as if she were going mad, trapped herself with nowhere to run.

Big Flo looked upon her daughter-in-law with a deeply sad expression in her tired old eyes. It was true they'd never been particularly close, them having such different views on religion, but her respect for the lass had grown tenfold over recent years. Polly was a worker, no doubt about that. She might be soft as butter on the inside, but outside she had some mettle, of which Big Flo approved. She was a woman of strength and courage. But scratch that surface too deeply and sparks would fly, as they had as a result of Joshua's latest interference.

'I reckon he's lost his marbles. He's so fastened his mind on looking after thee, since our Matthew isn't here to do it like, that he never stops to think what you might want.' It was the longest and fullest criticism Big Flo had ever made of one of her sons, and for all it wasn't entirely accurate, it left Polly dumbstruck.

'Look at it this road,' Big Flo continued. 'If you'd been meant to have that shop, you'd have got it. It's providence, that's what it is. Summat better'll turn up, you mark my words. You just have to keep your eyes open a bit wider, that's all.'

It was good advice which Polly followed, and with success, for some weeks later something better did indeed turn up. Something out of Ancoats altogether, just as she had once dreamed of.

While out and about looking for carpets, she found a three-bedroomed house to rent quite close to Cheetham Hill Road. Here there were open spaces, green fields and the scent of fresh air, the streets not being congested with motorbuses, motor cars and horse and carts. It would be as if they were living outside the city altogether, with an almost village-like atmosphere, just as she had always longed for. Cheetham Hill also boasted a rapidly developing parade of new shops, a prospect which greatly appealed to Polly. Perhaps, once she was better placed, that would be worth investigating.

The small terraced house she acquired at the exorbitant rent of thirty shillings a week had everything she could desire. Three good bedrooms, a front parlour and living kitchen, and, best of all, a bathroom with hot running water. She couldn't believe her good fortune. Outside was a tiny front garden complete with a gate she could latch behind her, providing a quiet haven of peace after the rigours of Dove Street.

She'd been nervous at first about whether she could afford such luxury, but the business was really starting to make a profit, aud it was worth the risk to get away from Joshua. Eventually of course, when she and Charlie married, they would have two steady incomes coming in, plus whatever the children earned. The depression seemed definitely to be lifting and things to be generally looking up, for them at least.

Benny was delighted by the prospect of a bedroom to himself, but disgusted to discover that a cinema seat costing fourpence in Ancoats, cost twopence more at the new Premier Cinema in the village. There was also a Public Swimming Baths which pleased him, and a Public Library which didn't interest him in the least, although Lucy meant to use it to seek out romances to sigh over. She could still savour the delights of open-topped tram rides with Tom, whenever she had an afternoon off, or simply browse amongst the many shops, not least Greenhalgh's cake shop which made her mouth water just to look at the French pastries in the window. It seemed like another world, far from the one in which Joshua Pride held sway, promising them all a bright new future.

-

Joshua's future was far from bright. So far as he was concerned, his life was falling apart. He had failed in his political ambitions, was still having no luck at finding employment, and despite thinking he'd curbed his sister-in-law's aspirations, she was about to escape his clutches entirely. He thought he'd succeeded in preventing her from walking out, but ever since she'd informed him of the house she'd acquired in Cheetham Hill, he'd been obsessed with devising some way to prevent the move.

She'd even won his mother over to her side.

'By heck, that's grand,' the old woman had said when Polly made the announcement. 'I'm made over for thee, lass.'

The woman was as slippery as an eel. He'd hurt her children, deliberately, in order to prove to her the extent of his power; even robbed her of her husband so that she could understand how it felt to lose someone she loved. He'd striven to restrict her everyday life, had put any number of obstacles in her path to prevent her from making friendships and building a new life for herself. He'd made it as clear as possible that she could no longer expect to have things all her own way, as she had with his foolish brother. But whatever he did, however much he hurt her, she came bouncing back, as lively and determined as ever, with her hunger to succeed all the greater for the difficulties she encountered.

In that devastating moment Joshua realised that for all his manipulation, his canting and preaching, the control and authority he'd exerted over the family, his labours had produced an effect exactly opposite to his intentions. He might have put her down for a while, but she'd come back fighting, and won.

Now the dratted woman owned a thriving business when others were still going bankrupt. She'd rented a house in a much improved locality, with the prospect of marriage ahead. His hatred and loathing of her had never surged more strongly through his veins than they did in that moment.

It was as he walked down Swan Street and saw the crowds gathering outside the Rising Sun, a pub which had never shut in living memory, that it came to him how he might put a spoke in the wheel of her progress.

'How do, Joshua,' said one man as he approached, while another merely acknowledged him with a nod of his head and a tug on the peak of his cap, as if touching his forelock. It brought a jolt of satisfaction to Joshua that they treated him with such respect.

'Let me buy you a pint,' he offered, surprising them both, for he was not known for his generosity.

'Thanks, mine's a pint of bitter.'

'Mild for me,' put in his mate.

With all the contacts Joshua now had through the NUWM, he was quite certain he would ultimately be successful. As he drank with his two companions and put a few tentative enquiries in motion, Joshua considered his plan. It wouldn't be easy to bring about, but he felt reasonably optimistic of success.

He had little to go on beyond the name 'Murdoch Shaugnessy' but hoped that would be enough. It was a name which should strike fear in Polly's heart since the man had entirely blighted her childhood and directly contributed to her own mother's death.

Once Polly's plans had been thrown into chaos, he meant to hit her where it really hurt. The second part of his scheme would naturally provide him with the greatest satisfaction, but then devising a punishment to suit any occasion had always been one of his strengths. He would take it step by step. The first task was to completely unsettle her.

He'd been watching his young niece for some time, and saw how she came home all flushed and excited, and always later than she should on a Saturday evening.

Following the occasion when she had bolted instead of coming to his study for her punishment as directed, he'd conducted a thorough search, not only of her bedroom but of the back yard too, since she always insisted on returning home that way. It hadn't taken him long to discover the scarlet dress and shoes. And, an even worse sin to Joshua's puritanical mind, he'd also discovered lipstick and powder.

Lucy was undoubtedly an attractive young woman, but a foolish and wanton one also. He would take great pleasure in teaching her a lesson for miring herself in debauchery.

His intention was to humiliate and break her without contravening his own high moral code. It could be done. He was sure of it.

Having concluded matters to his own satisfaction at the pub, he was actually smiling by the time he reached the house where his latest conquest lived. 'Victim' was not a word which ever sprang to Joshua's mind, though this was exactly what the woman appeared when she opened the door, almost cringing at sight of him. Despite her proteste that she was not well, that her son was off school with a bad toothache, that she had not a crumb of food to offer him, he pushed her along the passage and bolted the door. It took no time at all before his spirits began to improve, having pumped out the worst of his ill temper into her defenceless body. By way of reward he left her a packet of chitterlings for her children's tea, and the name of an employer who might, or might not, be in a position to offer her work.

He walked back along Dove Street with a positively jaunty step.

Later in the week, as Polly prepared to move, he made not a single protest. He actually smiled to himself as he listened to her excited talk about how she and the wonderful Charlie had decided against a Christmas wedding, agreeing not to tie the knot until the following spring.

He studiously ignored the troubled glances shot in his direction by her pestilential children, even his own mother. If they were surprised that he made no comment, curious as to the reasons behind his apparent complacency, let them wonder. Joshua refused to respond. He was content to bide his time, to wait and watch how this romance would survive echoes from the past.

He may have suffered a setback but the battle wasn't over yet and he meant to win. He would teach that woman a lesson she would never forget.

—

Polly placed the tin trunk containing all her most prized possessions in pride of place in the bedroom which she hoped one day soon to be sharing with Charlie. It seemed strange to remember a time when that trunk had been all she had possessed in the world, to recall how she'd sold their furniture and been content to live on orange boxes to cope with the shame of living on bare stone floors. And although Polly did think in retrospect that perhaps she should have discussed it with him first, knowing he would have disagreed and that she would be forced to defy him, how could things have worked out differently? How else could she have raised the capital for her business?

Her sacrifice was now paying off. She was doing well, could afford to rent a home of her own, one for which she had bought brand new beds and mattresses, even a large commodious double bed with a feather bolster for Charlie and herself to share when they were man and wife. She purchased new sheets and pillowcases, fluffy blankets and an eiderdown for each of them. What delights!

Despite a thorough search of all the likely shops and markets, she had found no trace of Matthew's beloved sideboard. Perhaps it was just as well. It was time to put the past behind her and begin anew.

She and Lucy scrubbed the little house from top to bottom. Then she paid Stanley Green to paint every room with white distemper, and finally black-leaded all the grates and the big old range herself, thrilled by how clean and fresh it looked when they'd finished.

Together, she and Charlie had great fun choosing furniture from the second-hand market stalls for the parlour and live-in kitchen. Polly naturally provided carpet rugs to cover all the flag floors.

And Charlie was delighted to see her free from her brother-in-law at last, agreeing whole-heartedly that it was important for her to set up home alone first, for the sake of her children.

He pulled her on to his knee on the night she moved in and for a long time they sat snuggled in the wing-backed chair he had bought for her, covered in a deep wine red moquette and in excellent condition. With their arms wrapped about each other, they dreamed of their future together. There was nothing they liked more than to discuss how they might develop the business, how well the sale days at the warehouse were going, whether they should take on more market stalls as Dorrie Hughes had done, or wait till they could afford to rent a shop, perhaps one day in the centre of the city.

His own bric-a-brac barrow was doing well enough in its own small way, particularly in household items, but he and Polly dreamed of Charlie managing the retail side of the operation, perhaps even moving into new carpets one day, if they could raise a loan for the stock.

'A fine team we'd make, to be sure.' Polly sighed with pleasure, then tried to wriggle free from his grasp. 'Aw, but I've no time to be chattering here. Isn't there work to be done in plenty? I've surely brought home enough bills and accounts to keep me going half the night.'

But he wouldn't let her go. He meant to keep her all to himself for this evening, while he had the opportunity. With Lucy out with her young man, Benny fishing in the canal, and no Joshua likely to walk in at any moment and discover them, this was the first time they'd been alone together indoors.

'I don't mind whether we wed in your church or at the register office. It's up to you, Polly. I'll change for you, if it'd make you happy. I'm not certain what religion I am in any case, so it'd happen do me good to start over again.'

She gathered his hands between her own, kissing each precious thumb and finger, giddy with love for him. 'I wouldn't ask unless you really wanted to, but bless your kind heart, wouldn't that make Father Donevan happy? Me too, for that matter. I think I've missed me own church more than I've realised. Anyway, we can decide all of that later.'

They celebrated with a glass of stout each and pie and peas, eaten off their knees before a blazing fire. It was the most delicious meal she had ever tasted. Charlie wasted no time in finishing his meal so he could start kissing her all over again, whereupon Polly began having second thoughts about waiting even a day before marrying him.

The evening continued with enough gentle bantering and kisses to make Polly's face rosy with love, and her heart beat far too fast. Life seemed utterly perfect. Later, after Charlie had gone, Benny and Lucy arrived home to find her singing 'The Rose of Tralee' at the top of her voice.

The next morning Polly was still singing as she cooked breakfast and saw them on their way, Lucy to the barrow in Oldham Street and Benny to school. He seemed to be growing taller by the day, changing from a boy into a gawky youth with legs too long for his scrawny body. But he was far more cheerful than he had been in months. He'd confessed to her that he avoided Georgie Eastwood as far as was reasonably possible, and had made no further efforts to join his or anyone else's gang. Polly agreed this was wise, but had never told him that she'd once had a quiet word with the boy's mother, hoping they could settle the matter peaceably between them. The woman had promised to do her best, though admitted that with a bully of a husband to deal with as well, she had little control over her son.

As Polly saw her own son out, she again reminded him that if there was the least sign of any further bullying, he should tell his teacher. Benny simply looked at her with disbelief on his young face, and said nothing.

'Can I bring Tom home for tea?' Lucy asked, as she pushed the sandwiches her mother had made into her bag.

Polly sighed with pleasure as she gladly agreed. It was so wonderful to be free from Joshua's glowering presence and for life to be normal again. She felt as if a heavy load had been lifted from her shoulders. She was still singing as she washed up the few breakfast dishes, mind rushing ahead to the work she planned that day. When she heard the knock at the door she didn't even trouble to stop or to turn around, simply sang out, 'Come in, why don't you, the door's open.'

'Well, isn't this grand, Mary Ann? Here we are together again, after all these years.'

As she swung round to face her father, the dish she'd been washing fell to the floor and smashed into a dozen tiny pieces.

Chapter Twenty-Seven

He came whirling into her life like a dervish. That very first night he came in rolling drunk, singing 'Danny Boy' at the top of his lungs. Polly would have liked to lock the door on him, leave him in the gutter where he belonged, but mindful of her new neighbours she dragged him into the front room and left him there, unconscious. The next day she found him still sprawled out, seemingly dead to the world, except that he'd spewed the remnants of several pints of beer all over her new carpet.

'Sweet Jesus, will you look at yourself? Why do you do it, you great Irish eejet?'

She marched into the kitchen, filled a jug with ice cold water and flung it over his head. Murdoch shook himself like a dog and got unsteadily to his feet to stand swaying slightly before her. Even his grin was lopsided and spaniel-like, as if wishing to ingratiate himself for his misdemeanour.

'Shorry,' he said, and hiccupped rudely, earning himself a further glare of disapproval.

'I'll have no drunkenness in my house.' Even as Polly spoke she recognised the futility of her words, remembering how her mother would say the very same thing. Murdoch had never managed to stay sober in all his long life. He certainly wasn't going to start now.

'Shure and would you deny me a few shimple plesh – plesh – me bit of fun?'

'Fun. *Fun?*' Polly's hands itched to slap him, to knock some sense into that ignorant fool's head. Turning from him in her exasperation, she began to pace the small room, back and forth, back and forth, her fury as sharp as a spitting cat's. 'You and your so-called "simple pleasures" ruined my life when you killed my lovely mother.'

He stared at her in shock, struggling to focus his befuddled mind. ''Tis a cruel hard thing you're saying to me, Mary Ann. Sure and I wouldn't have hurt a living hair on that good woman's head. Any more than I would yours. It's only the drink that let's me down now and then, and for sure I'd never touch another drop so long as I live, if'n you asked me to.'

'Like hell you wouldn't!'

How many times she'd heard his promises, to herself and her brothers and sisters, most of all to her mother. Within days or even hours of swearing unfailing abstinence to his dying day, he'd be found rolling out of some pub, roaring drunk and waking all the neighbours, or else collapsed senseless in the middle of the street. He'd become more familiar with the insides of the local police cells than any burglar. Whenever Polly's mother tried to save him from himself, she'd earn herself a hail of abuse, or more likely across the mouth. In drink, Murdoch Shaugnessy went right back to his bare-knuckle fighting days.

Polly, unlike her siblings, who perhaps because they were older were better able to cope, had been hurt beyond measure to see her parents constantly at war. She'd lost count of the number of times she'd run to her mother's aid, held her close while she sobbed, or even acted as nursemaid, tending the wounds inflicted during her father's mad rages. There were other times she'd helped her mam to pack their meagre belongings so they could do a moonlight flit, escaping before the folk to whom they owed money could catch up with them, only to have the same thing happen all over again in the next place, and the next. Every penny Murdoch possessed, and whatever he could borrow when his pockets were empty, he spent in the local hostelries.

It had been Polly who'd gone round begging them to stop serving her father. And Polly who'd found her mother stone cold in her bed one morning, driven to an early death by the disappointments, unfulfilled dreams and constant battles. It had been clear then, as it still was now, that her mother had simply lost the will to live, something Polly vowed she would never do, if only for the sake of her children. A philosophy of life to which she'd resolutely kept.

As a young impressionable girl, she'd grieved deeply over the loss of her mother, laying the fault entirely at Murdoch's door. Now a mother herself, the anger still churned in her. How dare he throw her life into turmoil yet again, just when she'd was getting back on her feet?

Murdoch promised Polly that he was a reformed character, wanted nothing more than to be friends and make up for all his past mistakes. He said he'd no wish to hurt her or interfere in her life in any way. Polly merely snorted with disgust, told him to clean himself up, and walked away.

He came to her again, hours later, showing every sign that he had done just that. His shirt and muffler were spanking clean, his bowler hat set square upon his head and the face beneath glowing from a judicious ducking and scrubbing. Even so, Polly barely lifted her head from the accounts she was working on, let alone comment upon this metamorphosis.

'I'm thinking I could help by working for you, rather than being stuck in the house on me own or working for strangers,' he blithely informed her. 'I can allus carry the carpets, mebbe?'

'I have Benny to do that,' Polly said, adding more succinctly, 'and all you've ever managed to carry in your entire life so far as I can recall is a pint glass.'

He offered up his saddest expression, as if she had wounded him to the heart, repeating his earlier assurance that he was indeed on the wagon now, and if she wasn't kinder to him, wouldn't he fell off it again?

Polly remembered only too well how he'd always claimed it was the loneliness in him, and the hard life he'd led that drove him to the nearest bar quicker than you could say 'God Bless the Irish'. Even so, she could barely find the patience to respond. Didn't she have enough to worry over, without a drunken father?

Charlie was concerned. Polly had become far more withdrawn and touchy since Murdoch's arrival, and seemed to be taking out her frustration on him. Nothing he said quite pleased her. She had entirely lost her ability to relax, or even to laugh, and would fly into a temper in a second. He wished the old man no ill, for all he had grave difficulties keeping on the straight and narrow. Charlie did his best to help, to give Polly a break by taking him out fishing in the canal or to a football match once in a while. But even that didn't seem to suit.

'Don't pander to him,' she stormed after one such outing. 'Once Murdoch has his feet under our table, he might never take them out. And I want him out of here!'

'He's your da,' Charlie softly reminded her. 'I thought you'd promised to give him a chance? He hasn't had a drink for seven days now. Perhaps he'll make it this time.'

Polly clenched her fists, restraining her fury with difficulty. 'Ye can't believe a word he says. The man destroyed me mother's life. D'you want me to put out the welcome flags? Say I love him? Well, I don't.'

Charlie shook his head. 'I can understand how you must feel. But it might help if you mebbe let bygones be bygones. Let the past be forgotten.'

Polly made a sound half under her breath that Charlie thought just as well he hadn't quite heard. Then she grabbed a loaf of bread and started to hack it roughly into pieces. He gently took the knife from her hands. 'Shall I do that so you don't hurt yerself, or even the bread? You put the kettle on, love.' A thought struck him. 'Where's he sleeping – with young Benny?'

'No, he is not. For the first time in his life Benny has a bedroom to himself. I couldn't deny him that pleasure. Lucy has moved in with me.'

There was the slightest pause before he went on. 'I see. Well, that's all right for now, I suppose. But Benny will have to share a room with him eventually, after we're wed. I'm sure he won't mind.'

Polly stared at him wide-eyed. 'By the saints above, Da had better not still be with us by the time we marry! Sweet Mary and Joseph, aren't I tearing me hair out already?' She couldn't believe Charlie was even saying such things. Why couldn't he see that Murdoch had ruined everything? Tears of self-pity sprang to her eyes. 'I wanted to have some time on my own with my family about me. Now it's all gone wrong. Sure and I'll have him driven away in the paddy-wagon if he steps out of line just once.' She shook the knife so hard a great blob of margarine landed on the stone-flagged floor, and Charlie took that off her too.

'Whatever you say, Polly.' It seemed better to agree with her right now.

—

Big Flo and her fellow matriarchs were still working at the carpet warehouse, and Polly kept herself equally busy, either helping with the sewing, organising the next Sale Day, searching out more stock, or checking on Lucy at the hand cart on Oldham Street. It all added up to a considerable workload but she loved it and wouldn't have had it any other way. Once she had more money coming in, then she could afford to take on extra staff and life would get easier. For now she had to attempt to be in three, if not four, places at once. The one benefit was that the more she worked, the less time she had to spend in the house with her father.

Big Flo informed Polly, in her usual blunt manner, that although she was in favour of doing one's duty and honouring one's father and mother, Polly would do herself no favours by harbouring a drunkard in the house. 'Beware the demon drink, that's what we Methodists believe.'

Perversely, this made Polly jump to Murdoch's defence.

'He says he's reformed, that he'll never touch another drop. I've agreed to give him a chance.'

'Time will tell,' Big Flo sagely remarked.

Unfortunately Polly's lack of faith in her father was proved to be justified. She came to dread arriving home, despite her pride and joy in her new home, for she never knew what might be waiting for her. If she was lucky he was senseless, and she only had the bottles and mess to clear up. On other days, she found he'd generously invited some of his drinking pals round, irritating the neighbours with a noisy shindig the like of which they'd never before witnessed. On one notable occasion she found every cup and plate in her tiny kitchen smashed, together with two wooden chairs. The result apparently of a drunken brawl. Vomit and blood streaked the walls and the stink of the place almost made Polly want to throw up herself. She screamed at him, letting all her pent-up emotion and rage soar to the surface.

'Will you get out of my house this minute! Get out!'

This time there was no maudlin response, no begging for her to understand or promise to be good. Instead he pushed her roughly out of his way, knocking her back against the wall. 'Shut your blathering and make me some tea. I'll not be told what to drink, or which friends I might invite home by me own daughter,' he informed her, arrogant in his drunken state.

Polly could see the danger signals in his eyes, recognise the spark of stubbornness that indicated the depth of his addiction, but she stood up to him, as she always had done.

'This is my house. I pay the rent. I haven't worked hard all these years to have you mess it up for me.' Had she not been so filled with rage, she would have wept at the utter destruction around her. Any moment now Benny or Lucy might walk in. What would they think she had brought them to? Jumping from the frying pan into the fire evidently. Would she never be free?

Murdoch was still talking, speech slurred and well-nigh incoherent, but louder in consequence as if to compensate. 'Aren't I your bleshed father? A man you should honour. Don't you forget that shmall fact, Mary Ann. I've had a hard life, to be shure, but I've allus done me best by you.'

'You've never given a thought to anyone but yourself.'

He wagged a finger furiously at her, inches from her face. 'I'm here to stay and there's not a damned thing you can do about it.'

—

Charlie arrived an hour later to find Polly weeping over her wrecked kitchen. Realising what had occurred, his heart filled with pity for her. He longed to put all her problems right, to make her life sweet and fresh and new. Surely he could do that for her.

On seeing Charlie she began to storm and rage, to tell him what he could plainly see with his own eyes. He waited till she ran out of breath then said in his quietest voice, 'I want to look after you, Polly. To be a part of this family. Isn't it time we set a date?'

Looking into his sorrowful face, all the despair and temper drained out of her and Polly wrapped her arms about him, resting her head against his chest.

'Aw, you see how the old drunken sot has come between us already.'

'We could be wed in three weeks or so, if you've a mind. Wouldn't that be grand?'

Sadly, the presence of her father had only confirmed Polly's determination to set her own life in order first. She pulled away from him, and struggled to explain some of this to Charlie, 'Sure and I'd marry you tomorrow, m'darlin', but besides not wanting to land you with the problem of Da, I must give me children time to get used to the idea, used to a life free from Joshua breathing down their necks. Lucy will be able to invite her young man home for tea, which is how things should be done. Benny can begin to feel strong and secure again. He's thrilled to have a bit of a job at the warehouse, but before you know it he'll be leaving school, then he'll find himself proper work and a young lady I shouldn't wonder, and I'll have lost him.'

Charlie looked startled, as well he might by this catalogue of events still some time in the future. 'What has all of that to do with us?'

'Don't we need time to get to know each other a bit better first? Can you not understand that? Just let me get rid of the old man, and me children established, and then I'll put it to them about you and me.'

'They're not daft, either of them. They know we mean to wed. And I don't mind about your da, really I don't. He'll no doubt take himself off one morning as suddenly as he came.'

'I wish I could believe that.' Charlie saw again the dark clouds gathering in her greeny-grey eyes at the very notion of Murdoch's becoming a permanent fixture.

'We can't keep letting other people dictate our lives for us, Polly. I want you for my wife.'

But she refused to discuss the matter further. She felt too tired from the disturbed nights of hearing her father come home the worse for drink; exhausted from lying awake worrying about her future with him; worrying over Joshua; the commitments she had taken on; even the children. So instead she simply kissed Charlie in an absent-minded fashion, to cheer him even as she gave her refusal. 'And so I will be. Just give me a wee while to sort this whole mess out.' The kiss didn't seem to have done its work for he was frowning down at her, looking disappointed and hurt. Then he voiced the worry that had niggled at the back of his mind for weeks. 'Don't you think it mighty odd that Murdoch should appear so unexpectedly, out of the blue like that? How d'you reckon he found your address?'

Polly swept up the last of the broken shards of crockery and dumped them in the bin. She was hardly listening, certainly not taking in the implications of his words. As she reached for a cloth to start cleaning the mess off her newly painted walls, she was concerned only with the agonies of daily life with her despised parent.

'Don't you see, this could all have been planned?' Charlie persisted. 'It's Joshua who's set this up. And if you let the wedding be put off, then he'll have won.'

For once, Polly refused to place the blame upon her brother-in-law, being far too determined to cast her own father as the villain of the piece. As she sloshed soapy water into a bucket, her words came out all tight and clipped. 'I've no time for the fuss of a wedding just now. Haven't I the warehouse to see to, as well as everything else? I've to work even harder to pay all this rent I've taken on. So will you stop harassing me, for pity's sake!'

He stepped away from her. 'Drat your stubbornness, Polly. You're a fool to yourself at times.'

They both fell silent, hot and bothered by the path down which their heated words had led them. Charlie glowered and sulked; Polly, half glancing at his face, recognised the depth of his hurt and anger by the hard set of his jaw. Oh, but wasn't it her and Matthew all over again? Why couldn't a man ever understand that sometimes you had to trust to instinct, and hope that time would resolve matters? She felt utterly devastated, stretched to the limits of her endurance, as if she'd been put on a rack. Her life seemed to consist of walking on tightropes, desperately trying to keep everyone happy.

And where was the hurry anyway? She felt quite secure in his love for her, certain he would wait, no matter how long. She knew that Charlie needed her, that he would always be here by her side. There really wasn't any need for her to worry about him. But his next words challenged even this long-cherished belief.

'I have to go away on a bit of business,' he suddenly announced, voice strangely cool and distant. 'Perhaps it's no bad thing. It'll give us both time to think.'

She stared at him. 'Think? About what?'

'About us. About how important we are to each other.'

Polly fell silent, struggling to absorb the message he was giving her and not much caring for it. 'Where, are you going exactly? What kind of business?' Fear was closing her throat and she could hardly believe what she was hearing.

'Liverpool. There's a bloke I need to see.'

'Why would you have to go to Liverpool?' It might have been the ends of the earth.

'I've told you, a bit of business has come my way. You don't mind?'

'Ach, why would I mind? It's no business of mine what you do.' And she turned away, dipped the scrubbing brush in the soapy water and began to scrub.

It was their first real quarrel and it ended with Charlie marching away and Polly bursting into tears.

–

Lucy hugged herself with delight. Life was so much easier now that she wasn't glancing over her shoulder half the time. With a home of their own, Uncle Joshua couldn't watch her every move as he had before.

Tom continued to take her regularly to the Picture-drome or to the Palais. Sometimes they went to Joe Taylor's dance hall or even as far as Belle Vue. Nothing was too good for her, so far as Tom was concerned. And no longer did she have to hide the scarlet dress and shoes behind the lavatory, but was able to walk out in them bravely, knowing that although her mother would also probably disapprove, she was too absorbed in her business, and with the unexpected arrival of Murdoch, to notice what her daughter got up to.

Lucy could meet Tom whenever and wherever she wished. There were many days when he didn't have much money at all, and they'd have to be content with a walk by the canal or a tram ride. But it didn't matter to Lucy, so long as they could be together. Life was sweet.

–

Polly was missing Charlie more than she'd thought possible. He'd been away for two whole weeks and she couldn't understand what was taking him so long. It frightened her that they'd parted on a quarrel. Was he staying away deliberately? Would he perhaps find himself another woman, one without the encumbrance of a drunken father and two youngsters hell-bent on growing up too fast?

In truth, if it hadn't been for the fact that she was kept so busy she might have felt a good deal worse. Improved relations with her mother-in-law helped and the two women would often sit and eat their sandwiches together at dinner time, chatting over the morning's work and whatever the next task of the afternoon would be. Without Big Flo's sensible, down-to-earth good humour, Polly felt she might not have survived Charlie's absence half so well.

'And how's your dad shaping up?' Big Flo asked. 'Still keeping off the bottle, is he?'

'He's been sober for a whole week, which is a record so far.'

'He'll have to join our Band of Hope or the Reccabites. They'll help keep him on the straight and narrow. Trust in the Lord, that's what I say,' which made Polly giggle. The thought of her father joining a non-conformist temperance organisation was beyond even her hopes.

'We're having a meeting soon, matter of fact I'll ask him to join us,' Big Flo magnanimously offered.

'Thank you. Not that I could guarantee he'd come.'

'Doesn't hurt to ask. He needs to repent and sign the pledge. He can start by coming to our coffee and bun evenings. That might do the trick.'

Polly couldn't hold back her mirth any longer and burst out laughing at the very thought of Murdoch consuming coffee and sticky buns with a gathering of Methodist matrons. Big Flo stared at her perplexed, one huge hand poised with a sandwich halfway to her mouth. 'Have I said summat funny?'

Polly was wiping tears of joy from her cheeks. 'No, Flo. There's nothing funny about such worthy causes, except the idea of my father joining them. I'm thinking he can't hold out much longer. He must be dying for a good soaking.'

A few nights later she heard the too-familiar scratch of his key at the front door, and her father's raucous voice giving a loud rendition of 'When Irish Eyes'. Murdoch Shaugnessy was roaring drunk.

How many times as a child had Polly lain listening to his tuneless singing and his pathetic struggles to find the lock? How many times had she got up from her warm bed to let him in, only to have her head knocked for her trouble? Now Polly didn't move but continued to stay curled beside the body of her daughter, listening intently until she heard the door bang open. She almost turned over then, to drift back to sleep, when she realised she hadn't heard it close again. Only then did she resignedly climb out of bed, pull on her dressing gown and make her way wearily downstairs in the semi-darkness.

Outside the night was dark and still, a shaft of moonlight slanting across the road. For a fleeting second Polly thought she saw a figure standing beneath the lamp-post, but she'd already pushed the door closed with her toe. By the time she pulled it open again to check, the pool of light below the lamp was empty, as it should be. It probably always had been. She was so tired she was imagining ghosts now. She made sure the door was locked, then started back upstairs, eager to return to her warm bed and much needed sleep.

Chapter Twenty-Eight

Murdoch's period of abstinence was soon over. Only days later on her way home from work, Polly heard the row long before she reached the street corner. Sure enough there he was, fighting drunk, throwing punches at some other unfortunate inebriate who had happened to displease him. Within seconds the pair of them were rolling in the dirt, arms clasped tight about each other as if for support. The evidence of this latest failure was yet another bitter pill for her to swallow. Rage threatened to choke her. How dare he do this to her? How could he behave in such a manner in front of her new neighbours? She didn't need to glance about her to know that the lace curtains would be twitching and folk would be speculating on this new resident who had brought disorder into their peaceful lives. Scarlet with temper and embarrassment, Polly marched straight up to her father and yelled at him.

'Can I not trust you to stay sober for even a few hours while I'm at work?'

Flat on his back, he beamed happily up at her. 'Polly, m'darlin'. Is it dinner time already?'

Were it not for the gathering audience of curious onlookers she might well have slapped his silly face. Years of listening to his useless promises stabbed her to the heart. What a fool she had been. Why had she ever let him stay, or pretended to believe in him? If she didn't watch out she'd end up just like her poor mother.

Reaching down, she grabbed him by his coat collar and started to yank him to his feet. 'May the good Lord forgive you, great useless good-for-nothing drunkard that you are. Get out of my life before I do something I'll be sorry for.'

'Aw, Mary Ann, don't take on so. Sure and you make me head ache.'

She swore at him, loudly and comprehensively, telling her father she would knock his head off his unmentionable shoulders if he didn't pick himself up and move.

He staggered to his feet, only to sag on to the doorstep and flop, eyes half closed, focusing upon some unseen place in his head. She made to lift him up, to get him into the house, out of sight of her neighbours, but it was then that Polly learned an unpalatable fact. One, she'd much rather not have heard yet recognised as the truth at last, for it confirmed Charlie's warning.

'Sure and wasn't Joshua right in what he told me?' grumbled her father. 'Ye've the meanest temper of all the Irish in Manchester, and isn't that saying something? He said I'd have me work cut out to make you happy.' Murdoch put one hand to his head, as if to make Sure it was still there. 'The divil take it, I'm that tired I could sleep for a week.'

'Who told you what?' Polly's voice had grown ominously quiet. 'Are you saying that you had a conversation with my brother-in-law? About me?' When he didn't answer but looked like slipping into sleep, she reached out, grasping his arms and shook him. '*When*? Will you answer my question? When and where did you discuss me: with Joshua?'

'Will you stop your, blathering and leave go of me, girl?' He swiped at her, catching her off balance so that she fell sideways, bruising her cheek on the stone wall. Polly put up a hand, feeling the warm'sting of blood but not stopping to staunch it or care who witnessed their quarrel, not any longer.

'Tell me what Joshua asked you to do.'

'Sure and didn't he offer me this accommodation in the first place? A gennelman to be sure. Bought me a Guinness and a chaser to help me on my way. Generous to a fault he is. Oh, me bleedin' head's fallin' off, Mary Ann. Let me lie down, for pity's sake.' He flung a punch at her again but this time she was ready for him, and ducked neatly out of the way. Having missed his target he lost his balance and sprawled headlong down the path. Polly stood over him, her face a picture of cold fury.

'Joshua offered you accommodation in my house, did he?' She was beside herself with rage. Charlie had been right. The whole thing had been a set-up. She'd been made a fool of, manipulated yet again by her oh-so-clever brother-in-law.

—

Joshua appeared entirely unconcerned, insisting he was doing Polly a favour by finding her long lost father, after all these years.

'Ye did it deliberately! Don't take me for a complete fool.' Polly paced the tiny kitchen, almost demented with fury. 'You thought you'd put a spoke in my wheel now I've got a place of my own at last. Not to mention stirring things up between me and Charlie by sending me drunkard father back into my life. You knew how I felt about him, and that he could never stay sober. But you also guessed, very cleverly, that I'd be too soft to throw him out.'

Joshua leaned back in his chair, rubbed his index finger slowly over the bridge of his nose and smiled. 'Dear me, what a sad state of affairs. And there's me thinking you Catholics always stick together, as we Methodists do.' He looked so self-righteous and full of himself in that moment that Polly came close to striking him.

'You're twisting me words, drat your eyes. D'you think I came down with the last snow fall?' She wagged one finger at him. 'I know your little game. What I'm saying is you didn't send him to me out of generosity but as a deliberate ploy to upset me and ruin my life.'

'Don't unload your sense of guilt on me.'

'Guilt?' Polly clenched her small fists then raised them high, eyes closed as if praying for patience. 'Dear God, you'd drive a saint to murder, so you would.'

It was Big Flo who saved the situation by stepping in to calm tempers all round. 'I'm sure he only meant it for the best, Polly. And you did at least try, as I did, to persuade your father on to a more sober path. But thee were quite right, he did refuse to come along to our meetings. Happen he'll see the light one day. We can only hope so. Don't blame yourself, lass.' And, reaching out, she put her great arms about Polly's trembling frame to hold her close. Polly was grateful for this unexpected comfort, but finally shook herself free of her mother-in-law's embrace and faced Joshua again, her gaze unswerving.

'Let's make this absolutely clear. I'm Catholic. Always was, always will be. Your brother, my lovely husband, was not. It didn't trouble us, so it shouldn't have bothered you; Now Matt's dead and none of this matters any more. I've taken my children away for their own good. From now on I mean to lead my own life and I'll suffer no more interference from you or anyone. Is that clear?'

'As crystal.'

She was surprised by his placid reply, almost hesitated before pushing on with her prepared statement. 'I want you to understand that it's over. You must leave us alone so we can be free. Right?'

Big Flo was looking anxiously from one to the other, wringing her hands. When Joshua did not immediately reply, she gave him a nudge with one clenched fist. 'Go on, lad, say you will. What the lass says is fair enough. Our Matt has been dead a while now. She's a grown woman and should be free to start afresh, in another house, with another chap. It's only right and proper. And it's time we had a bit of family peace. Is it agreed?'

Joshua looked into his mother's face, and then into Polly's, striving to mask the loathing he felt for her. Now was not the moment for a showdown, not with his mother present. Besides, there were better ways. Slowly, very slowly, he smiled as calmly and benevolently as he could manage. 'Of course. I too wish for family harmony. How could you imagine otherwise? Polly is perfectly free to do as she pleases. I only tried to do what I thought best for them.'

''Course you did.' Big Flo folded her great arms as if she'd just won ten rounds in a wrestling contest. 'There we are then. All mended, done and dusted. Isn't that grand? Now, shake hands, the pair on you. It's time breaches were healed.' And she smiled with pleasure as, after some initial on Polly's part, this was brought about.

–

When Charlie came home Polly ran into his arms and begged him never to go away again. 'Aw, didn't I miss you every waking moment? I'm sorry we quarrelled. What an old gripe I am. Will you forgive me?'

He seemed to have forgiven and forgotten already for he was kissing and hugging her as if he might never let go. Later, much later, he told her all about his trip to Liverpool. He'd seen a man, he said, off whom he'd bought a load of brushes, brooms and wash leathers which Charlie was certain would sell well on his barrow. 'He also gave me an interesting piece of news.' And he began a tale which held Polly enthralled from the first word to the last. She wasted no time when he was done in going straight to her children.

'Lucy, will you keep an eye on Benny for me? I have to go away.'

'Go away where?' Her daughter looked concerned.

'Don't fret, it's only for a little while. To Liverpool, to see a man about a ship.'

Benny, who had been taking an interest in the conversation since it concerned him, opened his eyes wide. 'What sort of ship? Can I see it?' He was considering a change of career if he ever got bored with his mam's warehouse, perhaps in the Navy instead of the railway. He didn't feel quite the same about trains as he used to.

Polly tweaked his nose. 'No, you can't see it. You still have to go to school. It's a liner about to be decommissioned. That is, broken up. And isn't it filled from stem to stern with fine things which have to be auctioned?'

'You mean, carpets?' Lucy asked, excitement in her voice.

'I do indeed. The finest the steamship company could buy. Sure and if I manage to get a fraction of what's on offer at a bargain price, won't we make a small fortune?'

Lucy's jaw dropped. She was trying to imagine the size a ship's carpet might be. 'Will we be able to cope with it?' But Polly only chortled with glee at the prospect.

'Let's say it'll be a challenge, but one we can meet. I haven't the smallest doubt of that, m'cushla.'

And so it was agreed that she and Charlie would go to Liverpool to bid for as much of the ship's carpet as they could get. Benny and Lucy would continue to help Big Flo at the warehouse, and Lucy would see to Benny's meals and that he went to school on time, despite his protests that he didn't need any girl to tell him what to do.

'And what about your da?' Charlie mildly enquired, blue eyes twinkling.

'We were both right – me about him being completely unreliable and forever falling off the wagon, and you about Joshua having planned the whole thing. But we've made a pact. My brother-in-law has promised faithfully to stay out of my life in future. We're free of him at least.

'As for me da – sure and I've no idea what'll happen to him, nor do I care.' But a frown of concern gave the lie to that statement. By the next day she had her answer, in part at least.

Polly and Charlie were packing their bags ready to depart when they saw him. Murdoch was dressed in his smartest derby tweeds and bowler hat, a blue collar and tie instead of his usual muffler, face scrubbed clean and shiny. The very picture of sobriety.

'I'm off now, Mary Ann. Have a good trip,' he said in his cheeriest voice.

'Off where?' She thought for a moment that he meant he was leaving and felt a jolt of unexpected disappointment. In that instant Polly realised she'd no wish for him to go. She wanted to get to know her father better, to find a way of helping him to overcome his problem, perhaps even one day learn to forgive him for what he'd done to her mother. Before she had time to express any of these jumbled thoughts, she heard the click of the front gate and saw Big Flo marching up the path.

She was dressed as if it were a Sunday, in her chapel black, though it was but Wednesday. On top of her frizzed grey curls was squashed a flattened pancake of straw masquerading as a hat. 'Now then, Polly. Mind what thee gets up to in that den of iniquity. Full of wicked sailors is Liverpool.'

Big Flo considered most places other than Manchester to be rife with evil. Polly struggled not to laugh as she solemnly agreed to 'watch her back', then looked from one to the other of her visitors with curiosity. 'And where are you two off to, might I ask?'

'Do you never listen to owt anyone says to thee, lass?' Big Flo said with a heavy sigh. 'Didn't I mention I was going on the Reccabites' Harvest Trip today? We're going to Bispham in a char-a-banc. Murdoch has agreed to accompany me.'

'Indeed, it is my great pleasure,' he said, bowing solemnly.

'Not only that, your da's planning to come to meetings regular like, aren't you, lad?'

'I am so. It'll be the making of me, will it not?' And before Polly and Charlie's astonished gaze, the pair of them said their goodbyes and set off down the street, walking arm in arm for all the world as if they were the most respectable couple on God's earth, and Polly's father the most sober individual.

'Will you look at that? Sure and I wouldn't have believed it if I hadn't seen it with me own eyes. The old besom has won!' And Polly fell laughing into Charlie's arms.

–

Benny was not taking kindly to being looked after by his sister, like a child who needed minding. There wasn't a minute of the day when she wasn't ordering him about.

Wash the dishes. Wash your face. Go to school. Go to bed. Get up. Benny was weary of it. And judging by her behaviour, he considered it was Lucy who needed looking after, not him. She was never in the house more than ten minutes together, always off somewhere with that Tom Shackleton, or else giving Benny a tanner to make him go off some place so they could be alone, kissing and canoodling like they did in soppy pictures. Benny and his mates always booed through those bits. To have such goings on in his own house was too embarrassing for words.

There were some evenings when she didn't look after him at all but stayed out far later than his mother would like. Benny made a point of telling her so, more than once.

'What would Mam say if anything were to happen to me while you were off courting?' he challenged her. 'It was half-past ten last night when you got in.'

But Lucy only tossed her pretty head, asking what could possibly happen to him, accusing him of sounding like Uncle Joshua. She also reminded her young brother that since he objected to being constantly watched over like a child, he couldn't have it both ways.

Her mention of their uncle made Benny warn her to take care Joshua didn't spot what she was up to.

Lucy sniffed, and indelicately thumbed her nose. 'See if I care. He's no control over us now we have our own house, so stop fretting. You're old enough to be left on your own for a little while, I'm sure, big lad like you.'

Benny watched in silence as she applied far too much scarlet lipstick to pursed lips for someone who was only going for a walk in the park.

'We're off to listen to the band, then we might take a walk or go for a cup of tea and a bun somewhere. After that... well.' She shrugged her slender shoulders, studying the effect on her new bias-cut frock with its wide cape collar. 'After that we might go to the pictures, or even to the Variety.'

'What about me? Mam said you were to look after me.'

'There's a cold meat pie in the larder for your tea, after you've finished those deliveries,' she told him. 'All you have to do is eat it.' She began to smooth her fair curls around her fingers, teasing each one into place. 'Don't take on so, Benny. You've spent most of your life living by your wits on the streets. A few hours here and there isn't going to make much difference. Mam fusses far too much. Parents do. Now scarper, will you? Tom will be here any minute.'

Benny scarpered, perversely relieved to be free from Lucy's tyranny, for all his complaints. He almost felt sorry for Tom Shackleton, being told where he must go and what he must do all the time. He decided there and then he'd have nothing to do with this courting business. Not ever. Not unless the girl was a lot less bossy than his sister, anyroad.

—

Lucy did not mean to be unkind to her brother but at seventeen, she was very much a young woman with a mind of her own and had far more important matters to concern herself with than whether a thirteen-year-old boy was supervised day and night. He'd be leaving school soon, then he'd have to get a job and join in the real world instead of being mollycoddled by his mother. Mam was far too soft with him in Lucy's opinion, never making him dry the dishes, peel potatoes, or even set the table. She conveniently forgot all the times Benny had kept the family supplied with wood and coal, not to mention Christmas dinner on one notable occasion. Boys, she thought, had things far too easy.

Now an autumn sun was shining guinea bright, and she was walking in the park with her arm hooked through Tom's, feeling very much the young lady about town. Children were scrambling over the old cannon, just as she once used to do. Today she sat with her young man upon a bench and listened to the band playing 'There's a Rainbow Round My Shoulder' and 'Somebody Stole My Gal', which got everybody in the park singing. Lucy couldn't remember ever having been so happy.

'Somebody had better not steal you,' Tom whispered in her ear, making her shiver with delight.

'They wouldn't dare. Not unless I wanted them to,' she teased, as carelessly as she could. Then, meticulously arranging the skirts of her dress, she went to sit on the grass and started picking daisies.

Tom looked stunned. 'You wouldn't, would you?'

'Wouldn't what?'

'Want them to?'

Lucy threaded two daisies before slanting a sideways glance up at him. 'Want who to do what?' But then, seeing his adorable young face looking so wounded and confused, she burst out laughing. 'Oh, Tom, you shouldn't let me tease you so easily,' as if it were all his doing. Mollified by her laughter, he dropped down beside her to plant a kiss upon her cheek.

'I don't care how much you tease, so long as you're my girl. Oh, you are, aren't you? I do love you, Lucy, and I'm saving like mad.' She lifted a pair of painstakingly plucked eyebrows to regard him with some surprise. 'Saving for what, might I ask?'

A bright crimson stain flooded his neck and cheeks. 'You know full well what I'm saving for.' And after drawing a deep and heavy sigh, 'For us to be wed, soon as may be.'

Lucy threaded two more daisies upon her chain, pursing her scarlet lips into a delightful moue. Her frequent visits to the picture-house, and the romances she devoured daily from the Public Library, had made a deep impression upon her. The heroines of these novels were always sophisticated, elegant and languid but extremely modern and glamorous. She read about them in such titles as *Love's Fool* and *The Flame of Youth*. They certainly didn't hang around waiting for a proposal. They took jobs in hat shops, if they weren't whisked off to the desert by an Arab sheikh. But failing either of these diversions, Lucy was well aware how vital it was for a young lady, when in the company of her admirer, not to appear too forward. Not if she was to bring him to his knees and get a proper proposal out of him, which was exactly what Lucy was getting at now, in a roundabout sort of way.

'Wed?' she enquired, wrinkling her pretty nose. 'I've no recollection of any conversation on that score. Did I miss something?'
And she turned to offer her suitor the full beguiling beauty of
her innocent blue eyes. Not having kept pace with the same kind
of literature or films, Tom was lost. He'd thought everything was
settled between them and, unfortunately for him, said as much.

'I thought it were all taken for granted like? You and me.'
Dramatically dropping the daisy chain, Lucy put her fingers to
her lips and gave a tiny gasp, rather as the heroine had done in
the last Annie S. Swan novel she'd read, just to let him see how
shocked she was. 'Never, Tom Shackleton, should you take a lady
for granted.'

'Oh, I didn't mean it like that.' Tom looked thoroughly miserable, as well he might, the whole sunny afternoon becoming dull
grey as every word he uttered seemed to be turned against him.
There followed a tiny disquieting pause while Lucy waited for
the expected proposal. Tom worried how it had all gone so badly
wrong and what on earth he could do to put it right 'I'm no good
with words,' he pointed out, in all fairness to himself.

'I think we are agreed upon that,' Lucy tartly remarked.

Perhaps it was the casual way she picked up the daisy chain
again that fired him, but in that moment Tom made a decision
that was to affect his entire life. Ripping the flowers from her
grasp, he tossed them aside. 'I might not have much to say, but
I'm a man who knows what he wants. And I want you.'

Whereupon he swept her into his arms and kissed her every bit
as thoroughly as any heroine could dream of. Lucy melted in his
arms and returned his passion, kiss for kiss. After they had come
up for air, all pink-cheeked and breathing hard, it was a matter of
moments to fix a date not too far distant. And then, to seal the
bargain and celebrate their engagement, for surely that was what
it was, Tom bought her a strawberry ice cream as a treat.

Later that same evening, after a visit to the Princes Musical
Theatre in Oxford Street, they dawdled slowly homewards, hand
in hand, lost to the world as they planned and dreamed of their

bright future together. So absorbed were they in each other they were quite unaware that for much of the day they had been followed.

Meanwhile, tucked up in his bed at home alone, Benny struggled to stay awake so that he could tell Lucy off for being late home yet again. But, tired after a long day delivering, his eyes drooped and within moments he was asleep.

−

The next day, being a Sunday, Benny didn't hang around waiting for his sister to nag him over breakfast. He hoped she'd sleep late and not miss him, following her evening out. Quietly he tiptoed past her closed door, making sure he didn't wake her, and fled.

He was revelling in the sensation of unaccustomed freedom. His mam and Charlie would be back soon, of course, but probably not until evening. And since Uncle Joshua was no longer in a position to force him to attend Zion Methodist, a wonderfully free Sunday stretched out before him, long and bright and unseasonably warm, his to do with as he pleased. While he considered various possibilities, he decided to go for a walk.

He walked the length of Ancoats Lane with no particular destination in mind, whistling a merry tune as he strolled along, though inside he felt just a little bit empty. He hadn't seen Liam, Don or Joe for longer than he cared to reckon. Ever since his mistaken effort to get round Georgie Eastwood by joining his gang, Benny had been treated as an outcast by all his former mates. It had been a great blow, and totally unexpected. He'd thought they would understand what he'd been about, but no, they saw him as a traitor. And a cowardly one at that.

So now, as per usual, even as he revelled in the freedom of a whole day to himself, loneliness niggled within.

He found himself nearing the Medlock, its swirling brown waters now clearly visible. As it rushed under Pin Mill Brow Bridge, all sorts of rubbish came with it, ropes and boxes, old boots and cart wheels. It was a favourite occupation of the local children to scavenge the river, where they could reach it, for anything of value. So it didn't surprise him to see a group of them laughing and arguing over some supposed prize as he neared the bridge. And then he realised who it was and his steps instinctively slowed.

It was Georgie Eastwood. His henchmen were with him, as usual, and Benny glanced nervously back over his shoulder, wondering if there was some way he could escape before they spotted him.

And then he saw who they were teasing.

It was Daft Betty. He could see her straight brown hair and round face, hear her piping voice. She sounded quite unlike her usual cheerful self, distressed and afraid. She was shouting something about jam jars, offering to give them some if they would let her go. But Benny could see that they had no intention of doing that. These lads enjoyed pulling wings off flies and legs off toads, and were clearly capable of far worse. Poor Betty Sidebottom didn't stand a chance. Even as he stood, frozen to the spot, wondering what best to do, he saw them push her to the lip of the bridge. Seconds later, to his horror, he heard a terrifying splash. They'd pushed her in! Without considering whether or not she could swim, they'd thrown Daft Betty into the river.

Without any thought of escape now, Benny started to run to the side of the bridge where the lads were hanging over the parapet, watching her thrash helplessly below. They were laughing as if they'd done something clever.

'You lot want your heads seeing to,' was all Benny had time to yell before kicking off his clogs and, without a second's hesitation, flinging himself into the mucky depths.

Chapter Twenty-Nine

Somehow, against all the odds, Benny managed to grab the woman and hold her head above water while he swam as best he could, despite the fact that she was bigger than himself.

'Don't worry, Betty, I've got you,' he yelled, getting a mouthful of filthy water for his pains.

Yet it felt like a living nightmare, as if they'd be trapped forever by the rushing waters of the Medlock as it raced along carrying them with it, with no hope of escape as dark mill walls lined its edges like great black cliffs. Then just as he felt he couldn't hold on to her solid body for a minute longer, Benny saw what he was looking for – a break in the wall where a boat was tied up. Kicking his legs like fury, arms entirely devoid of sensation by this time, he managed to pull Betty to the side and helped her to hold on to the mooring rope.

'Hang on, hang on!' he kept shouting, whenever he feared she was about to go under. His own lungs were bursting, and he felt sure he'd soon sink beneath the brown slimy water any minute from pure exhaustion. His eyes were stinging so much he could barely see. Then, inch by inch, he persuaded and cajoled, pushed and shoved, till he edged Betty round to the stone jetty. And wasn't he glad to hear the sound of clog irons ringing on the steps above as people came running to help!

By the time they were safely on the jetty quite a crowd had gathered, including Liam, Don and Joe, watching the scene in utter amazement. His picture would be in the paper, they told him, since a man with a camera had just taken a snap of him. Benny was a hero.

Betty had proved not to be so daft after all, since she'd done exactly as he'd told her to and not panicked at all, paddling her feet as instructed and keeping her chin up. She'd trusted in Benny completely, even though she couldn't swim a stroke on her own. She even kissed him when they were both safely on dry land, and the man with the camera snapped that too. Benny only grinned, not minding a bit. He was thrilled that all the swimming he'd done in the canal over the years, quite against Polly's orders, had finally paid off.

Despite the fact that he was soaked to the skin and shivering with cold, he had the immense satisfaction of seeing that Georgie Eastwood and his mates were looking even sicker than himself. Benny might have been the first one to act, blit he wasn't by any means the only one to have spotted the perpetrators of the crime, Georgie was in for a severe wigging from the constable, who was even now striding purposefully towards them.

When statements had been taken and Betty led off home by two kindly ladies, Benny found himself suddenly clasped to Grandma Flo's well-upholstered bosom. Alerted by a neighbour she'd hastened to the scene to revel in her grandson's glory. When finally Benny managed to extrireluctantly agreed to be marched off to her kitchen to be dried, 'before he caught his death'.

Wearily he knew this would mean more Fenning's Fever Cure, and yet another plastering of goose grease and brown paper. Georgie Eastwood and his cronies, however, were being marched off in quite a different direction.

As Benny set out for home with his grandmother, Liam stepped quickly forward. 'See you tomorrer then?'

Benny looked at these one-time friends of his, who'd never quite been there when he'd needed them. 'Happen,' he said, 'Then again, happen not. I've better things to do than play daft kids' games.' And linking his arm in Big Flo's, he strode away, head held high, enjoying every clap upon his back, every cheer and every 'well done, lad' as he went his way. No one could ever call him a coward again.

Polly felt as if a great black cloud had lifted from her. Her life at last seemed to be on an even keel. She felt so happy and carefree she kept bursting into song for no apparent reason. But then, she told herself, perhaps she did have every reason.

A successful trip to the auction in Liverpool had resulted in their buying up all the ship's carpets at an unbelievably low knock-down price. These were to be delivered, via the Ship Canal, the very next week and Polly was anxious to get to the warehouse and make provision for the new stock. Once she had seen her lovely family again, of course.

In addition to this success, she and Charlie had snatched the opportunity to enjoy a precious few days together, giving them time to relax and talk, to browse among the shops in Liverpool as well as down by the docks. It had proved to be a time for them simply to be a couple. He bought her a lovely ring that might or might not be a genuine sapphire. Polly really didn't care. To her it was the most beautiful piece of jewellery she'd ever owned. Being so far from home, they'd risked offending convention and signed into a small hotel as Mr and Mrs Stockton. If this made her a wicked woman in Big Flo's eyes, so be it. Though Polly would make certain that the old woman never got wind of this particular show of rebellion.

For Polly and Charlie it had been a dream come true, like a honeymoon, albeit before the wedding, which made it all the more deliciously enjoyable. He'd held her in his arms all through the softness of a mellow autumn night, stroking the silky smoothness of her skin, the glossy satin of her dark hair, and loving her as she had so longed to be loved.

After they had slept, limbs entwined, fingers still linked in sleep, they'd woken at dawn to a sky that seemed bluer, a sun more bright and golden, and even the hoot of ships in the pool sounding almost musical to their ears. To find themselves in bed together, and at such a time, meant they must once more demonstrate their love, each drawing the other ever closer in an unbreakable bond that would last a lifetime.

Now, Polly too was eager for an early wedding. What was there to wait for? Everything was going well for her at last. She had the privacy of a home she could call her own, where her children were free to grow unshackled by prejudice or Joshua's bigotry. Even her own father had been taken in hand by Big Flo. Deep down, Polly felt glad that Murdoch had come back into her life, despite her reservations when he'd first arrived. Perhaps it was time for old hurts to be forgotten, with her father and with her brother-in-law too. Joshua certainly seemed to be keeping out of her hair at last.

They found the house locked and empty on their return, with not a sign of either Benny or Lucy. Leaving their bags to be unpacked later, they hurried round to number twenty-three, assuming they might find them there. Instead they found a pile of wet clothing lying on the flagged floor. A pan of hot water had clearly been bubbling on the hob, and a wad of Big Flo's pink lint stood handily by, as if she'd been about to use it on someone.

'Benny?' Polly half whispered the words. 'What has the boy been up to now? Oh, Charlie, that lad'll be the death of me.'

'Don't panic. We've no proof anything is wrong yet,' he cautioned, but a thorough search brought no answers so they set off up Dove Street, seeking news from anyone who could tell them. As luck would have it, Vera Murray was polishing the windows of her toffee shop. She spied Polly at once and came trotting over in her busybody way. 'Now don't get yourself in a lather, you. Nobody's hurt.'

'What do you mean, nobody's hurt? What's happened?'

'That lad o' yours has only turned out to be a right little hero, hasn't he? You should be right proud of him.'

'Benny?' Polly was gaping, and could hear Charlie start to chuckle. '*Benny* a hero?'

'Saved Daft Betty from almost certain drowning he did.' The chuckle swelled to a great guffaw of laughter and Polly was slapping him, telling Charlie to hush, didn't she want to hear the whole story?

Vera turned back to her window cleaning, and then as if the thought had only just struck her, stopped and gave her duster a little shake. 'I shouldn't worry too much about your Lucy either,' she said. 'I'm sure they'll find her. Turn up like a bad penny no doubt as they allus do, eh?'

Before Polly had time to tune in the hill import of this devastating piece of information, Nellie Sidebottom came huffing and puffing down the street towards her. She was a large woman, not built for running, and with a face as red as a turkey cock's she was clearly in some distress. Without even pausing to comment on the dramatic events involving her sister Betty and Polly's son, she barked loudly while still some, twenty yards distant: 'Get to the warehouse, Poll. At once. Lucy's in trouble!'

—

The great double doors of the warehouse were locked. Standing outside in the dusk of a warm September day was an anxious-looking Benny, with an equally distressed Big Flo and Murdoch. Just looking at the expressions on all their faces filled Polly with fear.

'What is it? Where is she? Is she inside?'

Big Flo grabbed both Polly's arms in a grip that wrung the blood from her fingers, though she barely noticed. 'He's gone off his head! He's gone barmy, Polly. I don't know what the heck to do with him.' Such despair from Florence Pride was unheard of. Polly found herself in the unlikely position of calming the old woman and offering the sort of platitudes that were usually her province. 'Tell me slowly and calmly what's going on.'

'Joshua's in there with the child. And t'door's locked. Run mad he has.'

Today Big Flo hadn't even the strength to call upon her Good Friend for help. She stood wringing her hands, the lines on her worn face scored deeper than usual.

Charlie stepped forward. 'Let me tackle him. I'll wring his bleedin' neck!' He was all for fetching a battering ram and breaking the door down, but Polly wouldn't let him. It took some precious moments to calm him too, but finally she persuaded them all to leave the matter to her.

'We don't want any fisticuffs, or any more danger to Lucy. It's my daughter he's got in there, but it's me he's got the quarrel with. So it's time Joshua and I had a little heart to heart as it were, and settled this matter between us once and for all.' Then she kissed Charlie and pressed a finger to his lips. After a long moment looking into her eyes, he let her go.

If only she felt as confident as she sounded, Polly thought. She could hear her own heart pounding as she rapped on the door, rattled the handle and finally shouted through the letter-box. 'Joshua! If you can hear me in there, let me in.'

After what seemed an eternity, she heard the turning of a key in the rusty old lock and the door swung open a few inches. She had time to cast back one lingering glance, seeing Charlie's anguished face, Murdoch giving her a huge wink and Big Flo holding her grandson close and Benny for once not protesting. Then the door had clanged shut behind her, the key turned and she was locked inside the warehouse with Joshua.

Through the thick rough panels of the door she heard Charlie's furious shout. 'Lay one finger on her and I'll personally take you apart, inch by bloody inch!'

Joshua only smiled and jerked his head, indicating she should precede him up the stairs. Polly didn't hesitate. She was anxious to find her daughter.

When she did, she jerked to a halt in shocked silence, struggling to make sense of the picture before her eyes.

Lucy was not in the part of the warehouse they used for cutting the carpets. Nor was she in the office. She was in the tiny cupboard-like kitchen. A pan of water was boiling furiously over the single gas jet.

Lucy was sitting cross-legged on top of the deal table and Polly's eyes went straight to her daughter's face, to find there the brightest red lipstick she'd ever seen, which seemed to extend far beyond her small pretty mouth. A mouth that was, in fact, trembling while the blue eyes glistened with tears.

Polly glanced again at the stove. 'What's the pan of water.'

'Your daughter needs a good scrub, a thorough cleansing, more spiritually and physically.'

It was then that Polly noticed what Lucy was wearing. She was dressed only in a sack, her legs and feet were bare and upon her beautiful hair lay a scattering of grey dust.

'She is learning the true meaning of repentance,' Joshua's explained. 'By wearing sackcloth and ashes.'

'*Sackcloth and ashes*?' Polly turned to stare at him, feeling her mouth fall open in a foolish gape.

'She spent much of yesterday cavorting in an immoral way with a young man in the park, and the evening in a theatre – surely a palace of sin if ever there was one.'

Polly heard a muffled protest from Lucy, quickly stifled, as if she'd learned during the time she had spent sitting on that hideous table that no matter what defence she offered, Joshua would not heed it. Frowning, Polly took a step towards her, only to have her way blocked, as it had been once before when she'd tried to protect her son.

Joshua held up his hands, like a barrier before her. 'No, do not interrupt. I brought her here last night while the sin was ripe upon her. The girl needs discipline. She is also learning the valuable lesson that we, as mere mortals, cannot improve on nature. Had the good Lord wanted young women to have scarlet mouths, I'm sure he would have made the necessary provision.'

Polly longed to smack his hands away but had learned from bitter experience that Joshua did not react well to a display of temper. 'She's but a growing girl, Joshua, finding out about herself and what life has to offer. If she makes any silly mistakes with clothes or lipstick, sure won't she learn sense as she gets older? As for her friendship with young Tom Shackleton, I know all about that and see no harm in it.'

'Because you have no judgement yourself.'

Polly told herself to stay calm and not rise to his bait. He was deliberately provoking her, so she merely smiled while edging a step closer to the table and a now openly weeping Lucy. 'It's because he's a fine young man. But this isn't about Lucy, is it? I thought we had this matter all sorted between us, Joshua? We do appreciate the care you took of us in the months following Matt's death, but that's past now, and time for you to stop. The responsibility for my children's behaviour, including any punishment they might require, is mine, not yours. Wouldn't you say that was fair?'

There was a long telling silence and then, to her great alarm, Joshua began to laugh. The sound, coming from his thin lips sounded so unreal that it sent a chill running the length of Polly's spine.

'Joshua,' she coaxed, 'let her come to me. I'll give her a good talking to, about the lipstick and all.' Then the laugh stopped as quickly as it had begun and the silence following it was even more deadly.

'To allow you control over your own children would serve only to perpetuate the sin. By becoming a part of our family, you corrupted and shamed it. But your marriage didn't work, did it? Matthew learned sense in the end and abandoned you.'

Polly bit down hard on her lip. 'Because you dripped your poison into his ear. I can see that clearly now.'

'You brought nothing but problems. Now your daughter is about to commit the same mistake by seducing a Catholic boy, when really she should marry a Methodist.'

'I'll never marry anyone but Tom!' Lucy's anguished cry echoed heart-breakingly in the tiny room. Polly's whole body shook as she witnessed her daughter's pain. But still she held on to her temper.

'I created no problems for this family, Joshua, nor for Matthew. Weren't we always happy, until poverty and our different ways of dealing with that came between us? A problem we might have overcome had you not interfered.' Joshua advanced to within an inch of her, and leaning close spat the next words in her face. 'You *ruined him,* Jezebel that you are! Because of his ridiculous passion for you, Matt was more concerned with saving his own skin than rescuing our younger brother from the dangers of battle.' It all came out then, the hatred and the venom, the bitter resentment he had stored up over the years. Joshua poured out his version of events, how he was certain that Matthew could have saved Cecil, could have gone back and carried him from the field of battle.

His eyes were glittering like glass, and though they gazed upon her, failed to quite focus.

Polly stated at him, transfixed by horror. The terrible tragedy of poor Cecil's death was being set firmly at Matthew's door, and her own too. Young though she'd been at the time of the Great War, Matthew had told her then of Joshua's accusation, but she'd never dreamed it could turn into a feud, almost an obsession. As if Matthew would have abandoned his dying brother in order to save his own skin! The very thought made Polly steam with anger on his behalf. But Joshua evidently believed that he had, and clearly laid some of the blame upon her too, simply because Matthew had loved her. However unfair, Joshua hated her because she was alive and Cecil was not.

Polly was shaking her head. 'Actually you're wrong. Matthew did go back. Didn't he tell you? Perhaps because he was such a modest man, and the pain of his failure cut so deep, he may not have done. Of course he tried to save his poor brother, for all he was ordered not to risk trying by his commanding officer. He ignored the order, as did one or two others. Despite lying injured for hours and needing urgent medical attention himself, Matt searched among the dead and dying, saving a few, thank God, but Cecil was already dead when he found him.'

'Because he went back too late. Coward that he was!'

'No!' Now it was Polly who was shouting. 'My Matt was not a coward. The situation was always hopeless but at least he tried! Look how he saved Tom Shackleton, and died as a result?'

'He deserved to die.'

331

Something in the tone of his voice brought Polly to a new and terrifying realisation. She recalled how once she'd suspected that Matthew's death might not have been entirely an accident, but had dismissed the idea as the product of her own overwrought imagination. Now she looked into her brother-in-law's frozen expression and knew that was not the case. 'You killed him, didn't you?'

'I left him to die. In exactly the same way that he left Cecil. It was only right and proper. Justice for his cowardly neglect of our brother.'

While Polly stood in a daze of shock, Joshua swivelled on his heel and reached for Lucy, pulling the screaming girl from the table by her hair, as if she were a rag doll. One hand smoothed down the rumpled sack, his fingers lingering over pert young breasts, savouring the pleasure of that moment before he moved on to grip Lucy's slender arms. 'And now it is your turn. You, the Irish bitch who first turned him from his family, and this child, your whore of a daughter. She's as worthless as the muck on this floor.' So saying, he flung Lucy to the far corner of the room, where she crumpled in a heap as if she were indeed no more than a sack of rags.

Without stopping to think, for surely she would never have done such a terrible thing if she had, Polly picked up the pan of boiling water and tossed it into Joshua's face. She didn't wait to check the result of her action as his screams filled the room, but grabbed Lucy's hand and ran. It took several frustrating moments before she managed to get the key to turn in the lock, her hands were shaking that much. Then the door banged open at last and she was half-carrying, half-pushing her daughter out into the open where they were both gathered safely into Charlie's arms.

–

Polly and Charlie were married by a delighted Father Donevan just a few weeks later. Not only had he the pleasure of welcoming Polly Pride and her children back into the Faith, but a new member as well. Charlie had willingly attended classes every Thursday evening with the old priest in order to make this change, which he saw as a new beginning for himself. Polly was also delighted to be at last returning to her Church, which felt like coming home in a way. Strangely, in the end, it seemed Joshua's quarrel with her had not been about religion at all, but a bitter feud of his own making.

She lit a candle in memory of Matthew, as she would do every year at the anniversary of his death.

She and Matthew had been happy until poverty and his pride had got in the way. But then she was not without the sin of pride herself. Nevertheless, they would have overcome their difficulties, in time, if Joshua's obsession hadn't twisted Matt's mind against her. But whatever had happened in the past could not be altered, simply endured. Now it was time to move on and face a new future. She'd been given a second chance to love and be loved by another good man. Oh, indeed, she was a lucky woman.

As she walked down the aisle on the arm of the man she loved, Polly looked upon her family with pride and joy.

There was Benny, seated beside Tom Shackleton in the front pew, looking quite the young man in a new grey suit, and giving her a wink as she passed by. He would be coming into the business full-time at Christmas, or so he'd informed her. Polly had welcomed the idea, for wasn't he a great asset? Charlie too had plans for a big carpet store in the centre of the city, given a year or two's good trading.

She could see Big Flo grinning from ear to ear, refusing only to kneel along with the rest of the congregation as she preferred to sit with her back as ramrod straight as her morals, so that she could talk to her God face to face.

Polly knew that her mother-in-law was not quite the woman she'd once been. A part of her robustness had gone, perhaps forever. Her large frame seemed to have shrunk a little, although not for a moment did she complain. Watching her only remaining son struggle with those scalding burns after that terrible day in the warehouse should have filled her with compassion. But she'd shown no sign of such an emotion.

When Joshua had recovered sufficiently to leave hospital, Big Flo had looked at the scars on his face and told him that they would forever be a warning to him that he had no understanding of the words 'love' or 'compassion.'

She'd gone to see him off when Joshua had left on a cheap passage to Canada, Polly by her side at the dock on the Manchester Ship Canal, as support. But not a single tear had touched her mother-in-law's cheek, nor had she waved, or wished him well as she'd stood, hands folded, spine rigid. She'd watched the ship carry her last son away, knowing she would probably never see him again, and that he was the cause of her losing her second son.

'You still have us,' Polly had told her.

'Aye, lass, I know. I take great comfort from my two grand-children, and my brave daughter-in-law.'

They'd smiled at each other then and walked home together arm in arm.

'Are you happy, Mrs Stockton?' whispered a voice in her ear.

'How could I not be?' Polly said, sighing.

They stepped outside of the church to be met by a sunburst of brilliant light and smiling faces, everyone laughing and throwing rose petals and confetti. A cameraman with a tripod called instructions for the bride to look his way.

But turning her head in quite the opposite direction, Polly sought out Lucy, who looked enchanting in a soft blue satin bridesmaid's dress that exactly matched her eyes.

'Catch. You next!' she cried and tossed her wedding bouquet of roses and lily-of-the-valley. But she was too happily engrossed being kissed by the groom to check whether her daughter actually caught it.